"You underestimate yourself, Amanda. No man needs any such reason to try to get near you."

She hadn't realized how close he was. Suddenly he was there, beside her. She could feel the light hairs on his arm next to hers, smell the citron on his skin mingling with the faint pungent odor of tobacco. The air between them came alive; she could sense the throbbing warmth of her body calling to his.

This would never do! "Good night. I'm going to bed," she snapped and started toward the door of her room.

Cole watched her for a moment while his blood surged with his desire for her. He darted after her, catching her next to the door where he spun her around.

"Let me go!" Amanda cried.

"Not yet. Tell me not to touch you, not to kiss you, not to hold you in my arms ever again. Tell me I'm nothing to you and then I'll walk away."

Amanda opened her mouth, but the words would not come out. She looked into his dark, burning eyes, wanting to tell him and wanting not to, but most of all, wanting him with a longing that cried for him to fill all the empty places and do away with all the hurt.

"Tell me, Amanda," Cole whispered, leaning into her, his lips brushing her skin like brands of fire. "Tell me."

Amanda's free arm went around Cole's neck and wildly, wantonly, she opened her mouth to his.

ASHLEY SNOW

OUTLAW'S EMBRACE

ZEBRA BOOKS
KENSINGTON PUBLISHING CORP.

For Bill

ZEBRA BOOKS are published by

Kensington Publishing Corp.
850 Third Avenue
New York, NY 10022

First Printing: June, 1994

Printed in the United States of America

One

Arizona Territory
March 18, 1880

Dear Robert:

You will, no doubt, be surprised to receive a letter from me after all these years. I know it has been an age since we were last in touch, but I find as I get older, I long to rekindle the bonds of family; and you, dear brother, are all the family left to me, as I am to you.

For over a year now I have lived in this new, tiny, god-forsaken desert oasis they call 'Tombstone,' where I make a barely substantial living dispensing drugs and medicines. It is a wild place but exciting, and with silver ore being mined to the tune of thousands of dollars every day, you can imagine that fortunes are being made. And lost, too, thanks to all the temptations that swarm to miners like fleas to a dog.

We have at the moment only one doctor in this town, and he is much given to imbibing the barleycorn a little too freely. I mention this because it occurs to me that you might be ready to move your practice to a new place and this one would be worth pursuing. Between us, we could supply most of the medical needs of this town of over two thousand souls.

The dry desert air would also benefit your little Amanda. I recall how she suffered with the asthma when I visited East. Such a pretty thing she was, with her long pigtails and sprinkle of freckles across her nose.

I suppose you can read between these lines how much I long to be reunited with you and to have kinfolk nearby. Sometimes I think in this impermanent world, family is the only permanence we can rely upon.

I am assuming you still practice doctoring in Cincinnati and am writing to you there. Say you'll come, Robert, if only for a visit. I eagerly await your reply.

Your loving brother,
George Lassiter

P.S. Robert, on the happy chance that you agree, I am enclosing a list of drugs which I need in my dispensary. Some of them, like quinine bark and sodium nitrate are almost impossible to get out here.

Two

Office of the Bishop
January 20, 1881

To Mr. Leander Walton
Tombstone, Arizona Territory

My Dear Mr. Walton:

I am writing to inform you of the happy news that we have at long last determined upon a young clergyman to carry the mantle of Our Lord into the desert wilderness.

The Reverend Cabot Phinias Storey, a fine young man of sterling character and an excellent preacher, should arrive in Tombstone within the next two months to take up his duties at St. Anselm's parish. As senior warden, I know you will make sure that Reverend Storey is welcomed and given suitable arrangements. We have made Reverend Storey aware that his first, most pressing obligation will be to see that a permanent, proper house of worship is erected for the congregation.

Be assured that our prayers continue for your church and your new leader.

The Right Reverend Geo. K. Dunlap
Bishop of Arizona and New Mexico

Three

Tombstone
February, 1881

Cole,

Don't know if this'll find you, but will send it out and hope. You ought to know there is plunder and spoils aplenty just waitin' in this town. Silver ore comin' in and goin' out and lots of it lost on the way. More gamblin' then I ever seen, which is okay for me, ha! And some interestin' under the table doin's as well.

If you decide to come, I can get you in on some easy pickins.

Aces Malone

Four

Amanda Lassiter absently ran a finger across the bridge of her nose. Those awful freckles! How ironic that they, of all things, should be what Uncle George remembered—and after all the years she had worked so hard to get rid of them.

But, then, she had been a child the one time Uncle George came East to visit Papa. Now the freckles only reappeared on those infrequent occasions when she forgot to wear her bonnet outdoors. And the pigtails had made way for the fashionable and sensible bun at the nape of her neck.

"If you keep handling that letter you are going to wear it to shreds. You must have it memorized by now."

Amanda glanced guiltily up at the round, pink face of her neighbor, Mrs. Abernathy. She saw a tiny smile crease the woman's broad lips as her china-blue eyes peeked over the rim of her round glasses, assessing Amanda with her usual shrewdness. Her knitting needles had stopped their clicking and lay silent in Mrs. Abernathy's broad lap.

"I do have it memorized. I only read it to convince myself I'm doing the right thing." The pages fell into their worn creases as she tucked the letter back into her pocket. *Am I doing the right thing?* she wanted to add. Yet she didn't ask because she did not want to let even her closest friend know how uncertain she was about this step she was taking. The question might reinforce her own deep fears. She had to do this. To be unsure of herself now would only make everything that much more difficult.

Mrs. Abernathy rearranged the pile of knitting in her lap. "My dear, I wish you would reconsider. It would be different if your father were still alive. But to start out on a journey like this alone and unprotected—it just doesn't make any sense."

Amanda turned from the window where she had been standing and folded her arms defensively across her chest. "It makes perfect sense. Uncle George offered Papa a chance to start a new life, why shouldn't he do the same for me? He couldn't know that Papa would die before his letter arrived."

"But that letter was written almost a year ago. Who knows what changes might have occurred since then? By now your uncle might not even be in the Arizona Territory."

Amanda's jaw assumed the stubborn lines her neighbor recognized so well. "He had already been there a year. And he runs a business. Why would he move? His letter took so long to reach us only because he didn't know we had moved to St. Louis."

"You really are determined to go, aren't you? I don't understand it. You have a home here, friends . . ."

A sharp pang tore at Amanda's chest. She turned away, lifting the lace curtain at the window to stare absently into the dusty street that fronted the house. The little sign her father had put up swung and squeaked in the stiff breeze. The words—*"Robert Lassiter, M.D. General Doctoring"*—were faded now by last summer's harsh midwestern sun. She must remember to take that sign down.

"Now, Mrs. Abernathy, you know very well I have no friends here in St. Louis, apart from you and one or two people who knew my father well."

"Yes, and many's the time I told your Pa he ought not to keep you so busy. A pretty young girl ought to be out sparkin' and enjoying herself, not fussing about with a dirty, grimy business like doctoring . . ."

"I wanted to help Papa," Amanda said, firmly cutting her off. Immediately she felt remorse at being so short with this friendly woman who had given her such staunch support through her father's final illness and death. She moved to the old rocker opposite her friend, sitting down and clasping her hands in her lap.

"You know I never begrudged helping Papa. He taught me so much and it meant so much to him. We had only each other for so long that he depended on me. He knew I would never let him down. But now, with him gone, I really have nothing else to pursue."

"Yet surely he left you enough to live on until . . ."

Amanda smiled. "Until I find a husband?"

A tinge of embarrassment flickered over her neighbor's face. "Well, that's usually what young ladies look for."

"Perhaps. But I have no prospects here in St. Louis and no fondness for this town. I'd rather try a new place and a new profession. I'm certain I know enough about dispensing drugs to help my uncle, and he can teach me what I don't know. He said the territory was 'wild but exciting.' I think I'd like that."

Mrs. Abernathy reached out and clasped one of Amanda's hands in her plump fingers. "Oh, my dear. I don't think you have any idea of the dangers involved in this move. You'll be a lamb thrown to the wolves."

Amanda's laugh lit up her lovely face. "Not quite. After all, I took care of myself and my father for quite a few years after Mama died. I'll manage."

The knitting needles began their rhythmic clicking as Mrs. Abernathy gave up the hopeless pursuit of trying to change Amanda's mind. The girl was headstrong when something took her fancy. If only that letter had arrived from its long journey before Dr. Robert passed away, he might have put the whole thing to rest. Now, nothing was going to deter this pretty, vulnerable young girl from striking out for the West, with its terrible dangers from gun-shooting brigands on the one hand and wild, savage Indians on the other.

Amanda sat back in the chair, rocking slowly. 'Wild' and 'exciting' sounded like something she needed right now. Something to erase the pain of her father's loss and the prospect of bleak, empty, spinsterish years that stretched ahead. Anyway, now that the house was sold, she had no place to live. She had to move on. Besides . . .

She caught her full underlip lightly in her teeth and stared toward the window. How could she tell her matronly friend that one of her reasons for seeking a new town was the burning desire to find the man she dreamed was waiting for her? How often she had imagined him—strong, virile, maybe just a little bit dangerous, like the heroes of the dime novels she so loved to read. Yet underneath he would be a man of impeccable character, with an idealistic desire to serve others. A doctor! Yes, that would be perfect. They would work side by side bringing healing and hope to the grateful people of a wild, primitive society.

He needn't be handsome in the classical sense, but his open, honest face should reflect firmness and, at the same time, gentleness. And a sensitivity to beauty—to a lovely song or a breathtaking sunset—would be nice, too. He would be tall with broad, firm shoulders and a slim waist tapering to narrow hips, and he would wear tight, leather pants which accentuated every swelling contour . . .

Tremors of warmth stirred in her body and brought a flaming red blush to her cheeks. She gave herself a mental shake and forced her mind back to reality.

Her fingers slid into her pocket where she could feel the sharp edges of Uncle George's letter. She had enough money to pay her way on the train and the stage, with enough left to bring the medicines her uncle had asked for. Once there, surely he would help her find a place to live and pay her some kind of wage to work in his drug store. If not . . . well, she would do something. Life with Dr. Robert Lassiter had taught her to be resourceful.

It was a little disturbing that the letter she had sent off to her uncle had, as yet, brought no reply. But that could be due to the uncertainty of the mails. After all, look at the months it had taken Uncle George's letter to reach her.

The creak of the rocker made an accompaniment to the staccato click of Mrs. Abernathy's knitting needles. Amanda smiled to herself. It was going to work out. She just knew it.

Five

He was singing. Singing! And at the top of his lungs.

His horse ambled down the narrow dirt path as casually as though its rider were out for a stroll in a city park. The man astride it wore his fine Stetson hat pulled low over his eyes against the merciless sun, but sat straight in the saddle, the reins carelessly draped in one hand. Every now and then he would throw back his head to reach some high note of the song he was bellowing. Cole recognized the old hymn at once.

"Rock of ages, cleft for me.
Let me hide myself . . ."

"He'd do better to hide," Cole muttered to Floyd Barrow, who crouched beside him, peering over the rim of the hill and looking down on the road. "Roaring like that, he might as well send out an invitation to come and get him. This fool deserves to be robbed."

"I wonder that Heronimo hasn't already done the honors," Floyd murmured. "He must know he's here."

"Oh, he knows all right. I think he left him for me."

Floyd nodded agreement then scrambled down the hill just far enough to still be out of sight of the road. Pulling off his hat, he wiped off the sweat on his forehead with a bandanna. Coming from any other man, Cole's statement would sound like foolish bragging. Yet Floyd, more than the others in Cole Carteret's gang of brigands, knew that the Indian renegade Heronimo had some kind of special friendship with his boss. He still didn't know why—Cole was closemouthed about it—but he had seen too many instances now to doubt it was true. Otherwise, that foolish, solitary rider would have already been staked out on an anthill.

Cole took a last glance at the rider below, then scrambled down beside Floyd. For a moment he wondered if this idiot greenhorn was worth bothering with. His clothes looked expensive, and there was probably a gold watch in his vest pocket. But he had only a thin pack tied behind the saddle and nothing else. Not even an extra pack horse.

Still, any activity was better than none. There had been too much sitting around lately.

He pulled his neckerchief up over his nose. "Well, let's get to it," he said. "We ought not to even raise a sweat on this one." The cotton square protruded over his thick moustache and heavy beard, making an uncomfortably hot disguise. Yet it would keep off most of the dust and was necessary just in case his victim had ever seen a wanted poster of "The Casket Kid." How he hated that nickname! Just because he had a deadlier aim than most men with a Colt .45, he was stuck with a constant reminder of the number of men he had been forced to kill in foolish challenges. His rightful name was Cole Carteret. Why couldn't they leave it at that?

The boots of the two men crunched on the rough

gravel as they made their way to a clump of scraggly trees where two other men waited with the horses. Swinging easily into the saddle, Cole pulled his long-barreled Colt Frontier from its holster and balanced it easily in his hand. From over the hill the dim notes of the hymn told them their prey had advanced along the road.

> "All for sin could not atone:
> Thou must save, and Thou alone . . ."

"We'll wait by the outcrop where the road bends," Cole said, turning his mount. The others nodded and fell in behind him. The jagged growth of rock that rose abruptly out of the desert floor was the perfect hiding place. Especially since this nincompoop rider did them the service of announcing his approach.

Though their horses' hooves swirled up a cloud of yellow dust, it was obscured from the road by the high rocky elevation. They slowed to a walk as the horses moved down out of the hill's protective shield to quietly approach the shelter of the outcrop. Cole reined in, knowing without looking around that his companions had eased up behind him. As he waited, one hand resting on the pommel of his saddle, he mused once again over whether they could be trusted. Floyd had been with him since Albuquerque, long enough for Cole to feel he'd probably stand by when things got tough. The other two were still unknown factors. Jim Reily's hard face and cold eyes bothered Cole. He knew the type. A drifter who never managed to be successful at anything on his own and so wandered from gang to gang, picking up a share from schemes dreamed up by better men. Such a life had left him hard and bitter. Jim was the kind of man who would shoot you in the back without a flicker of conscience. He'd earned the nickname "Scorpion" for his scuttling ways and lizard-like features. Still, he obeyed orders pretty well and, as long as no fights were picked with him, he probably wasn't a bad man to have along.

Grady, the other rider, was more of a gamble. Young and inexperienced, he had joined Cole's outlaws more to seek excitement than to make a living. Cole still couldn't tell how he would react in a real fight. And this easy bit of business would not be likely to show him.

They could hear the singer's voice growing louder as he rounded the bend just beyond the rocks. Cole glanced around to see the others covering their faces, then motioned them to be ready for his signal. He waited until the rider was almost abreast before throwing down his hand and galloping out into the road, taking his place in front of the startled victim while the other three moved to surround him.

The startled horse reared and snorted, nearly unseating its rider. The song broke off abruptly. Cole balanced his gun on one arm, pointing it at the man who struggled to calm his horse, and absently noted it was a fine animal. There might be more riches here than he'd thought.

"Oh, my goodness!" the man cried, looking around. "Robbers? Outlaws?"

Cole expected him to go for a gun beneath the long,

black frock coat he wore. Instead the man patted his mount's sleek neck and leaned over it to peer at Cole.

"Are you really a western gunslinger?"

Cole stared at him. This was the last response he expected. "Get off," he snapped, motioning him out of the saddle.

"I've never met a real outlaw. I've read about them, of course, but I never thought to see . . ."

"On your feet!" Cole yelled. This fool didn't even know enough to be frightened.

"Well, of course. If that's what you want, I'll be happy to oblige you."

He swung down out of the saddle with a grace and ease that gave Cole second thoughts about this being a greenhorn. "What is it you want?" he asked, looking around at the others. "My, I didn't really believe you'd wear those handkerchiefs over your faces. You've nothing to fear from me, you know. I'm certain I'd never recognize any of you."

Cole caught Floyd's eyes staring at him over the rim of his kerchief, full of incredulity. "Grady, go through his pockets," he demanded.

"Oh, there's no need for that, dear fellow," the man replied as Grady jumped down to grab him. "If it's money you want, here." He pulled several of his pockets up out of the lining of his coat, holding out a fistfull of bills. "It's not so much really but it's all I have. You're welcome to it."

Grady threw Cole a questioning glance. "Go through the pack," Cole muttered.

"Well, really! You won't find much of value, but have a look if you want. I carried a few sleeping things and a pot or two. Just enough to get to Tucson where I can pick up the stage."

Grady threw the pack on the ground and spread it out. He picked up a worn, leather case but found it to be only a book.

"That's my Bible and Prayer Book. You're welcome to it, if you like, though I confess I'd hate to part with it. But perhaps it would do you more good than me."

"Will you shut up!" Cole cried in exasperation. He looked closer at the man, seeing for the first time that he was very young. He had a long, rather pale face and deep-set eyes. Apart from his horse, they were wasting their time.

"Oh . . . well, all right," the victim said, looking around. He seemed a little startled when he caught Jim Reily's cold eyes assessing him, but turned back to Cole as ebullient as ever.

"Grady, check his vest," Cole snapped. Grady stepped up and rifled the man's vest pockets, pulling out a round gold watch. A smile flitted across Grady's thin lips.

"Well, at last. Here's something, boss," he said, throwing the gold watch and chain to Cole, who caught it deftly. He turned it over in his hand. It was elaborately carved and very heavy—a fine, expensive watch. He glanced up to see that for the first time a look of dismay had come over the victim's face.

Flipping up the lid, Cole lifted it to read the inscription engraved on the inside.

"To CPS from JDS
God bless and keep you"

Cole smiled thinly. "It looks like God's not doing too good a job."

"On the contrary," the young man smiled back. "Perhaps He wants you to have that watch more than me. I admit I hate to give it up; but if that is His will, I will not complain."

Floyd spoke up. "What are we going to do with this greenhorn, boss?"

Reily leaned forward over his saddle. "I say we shoot him and leave his body for the coyotes."

Cole silenced him with one hard glance. "I'll decide that."

"He hasn't got anything much worth having," Floyd said. "We can take his horse and leave him to walk to Tucson."

Grady laughed. "Which means the Apaches will have him staked out before dark."

The young man's already pale face turned a shade lighter. "Apaches? But they're all on the reservation, aren't they?"

"Somebody's not giving you the right information, greenhorn," Cole said, resting his hands on the pommel with his pistol still pointed at the young man. "Don't you know Heronimo has a renegade band savaging these parts? He'd just love to come across an innocent white-eyes like you to practice a little revenge on."

"Heronimo? Oh, you mean Geronimo. Yes, I did hear about him, but I thought he was in the mountains farther south. My goodness . . ."

"Your goodness would have been scalped long ago if Heronimo hadn't left you for me to take. Who the hell are you, anyway? What are you doing crossing this desert alone?"

The young man smiled broadly, back on familiar territory. "Allow me to introduce myself. The Reverend Cabot Phinias Storey, out from Boston, come to take over my duties at St. Anselm's Church in Tombstone, Arizona Territory." He gave a ridiculous little bow toward Cole. "I admit I came here knowing little of the ways of Indians and outlaws, yet I came believing God intends to use me to build up his church in this virgin territory."

"Virgin?" Floyd turned to Cole. "Did he say something about virgins?"

"He's a preacher!" Grady exclaimed. "I didn't count on robbin' no preacher."

"I still say we leave him for the coyotes," Reily muttered.

But Cole did not hear them. He had heard little else beyond the mention of Tombstone in the Arizona Territory.

How long had it been since he received that letter from Aces Malone? How many nights had he pondered on it, trying to think of a way to slip into town without Sheriff Behan knowing he was there. John Behan, who would like nothing better than to hang him from the nearest gibbet. One whiff that the Kid was in town, and he'd do it without ever bothering with a judge or a court. And all because of that pimply faced cousin of his who tried to make his reputation by outshooting The Casket Kid. Of course, Behan wouldn't admit his real motive. He'd say he was out to get Cole Carteret because of that robbery of the Cortez stage last year and the accidental shooting of a passenger. And he'd have that awful wanted poster to back him up. But Cole knew what was really behind John Behan's crusade to throw him in jail, and he knew he'd be wise to stay as far away from the sheriff as possible.

All the same . . .

Cole sat, staring at the young man, clicking off ideas through his mind. Finally he slipped his pistol back in the holster and picked up the reins. "Get back on your horse," he snapped.

All three outlaws muttered in exasperated surprise. Floyd turned incredulous eyes on his boss.

"You're not going to let him go just because he's a preacher, are you?"

"No, I'm not. Grady, tie his hands to the pommel. Jim, lead his horse. We're taking him back to the camp with us."

"Dammit, are you out of your mind, Cole?" Floyd cried. "What in hell do you want with him?"

"I'm not sure. Mostly I want time to think about it."

"It's crazy." Reily spit out the words. "Letting him see where we keep camp. And for what? A gold watch, a horse, and a few dollars."

"I make the decisions here," Cole yelled in a sudden burst of fury. "If you don't like it, move on."

Reily's eyes blazed but he dropped them when he met Cole Carteret's cold, steely look. Turning his horse, he started back up the path while behind him Grady jostled the Reverend Storey up into the saddle and tied his hands to the pommel with the preacher's own rope.

"I must say, I do appreciate that you didn't shoot me," the young man said to Cole. "And I've never seen an outlaw's lair before. This should be very interesting . . ."

"Just shut your mouth before I change my mind." Cole pulled his horse around, as much to avoid Floyd's accusing gaze as anything. "And for God's sake, no more singing!"

Six

"Your stage just pulled in, ma'am."

Amanda looked quickly up from the dime novel she was reading. The young station attendant's earnest, pimply face bent close enough to her own to allow her to catch a whiff of his unpleasant breath.

"Oh, thank you," she replied, shoving the paper novel deep inside the large cloth bag in her lap. "I was so engrossed in my book I didn't hear it."

"That's what I thought. I said to myself, 'Jimmy, that pretty little lady probably didn't even notice the Tombstone stage has pulled in, and you ought to amble over and let her know, just in case.' "

Amanda gave him a grateful smile. "You're very kind. I'll go right out."

As she rose from the bench, the young man reached to take up her bag. "It's just this way, ma'am."

She followed in his wake, out of the dark, depressing wooden structure that served as the way station for the stage. As she emerged onto the porch, the sudden bright sun transformed the roadway into a blaze of light. Dust swirled ankle-deep around the wheels of the large cumbersome vehicle that was pulled up in front of the building. In the road behind it, another yellow cloud—

churned up by the traffic of horses and riders, wagons and buggies—forced Amanda to raise a gloved hand to her face. The blinding sun reflected on the whitewashed fronts of the buildings across the street, and dimmed the names of the various proprietors painted on the facades that reached up two or three stories high.

As Amanda shielded her eyes against the sun, a figure rode close to the walk, materializing out of the light. As her eyes adjusted, she found herself looking up into the frank gaze of a man riding a beautiful sorrel horse. He sat straight and tall in the saddle, with an easy grace that melded rider and mount. His black Stetson hat was pulled down over his forehead; the long tails of his coat spread out over the sorrel's rump, and his muscular thighs were encased in tight breeches above high boots ornamented with silver spurs.

Amanda felt her pulse quicken, and a smile lifted the corners of her lips. She looked closer at the clean-shaven, firm jaw; the long, aquiline nose; the dark brows. Beneath his hat, his hair fell in waves a woman might envy to strong, powerful shoulders. One graceful hand casually held the reins while the other was poised on his hip in a gesture of defiant assurance.

Her heart gave a sudden twist. This was what she had come West hoping to find—this beautiful, self-contained, virile kind of man. Her eyes lingered on the rider as he passed on, then returned to the group of men clustered around the stage—men in stained vests, with stubble on their chins, who leaned over between sentences to spit a stream of tobacco juice into the dirt.

How ridiculous! She must stop allowing her romantic notions to cloud her judgment when reality stood there before her. She covered her mouth with her lace handkerchief against the choking dust and stepped down the low stairs to the street.

"Do you want your bag tied behind, ma'am?" the station assistant asked her, touching the rim of his cap.

"How long will we take to reach Tombstone?"

"Oh, several hours. You're not like to get there before this afternoon."

"In that case, perhaps I had better keep it with me," Amanda said, remembering the dime novel as well as her other precious cargo.

"Whatever you want. Let me have your ticket, and I'll check it in with the stage driver."

Amanda handed Jimmy her ticket, then waited while he walked over to speak to a heavyset man with a beard covering the lower half of his face and a battered felt hat nearly eclipsing the upper half. He took the ticket, glanced in her direction, and nodded to the assistant, who hurried back to her.

"It'll just be another ten minutes until they change the horses. That's Mr. Jameson driving. He'll see you get aboard."

"Thank you. You've been most kind."

The young man smiled and touched his cap again. "My pleasure, ma'am. I hope you'll come back to Tucson again soon."

Not very likely, Amanda thought as she watched him hurry off. Not that everyone hadn't been pleasant to her—a surprise after Mrs. Abernathy's dire predictions. By this time she had expected to see brawls, gunfights, and dead outlaws lying in the streets, when, in fact, she had seen none of those things. The train ride from St.

Louis had been a long, uncomfortable, boring trip interspersed with poor meals in shabby way stations. The only relief had been in Denver, which appeared to be a growing, exciting city. Even there she had not stayed long enough to really see it, but had been forced to hurry out on the first train south to Tucson.

She looked around at the busy road. Tucson, at least, appeared to be what she expected in a western town. It was fairly large—she had noted that from the train—and certainly it bustled with life. There were woman wearing sunbonnets ambling along the walkways and children dodging the traffic in the streets. The men were a mixture of business types in black coats and cowboys in tall boots and wide, battered hats. Now and then a flamboyant figure in tasseled buckskins swaggered down the walk, and once she even spotted an Indian family swathed in dirty blankets and looking completely confused by their surroundings.

Yet, for the most part, it had been a long three hours' wait at the stage station, and she would be thankful to leave. She had been traveling nearly a week, and the end of her journey was finally in sight. She could not wait to get there.

Absently she noted the group of people standing near the stage. They were all men except for one woman waiting patiently near the open door. The men smoked cigars and exchanged comments with Jameson, the driver, and a smaller, wiry fellow cradling a rifle in the crook of his arm, who was probably the guard. She had read enough dime novels now to know that every stage carried one. Someone had brought Jameson a tankard of beer from which he took long drafts in between comments.

The woman worried her more than the men. She was tall, with a long face more highly painted than any Amanda had ever seen. She wore a green-velvet dress with a large bustle of drapes behind, had flaming red hair that cascaded down her back in long swirls, and her head was topped with a green-velvet pointed cap clustered with trailing feathers that suggested some exotic bird. She did not look exactly respectable, and Amanda found herself hoping the woman had come to see someone off and not to take the stage herself.

She saw Jameson hand someone the tankard and motion her forward. Her heart sank as she saw him reach to help the woman in the green hat up the steps and into the stage while the rest of the men fell back.

"Miss Lassiter, is it?" Jameson said, as she came abreast. He took her hand to assist her into the stage.

"Yes. And you'd be Mr. Jamison. I'm pleased to meet you."

The body of the vehicle swayed on its springs as she climbed aboard. She glanced at the other woman briefly, gave her a tentative smile, then took the seat opposite, setting her bag down beside her. The woman looked around long enough to give her an appraising glance and a casual nod, then went back to staring out the window.

"Is this your first trip to Tombstone?" Amanda asked in a shy attempt to be friendly.

"Yes." There was a long pause as the woman appeared to struggle with an unwillingness to talk. "What about you?" she finally added.

"Yes, it is," Amanda said, settling back on the hard seat. She gave up her brief attempt at friendly conversation and hoped her companion would become more talkative as the journey commenced. She was disappointed, though, that none of the men joined them. She felt certain that the lady in the green dress was no shrinking violet, but it wasn't encouraging to think this stage would be heading into the desert with only two women aboard. She winced as Jameson closed the door with a bang then leaned through the open window long enough to say, "Make yourselves comfortable, ladies. It's two hours to the next way station."

The stage wobbled back and forth as the driver climbed up to his post. Amanda settled back against the horsehair cushion, her hands folded in her lap, trying not to think of what she would do when she finally reached Tombstone. Would Uncle George be glad to see her? Would the packets of drugs he had requested, which were snuggled deep in the bottom of her carpetbag, make the surprise of her arrival more agreeable to him? Would he let her stay or order her back East on the first stage out? The coach jerked forward, and she clutched at her bag.

"Driver! Hold! Wait a minute!"

With a sharp cry from the driver to the horses, the stage pulled up. Jarred out of her thoughts by the cries from the porch, Amanda leaned forward and peered out of the window. A late arrival came running out of the station, waving his ticket and calling frantically to the driver. The body of the stage rocked gently back and forth as she heard the man talking to Jameson, still sitting on his perch with the reins in his hands. Then the door was pulled open and a man in a black frock coat filled the narrow space as he climbed inside.

He glanced around long enough to see that Amanda

and her tapestry bag took up most of the room on one side of the cab, then took a seat in the corner beside the lady in green. This lady, who had barely acknowledged Amanda's presence, fastened an appraising gaze on the new arrival that grew in interest the longer it lasted. The cab swayed as Jameson climbed down and walked back to lean in the window.

"I'll take your ticket, if you please, sir."

"Oh, of course. Here you are."

Jameson glanced down at the paper. "A reverend, is it?"

"Yes," the man smiled thinly. "The Reverend Cabot Phinias Storey, on my way to my new church in Tombstone."

Jameson shoved his hat back an inch. "That'll be St. Anselm's. They've been waiting for you."

"So I've been told," the young man answered.

"Well now, Reverend. You take care of these two ladies, you hear."

Having done his duty to his passengers, Jameson moved off to climb back to his perch. Amanda, without, she hoped, seeming too obvious, peered up from under the brim of her bonnet, taking stock of the new arrival. Intrigued that a real preacher would be traveling with them, she noted the long black coat, the string tie, the fine-quality Stetson hat, the tall, black boots, and silver spurs. With a skip of her heart, she recognized the rider she had seen earlier and leaned forward to examine him more closely.

He had a pleasant-enough face—clean shaven, with a wide, square jaw, framed by sandy hair that fell neatly to his shoulders. Though she had never really known a clergyman, she'd always thought of them as either old and fatherly or young and naive. This fellow was neither. He was sun-burnt, and his lean face had a strength that suggested there wasn't much he didn't know about life. He settled himself back on the seat as though he rode stage coaches every day, and the smiling glance he gave to his fellow travelers was as challenging as it was friendly. When he abruptly caught her looking at him, he gave her a smile that set her blood simmering and brought a blush to her cheeks. His gray-green eyes were almost faded, as though they had seen too much desert sun.

Embarrassed to be caught staring, Amanda managed a shy smile and quickly reached for her book.

"Reverend Storey," the man said, lifting his hat.

"How do you do. Miss Amanda Lassiter."

He turned politely to the other woman as the stage went bouncing off down the street. She reached out a languid hand which he took briefly.

"Mrs. Tilly Lacey," she said in a husky voice. "The *widowed* Mrs. Lacey."

"Pleased to meet you Mrs. Lacey. And you, Miss Lassiter. You did say *Miss* Lassiter?"

Amanda raised her book to hide her face. "Yes," she murmured.

"Well," he said, settling back. "It seems we shall be traveling together for some hours. I hope you won't mind if I raise this window against the dust. Just let me know if it gets too warm for you."

Amanda nodded while Mrs. Lacey, still appraising the interesting young preacher, gave a short laugh. "I don't care what you do, as long as you don't pray."

Amanda caught her breath at the woman's impudence, but the preacher only smiled good-naturedly.

"Only to myself," he said, settling back against the seat. "Only to myself."

Cabot. Cabot! He must remember that name.

For a split second there he had almost called himself 'Reverend Cole.' He would have to be constantly on his guard if he wanted to carry off this crazy masquerade.

Cole lounged back on the seat and yanked his hat down over his eyes to give the impression he was dozing. It might seem more natural to pull out the Reverend Storey's Bible and read from it, but he decided he was not really interested in doing that. It had been an impulsive decision, taking on this preacher's clothes and identity in order to sneak himself into Tombstone. The warm air still felt unaccustomedly cool on his newly shaven cheeks. Yet it had been necessary to rid himself of his fine moustache and heavy beard if he wanted to keep Sheriff Behan from recognizing him since in the wanted posters he was pictured wearing both. Without them, at least there was a chance of going unrecognized long enough to contact Aces Malone. Once that was done, he would be out of there and back to his hideout where, with any luck, that preacher could be sent on his way. That is, if Floyd could keep the man safe from the rest of the gang.

Cole peered through narrowed eyes from under his hat. He could feel Mrs. Lacey's curious glance still on him, and he hoped his lack of interest would soon bore her enough to ignore him. He had heard of Tilly Lacey.

She used to run a notable brothel in the red-light section of Newton, Kansas, some wag had dubbed 'Hide Park.' She was either on her way to set up a new establishment in town or returning to a going business. Either way, she obviously had a too-curious interest in the Reverend Storey. Cole knew he had never met her, however; and if she had heard of 'The Casket Kid,' surely she would not link him with a preacher.

He was relieved to see that Tilly had gone back to looking out of the other window and turned his gaze back to studying the young woman on the opposite seat.

The truth was he had barely been able to take his eyes off her since he boarded the stage. For a fleeting moment, he wondered if she were traveling with Tilly or perhaps were one of her 'girls.' But he soon ruled that out. She was far too wholesome and lovely to be one of the ladies of the line.

His eyes lingered on her small, pixie face. She had the longest lashes he had ever seen. They lay in a crescent slightly above her cheek as she looked down at her book. Her mouth grew pursed as she read, the full, shapely lips trembling into a smile over something on the page. Her skin reminded him of the creamy sunset over the desert hills—the russet tones of her luscious mouth against the dusky rose of her cheek and the pale pink of her throat above her lace collar.

Even the faint sprinkle of freckles across the bridge of her nose gave a piquancy to her face that was endearing. She had hair the color of a dark creek after a rain—brown and red mingled together and shining like the sun sparkling on the surface of the water. It had to be long and thick, and though she had caught it in a full bun at the nape of her neck, wavy tendrils fell on her forehead below the rim of her bonnet.

Oh hell, she felt him watching her. He intended to quickly close his eyes when she looked over at him, but he couldn't tear his gaze away. He was rewarded with a shy smile that creased a dimple in her cheek, and he saw that her eyes were the color of new honey and flecked with gold.

Good God, what was happening to him? There was a peculiar murmur in his chest and a spreading warmth lower down which he resolutely forced away. Imagine Cole Carteret going all watery over a neat little lady who was probably a schoolteacher or some other respectable creature. And especially now, when he needed his wits about him. This was impossible!

He forced his eyes closed. No use talking with her now since it might only encourage Mrs. Lacey's interest. They had a long journey ahead. He'd find some way to have a conversation before they reached Tombstone.

By the time the stage reached the first way station where they were to change horses, Amanda had a painful crick in her back from being jarred by the rough road. She entered the low, adobe building just long enough to have a cool drink, then walked outside, surveying the area. The small building sat close to one other, which was obviously some sort of stable, and was enclosed on three sides by a fenced corral. Beyond that, in all directions, stretched the desert, its graveled surface dotted with clumps of green, thorny scrub grass that looked as though it could not sustain any form of life. The mid-day sun made the heat a living thing that set the horizon wavering. One solitary tree struggled beside the stable, casting its weak shadows over one end of the corral. Several horses stood grouped there, their tails swishing against the flies.

Stiff from sitting on the stage, Amanda felt she had to walk, even in this heat. She set off with long strides, back down the road they had come, determined to go only a short way, then return in time to climb aboard again.

She had taken only a few steps when she heard someone behind her. Before she could turn to see who it was, the Reverend Storey stepped up alongside.

"You ought not to go wandering off alone, you know," he said, smiling down at her. "There are rattlesnakes out here."

"I only wanted to get a little exercise. One gets stiff sitting for so long. I'll stay on the road."

She hoped he would realize he was being dismissed; but if he did, it did not discourage him.

"Do you mind if I join you? I'd like to stretch my legs a little, too."

"Well, of course. If you want."

Amanda looked down, embarrassed. Though at first she had quietly studied the preacher on the stage, afterwards he had kept his hat over his face so long that she couldn't really see what he looked like. Now she knew his smile was engaging and his eyes sparkled with life. Quickly she turned her face away to hide the sudden flush that rose to her cheeks.

He fell in step beside her, gazing out at the low rim

of purple mountains on the horizon. "There are Indians out there, too, you know. It's not a hospitable country."

"You sound as though you know it well."

Cole caught himself, remembering that Cabot Storey was a greenhorn. "Well, although I am just coming from the East to take up my duties in Tombstone, when I was younger I spent some time out here. On . . . a ranch. Yes, getting to know the country. And I've read a lot about it, too."

"Was that to prepare yourself for your new church?"

"Yes, that's right. I believe one ought to learn all one can about a place before taking it on."

"That's very wise. I wish I had read more about the Arizona Territory before I left St. Louis. If I had, perhaps I would be more prepared. Somehow I didn't think it would be so . . . so desolate."

"It's not as desolate as it appears to be. The desert is full of life. The Indians know that. They can walk across this flat space and find water and food with no trouble at all."

"Food?"

"Yes. Mesquite beans, agave hearts, saguara and cholla fruit, juniper berries, and piñón nuts. And occasionally, even meat."

She looked up at him, smiling shyly. "Rattlesnakes and scorpions?"

"Don't laugh. Rattlers can make a tolerable stew."

"I don't believe it."

Cole realized they had gone far enough and lightly pressured her arm to turn back, leaving his fingers to cradle her elbow, enjoying the warm sensation it gave him to touch her. "It's true. Every word."

Amanda eased her arm away from his touch. "How do you know so much about the Indians? I thought they were all on reservations by now."

"I have a friend who works at Fort Apache," he lied. "Most of them now live at the San Carlos; but a few refuse to remain there and simply walk away, hiding in the mountains. Heronimo is the most famous. He's a Chiricahua war chief who refuses to be subdued. He keeps a band with him in the Coronados, managing to stay out of the way of the army that's always on his tail."

"Would he bother a stage like ours?"

Cole peered out across the desert, suddenly serious. "He might. He likes to go after small prey like a solitary traveler or stage."

Amanda's hand went to her throat. "Oh, dear . . ."

He smiled down at her. "Don't worry. We have a guard, and I'm not a bad shot myself. We'll get through all right."

They were nearing the corral where the stage stood, fresh horses already hitched. Jameson came striding from the station house to open the stage door for Mrs. Lacey, who was close behind him. She paused as she saw Amanda and Cole approaching.

"Out for a little meditation, Reverend?" she asked.

Cole ignored the faint irreverence in her manner and assumed what he hoped was a pious face. "Many people, Mrs. Lacey, feel that the Creator forgot about this country when he made the world. But I was just showing Miss Lassiter that the Lord put great beauty in the desert, as well as . . ."

"Yes, yes . . ." Tilly said, hoisting herself up into the body of the stage.

Cole smiled to himself. With any luck, his verbosity would discourage Tilly Lacey and that would give him a chance to get to know Amanda Lassiter better. And he would not have to pretend to sleep the rest of the afternoon.

Yet, as it turned out, there was little conversation in the coach for the next two hours since the tedious, slow journey worked on all the passengers to draw each of them into their own solitary thoughts. Amanda pulled her carpetbag into her lap and, with her arms protectively over it, leaned back to doze fitfully most of the way. Now and then, when the wheels hit a gaping hole in the road or struggled through a patch of heavy sand, the coach would jar strongly enough to wake her. But for the most part, she closed her mind to any concerns over her reception in Tombstone and gave way to the weariness compiled from a week of traveling.

Cole was grateful that she did, for it gave him an opportunity to study her face and the way her firm breasts lifted over the rim of her huge tapestry bag. She wore a drab brown dress, tightly buttoned down the front, that gave tantalizing indications of the high, rounded contours beneath. Unfortunately, focusing on them brought on such uncomfortable sensations that he was forced to pull out Cabot Storey's worn Bible and pretend to read from it. Though he felt like a hypocrite to do so, at least it seemed to turn away Mrs. Lacey's frequent curious glances.

When the stage drew to a complete and sudden stop in the middle of a barren patch of desert, Amanda awakened, wondering why. Then the door was pulled open, and Jameson appeared to speak to the passengers.

"We're about to cross the last group of hills into Tombstone," he said, leaning on the door frame. "The stationmaster told me earlier that Heronimo's Apaches have been seen around here recently, so we may have to make a run for it. I just want you to be prepared in case we do."

"Wild Indians?" she breathed.

"I'm afraid so. But don't be alarmed. We have good horses and a guard who is an excellent shot. We'll get you through safely."

Cole leaned toward the driver. "I'm a pretty good shot myself, if you have an extra rifle."

Jameson glanced skeptically at the preacher, wondering if he were speaking the truth or just trying to impress the ladies. "I never knew a preacher who could shoot straight," he murmured.

Cole smiled. "Well, there's always the exception, isn't there?"

"Okay, Reverend Storey. I guess we can use all the help we can get." He reached out and caught the rifle the guard threw down to him, handing it to Cole. "Just don't let it go off inside the coach."

Cole bit his tongue to keep from telling him he knew more about guns than this driver ever imagined. "I'll be careful," he muttered, looking to see if the rifle was loaded.

Jameson slammed the door and climbed back to his perch. As the stage started off again, climbing slowly along an incline, Amanda glanced over at the man who seemed so knowledgeable about the rifle in his hand. It made her a little more confident to know he had it, yet, like Jameson, she wondered at a Man of God's being so sure of himself with a shotgun. Perhaps in this wild country everybody had to know how to shoot. Even preachers!

"Is St. Anselm's your first church, Reverend Storey?" she asked, hoping casual conversation would take her mind off the dangers that might lie ahead.

Cole pointed the rifle out the window and squinted down the sight. "Uh . . . why, yes. It is."

"Is it a large congregation?"

He hesitated, cradling the rifle in his arm, trying to remember what he had learned from Cabot Storey. "Well, to tell the truth, Miss Lassiter, I don't know too much about it yet, except that I'm supposed to help them build a church. They've been worshipping in a hotel, you see, and they really want their own building."

"I'm sure they'll be grateful to have their own pastor as well. I mean, I don't know much about churches, but I would suppose it is important to them to have a regular leader."

"Mmm," Cole murmured. "A leader, yes. Churches need that."

"I suppose you'll be organizing a lot of fund-raising events to raise money to build the church. My neighbor in St. Louis often told me about the events her parish held. Potluck suppers, raffles, circuses . . ."

Cole suppressed an inward groan. The idea of The Casket Kid presiding over a potluck supper or leading a raffle was too ridiculous, too nauseating to contemplate.

"As a matter of fact, I hope to bring in some new ideas

for raising the money," he said, hoping she would not ask what they were. One good robbery would do it.

The stage hit a level plateau and picked up speed. Amanda leaned closer to the window to peer out at the scenery. A wall of sandstone blocked her view to the side, but far out in front she could see a level spread of green prairie with a ribbon of white road winding across it. She had just settled back against the seat when she heard the first terrifying howl. For an instant, she thought it might be a wild animal, but when it grew in intensity and the preacher leaned to the window, balancing his rifle on the rim, she knew it had to be Indians.

A shot rang out from the guard. "Get down on the floor," Cole ordered. Terrified, Amanda scrambled down, crouching beside Tilly Lacey as the stage careened forward, the horses speeding between the canyon walls and heading for the open ground. The cab swayed and rocked, jostling the two women together. Clutching her precious bag, Amanda looked up to see Cole balancing himself against the door, raising his rifle to point toward the top of the hills and getting off round after round.

The howling grew louder, and the ping of gunshots resounded against the coach. With hooves flying, the horses raced from the wall of the surrounding hills and out onto the flat prairie, careening down the road stretching across it and tearing out over the bumpy terrain.

As the howling grew fainter, Cole switched his position in order to fire back the way they had come, methodically picking his targets, cocking and firing his gun with a casual ease and an indifference to danger that took Amanda's breath away.

As the distant howls of the Indians faded, he sat back

on the seat and gave Amanda a hand up. "You can get up now. They've gone."

The two women climbed cautiously back on the seat, Mrs. Lacey adjusting her hat, which had been knocked askew. "It's an outrage. Why aren't those savages on the reservation like they're supposed to be? We could have all been killed!"

"Oh, I don't think so," Cole muttered, laying the rifle across his lap. "They were only trying to annoy us. If Heronimo really wanted to destroy this stage, he would have picked a better place to attack. This was more like a warning."

"Well, it seemed serious enough to me," Amanda breathed, her heart still pounding. She looked with awe at the man opposite, her admiration swelling. It was amazing to her that a man of such high moral fiber could be this strong and brave, facing death to lean out a window and fire at savage hordes. Cabot Storey was certainly nothing like she ever imagined a preacher to be. He had not only protected the stage, he seemed to actually enjoy it in a decidedly unpastoral way.

"Were you able to hit any of them?"

Cole shrugged. "I wasn't really trying to," he said, looking away. He could see the admiration in Amanda's eyes. Let her believe he didn't want to kill another human being. The truth was he didn't want to kill one of Heronimo's band of renegades.

The coach continued at its fast pace across the desert as Amanda gripped the seat and watched the gray-green of the desert floor flying by. At length she felt the horses slowing and saw that they had just passed a clapboard building. "Oh, we're here," she cried, leaning forward to peer out of the window. The stage had indeed pulled onto a road that was lined with ramshackle adobe and clapboard buildings. As it slowed to a halt, people began to appear on the streets, walking along the low walkways. Children came running along after them, crisscrossing the wide dusty street. At length, with a tug on the reins and a loud 'Whoa!', the driver pulled the horses up and the stage jerked to a stop. By the time Amanda had gathered up her tapestry bag, Jamison was yanking the door open.

"Well, here we are, little lady."

"Allow me," Cole said, moving ahead of her to jump out. He reached for Amanda's bag then offered her his hand.

As she bent to move out of the coach, a loud, noisy caterwauling struck up, thundering against her ears. She stepped onto the dusty street and looked around at a group of people standing nearby who applauded and smiled at her. The racket behind them, she saw, came from a small band—a loud thumping bass drum and several squawking horns.

Amanda smiled at the group, thinking that this must be a nice town indeed to give new arrivals such a warm reception. A small man in a black suit with a derby perched on his head came striding toward her, his hand outstretched. She had her arm raised to accept his handshake when he passed right by her and walked up to the preacher.

"Is it Reverend Storey, sir?" he asked in a booming voice.

Amanda shrank back in embarrassment as she watched

her traveling companion stare at the man in surprise. "That's right."

At a wave of the man's hand, the band grew mercifully quiet.

"Reverend," the pompous little man said loudly, reaching for the preacher's hand and pumping it energetically. "I'm Leander Walton, your senior warden. These good folks of St. Anselm's Congregation have been meeting every stage for the past two weeks hoping you'd be aboard. Welcome to Tombstone, sir!"

Still embarrassed by her mistake, Amanda slowly faded into the crowd. For the most part these people appeared to be the respectable citizens of the town, men in dark coats or shirt sleeves with bands on their arms, women in calico dresses and sunbonnets, holding babies or clutching children by the hand. Judging by the smiles on their faces, they couldn't be more delighted by the arrival of their new minister.

Leander Walton turned to the crowd, raising high the Reverend Storey's hand in his own. "Here he is, folks, at long last. The new pastor of St. Anselm's Church. Let's give him a warm welcome!"

A loud round of applause and huzzahs swept the crowd, but was almost drowned out when the band struck up its caterwauling once again. Clutching her carpetbag, Amanda stepped up on the low walkway and edged around the bass drummer who was energetically pounding away at his drum. She would just make sure her trunk was stored in the station house and then ask directions to her uncle's store. After all, this was not her celebration.

At the door she paused and looked back, curiously

noting that the new pastor was still staring at this enthusiastic crowd with a bemused, open-mouth, stricken face.

How strange, she thought absently as she started inside, that a man who had faced wild Indians with such confidence should be made so uncomfortable by a welcoming party.

Seven

Cole glanced behind him at the open door of the coach. The fresh horses were already in their traces. If he made a run for it just as the stage pulled out, he might be able to roll out of town before these people caught on to what was happening. It was a long shot, but compared to this . . .

"Now, everyone . . ." the little man in the battered derby hat shouted, silencing the crowd with an energetic wave of his arms. "Now, everyone, let's give the preacher a chance to catch his breath." He turned to Cole, beaming. "I'm sure the Reverend Storey has a few words he'd like to say to his new flock, don't you, sir?"

"No. That is . . ." Cole murmured.

"Of course you do. Our little welcome has taken your breath away, I can see. But I've never known a preacher at a loss for words, have you?"

Leander Walton beamed at the crowd, which responded with good-natured laughter. "You just go ahead and have your say, Reverend Storey, and then we'll get to the *important* business."

More laughter. The stress on the word 'important' gave Cole a momentary pang. Good God, what else could they have in mind?

At a wave of Walton's hand, the crowd grew silent, turning expectant smiles to Cole.

He looked around at their faces—kind faces, sympathetic faces. How long would that last? he wondered. Still, he ought to be able to say something that would satisfy them—at least until he could escape their clutches, find Aces Malone, and get out of this town. He searched his mind for long-forgotten sermons from the tiny clapboard church his mother forced him to attend as a child.

"Good people," he intoned. Encouraged by the broadening smiles, he raised his voice to carry over the crowd. "Good people, strange circumstances have brought me here." *Stranger than you'd ever guess.* "But it was always the will of the good Lord that guided me right to this spot to help you with your church."

"Amen" echoed through the crowd. Encouraged, Cole's voice took on more enthusiasm.

"Here, in this godless town . . ."

"That's for sure," someone shouted.

"You don't know how godless . . ."

Cole gave them the kind of indulgent smile he imagined to be typical of that clergyman back at camp. "Here in this godless town, we'll build a little haven of respectability."

"Amen . . . amen . . ."

"Praise the Lord!"

"We'll make the desert bloom with the glory of God!" A nice touch, he thought.

"Praise God . . ."

"We'll build the prettiest, the strongest, the . . . the best put-together little church building that ever graced the prairie."

Applause swept through the crowd. Encouraged by their enthusiasm, Cole beamed at the delighted faces of his congregation. "And now, let's thank the Lord for his blessings, ask forgiveness for our sins, and . . . go on with our lives."

As he moved toward the low walkway, the crowd, still applauding, made way for him. Feeling a tug on his arm, he looked down at Leander Walton, walking beside him.

"Wait, Reverend Storey. We can't go on with our lives until we take care of the important business that's waiting for you."

"Business?" Cole asked uneasily, hoping he wouldn't be asked to lead them in prayer.

"Why, yes," Walton said, stepping up on the wooden walk. As if it had been planned, the congregation grouped themselves in the street facing the walkway, while the town band spread out behind Cole and the senior warden.

"Step on up here, you folks," Leander cried. Working their way through the crowd, six young people, giggling and smiling, came forward to stand before Cole. He glanced down at them—three men in short coats, battered cowboy hats, and dusty boots; three women in beribboned straw hats and calico dresses, with pink spots of embarrassment on their pale cheeks.

"I don't understand," Cole murmured, looking at Leander.

The senior warden drew himself up proudly. "These good people have been waiting over a month for you to arrive to marry them up. 'Course, they knew all they had to do was go round to Judge Wilkerson at the courthouse and tie the knot; but no, that wouldn't do. They're good, God-fearin' people, and they wanted a proper weddin' with a proper clergyman.

"But now you're here, they can't wait no longer. So I says what better way to welcome our new preacher than to set him to marryin' right here the minute he arrives?"

"Marryin'?" Cole said weakly. "A wedding?"

"That's right. So if you'll just go ahead and do the honors, then we can all move along to the Widow Jasper's and wet our whistles with a little punch. Fruit punch," he added hastily.

Cole glanced around, wondering where he could run. He tugged at the strong grip Walton had on his arm. "Well, now, you see, I haven't been a preacher very long and I really don't know about doing any weddings."

"You mean these three good couples here will be your first?"

"That's right. I've never married anybody before." That was true, anyway.

"Why, that's wonderful! Look here, Janelle, Ted, Charlie, Jane, Horace and Clara. Not only are you goin' to be the first couples from St. Anselm's to be married here in Tombstone, you're gone to be the first for the preacher here! Ain't that somethin'!"

"I really think they should go see the judge," Cole said, trying to pull away. "I'm not really qualified . . ."

"Why, you're a clergyman, ain't you? That makes you qualified."

"But I don't know the words."

"Why that's no problem. Here, someone hand the

preacher a Prayer Book." He opened the book and jabbed at the page with his finger. "It's all right there. All you have to do is follow it, which I'm sure you know. You're just pullin' our leg here, aren't you, Reverend Storey?"

Cole turned to look down the street, wondering how far he might get if he made a break for it. Even as he wondered, two men ambled through the swinging doors of a nearby saloon and sauntered toward the crowd. They paused as they neared the stage house, looking over the group with a bemused curiosity.

The taller of the two men leaned one shoulder against the wall and stuffed his hands in his pockets, smiling thinly. Cole recognized him at once from his photographs—the long face; dark, drooping mustaches; heavy brows; and thin, agate eyes that stared coldly out at the world. Wyatt Earp, erstwhile gunfighter, lawman, gambler, and all-round hell-raiser. The stocky, shorter man beside him had to be his brother, Virgil, judging from the star on his chest. Cole remembered hearing that Virgil Earp had been appointed the deputy marshal of Tombstone.

Automatically Cole reached up to pull his hat down on his forehead, casually turning so the two brothers could only see his back.

"All right, folks," he intoned. "Draw right up here now and we'll get this deed done. Just remember though, this is my first wedding, so be patient if I stumble a bit."

Leander Walton slapped him on the shoulder. "That's all right. You're among friends—ain't he, folks?"

Cole glanced down at the words on the page. "Dearly

beloved, we are gathered together here in the sight of God and this company . . ."

A long-forgotten memory stirred in his mind, a memory of the preacher's voice intoning the words of the marriage ceremony in the old clapboard church while he sat squirming next to his mother's stiff body. This sounded like the right ceremony, if only he could remember how it proceeded. He took his time, reading slowly and scanning the fine print for directions. The three couples stood properly serious before him, bringing out the rings at the appropriate time and carefully whispering their names when they were instructed to say their vows. Cole stumbled several times over some of the words, but managed to put a good enough face on it that the sympathetic crowd took it in stride. By the time he had finished, to the applause and good wishes of the congregation, he saw that the Earp brothers had moved on down the street.

Closing the book, he leaned down to instruct the three couples in a low voice, "It might not be a bad idea, folks, to go along to the judge and have him read a civil ceremony. Just to be on the safe side."

All six of the newlyweds were so busy bestowing marital kisses on each other that they barely paid him any attention. But at least, he thought, he had tried. Now if he could only get away from this crowd . . .

"You're coming to the Widow Jasper's, aren't you?" he heard Walton ask at his elbow.

"Well, as a matter of fact, I'm kind of tuckered out."

"Well, that don't matter, 'cause you're staying at her house anyway. Just until we can get you a proper place.

You can come and celebrate with the happy couples here, then go on upstairs and settle in."

For the life of him, Cole could not see how he was going to get away from these people. He shrugged. "Sounds good. I wouldn't mind a little drink. Fruit punch, of course," he hastily added.

Leander took his arm and led him off down the street while the others followed in their wake. "We can't have anything stronger," he muttered, leaning close to Cole's ear, " 'cause the Widow don't hold with hard liquor. But sometime if you want a little more than weak tea, well, you just let me know. I keep a good store of Kentucky Rye, just for a nip now and then. I hope that don't shock you."

"Why, brother Walton," Cole answered, deciding to make the best of his situation. "The Good Lord won't fault a man for having a nip of good whisky now and then, long as it doesn't cause him or anyone else any harm."

Leander's narrow face creased with a broad smile. "Reverend Storey, I can see that you are my kind of man. We're going to get along very well."

They turned down one of the side streets that led away from the main section of the town. It was lined with small square houses set between vacant lots. Some of the lots were nothing but encroachments of the desert upon the town, but others had new houses in the first stages of construction. Though most of the occupied homes still had a raw, recently built look, in a few, efforts had been made to create civilized front yards with struggling grass lawns and colorful flower beds.

The Widow Jasper owned an imposing two-story

frame house with frilly lace curtains in the windows. She met Cole at the door—a round, plump woman with white hair neatly caught in a bun at the back of her neck and a sweet, matronly smile. She was obviously proud that her home had been selected for the temporary housing of St. Anselm's new rector.

"I serve supper promptly at six every day, but beyond that you're on your own," she said, welcoming Cole into the parlor. It was a narrow room made even smaller by festoons of paper garlands hanging across the ceiling. One table against the wall, covered with a lace cloth, held an enormous punch bowl surrounded with glasses of every size and shape. Above the table someone had hung a banner with the inscription: WELCOME REVEREND STOREY!

"This is all very festive," Cole murmured, looking around. "Is all this for me?"

"Oh no," the Widow responded as the rest of the congregation crowded inside the room. "It's for you and for the young folks who finally tied the knot. They've been patiently waiting for you, you know. We've all been waiting."

Leander Walton handed Cole a glass filled with a red liquid. "Here, you are, Reverend Storey. Wet your whistle, then I'll introduce you to the rest of the congregation."

Cole groaned inwardly. But, for the time being at least, he was stuck here with these people so he might as well try to act preacherly. He barely paid attention to the names or the faces of the people that crowded around him. A few stood out, of course. Mrs. Stone was a fierce-looking matron who let him know right away she was put out that he wasn't staying with her. She also had an unmarried daughter, Alice, dragged forward by her mother and so shy she was barely able to look him in the eye.

There were two other young, unmarried daughters whose mothers clearly had that matchmaker's gleam in their eyes. Of the two, one was nearly as shy as Alice Stone, but the other gave him such a brazen, appraising once-over that he had to turn away to keep from returning it. Lucy . . . Lucy Ellis. That would be one to watch out for.

In addition to Leander, there were five other men who had been elected by the congregation to run the church. Cole recognized their small-town, respectable type right away. One was the telegraph agent in the town, another a clerk at the stamp mill. Only one of them appeared to have a place of importance among the town hierarchy—Joseph Donnely, the assistant manager of one of the banks. Of the other two, one worked at Bauer's Market and the other at the barber shop.

Reverend Cabot Storey had his work cut out for him, Cole thought to himself, if he planned to build a prosperous church with this bunch. But Cole kept a kindly smile on his face and tried his best to make casual chitchat with the men and their matronly wives while he watched all the time for an excuse to dash upstairs and be alone. He could always plead fatigue—and, in truth, he was a little tired from the long trip. But more than that, he needed time to think through a way of getting out of this trap that had been closing around him ever since his arrival in Tombstone. Something of his concern must have finally showed in his face, for Leander

Walton, who had assumed the unofficial position of keeper of the new rector's well-being, finally took his arm and drew him toward the stairs.

"We've put your trunk in your room already, Reverend Storey, so you can go on up and rest yourself a while. Come on, I'll show you where you're to bunk."

"I'm obliged," Cole said, following Walton up the narrow stairway. There was a hall at the top which stretched the length of the house. Walton hurried him down to the end where the last of three doors stood ajar.

"Here you are."

Cole stepped into a room neater and cleaner than any he had seen since he was a child. The plank floor was scrubbed to a honey-colored sheen. The walls were freshly painted and decorated with several small, framed pictures. A narrow bed on a white frame stretched against one wall while a heavy dresser and a table with a porcelain pitcher and bowl sat against another. There was one window, the top half shuttered, the bottom framed with a starched white curtain. Someone had even thoughtfully put a small vase with a handful of brightly colored flowers on the dresser.

"Why, this is mighty nice," Cole said, looking around. "I didn't expect anything this pleasant." That much was certainly true.

Leander beamed. "I'm glad you like it. The ladies worked hard to get it ready for you. Now, I'm sure you want some privacy and some rest."

"That would sure be nice," Cole agreed, sitting on the bed and finding the springs comfortable.

Leander already had his hand on the door handle.

"Besides, I know you'll want some time to work on your sermon before tomorrow's service."

Cole's head shot up. "Sermon!"

"Well, after all, Reverend, tomorrow *is* Sunday. And good preachin' is something we have wanted for a long time. We're really looking forward to hearing you."

"Wait a minute," Cole said, jumping to his feet. "Preaching a sermon . . . I don't know. I'm not really used to it . . ."

Leander frowned. "Come now, Reverend Storey. Preaching's the one thing all ministers learn in seminary. I can see that you might be uneasy about readin' a weddin', but I never heard of no preacher that couldn't preach! And the bishop said in his letter you was good at it."

Cole could sense the first cracks in the welcome he had received, and he quickly backed down. "Well, of course, I know how to preach and everything, but I was just wondering what kind of sermon you folks like. You know, different churches like different things."

He was relieved to see Walton's smile return. "Oh, we like everything," the warden said, "but if we had a preference, well, I'd say the more fire and brimstone, the better."

"Fire and brimstone. Of course. My preference as well."

"Good. I'll be by early tomorrow to take you along to the hotel where we hold service. Good night, Reverend Storey."

"Good night," Cole muttered, sinking back down on the bed as the door closed behind the senior warden.

A sermon! Now he knew he *had* to find a way out

of this place. He moved to the window and looked down. The sloping roof of a woodshed just below would give easy access from the house. Once it was dark he could slip out the window, find Aces Malone and then ride out of Tombstone before the little congregation of St. Anselm's knew they had lost their new preacher. Yes, that might work.

A sermon. Fire and brimstone.

He smiled thinly to himself. It might have been fun, at that.

Eight

Dead!

The word hung on the air—unreal, preposterous, terrifying. Amanda gripped the edges of the tapestry bag in her lap, her fingernails digging into the heavy fabric.

"He can't be dead. I have a letter from him."

Across the desk from her, Lawyer Warren Peters watched her face drain of color and leaned forward, ready to reach for a glass of water from the sideboard.

"Let me see it."

Amanda dug into the bag and brought out Uncle George's dog-eared letter, stained and creased from much handling. The lawyer took it and spread it out on his desk.

"But this is dated over a year ago."

"I know. He sent it first to Cincinnati and it took some time to get to St. Louis. By the time it arrived, my father had succumbed to an attack of typhoid."

"So you are George Lassiter's niece?"

"Yes. I thought since my father could not respond to his invitation to come to Tombstone, that I would. You see, he is my only living relative. Or, at least, he was . . ." Her voice broke and she looked down trying to hide the distress she felt. "If only I had known . . ."

"It was sudden. A heart attack, Dr. Goodfellow said. But he left a will. Let's see, it's here someplace."

He pulled out a drawer and leafed through the papers stacked inside. "I drew it up myself, so I'm familiar with the contents. He didn't have anything much of value apart from the store. He rented a room at the Cosmopolitan Hotel the whole time he lived here and didn't seem to care about belongings. Even rented a horse when he needed one. He put everything into that drug store. It was all his, with no encumbrances."

Amanda fought against the sense of hopelessness that threatened to overpower her. "I brought some drugs he asked for," she murmured. "He sent a list."

Peters extracted a thin sheet from the pile and opened it, settling a round pair of steel-rimmed glasses on his nose.

"The store is left to his brother, Dr. Robert Lassiter, and, after him, to his surviving heirs. I guess that means you, Miss."

She glanced up quickly, her eyes obscured with unshed tears. "What?"

"You are the new owner of Lassiter's Drug Store. I have to warn you it's not much to inherit. Once George died, we sealed the door and left it to collect dust until we could hear from your father. I wrote to him, but I suppose my letter arrived after you left, since it also was sent to Cincinnati."

Far from being a comfort, the news that she now owned her Uncle George's store only increased Amanda's confusion. She was in a town where she didn't know a single soul. What did it matter what she owned?

"It's a tiny place," Peter's voice droned on. "Not

much more than a hole in the wall, but it served a useful purpose and had a faithful clientele. Without it, the only medicines in town repose in the doctor's saddlebags. You could probably sell the store. That is, if you don't want to set up shop yourself."

Amanda shook her head. "No. That is out of the question." Through the window behind Mr. Peter's head she could see the long russet stripes of sunset beginning to appear over the desert. Soon it would be dark and she had no place to stay and no one to advise her. Her heart sank as she recalled Mrs. Abernathy's dire predictions. Her friend had been right. Coming out here alone was a crazy thing to do.

"Well, at least you'll want to see the place," Peters said, folding the will and handing it to Amanda. "And I've a chest stored in the back with Lassiter's belongings. You'll want to go through them, I'm sure. There's little of value beside his pistol, but you could probably get a good price for that."

"Yes, I suppose I should do that," she murmured. "Perhaps I could rent a room for the night at that hotel you mentioned."

"The Cosmopolitan? No, that wouldn't do at all. You'd be better off at the Union." As he studied her pale face, he found his sympathy for her increasing. Not that he wanted it to. Since the moment he heard her inquire about Lassiter in the stagecoach station, he had hoped to turn over the will and the key to the store and be done with this whole thing. He certainly did not want the burden of sheltering a respectable young girl who ought to have better sense than to come to this wicked town alone and unescorted.

And yet . . . she was so pretty, and she looked so vulnerable. She would be eaten alive by this place unless someone protected her. Perhaps he owed George Lassiter that much. And with any luck, she would be out of here in a day or two.

Peters reached for his round felt hat. "Come along then, Miss Lassiter. I'll show you the store, and then we'll go around to the Union and rent you a room. Martha Poole runs it. She'll take care of you."

Amanda felt the pall of anxiety lessen a little. "Thank you, Mr. Peters," she said, smiling up at him. "I'm grateful. I had kind of planned to stay with Uncle George, you see."

The lawyer clamped his black hat on his thick white hair. "I know," he said, opening the door for her and reaching for her bag. "I'm certain if George were still here, he'd have taken you around to Martha Poole himself."

They descended a flight of narrow, unpainted stairs that opened onto the wooden walkway beside the stage station. Peters turned Amanda so that she would be walking next to the wall, then took his place beside her as they started along the walk. They hadn't gone ten feet before the swinging doors of a saloon jutted open in front of them and two men came careening out, clutched in a wrestler's grip that sent them staggering down the low steps and into the street. Pounding each other with their fists, they fell into the dust and rolled over and over. A stream of men, hollering encouragement, flowed after them to watch. Peters pushed Amanda against the wall of the saloon and took his place protectively in front of her.

The shouting and laughing grew more ribald. Amanda peered around the lawyer's shoulder and saw one of the men punch the other in the teeth and send him sprawling flat on the ground. Standing up on his knees, the man laughed—while his victim rolled over, sat quickly up, and reached around his back. Pulling out a short-barreled revolver, he blasted away. Amanda hid her face in Peters' broad back, but not before she saw the spurt of blood spread across the first man's chest. A roar went up from the crowd as they swelled out into the street. Taking advantage of the open space before the saloon, Peters grabbed Amanda's hand and pulled her down the sidewalk, crossing a side street and hurrying along.

"Merciful heavens!" Amanda cried. "What kind of place is this?"

"It's Saturday night," Peters muttered. "Pretty soon the miners will start arriving, ready to let off steam and raise a little hell. You'd better get accustomed to hearing guns go off."

"But that man shot the other one. Won't he be arrested?"

"Oh, yes. And tried, and probably released for defending himself. No one's supposed to wear guns in town, but that's one law that's frequently broken."

Amanda hurried to keep up with Peters, looking nervously around as they trotted along the walk. It seemed to her that every other store was a saloon, with lights blazing inside and the music of a piano or a fiddle keeping time beneath the crowd's shouting and laughter. Men on horseback rode wildly down the wide street, hollering and waving their hats in the air—probably the workers from the surrounding mines coming into town for a little Saturday evening recreation. There were women on the walkways as well, most of them tawdrier versions of Mrs. Lacey. Amanda thought longingly of the women in sunbonnets who had met the Reverend Storey. As the dusk deepened, there were none of them to be seen on the streets of Tombstone.

And over all was a constant, loud pounding from the edge of town, like the beat of a huge heart. When she inquired about it, Peters told her it was the stamp mill that turned the silver ore into bars which could be carried into Tucson.

"Does it never stop?" she asked.

"Never. It's the life blood of this town. If it stops, the town stops."

Amanda followed him as he turned off the main street and down one of the narrow side roads. How could anyone live with such noise and violence? she wondered. How did Uncle George manage to stay here two years?

They walked along the side of one of the saloons and in front of two stores with shuttered doors. As Peters started across the street, he paused to wait for a small, dark-green buggy that was just passing. The driver was a short little man with a Vandyke beard and a ramrod stance. Beside him sat a chubby woman in a flowered bonnet. Peters smiled and lifted his hat.

"Afternoon, John. Mrs. Slaughter."

The driver waved his whip and moved on while Peters took Amanda's elbow to help her across the street.

"That was John Slaughter. He owns one of the biggest ranches around these parts. Nearly forty thousand head of cattle and almost five thousand horses. He doesn't come into town very often, but I suppose he's here today to testify about the stage robbery."

"Stage robbery?"

"Oh, yes. They happen all the time, but the one last month was worst than most. The driver, Bud Philpot, was shot dead, along with a passenger in the dicky seat. Talk around town is the robbers were really out to shoot Bob Paul, the Wells Fargo agent who was riding shotgun messenger. But Paul and Philpot had changed places, more's the pity for Bud Philpot. Well, here we are."

Peters came to a stop in front of a narrow shop in the middle of the block, with its only window boarded up. Pulling out his key, he opened the door and turned to Amanda.

"It's been empty for some time. Maybe I'd better go first."

The door creaked open revealing an interior so dark and gloomy she gladly stepped aside to let the lawyer enter. She could smell the fetid air oozing into the street from the shuttered building She waited while Peters rummaged around, found a piece of a tallow candle, and lit it. He pulled the door open wider and beckoned her inside.

Dust motes circled in the light from the candle. Amanda looked around the shop with dismay swelling like a sickness in her stomach. She saw a long, narrow room, lined on both sides with mostly empty shelves. At the end of the room, the iron lid of a fat, round stove glinted in the light. A square box of sand sat on the floor near the stove and, beyond that, two spindly chairs lay upended on the floor. A long table, which had obviously served as a counter, was also tipped over, one leg missing.

The floor was so littered with bottles and tins that Amanda could barely take a step without kicking one of them. Some of them had spilled out powders and liquids, long since merged to form a sticky morass underfoot.

"I might have guessed," Warren Peters muttered, looking around. "I thought since it was boarded up, it would be left intact. I ought to have known drugs would attract thieves."

"What an awful mess!" Amanda breathed. "Surely Uncle George . . ."

"No, he kept it neat enough. This is vandalism, pure and simple. I'm sorry you have to find it this way. If I'd known you were coming, I would have had it cleaned up."

Amanda grabbed a handful of her skirt to keep it off the floor. "That's all right. I might as well know the worst. But it will have to be improved before anyone will think of buying it."

"Yes. Well, I'll set a crew to work first thing Monday morning." He touched her elbow, turning her back toward the door. "There isn't much to see here now, and it's getting dark. I suggest we go along to the hotel and get you settled."

"All right." Amanda sighed. "But I'd like the key, please. I want to take a closer look in the morning to see if I can salvage anything."

The cool evening air seemed heavenly after the close darkness of the drug store. Amanda was relieved to see that they headed away from the riotous main street they had come down earlier and which sounded even more boisterous now than it had before. She followed the lawyer down the side road to turn onto another wide dirt street. One block down they came to the hotel, a pleasant-looking building with stout double doors. The welcoming interior with its flowered carpets and gleaming wooden counter reminded her how weary she was.

She began to feel better about Tombstone when she met Martha Poole—a round-faced, motherly woman, who greeted her like an old friend.

"Your trunk has already been sent around, Miss, thanks to Mr. Peters, here. I put it in your room on the second floor, at the end of the hall. We run a respectable place, so you've nothing to fear from the rowdies. But it is Saturday night, so I'll apologize now for the noise. I hope it won't keep you awake."

Amanda gave her a tired smile. "I don't think anything will keep me awake tonight, Mrs. Poole. I haven't slept in a real bed for a week."

It was a small room that, even though Spartanly furnished, looked both clean and comfortable. Once Amanda was alone, she laid out her few toiletries on the dresser, splashed some water on her face, and slipped out of the confining, dusty traveling dress she had lived in for days. After shaking out a flowered dimity dress to wear tomorrow and smoothing a bonnet of the creases from the trunk, she slipped on her nightdress and sat on the bed, knees drawn up, brushing her long hair and thinking.

Perhaps it was just as well Uncle George's store had been vandalized, since that made it easier to sell it and walk away. Of course, she still had all the supplies she had brought with her, but perhaps the new owner would want to buy them. The old store was such a wreck it would have had to have been completely restocked anyway.

Tombstone was certainly different from any town she had ever seen, she thought, expertly braiding her hair into one long strand. It appeared to be as violent, unrestrained, and wild as any of the places she had read about in those dime novels. And yet there were kindly people here, like Warren Peters and Martha Poole. And respectable people, too, as that welcoming committee from the church testified.

A smile trembled at the corners of her lips as she recalled the new minister's astonished face. He obviously had not expected such an effusive welcome from this town of miners and gunfighters. And it was such a handsome face, too. The wide, shapely mouth, the square chin, the deep-set eyes, the lean cheeks . . .

She felt a shiver course through her body. The wide, firm shoulders, narrow waist, lean hips . . .

This had to stop! Leaning over, she turned down the kerosene lamp beside her bed and scrunched down under the covers, relishing the comfort of soft mattress and pillow, the clean smell of the sheets. Her eyes closed and her thoughts drifted away into drowsiness.

He really was attractive. Too bad he had to be a preacher.

Amanda woke the next morning to bright desert sunshine streaming through her window to form golden pools on the floor. She came awake immediately, realizing the hour was late and that she was starving. She dressed quickly, praying she had not missed breakfast, brushed out her hair and pulled it into a netted chignon at her neck, splashed water on her face, and hurried downstairs.

To her dismay, the dining room had been cleared and set up to resemble a meeting roam, with chairs set in orderly rows facing a small table at one end. She turned away, resigned to seeking out one of the town's cafe's, when Martha Poole came bustling out from behind the gleaming wooden counter.

"I forgot to tell you, Miss, at ten o'clock the dining room is taken over on Sunday mornings by St. Anselm's. But I thought you might be hungry so I saved you a plate in the pantry. Would you be wanting some breakfast?"

"Would I! I'm starving. Thank you, Mrs. Poole."

"Oh, please, it's Martha. Just come along, and I'll have Henry fix you some of his Mexicali fried eggs. You never tasted better."

She was ushered to a small round table in a secluded alcove usually reserved for dishes coming into and going out of the kitchen. A steaming cup of coffee was put before her almost as she sat down. It was quickly followed by eggs, thick slices of fried bacon, hot rolls, and potatoes fried with onions and peppers. Amanda ate every bite, even though the total meal was swimming in more grease than she usually consumed in a week.

By the second cup of coffee, she could hear muffled singing coming from the dining room. She recognized the strains of one of Mrs. Abernathy's favorite hymns, "Peace be Still," followed by voices reciting a prayer.

Amanda lingered a while before curiosity drove her to venture out and observe the service. After all, it was Sunday morning.

Gathering up her bonnet, she tied it under her chin and walked around to the dining room. Grateful to see an empty chair in the last row, she quietly slipped into it. When the woman next to her smiled and offered to share her Prayer Book, Amanda gladly accepted. This kind of worship was new to her, and it helped to be able to follow the words, even though the small, fine print was difficult to read.

When the congregation finished reciting, they took their seats, looking expectantly toward the front of the room where their new minister rose to begin his sermon. Amanda's heart gave a little twist as she saw the tall figure of the Reverend Storey, attired now in some kind of long loose, white tunic and looking more striking than ever. He walked around the table and stood in the center of the room, looking out at the group of expectant faces.

For a long minute he remained silent and impassive, as though waiting for heavenly aid. Then he raised his arm, pointed one long finger at the congregation and spoke in a voice loud and assured.

"SIN!"

Amanda jumped, along with the rest of the people around her. Her gaze riveted on the rector's flashing eyes as she waited for the next outburst.

"This morning I want to talk about *sin,*" he went on. Amanda strained forward.

"Sin is something we all know about. I know about it, too. Oh, yes, brothers and sisters, even a good pastor knows about sin, because it is everywhere. It is all around us. It tempts us, drags us into its evil web, whispers at us all the time to just give in, or forget, or take what's not ours. Like a loose woman, it tempts us, lures us into evil, seduces us with its promise of pleasure.

"I suspect that sin is especially strong in this town of Tombstone."

Mutterings of "Yes, yes. . . . That's right. . . . Amen," came from the congregation.

"I see it in the gambling halls, the billiard tables, the saloons, the Bird Cage, and the cottages at the end of Allen Street."

"And the gunslingers," someone called out.

"Yes, the gunfighters are the worst. A Colt .44 or .45 is the devil's handiwork, bringing sorrow to men and their widows and fatherless children alike. I've been told that this town serves up dead men for breakfast . . ."

"Just about!"

"But, brothers and sisters, sin is not just in these places. Sin is right here, in the heart."

The rector pounded his chest for effect while the congregation nodded knowingly.

"We're all to blame. The Good Book tells us that if we lust in our heart, we sin just as much as if we put down our quarter at the Bird Cage."

There was an uncomfortable shuffling around the room.

"If we are angry at our brother, we might as well have murdered him."

A voice spoke up. "Them are hard words, Reverend Storey."

"Yes, they are hard. They were meant to be hard. But

what they also mean is that none of us is free from the taint of sin. None of us. Not me, and not you."

People around Amanda nodded their heads in sorrowful agreement. She sat back in her chair, listening as the handsome clergyman went on extolling the frightening consequences of sin, watching him in an objective way as he carried the congregation along with his words and his forceful delivery. He was a good speaker, she had to admit. She wondered if all sermons included so much hammering about sin and its effects, rather than touching on remedies or hope. She wondered, too, just what sins this attractive young clergyman could be guilty of? Weren't ministers generally supposed to be above all the frailties and weaknesses of lesser mortals? The thought of this man giving way to fleshly indulgences brought a warm simmer to her blood, and she sank down in her seat, looking guiltily around to see if anyone noticed her straying thoughts.

The service concluded shortly after the sermon. Amanda stood by her chair and spoke to the few people who were kind enough to step up to her and make her welcome. In a vague way, she had hoped to speak to the minister and renew their acquaintance. After all, they had traveled from Tucson on the same stage.

Instead she saw that he was immediately surrounded by members of his flock, among them two young women who looked up at him with such adoration in their faces that she felt he would probably not even remember her. A little disappointed, she slipped quietly out of the room and went to inquire of Martha Poole how she could get some of her laundry done before starting back for Tucson.

* * *

Cole watched her go, staring at her over the heads of the people who crowded around him. It had been something of a shock to see her join the members of his congregation. He hadn't been at all sure he could carry this performance off, and to have Miss Lassiter there, watching him, had made it even more uncertain.

He had never intended for things to go this far. If only he had been able to speak to Aces Malone last night, it never would have been necessary. Instead, he had sneaked out of Mrs. Jasper's house and gone into town only to learn that Aces had traveled somewhere, possibly down to Mexico, and would not be back for two weeks. Slipping back to his room, he had spent a good half hour trying to decide whether to leave the town quietly or go on with this charade. Then it had occurred to him that if he could carry off this deception, it would be the greatest challenge of his life. Then and there he made up his mind to see it through. He really did want to talk to Malone. And, of course, he also intended to get to know Amanda Lassiter better. A lot better.

His biggest problem had been the sermon, until the word 'sin' leaped into his mind. After all, clergymen were always talking about sin, and he ought to know more about it than anybody. After that, the rest was easy.

Mrs. Ellis leaned into his face, interrupting his thoughts. "You are coming to lunch with us, Reverend Storey, aren't you? My Lucy made an apple pie especially for dinner. She's a very good cook, my Lucy."

Cole gave her a wan smile. "Of course, Mrs. Ellis. I'd be proud to have dinner with your family."

If he knew anything about women, pert, pretty Lucy Ellis was a lot more than a good cook!

Nine

Monday morning dawned clear and sparkling, the desert air as fresh as the new day. Amanda dressed in her work clothes, ate a hasty breakfast, and—armed with brooms, empty boxes, and a mop borrowed from Martha Poole—made her way back to her uncle's drug store.

The shambles inside seemed even worse in daylight than it had that dusky evening when she had gotten her first look. She despaired at first of getting the boards off the window since she had not thought to bring a claw hammer. But on closer inspection she found they were so poorly nailed in place that with a little effort she could pull them away. As the light illuminated the store, she could see clearly that this mess would not be cleaned up in under a week.

Tackling the tins and jars on the floor first, she soon grew so fascinated at reading the labels that she forgot her dismay. The assortment of powders and tonics Uncle George had stocked in his store amazed her. She had packed her father's saddlebags often enough to know the basic drugs a doctor relied upon in treating the sick—items such as mercury, jalap, morphine and opium, ipecac, Epsom salt, borax, Spanish fly, Peruvian bark, rhubarb, and calomel.

But Uncle George had gone far beyond that. She found tins with labels of "sulphur and lard," senna, sugar candy, spirits of scurvy grass, cochineal. Dover's powder, dragon's blood, and tartar emetic. Some had convenient directions for a specific aliment—alum for gargles in respiratory difficulty, Seidlitz powders for measles, linseed for poultices, white incense for sore eyes, olive oil for insect bites.

Amanda quickly decided that the only way to attack the pile of refuse was to begin sorting. When she dug out a jar or a tin, she would read the label and place it on the table, arranging similar drugs together. Once she had everything salvageable off the floor, she planned to tackle the debris that was left. With the floor finally cleared, the rest ought to be easier.

She was on her knees with her back to the open door when she heard a voice behind her.

"Hello, there."

Amanda jumped to her feet in confusion. Company was the last thing she expected this morning, unless Mr. Peters should stop by. But though the man standing in the doorway had his back to the light and she could not see his face, she could tell he was taller and stockier than the lawyer.

"May I come in?" he asked politely.

She brushed nervously at the dusty apron that covered most of her skirt. Her hand went automatically to the towel she had wrapped around her hair. She knew she must look a fright, yet on second thought, what did it matter? This fellow might well be one of those dreadful men who had created such a fuss on the main street of the town the day she arrived.

Without waiting for an answer the man walked forward, extending his hand and giving her a pleasant smile. "I'm Dr. Goodfellow," he said. "I heard you had arrived and thought I'd stop by to say a word of welcome."

Amanda felt a mixture of chagrin and relief. "Oh, please do come in, Doctor. I'm very glad to meet you." As he came closer she could see he had a round face decorated with a luxurious moustache and sparkling, pale blue eyes. He took her hand in a firm grip and shook it twice.

"You have quite a job to face here."

"Yes. It's rather daunting, but I'll get it done. Won't you sit down?" she asked, indicating the two chairs near the stove.

"I'd love to," Goodfellow said and began picking his way over the debris to the back of the room. "I won't keep you from your work long. I knew your uncle—in fact, I treated him in his last attack. I thought you might want to know about that."

Amanda took the chair opposite the doctor. "I would, thank you. I don't remember Uncle George very well—in fact, I haven't seen him since he came East ten years ago. But I was looking forward to getting to know him again. It was something of a shock to learn he had died."

The doctor stretched out his legs toward the cold stove, locking his fingers over his vest. "It was very sudden. I told him his heart wasn't good, but he didn't like advice much. And for a man who knew remedies as well as he did, he was uncommonly stubborn about using any. 'All fools' tales,' he used to say. A lot of them are, of course, but he knew as well as anybody that some of them work."

"He sounds a lot like my father. They were brothers, you know. Papa had a reputation for relying on the natural healing properties of the body. It sometimes turned people from him, especially those who thought any kind of medicine was better than none."

"Was your father a druggist also?"

"No. He was a doctor. He used to say Uncle George could have made an even better doctor, had he ever wanted to become one. I suppose my uncle enjoyed mixing powders and running a business better."

Goodfellow gave a snort. "It wasn't much of a business; and, if the truth be told, George Lassiter liked the billiard table far more than mixing powders." He paused as he saw Amanda lower her gaze to her hands twisting in her lap. "Oh dear, there I've gone and insulted the dead. I didn't mean to offend you, Miss Lassiter, but old George would be the first person to agree with me."

"Did you work together?" Amanda asked, looking up at him from under her lashes.

Goodfellow melted a little. George Lassiter's little niece was a pretty thing, even though much too innocent for this wild town. "Oh, yes. I relied on him a good deal. He had a real knack for finding the medicines I wanted, no matter how peculiar or hard to get. I've missed him a lot since he passed on. It was a real relief to hear you had come to Tombstone to open up his store again."

Amanda felt her cheeks coloring. "I'm afraid you have been misinformed, Dr. Goodfellow. I intend to clean this place up so I can sell it and leave Tombstone. The sooner the better."

The doctor sat forward, genuinely surprised. "You're not going to run the store? But I thought . . ."

"I don't know who told you I would. Warren Peters knows my intentions and he agrees with me that it's the right thing to do."

"But Miss Lassiter, there is a real need for a store like this. I admit that Tombstone is not exactly the place for a decent lady to start out in business, but you'll find it's pretty tolerant of new ways if you hang around long enough. And once you have something that other people need, they won't care if you're a woman or a gorilla."

Amanda looked away in confusion. "Really, Doctor . . ."

Goodfellow waved a hand. "You'll have to forgive my bluntness, Miss Lassiter, but that's my way. I'm like this town: stubborn, unconventional, and not given to passing judgment. Didn't your uncle tell you about me?"

"Well, he did write my father a letter inviting him here to practice. He mentioned there was only one doctor in town and that he . . ."

She stopped in embarrassment as Goodfellow laughed. "He said I was a drunk, didn't he?"

"Well . . ."

The doctor slapped his knee in amusement. "That sounds like old George. Well, none of it's true. In a town like this, doctors come and go, and there is usually more than one at any given time. Right now there're two, me and Gillingham. And I'm not a drunk, though I do enjoy a drink. But I have a hardfast rule that no doctor ought to take more than allows him to touch the fingers of his two hands together the next morning. I never break that rule."

Amanda found herself liking Dr. Goodfellow more and more. As he talked she realized he was younger than he seemed at first glance, probably still in his twenties. It was obvious he had done a lot of hard living in those years. Still, she liked his blunt, straightforward way. It reminded her of her father—another direct, stubborn man.

She leaned forward, resting her arms on her knees. "Dr. Goodfellow, my father died of the typhoid two months ago. I came here to Tombstone hoping to work with Uncle George and learn this business. Now, with my uncle gone, too, I have no one here to depend upon and I don't know enough by myself to run a drug store. It seems the wisest thing to do is to go back to St. Louis."

"Do you have family there?"

"No. In fact, I had no one but Uncle George. That's why I came."

"Well, if you have no one else to go back to, why not stay here and keep this place going? You must have learned something about medicine if your father was a doctor."

"Yes, but not enough to . . ."

"Nonsense," Goodfellow cut her off with a wave of his hand. "Anyone with a rudimentary knowledge can learn the rest by trial and error. That's what we doctors do. Your father might have relied on the healing powers of the body, but I can tell you that those powers need a little help when a .44 caliber bullet has torn through the sternum. I'm prepared to grovel at your feet to get you to stay. We doctors need a store like this."

"But surely a new proprietor could handle it as well."

"And where is that person going to come from? We don't turn up too many people who know enough about medicine to run a drug store. Besides, with your contacts back East, you might be able to bring in more of the supplies we need."

Amanda remembered the precious cargo in her tapestry bag. "As a matter of fact, I did bring some things my uncle requested."

"There, you see!" He sat back in his chair as though the matter were settled.

"But why can't you or the other physician take over the store? Some doctors do."

"I can't speak for Gillingham, but as for myself, I can tell you I have all I can do to take care of my patients." He leaned forward, resting his arms on his knees. "I tend people as far south as Mexico and as far north as Fort Apache. Half my life is spent out riding the desert. Sometimes I'll be called forty miles away to treat a sick child or a mother in a hard childbirth. Gillingham does the same. Trying to run a business as well would be crazy."

Amanda looked from his penetrating gaze to the clutter at her feet. In the distance she heard a loud howl followed by the rapid popping of a gun going off. "I understand, Doctor, but my mind is made up."

Goodfellow gave her a long, hard look, then reached for his hat. "Well, Miss, it's your right, of course. I'm sorry, because I think we might have worked well together. I would have liked having someone in town I could rely on when emergencies come up and I have to be away."

He rose to his feet. "I'm keeping you from your work," he said extending his hand. "If there's any way I can help while you're here, you've only to call on me."

"Thank you, Dr. Goodfellow."

She followed him to the door, feeling somehow guilty that she had disappointed him. He paused there and grinned as two more sharp pops came from the street below.

"Sounds as though I might have a new patient or two. Good day to you, Miss Lassiter."

"Good day, Doctor. I'm sure I'll see you again before I leave."

"Yes, indeed. In fact, I may be asking you for some of those drugs you brought in for your uncle."

Amanda worked another hour before her second visitor arrived. While clearing an aisle through the debris on the floor, she came across an old cash machine which her uncle must have used. Heaving it up on the counter, she was deeply involved in trying to figure out how it worked when a brisk knock at the door brought her head up.

She recognized him at once, even though, like Dr. Goodfellow, he was standing with his back to the light. His tall body filled the doorway, and with his high Stetson, he had to duck to enter.

"Reverend Storey," Amanda cried. Her heart gave a sudden leap which she tried to disguise by turning away to yank the towel from her hair. Smoothing it down, she smiled shyly as the parson came striding into the room.

"Am I disturbing you?" he asked, wading through the clutter.

"No, of course not. I'm glad to take a break. Come in, please."

"Mrs. Poole at the hotel told me you'd be here." His gray-green eyes glanced from the table piled with jars and tins to the piles of refuse on the floor. "Your uncle doesn't keep a very tidy shop, does he?"

Amanda caught her breath, then said in a level voice, "Uncle George died several months ago. The shop was boarded up, but it had been well vandalized all the same. Come along to the back by the stove where we can sit and visit."

Cole reached up to remove his hat. "I'd like that." He followed her to the rear of the room and sank into the chair recently occupied by the doctor, though with none of Goodfellow's relaxed ease. In fact, Amanda thought, he appeared to be almost as self-conscious as she as she primly positioned herself on the edge of her own chair.

"I guess I put my foot in it about your uncle," Cole said, laying his hat on the stove. "I'm sorry."

"That's all right. You couldn't know. After all, we both only arrived in Tombstone just two days ago." She looked down at her hands, wondering what to say next. Her mind seemed to freeze and her body felt disjointed and awkward, as though all her limbs were coming unhinged. Mentally she cursed herself for acting like a giddy schoolgirl. And just because she was alone with this attractive, eligible man.

"Has it only been two days? It seems longer." Cole tore his eyes from her lovely face, forcing himself not to linger on the delicious roundness of her close-fitting bodice or the way her white throat disappeared below the V-shaped collar of her dress. "Well, I was just out making a few calls and I thought I'd drop by and . . . and say hello again." He coughed nervously, wondering why he sounded so idiotic. "I saw you come into the service yesterday, but you left before I could speak to you."

Amanda looked up and gave him a dimpled smile. "You were surrounded by your flock. But it was nice—the service, I mean."

"Oh, thanks. I'm learning. This is my first parish, you know. I hope you'll come again." He didn't expect to be there much longer, but he hoped he sounded properly pastoral.

"I'd like that."

"In fact, there's a potluck supper tomorrow night. How'd you like to come with me?"

Her eyes fastened on his face. "With you? Why, I don't know . . ."

"Oh, come on," Cole said, sitting forward in the chair and beginning to feel more confident. "You'll be doing me a favor. There are two old . . . two ladies in the congregation who have me half-hitched to their daughters already. It'll help to discourage them."

Amanda stared at him in amazement. "Why, Reverend Storey, I should think you'd be flattered."

"Well, I am, of course, but it's also something of a

nuisance. Any encouragement would give them the wrong idea, and I want to avoid that as much as possible."

"And I'll be there to throw them off?"

"Well, not exactly. I'd really like to go with you. I'd like to get to know you better, Miss Lassiter."

She was pleased, in spite of the way he had worded his invitation. "Amanda," she offered.

"Amanda," he said, smiling at her. "And I'm Col . . . Cabot."

"Cabot. That's a very nice name."

Their eyes locked across the small space. The air between them came alive with a tingling with which they both felt, yet fought to ignore.

After a moment Cole gave another nervous cough and wrenched his gaze from her face to glance around the room. "This is a big job. You ought to get someone to help you."

"I plan to, once I have everything sorted out. I was able to save more than I expected when I first saw it. In fact, there is probably still enough here to run a respectable store."

"Well, you're not thinking of doing that, I hope."

She opened her mouth to explain that she wasn't, but something stopped her. "Why do you say that?"

"Because it's no place for a woman, running a store that sells drugs and medicines."

"Oh? Do you think I couldn't make a success of it?"

"Maybe you could, but it wouldn't be right for a pretty, unattached young girl like yourself. You'd have to deal with all kinds of people, some of them pretty low."

Amanda tried to smile. "Reverend Storey, are you one

of those men who believes women belong only in the kitchen?"

"Now that's not fair. I don't see anything wrong with Mrs. Poole managing a hotel or the Waverly sisters running a restaurant."

"Because those are feminine occupations—somewhat like keeping a home?"

Cole began to feel uncomfortable. "I suppose."

"And mixing powders and salves and rolling out pills is not."

"That's right."

Amanda got to her feet, shaking out her apron. "At this point, I don't know what I'm going to do with this store; but, I assure you, if I wanted to run it, I would make it the best drug store this side of Tucson."

"I'm sure you would," Cole said, admiring her spunk and the way her honey-colored eyes turned dark with flashing anger. He had sensed the fire beneath her prim exterior and was delighted to know his instincts were correct. "Now, you're not going to get so riled up at me you'll refuse to go to that potluck dinner, are you?"

She turned to him, seeing the mischievous twinkle in his eyes as he smiled up at her. Her indignation faded away. "You're teasing me, aren't you?"

"Perhaps just a little. But I really do need you to help me fend off those matchmaking mothers."

Amanda leaned against the counter, folding her arms across her chest. "You know, Reverend . . ."

"Cabot."

"Cabot, you're not what I thought a preacher would be like. You're . . . different somehow. Very different."

Cole quickly jumped up and reached for his hat. "Not all preachers are cut from the same cloth, Amanda."

Her direct gaze held him. "No. And neither are all women."

He gave a short laugh. *"Touché.* May I pick you up at your hotel about five o'clock then?"

"Five o'clock. I'll look forward to it."

To her surprise he reached out and took her hand, closing it in his strong fingers. His flesh felt rough and warm and sent a delightful tingle up her arm. He stood, holding her hand for several moments while she felt her cheeks coloring.

"Tomorrow, then," he said, giving her hand a squeeze.

She watched him make his way down the aisle toward the door where he turned back long enough to touch his hat. As he disappeared into the street, Amanda lifted her hand to her cheek, laying it there for a moment, relishing the warmth that still lingered from his touch, and smiling to herself.

Why hadn't she told him she had no intention of running this store, that she meant to sell it as quickly as possible and leave town? Partly because he had got her dander up with his arrogant assumption that she couldn't do it. If she wanted to try, she knew she could make a success of this store, even with her limited knowledge of medicines. Hadn't Dr. Goodfellow practically begged her to stay and keep it open?

Then, too, arguing helped to diffuse the heat that was building between them. The attraction she felt for him was too strong, too enticing, too dangerous. It weakened her determination to go back to St. Louis as quickly as possible. It opened up too many possibilities. It gave rise to too many dreams.

Quickly she rubbed her hand against her apron. What nonsense! Cabot Storey, for all his good looks, was just another man trying to keep a woman in her place. She would enjoy being around him while she remained in Tombstone and forget all about him once she rode out on the stage.

All the same, without even being aware of it, she began humming every time she thought of going to the supper the next evening.

By four o'clock Amanda felt she had done all she could for that day. The long table was covered from end to end with containers saved from the floor. The floor itself was half-cleared, with piles of debris to be carted away stacked along both walls.

She was packing up the broom, mop, and buckets when a soft cough near the door signaled another interruption. Looking up, Amanda saw a woman standing there watching her. She was small and thin with a large woven shawl draped around her faded, white-cotton dress. The woman stood without speaking, waiting for some sign from Amanda, as though she were unsure whether to come in or turn and run away.

"May I help you?" Amanda asked, curious enough about who she was to encourage her to stay.

"If you're busy, I can come back later."

Amanda laid the broom aside. "No, please, come in. I was just finishing up." She watched as the woman approached her across the room. "I'm Amanda Lassiter," she said, extending her hand. The woman clutched tighter at the shawl bunched across her breast, refusing to take her hand. Amanda peered closer and realized why.

More a girl than a woman, she had a small, oval face with large eyes that were framed with dusky shadows—partly from the smudged kohl she used to outline her eyes and partly the result of ill-health. Her skin was like clear porcelain and stretched thin across the bones of her face. Her black hair, pulled severely back to expose small ears, shone in the light. She had caught it at the back in a band that left a long strand trailing nearly to her waist. From the shabby clothing that resembled a nightdress, the weary attitude, the eyes that had seen too much, Amanda gradually became aware that this woman had to be one of the town's prostitutes. She automatically shrank back before catching herself.

The woman seemed to find nothing unusual in her attitude. "My name's Nora. I'm one of Big Gert's girls over at the Bird Cage."

Amanda felt the color warm her face. Never in her life had she been this close to a 'scarlet woman,' and it was all she could do not to turn away and walk to the other side of the room. Outrage and pity warred inside her; and, for the moment, outrage seemed to win.

Nora glanced down at her feet. "I want to buy some medicine."

"You can see that the store is not open."

"Mr. Lassiter, he sold me some; but it's gone now."

Her voice was low and not unpleasant. Amanda folded her arms protectively across her chest, wishing the woman would just leave her shop. "George Lassiter was my uncle. He's dead now and the store is mine. But I'm not selling medicines."

The woman turned away as a brief coughing spell bent her slight frame. When she could speak again, she said in a near whisper, "I really need it."

That was certainly true, Amanda thought. "I'm sorry."

The pale skin had turned translucent with the coughing. "Please . . ."

"I'm sorry, but it's impossible. Half the supplies are gone, and I don't have the expertise to mix anything for you. Why don't you ask Dr. Goodfellow or the other physician?"

She shook her head. "No, no doctors. They don't do no good."

"I'm sorry," Amanda repeated. Compassion for the woman was beginning to soften the edges of her initial distaste. "Truly, I'm sorry."

Without answering, the woman turned to make her way back to the door. She had only taken a few steps when another fit of coughing began to rack her body. Reaching out, she grabbed for the table, knocking over a row of tins as she bent over it. The fit grew into such a hard, desperate struggle for air that Amanda could finally stand it no longer. She hurried to her, laying a hand on her shoulder and guiding her back to the chair. "Here, come sit down, at least until this passes."

Nora gave her a grateful glance as she sank into the chair. Bending over her knees, she clutched a dirty handkerchief to her mouth until the coughing subsided. Then she sat back, her eyes closed, her chest heaving.

"That cough sounds like consumption," Amanda said

gently, noting with horror the brown smudges on Nora's crumpled handkerchief. "Is that why you want the medicine?"

"No. There's nothin' that helps that. It was for . . . something else."

Amanda took the chair opposite and studied Nora's white face. With those delicate features, shapely lips, and large eyes, she must have been pretty once. And not so long ago, either. With shock Amanda realized she was very young, probably not much older than herself. Yet there was a hardened edge to her, something indefinable that made her far older than her years.

The shawl had fallen away from one white arm, enabling Amanda to see that it was splotched with dark bruises. "You've hurt your arm," Amanda said. "Did you fall during one of these coughing spells?"

Nora glanced down at her arm and quickly pulled the shawl over it. "No. That happened the other night. Some cowpoke got liquored up and turned rough."

Amanda looked quickly away as she realized there were probably lots of other bruises on Nora's body hidden beneath her clothing. "How did you come to Tombstone?" she asked, more to cover her embarrassment than out of a real interest.

"Just wanderin'. I been all over. One place is about the same as another after you seen a few."

Nora looked as though she wanted to get up but couldn't summon the strength. Compassion for the poor girl won over Amanda's heart. She was sick, young, and in a profession that made her an outcast. Yet Amanda suspected that she might have been something better.

She had a vulnerable fragility that was very appealing. Curiosity as well as pity kept Amanda talking.

"How did you get to be . . . into this . . . I mean . . ."

Nora gave her a thin smile. "In the trade? It's hard to remember now, it's been so long. I grew up on a sod farm in Kansas. My mama died when I was little and there was a lot of young'uns to care for. When I began to get growed, my papa and my uncle just wouldn't let me alone, so soon as I got the chance, I run off with the first sharpy that stopped by. He wasn't such a bad man, treated me pretty good, in fact. We went to Denver, but he got shot in a saloon brawl. The madam there was nice to me and took me in. Gave me a job. After a while I got restless, though, and moved on."

"How old are you, Nora?"

"Don't know. About twenty-two or twenty-three, I guess."

Four years older than herself, Amanda thought. It might as well have been a hundred! She made a sudden decision.

"That medicine you wanted. It was for the pox, wasn't it?"

The large eyes fastened on her, filled with surprise. "Yes."

"I thought so. When you said it wasn't for the consumption, it had to be that." Amanda rose to stride a few paces up and down the room. "I don't know much about treating the pox, but I've heard that doctors prescribe arsenic, or mercury and bismuth, or all three. What did the doctor tell you?"

"Never saw no doctor about that. If it gets about that

a girl has the clap, it ruins her business. But Mr. Lassiter used to make me a salve for it."

Amanda paused, taking in the girl's clear skin and sleek, shiny hair. That salve must have been something with arsenic in it, she thought. Well, that was no problem. Arsenic had been one of the drugs her uncle requested and she had carried all the way from St. Louis.

"I tell you what," she said. "You come back here tomorrow around this same time, and I'll have something made up for you. I don't have a lot here to work with, but I'll figure something out."

Nora gave her a relieved smile that made her look almost pretty. "Thanks, Miss. I'm much obliged to you."

Heaving herself up out of the chair, she moved toward the door where she stopped and looked back at Amanda. "I'm glad you came to Tombstone, Miss. You seem like someone a girl can talk to straight. Not like most of the old biddies in this town. Don't think I'll abuse it, though. I'll only come when there's nobody else in the store. But I'm obliged. I really am."

"You're welcome, Nora. Maybe I can think of something that will help that cough as well."

Nora smiled and turned away. After stopping long enough at the doorway to make sure no one would see her leaving the store, she disappeared into the street. Amanda watched her go, wondering if she should be grateful or offended by the girl's friendly words.

What was she thinking of! There was nothing anyone could do to help Nora's consumption; it was too far advanced. Why hadn't she explained she wasn't opening the drug store and could not be counted on for help?

She picked up the broom and jammed it into the

bucket. Why indeed. Because compared to that girl's life, Amanda Lassiter's had been a bed of roses!

There must be other Noras in Tombstone, lots of them, in fact. Someone ought to help them. But should it be her? For the first time since she learned her uncle was dead, Amanda began to waver in her decision to go back to St. Louis.

Ten

Cole left Amanda's store feeling very satisfied with himself. He had convinced her to go to the potluck supper with him; he possibly might see her in church again, and—considering her determination to leave Tombstone once her store was sold—he knew now that his involvement with her would be quickly made and quickly ended. That was the way he preferred to be involved with women.

Imagine that spunky little gal thinking she could run a business! She probably could make a success of it if she tried somewhere else, but not in this wild town. These hard-fisted, hard-living gamblers and cowpokes would chew her up and spit her out for breakfast.

Still, she had looked so pretty with her eyes blazing and the color high in her cheeks that he could almost forget how annoying it was to have a woman snap back at him like that. He smiled to himself as he went striding around the corner and out on to Allen Street, thinking what a pleasure it was going to be to tame Amanda Lassiter. It might even make this crazy charade worthwhile.

"Mornin', Reverend Storey."

Cole looked up quickly, jarred out of his reverie and

back to the uncomfortable realization that he was supposed to be Cabot Storey. Just ahead, he saw a cowboy leaning against the wall of one of the saloons, a bottle in his hand and a half-drunken smile on his face. The cowboy gave him a silly grin, then reached up and tipped his hat to Cole with the top of the bottle.

"Good morning. A little early for drinking liquor, isn't it?" Cole said, trying to sound like a proper cleric.

The cowboy's smile widened. "Early? Oh, I ain't been to bed yet, so I figure it's still last night. The evenin's not over till you go to bed, you know, Reverend."

Cole grinned. "Well, I guess that's one way to look at it. But if I were you, I think I'd start looking for a mattress."

"Good advice, Preacher. Good advice."

As Cole passed on, the cowboy slid down the side of the wall to a sitting position and pulled his hat down over his eyes. That was as much of a bed as he was likely to get, Cole thought, still amazed by the respect even a drunken cowpoke showed a clergyman. For the first time he began to suspect there might be a few advantages in pretending to be the Reverend Cabot Storey.

He had not gone much farther before he saw a man coming straight toward him whose expensive coat and fancy top hat, gold watch fob, and neatly trimmed beard proclaimed him one of the town nabobs. Curious, Cole caught and held the man's eye as he lifted his hat. As he hoped, the gentleman stopped to speak to him.

"Reverend Storey, is it?"

"That's right. And you are . . . ?"

"Brody Hanlon," the man said, lifting his sleek, felt

derby. "I'm one of the owners and the director of the Amelia mine."

Cole pumped Hanlon's hand. "Pleased to meet you, Mr. Hanlon. I've heard about these mines around Tombstone. They're pretty rich, aren't they?"

"The Amelia's one of the newest and the richest. We heard you were coming to town. I'm a Baptist myself—or was, back in Baltimore—but it never hurts to visit another church. You'll find most of the town fathers happy to welcome you."

"I'm pleased to hear it, Mr. Hanlon. Of course, we don't exactly have a church yet."

"Oh, but I understand you've come here to build one." Hanlon puffed his chest a little. "When you start taking subscriptions, you won't find me ungenerous."

"Subscriptions? Oh, yes," Cole answered, seeing some interesting new possibilities in his role. "That's very neighborly of you."

"I'm late for a meeting at the bank right now, but I have an office in the adobe building next to the courthouse. Stop by some time, Reverend Storey, and I'll tell you a little more about the Amelia. You might even be interested in purchasing some shares. One good turn, you know . . ."

"Yes, well, I'll try to do that."

"Good day, Reverend Storey."

Hanlon tipped his top hat again and moved on down the walkway. He was a small man with a pigeon chest and a torso that looked too heavy for his short legs. Yet Cole wasn't fooled a moment by the natty air. Hanlon's tiny, shrewd eyes had taken in every detail of his appearance even while he spouted off about subscriptions and mine shares. Cole's instincts warned him this man could smell money a mile away. It might not be a bad idea to stop by Hanlon's office soon, although it would be a cold day in hell before he purchased any shares in the Amelia or any other mine. It was only the owners who got rich that way. He preferred to get his profits in a quicker, more certain manner.

He hadn't gone half a block before he was stopped again, this time by one of the women he recognized from church, who gushily tried to pin him down on a time to come to dinner. While he was talking to her, the proprietor of the barber shop came outside to introduce himself and offer Cole a free shave and haircut. And so it went, the length of Allen Street. Merchants and their clients were friendly and informative. Once they realized who he was, they pumped his hand and made him welcome. He even met one of the bankers who, spotting him on the sidewalk, hurried out to introduce himself and offer him his services.

They were honest, respectable people, but they were definitely in the minority when compared to the number of men he saw frequenting the saloons and hanging around the card rooms and billiard tables. Nearly every other building appeared to be one of these gambling and drinking establishments. He counted fourteen before he gave up trying to keep track. One of them was run by a Chinese fellow with a long pigtail, who ran out to bob him several bows. Cole was not surprised, either, to see a number of Mexicans lounging along the walk, given that Tombstone lay so close to the border.

But it was the gunfighters that gave him pause. He had heard that gangs of them had established themselves in Tombstone and knew most of them by reputation. He had already recognized the Earps, of course, one of whom wore an assistant marshal's badge. When a cadaverous fellow with a handkerchief pressed to his mouth crossed in front of Cole to enter the Oriental, he recognized Doc Holliday, that cold-eyed dentist who would as soon kill you as deal you a card. He'd been told that Luke Short and Johnny Ringo were also in Tombstone, aligning themselves with the Earp brothers, but he saw no one this morning who resembled them.

As he strolled down the walk, he mused over what he knew of the problems this outlaw faction had brought to Tombstone. He would have to walk carefully to avoid being drawn into them. Twice Wyatt Earp had lost elections to John Behan, and he hated him for it. The Earp faction was also at odds with some of the 'cowboy' ranchers who competed with them in relieving people of their money, even though they sometimes worked jobs together. These cowboys had a profitable game going smuggling beef and horses which they then sold to the army. So-called 'peace officers' like the Earp brothers tried to build a reputation as law men, but they really were nothing but gamblers and opportunists. The man who stood in the middle of all this intrigue was Sheriff Behan, the one person Cole most hoped to avoid. With any luck, Behan would be too busy fighting the Earps to pay much attention to the new clergyman in town.

By concentrating on the legitimate businesses as he made his way down Allen Street, Cole managed to avoid coming face to face with either the Earps or the sheriff. That would eventually happen, of course. Tombstone wasn't big enough to keep away from them forever.

Maybe by then, though, he would be so well entrenched among the respectable population they would not pay him any mind.

His most curious visit came when he finally reached the Bird Cage. He had heard tales about this fancy theater for a year now and he was anxious to see what it was really like. As he pulled open the door, it crossed his mind that most clergymen would probably never want to enter such a place. On the other hand, there were those who might make a point of going there in order to preach to the 'unconverted'. Cole decided he would be that kind of pastor.

He found himself standing in a narrow room with a gleaming mahogany bar at one end and a huge, gaudy portrait of a half-naked woman on the opposite wall. A man in shirt sleeves stood behind the bar, wiping a cloth over its surface. When he looked up in surprise, Cole smiled to himself at the bemused look on his face as he took in every detail of Cole's long black frock coat, string tie, and impressive black hat.

"Hello," Cole said, walking up to him and extending his hand. "I'm Reverend Storey. I'm new in town."

"Reverend?" The bartender's mouth gaped. "Jonas Dole, bartender at the Bird Cage." He paused. "We don't get many preachers in here."

"I suppose not. But I thought to myself when I started looking around this town, if I'm going to minister to the good people of Tombstone, then it might as well be to the sinners as to the saved."

Jonas gave him a crooked grin. "You came to the right place then, Reverend Storey. One thing we got is lots of sinners."

"Hello there," said a voice from a door beside the bar. Cole looked around to see a woman standing in the doorway that led back into the theater. Of medium height, with a chunky body encased in a tired satin dress, she stood with one hand on the doorframe and the other on her hip, slowly undressing him with her direct gaze. Cole had been in too many brothels not to recognize her type right away.

"Good morning to you, 'madam,' " he said, with emphasis on the last word. He was a little relieved to see her grin in response. At least she had a sense of humor—something not always found in the business end of a bawdy house.

"I'm Gert," the woman said without extending her hand. "And I got to tell you, if you came here to preach against sin to my girls, you might as well turn around and walk out now."

"Well . . . not so early in the day, at least. Pleased to meet you, Miss Gert. Reverend Storey." With exaggerated politeness, he reached for her hand and shook it.

Gert seemed pleased by his response. "Come on back then and meet a few of the ladies of the line."

Cole followed her into a large room situated behind the bar. At the far end, a deep, bare stage, framed by a painted curtain, took up most of the wall. Along both sides, high above the floor, were a series of boxes hung with burgundy-velvet drapes. The open space before the stage held several round tables covered with green baize, each with its coterie of slatted Windsor chairs. He recognized a roulette wheel and a faro cue box prominently displayed on one of the tables.

"I thought this was a theater," Cole said, looking around at the gambling paraphernalia.

"It is," Gert replied as a door at the back of the stage was thrown open and several women in various stages of undress spilled out. Giggling with curiosity, they hurried down the steps toward him, not in the least perturbed to see his clergyman's attire. Cole noted with distaste that their chemises and petticoats looked gray with grime and their faces still bore the tired debris left from yesterday's cosmetics.

Gert waved a languid hand. "Reverend Storey, meet Eugenie, Annette, Roxy, and Bertha. A few of our 'entertainers.' "

Annette, the loudest giggler in the group, drew Cole down into one of the chairs. "I had a reverend once who used to come see me regular." She lifted off Cole's hat and ran her fingers through his hair. "You're such a handsome fellow, I wouldn't mind if you was interested in doing the same."

"Now don't give the new preacher the wrong idea," Gert said, shoving aside the hand Annette had thrust inside Cole's collar. "It's true that now and then we get a preacher for a client. After all, they get lonesome sometimes, just like other men. But it don't happen often. It's more like to be that they come to shut down our business."

Cole ran a finger around his neck then wiped his hand on the front of his shirt. "You don't need to worry about that with me. Live and let live, I always say."

"Good for you," Gert said, slapping him on the shoulder. "Now come on, get off him, you girls," she added pulling away the women who were hanging over the handsome preacher. "Give the pastor a little room. Annette, go and get Reverend Storey something to drink."

"You want whisky?" Annette said, reluctantly pulling away the arm she had entwined around Cole's neck.

"It's a little early in the morning for whisky," Cole muttered.

"Well, we're fresh out of lemonade, ain't we Gert?"

"That's all right," Cole added quickly. "I don't really want anything to drink." He inched back in his chair, trying to distance himself from the girls who draped their bodies around him, shoving their bare décolletages as near his face as possible. He had come in here with the vague assumption that he might hire one of them during his brief stay in town. Instead, to his surprise, he found himself extremely uncomfortable, as if he might be doing the good Reverend Storey a disservice by being so chummy with these whores.

Still, he was in this town to dig out information, and getting on the friendly side of these sporting ladies seemed like a good way to begin.

Gert, to Cole's relief, appeared to read his mind. "This here is a legitimate theater, Reverend Storey," she said, pulling up a chair to sit opposite him. "I wouldn't want you to get the wrong idea. We book actors and shows right out of New York City—Eddie Foy, Nola Forrest . . ."

"Old Rubber Face," Roxy added.

"And don't forget the *Pinafore.* Now that was a real good show."

Gert nodded. "All kinds of fine entertainments take place here. And, if now and then, one of the members of the audiences wants a little more pleasure than he gets from watching an actor, we take him upstairs to the boxes."

"I get the picture," Cole said, noting how conveniently the burgundy drapes could be drawn across the front of a box.

Annette giggled and plumped herself across his lap. "Big Gert runs a good, clean house. You can count on her to be discreet."

Cole shrank back from the sweaty fumes emanating from Annette's lithe body. "Big Gert?" he muttered.

Roxy laughed and slipped around behind him to drape her arms over his shoulders. "We call her 'Big Gert' so she don't get confused with 'Little Gert.' "

"Yeah," Eugenie added. "Little Gert likes to call herself 'Gold Dollar,' but she ain't worth more n' fifty cents, if that."

"But you don't want to cross her," Annette said, wiggling farther down into Cole's lap. "She's got a wicked temper, that one. And she's mean with it."

"I'll remember," Cole said, getting to his feet and unceremoniously dumping Annette out of his lap. The other girls laughed as she fell to the floor. Reaching down, Cole helped her to her feet.

"I'd better be going. I have . . . other calls to make."

Gert shoved aside the other women to take possession of Cole's arm. "Now, Reverend Storey, don't you think you got to call on those whores in the cribs down Sixth Street? The Cage here is a high-class house, not like those other places that dirty old miners and smelly cowpokes like to visit. If you ever get lonesome, you come see us now, you hear?"

"Miners and cowpokes don't frequent the Bird

Cage?" Cole asked casually as he began to make his way toward the door.

"Well, a few. But mostly we get the better-class citizens of the town." She laughed and pounded his arm again. "I bet even a few of your nose-in-the-air parishioners come in now and again."

Cole stopped in the doorway. "Thank you, Big Gert, for making me so welcome."

Gert batted her false eyelashes. "I guess you'll be comin' back again?"

"Oh, sure. The next time you book an 'entertainer' I want to see."

Gert shrugged, thinking that was not exactly what she wanted to hear. "You're a good lookin' fellow, Reverend Storey. I wouldn't mind showin' you the inside of those boxes myself sometime."

Cole took a few steps away as the other women began to make catcalls at Gert for saving the good ones for herself.

"Thanks for the invitation, but I'm sure you'll understand if I decline. Reluctantly."

He slapped his Stetson on his head and, giving Gert a little bow, hurried out of the Bird Cage, ignoring the knowing leer from Jonas, who had been leaning on the bar and listening to every word inside the theater. Once outside, he stood on the walkway, lifting his face to the bright, warm sun and breathing deeply of the clean air.

Gawddamn, he thought. What had come over him? Any other time, Cole Carteret would jump at the chance to take advantage of four or five whores who threw themselves at him. Even now, remembering all that white flesh, he felt a spreading warmth in his lower parts. Yet, it was easily overcome. Something about the stale air; the tired, streaked faces; the false gaiety; the eyes that had seen too much; the bodies that had known too many hands . . .

He gave himself a shake and went striding off, back down Allen Street. He knew the real reason he was unable to enjoy Big Gert's sensuous pleasures. The memory of pretty Amanda was too fresh—Amanda with her lovely, honest countenance; big, innocent eyes; and clean-smelling hair. Her body was every bit as enticing as any of those on display at the Bird Cage, and it was not for sale. Still, he suspected he might be the lucky man to unveil and discover its mysteries, to awaken its delicious responses. She would be a far more enticing and satisfying pursuit than any shopworn whore.

He lifted his hat to a woman in a sunbonnet who smiled a greeting from the sidewalk. Though he beamed back at the woman, his smile was really for Amanda Lassiter and the delicious prospect of taking her to the potluck supper at St. Anselm's tomorrow afternoon.

Nor was the potluck supper far from Amanda's thoughts the following day as she returned to the task of cleaning up her uncle's store. She cleared the rest of the bottles scattered on the floor, then moved on to tackle several boxes stacked haphazardly against the back wall. Almost at once she made her most intriguing discovery yet—a dog-eared, burgundy-leather ledger with careful entries of all the sales for the previous eight months, including items and prices. She was busily turning the pages when her first visitors of the day appeared—a young farmer begging medicine for his sick daughter. For ten minutes she argued with him, trying to convince him that the store was not open and she was not in business. However, his stubborn determination, his concern for his child, and the fact that there was no other place to go prevented him from leaving. Finally Amanda gave in and mixed a simple cough medicine for him to take home.

He was barely gone before two more people appeared. Once again Amanda's arguments were overruled, and she finally relented, consulting her uncle's ledger for advice and prices. After that a steady stream of customers kept coming throughout the morning. She only turned three of them away—because she felt their ailments were beyond her limited knowledge. Rather than guessing, she sent them over to Dr. Goodfellow for a prescription, which she promised to try to fill. By two o'clock, when she laid aside her brooms and brushes, she discovered to her surprise that she had accumulated nearly ten dollars. It seemed like a fortune to Amanda, who had never earned ten cents of her own before. She returned to the hotel feeling a sense of pride and accomplishment that was very much at odds with the despair of the previous morning.

She had planned to quit early in order to wash and dress for the church supper later that afternoon. With Martha Poole's help, a big tin tub with hot water was laid for her bath. She washed her hair as well and leisurely allowed it to dry by sitting in a chair in the hot sun behind the hotel. One of Martha's maids pressed her best calico, a pretty gown with tiny white flowers on a cornflower-blue background. Amanda slipped into it, admiring her tiny waist and the way the skirt billowed around her. The maid offered to help her dress her hair, but she preferred to simply comb it back, tie it with a blue ribbon, and let the long wavy strands fall down her back.

When she finished, she stood before the mirror, turning this way and that, pleased with the result. Not that it mattered how she looked she added to herself. In fact, it was silly of her to get all gussied up just because a handsome young man had offered to escort her to this supper. Once they were there, he would probably have to spend the entire evening talking with his flock and she would look ridiculous standing by herself. Why should it matter at all what she wore or how she looked?

Amanda sat down on the edge of the bed and sank her chin in her hands. Why should it matter? Because, if she faced the honest truth, there hadn't been many young men in her life, handsome or otherwise. Of course, in spite of her pleasure in stepping out with him, the Reverend Cabot Storey was not a "prospect" for marriage. He was too handsome, too religious, and too traditional about a woman's place in the world to ever want her for a wife. There was also something disturbing about him, something that did not quite ring true. That vague feeling of unease had only surfaced once or twice when she talked with him, yet it was there nonetheless. No, it might be pleasant to walk out with Cabot Storey as she was doing tonight, but that must be the end of it. If she wanted to find a dashing, heroic, slightly wicked fellow who would win her heart and carry her off into the sunset on his white stallion, she would have to look for him elsewhere.

Feeling more sure of herself after this brave speech, she was able to walk downstairs to wait for the rector in the parlor without so much as a twinge in her stomach . . . until she looked up and saw him standing in the doorway, his sleek black Stetson in his hand and a delighted twinkle in his eye.

His long coat had been neatly brushed—she hadn't noticed before how it emphasized the broad sweep of his shoulders. He wore trousers over his boots instead of the usual riding pants, and the usual silver spurs had been left home. His hair fell in waves to his shoulders, and there was an enticing cleft in his square chin below his newly shaven cheeks. Amanda resolutely fought down the sudden surge of excitement that turned her stomach over and rose from her chair with as much careless dignity as she could summon.

"Ready?" Cole asked.

"Quite ready," Amanda answered casually, slipping the strings of her reticule over her arm. As they passed through the lobby, Martha Poole stopped them long enough to hand Amanda a large basket with a checkered cloth peeking from underneath the lid.

"What's this?" Amanda asked.

Martha gave her an indulgent smile. "Child, did it never occur to you that you can't go to a potluck without some kind of a pot? That's for the auction."

Amanda looked questioningly at her escort. "Auction?"

"I don't know anything about it," the young pastor replied, obviously as confused as she.

"Land sakes," Martha exclaimed, "a body would think neither of you ever went to a church social afore.

Go on with you, Reverend Storey. You'll find out soon enough why Amanda has to bring a supper basket. I'm just glad I thought of fixing one for her."

Still wondering, Amanda murmured her thanks and they stepped outside.

"That was nice of Martha Poole," Cole commented, holding the basket while Amanda tied on her bonnet against the afternoon sun. "I hope I wasn't supposed to bring a supper basket, too."

"You can share mine," Amanda said, smiling up at him as she slipped her arm through his, trying to ignore the delicious tingle that coursed through her body at his touch. "She didn't need to go to all that trouble though. I would have cooked something myself if I had known."

"Oh, can you cook?" Cole asked in a dry voice as they set off down the walk.

"Tolerably well. I was never interested in more than the basic things needed to put supper on the table. I preferred helping my father in his surgery to puttering around the kitchen."

Cole led her across Fremont to the opposite walk. For late afternoon, the road was unusually empty. "Surgery? What did your father do?"

"He was a doctor. And a good one, too. It was my responsibility to keep his saddlebags properly equipped with his tools and medicines; and, now and then, he would ask me to assist him in simple surgeries. I found it fascinating."

Cole made a clucking noise with his tongue. "I can't imagine what your father was thinking of. It doesn't sound like the proper place for a women at all, but it does explain why you like mixing powders and salves."

"Oh, I don't know," Amanda replied archly. "I think I might have made a good doctor if I had been given the chance to study."

Cole laughed. "A woman doctor! What an absurd idea. A wicked idea! Think of the things you would have to see and handle—a pretty little thing like you."

Amanda was torn between her annoyance at his arrogant belittling of women and her pleasure at being called "pretty." For the moment, annoyance won.

"You probably aren't aware of it, but there are several women doctors in this country. Not many, of course, thanks to the prejudice of most men, but those who do practice are well respected."

She gave a sudden gasp as a man stepped out in front of her from one of the alleyways, blocking her path. Amanda shrank back, gripping the rector's arm. The man was an Indian, dark-skinned with long jet hair that fell to his shoulders and heavy, thick brows over tiny, agate eyes. With his dirty cotton shirt and deerskin trousers, the long handle of a large knife protruding from his sash, and a necklace of animal claws around his neck, he presented a frightening, threatening appearance. This was as close as Amanda had ever come to a real Indian, and she fought an urge to turn and run. Instead, as she felt the minister's grasp tighten, she shrank protectively behind him.

"It's all right," he murmured. "He isn't going to hurt us."

He turned back to the Indian and mumbled a few words which were obviously in the man's language. The Indian responded with several guttural sentences, then turned and went loping off down the alley as quickly as he had come. Amanda stood looking from the retreating figure and back to the Reverend Storey. It had all happened so quickly she had to wonder if she had imagined it. Yet the lingering fear that cramped her chest left no doubt.

"It's all right," Cole said taking her arm and hurrying her down the sidewalk. "It was just a lone Apache wanting a handout. Nothing to worry you."

Amanda had to skip to keep up with him. "But . . . You talked with him. Where did you learn the Indian language?"

"I told you I spent some time on a ranch out here, remember? One of the hands was an Apache scout. I thought knowing a few words might come in handy sometime."

It sounded reasonable, and yet . . . She would have sworn the Indian and the clergyman had recognized each other. "But . . ."

"Look," Cole broke in. "We're here. And haven't they set it up nicely?"

Amanda looked up to see that two vacant lots on the edge of the desert had been set out with tables and chairs. Above them strings of lanterns and streamers added a festive touch. The tables, already loaded down with dishes, were nearly obstructed by the men and women milling around them. Some of the men wore long coats, while others had discarded them for the more comfortable shirt sleeves. Their wives and daughters were decked in dresses as variously colored as flowers in a garden. Children ran around and between them, playing games and chasing each other.

Amanda hesitated. The Indian was forgotten in her

sudden realization that she did not know any of these people. An unexpected shyness swept over her.

Cole seemed to recognize her hesitation. "Don't worry. I'll introduce you," he said, drawing her arm through his again.

"Please don't go off and leave me by myself," she breathed. "At least, not at first."

He laughed and drew her into the crowd.

Eleven

As it turned out, not all the people at the supper were total strangers after all. Amanda recognized Warren Peters' short, rotund figure among the first group she approached. He was accompanied by a plump, pink-faced woman in a dark-blue dress with a fashionable bustle at the rear and two rowdy, tow-headed grandchildren. Peters, who knew everyone, took an obvious pleasure in introducing her, and she soon became so engrossed in conversation that nearly an hour had sped by before she realized how much she was enjoying the party. The people of St. Anselm's were, for the most part, a total contrast to many of the residents she had met in Tombstone. They made her feel at home among them right away without any trace of proselytizing, and they seemed to have a genuine interest in the drug store and her plans for it. In fact, so many people expressed the hope that she would stay in town and reopen the store that Amanda began to wonder if running back to St. Louis would be the best thing for her after all.

She soon lost Reverend Storey to the determined attentions of some of the young ladies of the flock, but by that time she had met enough interesting people that she didn't mind. In fact, on the few occasions when

Cabot Storey threw her a pathetic glance that begged her to rescue him, she found herself more amused than sympathetic. He had promised to return to her side when the supper was served, so she left him to deal with his admirers alone.

She was sitting in one of the chairs set out under a tree when she looked up to see Leander Walton's wife approaching, holding two glasses of punch.

"I thought you might like a cool drink," Libby Walton said, handing one of the cups to Amanda. "May I join you?"

"Please do," Amanda answered, drawing her skirts aside to clear the chair next to her. "And thanks for the drink. One gets thirsty in this heat, even so late in the day."

Amanda liked Libby Walton from the first moment they met. Libby had a round, cherub face with tiny lines at the corner of her eyes from frequent smiling. Her matronly figure reminded Amanda of Mrs. Abernathy back in St. Louis. The two women had something of the same manner—warm, motherly, and completely without artifice.

"And how do you like Tombstone?" Libby asked, loosening the strings on her bonnet to let the air circulate around her face. "I hope you haven't been put off by its wild ways."

"Well, it is a little daunting. Everytime I walk down Allen Street I am nearly knocked over by bodies careening out of the saloons. And the gunshots never stop, do they? I heard them the whole time I was working at the store."

"Oh, that's just the cowboys letting off a little steam.

Not that we don't have our share of gunfights. There's a sayin' in town that we have a 'body for breakfast every day.' 'Course, they say that about Dodge City, too. It's not really that bad."

"Most people brag about how wicked the town is."

Mrs. Walton pursed her lips in thought. "I can't say it isn't wicked, of course, because there's plenty of wickedness here. But there's another side to Tombstone that no one talks about much."

"I think I'm seeing a little of it today," Amanda said, gesturing at the people clustered around the nearby table. "It makes me wonder if staying here would perhaps not be so bad after all."

Libby reached over to pat her hand. "I'm glad to hear you say that, because we need more good women like you. Those of us who are . . . well, respectable . . . want to make this a fine town with schools and churches and upstanding citizens. There is a lot of money to be made here. If we just get rid of some of the lawlessness, we would attract more families and a better class of people. We've already made a good start with you and Reverend Storey."

Amanda glanced over to see the handsome clergyman, who looked as if he were choking in his starched collar, backed up against a table by women on three sides who were chattering away at him. "Yes, I think the rector will be a great asset to the town," she said.

"We're sure of it." Libby beamed. "He is everything we wanted. A man of God who is also practical and strong. He'll do great things before he's through. And he certainly seems to be taken with you."

Amanda looked quickly away as she felt the color

rise in her cheeks. Her gaze fell on a woman in a plain calico dress walking along the edge of the street and looking over at the group on the lawn with a longing expression. "Who is that woman?" she asked Libby, anxious to change the subject. "Shouldn't we invite her to join us?"

Mrs. Walton's kind face took on a sad expression. "I'm afraid we can't do that. She's Allie, Mrs. Virgil Earp. Unfortunately, the Earp wives are so much a part of that gang that we don't dare risk our reputations by inviting them in. She probably wouldn't come, anyway. They keep mostly to themselves. I've been told their husbands insist on it."

"The Earp gang?" It was a new name to Amanda.

"Yes. There are four or five brothers and their wives and some of their close friends—Holliday, Ringo, a few others. They call themselves law men, and Virgil and Wyatt both have run unsuccessfully for sheriff and marshal. Virgil finally got himself appointed assistant marshal, but the others mostly work over in the Oriental Saloon, gambling and running faro games."

"That doesn't sound so bad," Amanda said. "It doesn't seem fair to punish their wives for that."

"No, you don't understand," Libby said, lowering her voice. "It's said that two of those women were 'on the line' before they were married. And everyone in town thinks that gang may be involved in some of the stage robberies that go on all the time. Of course, they've never been able to prove it."

Amanda's eyes grew round. "You mean, they're thieves?"

"And they're not alone, either," Libby whispered, leaning closer to Amanda. "They're one of a kind with another bunch called the 'cowboys' because they rustle beef and run ranches. They fight among themselves something fierce, but between them there's hardly a silver-mine shipment leaving Tombstone that makes it to Tucson. And some of those gunshots you hear are those fellows blowing off steam. There's not a one of them wouldn't as soon shoot you down as look at you.

"You see, my dear, we've got more than our share of gamblers, rustlers, gunfighters, and the women who cater to them. And the mines are so wealthy that they attract a lot of footloose miners trying to make a rich strike. But we've also got some fine people here who really want to make this a thriving, decent town. That's one reason we're all hoping you'll decide to stay on."

Amanda watched Allie disappear down the street toward the Mexican section. Though tiny and plain, there was a suggestion of pride in the woman's straight back and determined chin. Where had she come from? Amanda wondered. How did she get mixed up with the Earps, and was she one of those wives who had previously been 'on the line'? It all seemed kind of sad.

"I believe supper is about to be served."

Amanda looked quickly up to see Cabot Storey bending toward her, smiling and reaching for her hand.

"I've discovered what Martha Poole was talking about when she mentioned an auction." He drew her arm through his and started for the long tables that were covered with baskets of food. "Just remember, whatever happens, you're having supper with me."

"I've never been to an auction." In fact, she had no idea what it meant, though she felt a certain sense of security knowing Cabot would stay by her side. By the time they reached the tables, the rest of the crowd had gathered together with them. Leander Walton jumped up on a chair in front of one of the tables and waved his arms for silence.

"Now, folks, you know that the most important thing at St. Anselm's—next to having the Reverend Storey join us, of course . . ."

A mild chorus of hurrahs and scattered applause followed as Leander once again waved for silence.

". . . the *next* most important thing is to build us a proper church."

More applause and cries of "hear, hear."

"It's something we've wanted since the first day we organized ourselves into a congregation. A 'temple in the wilderness,' bringing sinners to salvation and constituting a haven for the righteous . . ."

"Get on with it, Leander," someone behind Amanda called out. The listeners laughed good-naturedly as Walton coughed and went on.

"Well, the preacher here could say it better, but, anyway, we all know how important it is to all of us. And this here auction is just one more chance to add to our growing fund to build us a church. So, step right up, all you gals and guys, and let's start the bidding!"

Cole turned to Libby Walton, who was standing next to him, and quietly asked how much had been raised for the building fund so far.

"I think it's about one hundred and fifty dollars," she whispered back.

A hundred and fifty dollars. Not a lot, but worth considering, he thought, especially if it were just lying around somewhere. Though he wasn't sure how much cash it would take to put up a building, he was pretty sure it would require more than one hundred and fifty dollars. A lot more. In fact, it would probably take so much more that this little sum would probably never be missed . . .

His interest in the money faded as Amanda tugged at his sleeve.

"I don't understand how this works," she whispered. "Do I need money?"

"I'm not sure myself. Do you have any?"

She remembered the ten dollars she had earned in the store that day, buried in the deep recesses of her reticule. "A little."

Leander reached for one of the baskets on the table. "Now, folks, you know we usually start off with bids for these lovely young ladies and the suppers they brought. But tonight, we're going to do something a little different first. My good wife Libby brought this here extra basket so's we could start off letting the ladies bid for our new preacher.

"Just think, ladies this is your big chance to sit down with the Reverend Storey and share this lovely basket of Libby's good fried chicken and biscuits. All you have to do is call out a price. Now, who wants to start?"

An embarrassed twitter swept through the women in the crowd, while Cole turned a panicky gaze on Amanda.

"I'll give fifty cents," said a woman's voice from the rear of the crowd.

Cole looked around with growing distress. "Wait a minute, Leander," he cried. "I didn't know I was going on the block here tonight. I brought a guest."

"Don't you worry, Reverend Storey, there's plenty of

young bucks here who'd would pay a pretty price to share a box supper with that charmin' little gal."

"I'll pay a dollar to have the preacher here sit with my family."

Recognizing that voice, Amanda looked behind her and saw Warren Peters give her a wave. "And another dollar for the gal with him—Miss Lassiter."

"That's two dollars. Thank you, Warren. We got the ball rolling here. Do I hear any better offer?"

"Two dollars, just for the rector!"

Amanda looked over to see a slim, dark-haired girl standing a short distance away from her. She remembered meeting Lucy Ellis earlier. It would be difficult to forget the black looks the girl had given her when she saw her walk up on Reverend Storey's arm.

"Quick, bid," Cole whispered, tugging at her arm and ignoring the provocative glances Lucy was throwing his way.

"Two dollars and twenty-five cents," Amanda cried in a tentative voice.

"Gee, thanks," Cole muttered as Lucy shouted out: "Two fifty!"

Amanda raised her voice. "Three dollars!" The girl's flagrant behavior was beginning to get her dander up.

"Three fifty."

Libby Walton leaned across to say quietly to Cole, "I wish I could help you, but this is too rich for my blood."

He threw Amanda a desperate glance which grew more desperate as her lips pursed. "Go on," he urged. "I'll pay you back."

"Three seventy-five," she cried, seeing her day's profits slipping away. Did she really want to give away so much money just to sit at this handsome preacher's side sharing a box supper when she could buy a very good dinner in town for fifty cents? That ten dollars was meant to help her get back to St. Louis.

"Three eighty-five," Lucy called, throwing Amanda a venomous glance.

"Say 'four,' 'four,' " Cole prodded, pulling at Amanda's arm.

Before she could open her mouth, Warren Peters's voice boomed from behind her. "Six dollars for both the pastor and his little guest!"

A murmur of approval and awe swept through the crowd. Six dollars was a great sum to make on the first box to be auctioned, and it promised much for the rest of the night.

"Going for six dollars," Leander called, waiting to see if the high-spirited Miss Ellis would match it. When the girl sulkily pursed her lips together, he waved again. "Going twice . . . three times . . . sold! To the Peters family—Reverend Storey and Miss Lassiter and my wife Libby's delicious chicken dinner."

Cole pulled out his handkerchief and wiped at his brow. He was sweating, though whether from the heat or the possibility of having to fend off Miss Lucy, he wasn't sure. That girl would be a handful. He knew her type well; and while, as Cole Cateret he might enjoy taking supper with her, as the Reverend Storey, he felt sure she would see right through him in a minute. Besides, he had long ago made up his mind that tonight was to be the beginning of his seduction of Amanda Lassiter, and he was in no mood to be sidetracked.

Taking Amanda's hand, he collected the chicken dinner

and joined Warren Peters, his quiet wife, and two young sons. They moved away from the rest of the group, chatting while they waited for the auction to finish.

"That was good of you, Mr. Peters," Cole said, taking a seat on the ground next to Amanda's chair.

The lawyer smiled at Amanda. "No offense, Reverend Storey, but I did it for Miss Lassiter. I figured she wouldn't want to be put up for auction before she even knew most of the people who would be doing the bidding. Even if it were for a worthy cause."

Amanda smiled her gratitude. "I'm grateful," she murmured. "And I'm kind of glad I didn't have to spend any of my first day's profits."

"You've opened the store then? Does that mean you've decided to stay?"

"I didn't open it. People just kept coming in asking for medicines. It got to be so much trouble to explain that I wasn't in business that I finally just gave up and served them."

Mrs. Peters leaned across her husband. "You see, Miss Lassiter, how much we need someone to run the drug store. We're all hoping you will decide to stay in business. We've sorely missed your uncle since he died."

Amanda looked away, embarrassed. "I still haven't made up my mind," she said hesitantly. "Of course," she added, giving Reverend Storey a teasing smile, "some people feel it's not a woman's place to run a business."

"Stuff and nonsense," the lawyer replied, reaching for a perfectly browned chicken drumstick. "Out here on the frontier, women do a lot of things they might not do back in proper New England. Running a much-needed drug store is not so farfetched, considering you have the knowledge to do it. You might even go in with one of the doctors, if you don't want to run it by yourself."

Amanda noticed that Cabot Storey had not replied to her provocative comment. It was just as well. Although she had not yet made up her mind about her future, she felt certain her decision would not be influenced by the preacher's provincial thinking. It would be her decision and hers alone.

Dusk was giving way to twilight by the time the congregation finished supper. Lanterns, strung on strings around the perimeter of the lot, were lit with candles, giving a festive air to the rapidly descending darkness. The tables were cleared away as someone struck up a fiddle and partners squared off for dancing. Amanda, who had never attended a dance in St. Louis, prepared to stand at the sidelines watching, but Cabot Storey would not hear of it. He pulled her into one of the squares, telling her to watch what everybody else did and follow his lead.

She soon found herself having so much fun that all her hesitation was forgotten. After two energetic rounds, she had to sit one out just to catch her breath while Reverend Storey went off to fetch her a glass of punch. Darkness had descended with a vengeance by then—the deep, velvet blackness of the desert. Above the twinkling lights of the lanterns, a vast spray of diamond brilliants scattered on the night sky. Amanda scanned the horizon, breathing deeply of the cool, crisp air. Glancing around, she saw Cabot Storey advancing toward her bearing two glasses of punch in his hands and laughing at some comment one of his parishioners called out. He moved with a strong, manly grace that made her skin tingle. His lithe body, handsome smile, and mischievous eyes made her heart turn over.

Happiness swelled within her. She was filled all at once with a singing joy like none she had ever known, a sense of well-being and of hope. She felt at one with the universe of vast spaces and stars, at one with the laughing, joyous group of people that surrounded her. It was as though she had taken a step in a new, unknown direction filled with risks—as the unknown always is—yet offering the promise of unhoped-for rewards. How could she even think of turning back?

It was nearly ten o'clock and the party was breaking up by the time Amanda and Reverend Storey started home. Once they left the golden glow cast by the lanterns around the empty lot, they found themselves engulfed in the vast darkness of the night until they turned the corner on to Fremont and looked up to see a magnificent, majestic golden moon, as yellow as spun gold, gradually rising over the black rim of the distant mountains. It was so beautiful they paused to stare in awe at its full, round body, hanging in the sky like a brilliant jewel and casting a glow around them that was almost bright enough to read by.

Amanda leaned against the adobe wall of a building and tipped her face to the sky, sighing at the beauty of it. Cole, watching her, felt he could have sighed with the loveliness of the moonlight on her face. The warm delight that spread through his body set his blood raging. He knew he should go slowly, but his desire for her overcame every hesitation.

Bending toward her, he laid one hand against the wall

beside her head and touched her lips lightly with his own. She gave a sudden, surprised intake of breath, but she did not pull away. He gave her a moment, unsure whether or not she might still move out of his embrace. When she did not, he sought her lips in earnest.

After her first shocked surprise, Amanda found herself enjoying the soft feel of his lips. She had never been kissed like this before, so deeply and so long. He moved sensuously against her mouth, lightly flicking her lips open with his tongue. A slow fire began to burn in her body, flaring from warm embers to excited desire. Her arms slid up to his shoulders, then around his neck, pulling him closer against her. Her fingers laced the long strands of his hair, which surprised her with the softness of its texture. She felt his hands, tentatively at first, lightly exploring her back as he pulled her into his embrace. His body felt hard against hers and she was keenly aware of its masculine contours. Her palm moved to his cheek, touching the skin where she could feel a light beard beginning. With a sudden rush of passion, her lips opened to receive his thrusting tongue.

Cole felt his control slipping fast. The hardness of her nipples against his chest set his blood roaring. When her lips opened, he dove his tongue within, tasting, exploring, searching her sweet depths in anticipation of that more exquisite entry his body longed for. His hand slipped to her slim waist, then slowly traveled upward to cup the fullness of her breast, so firm and round in his palm. He was not even aware that his thumb sought the erect nipple, stroking it gently.

"No!"

Amanda put both hands against his chest and pushed

him backward. She darted away from the building, putting space between them, and stood breathing raggedly while she attempted to regain a measure of composure.

Cole turned away, disappointed, but not really surprised. "I'm sorry," he muttered. "You looked so beautiful in the moonlight, and I thought you were enjoying it, too."

"I was," Amanda murmured. "It's just that. . . . Well, I'm not used to this kind of thing."

"Oh," he said, remembering he was supposed to be a clergyman. "Me, neither."

In the dimness of the moonlight, he saw her turn to smile up at him. There was a teasing lilt in her laugh. "That's not the impression I got," she answered.

Cole smiled back at her, relieved to see that she was not going to be prim and outraged. "Well, not often, anyway."

Amanda set her bonnet on her head and began to tie the ribbons. "Don't do that," he said, reaching to pull it off. "The moonlight is so beautiful on your face. You're not mad at me, are you?"

She felt her body warm with delight at his compliment. "Reverend Storey, how could I be angry when you say such nice things?"

He politely offered her his arm. "I think we ought to be on a first name basis after that kiss, don't you?"

Taking his arm, they started down the street to the hotel. "I suppose so . . . Cabot."

For the first time, he wished she could call him 'Cole.' He patted her hand. "Thank you, Amanda."

One gaslight lantern cast a bronzed oval around the entrance to the hotel. Cole kept Amanda just outside its glow, in the shadow of the building. Taking her hands in his, he lifted them to his lips. "I enjoyed being with you tonight."

"It was a lovely evening," Amanda breathed. Her fingers felt so warm and protected in his large hands. "Thank you."

"Would you like to ride out with me tomorrow? I'd like to see what some of Tombstone's famous mines look like."

"Oh, tomorrow? I don't think so. I've so much to do in the store."

"Friday, then? You can't spend all your time buried in that stuffy store."

She only hesitated a moment. "Friday sounds fine."

"Good. I'll rent a couple of horses and have Mrs. Jasper pack us a picnic lunch. We probably ought to start early, before the heat sets in."

She lifted her face to his invitingly, hoping he would kiss her and afraid he would. He bent to kiss her again, softly, gently, this time, with none of the fire of before.

"Good night . . . Cabot," Amanda whispered and darted inside the building. He stood looking after her, a thin, triumphant smile on his lips. She was everything he had hoped. Innocent, but not prudish, with fires banked beneath that trim exterior, and as drawn to him as he was to her. She had been good company this evening and a good sport in betting against Lucy when he asked her to. She grew more beautiful and more enticing the more he was around her. His body ached for her, especially after her response to his kiss. Just thinking about it warmed him up again.

My God, what am I doing! he thought, stopping

abruptly on the walk. Innocent? Banked fires? He hadn't bothered with women like that since his early teens. For years now, his women had been those whose desires were a roaring blaze, who knew what they were doing, who challenged him to seduce them. He wanted experience, maturity—not some unskilled, timid little respectable, church-going, straight-laced Puritan!

He remembered a saying they used to have about cowboys: that they only feared two things—a decent woman and being set a-foot. And now, with this crazy masquerade, he had gone and gotten himself involved with both!

As he started again toward home, it crossed his mind that maybe he ought to go round to the cribs and work off some of his frustration with one of those 'soiled doves.' He almost turned in that direction before he realized the thought of lying with one of those sweaty, shopworn bodies would be no substitute for Amanda's fresh loveliness. No, he would go home, take off his boots, and read awhile until the embers died and he got his mind straight again.

Not until later did it occur to him that the Reverend Storey would probably never have visited the cribs on Sixth Street and he might have given the game away had he actually gone there.

Twelve

Three days later, Amanda stood at the door of her shop with her hands on her hips and looked with satisfaction at the long, narrow room. The shop was beginning to look quite respectable. The floors had been cleared of debris and scrubbed to a satin sheen. Along one wall, rows of neatly labeled bottles stood side by side, arranged in alphabetical order. A large wooden cabinet lined with narrow drawers stood near the end, its small white shell knobs gleaming in the strong sunlight that streamed through the newly washed window. On the opposite wall, neatly stacked shelves were almost obliterated by a long counter with curving glass lids that exposed a row of trays beneath. Of course, they were empty now, but they cried out for all kinds of products, from rolled bandages to candy for the children who came with their mothers.

In addition to the metal cash register, she had discovered some other interesting artifacts buried beneath the trash on the floor of her uncle's shop—several stone mortar and pestles, small balance scales for weighing, two pill presses, tins of tobacco, and pressed soaps. There were even assorted implements which more likely should be found in a doctor's saddlebags—a rusty amputation kit, two scrapers for bloodletting, a scalpel, several needles, and a small ball of catgut for suturing. Uncle George must have been an invaluable aid to the town doctors, she mused.

There was even part of an old skeleton among the trash piled high in the narrow storeroom across the back of the store. She hadn't gotten to that room yet; but when she did, she was determined to mount the skeleton for display. It would add a professional touch to the drug store, just as the potbellied iron stove and its flanking chairs added a domestic touch.

Deciding she had earned a rest, she sank into one of the chairs near the stove and allowed her mind to wander back to the night of the supper. The happiness she felt when she remembered the feel of Reverend Storey's—Cabot's—hands on her body, his lips against hers, set her blood racing and filled her with warmth. She had forced herself to keep the memory at bay as much as possible; but in quiet times like this, it came sweeping back to fill her with delight. She leaned back and closed her eyes, dreamily smiling at the image of the his lean face bending close to kiss her lips. A delighted shiver swept through her body as she remembered the feel of her hands on his broad shoulders, his hands sliding up her waist to cup her breast . . .

No, no, this won't do, she thought, giving herself a mental shake. Storey was indeed a handsome, admirable man; but he was not for her, nor she for him. He needed a church-going girl who would share his concern for spiritual matters. Her knees might go all watery when he touched her, but she knew nothing about church ideology, nor was she very interested in learning. She wanted a man who could reveal the mystery of love to her in all its wonders—physical love more than spiritual love. She wanted the closeness and comfort of a lover who could teach her to match him step for step. If he had any idea how she felt, the good Reverend Storey would probably be shocked from the top of his Stetson down to the tip of his silver spurs.

Of course, she had to admit he hadn't seemed terribly interested in spiritual matters that evening in the . . .

"Miss Lassiter!"

Amanda jumped, opening her eyes. A man came bounding through the doorway, pulling off his plug hat. His checkered shirt stuffed into ragged pants suggested a mine worker. He wore a kerchief caked with dust around his throat, and his face was lined with dirt. His eyes were anxious and glittering.

"Are you Miss Lassiter? If you are, then come quick."

Amanda hesitated. "I am, but what do you want?"

The man turned his hatbrim nervously in his hands. "They sent me from the stamp mill. There's been an accident. You gotta come quick."

Amanda jumped up from her chair to stride toward the door. "But you don't need me. You want Dr. Goodfellow. I'm not a doctor."

"He's not here. He rode out to the Leslie ranch on Horseshoe Canyon. That's ninety miles there and back, and we can't wait."

"But Dr. Gillingham?"

The man reached for her arm, pulling her urgently toward the door. "He's ridden down to Mexico for a birthing. There's no one else, and the foreman said maybe you could help."

"Wait a minute," Amanda cried, grabbing at the door frame. "At least tell me what's happened so I can bring the proper medicines."

"It's Jody. He's my boy and works with me in the boiler room of the press mill. A pile of timbers slipped, and he fell under 'em and hurt hisself. He's in a bad way, Miss, and somebody's got to help him."

Amanda thought a moment. "All right. I may be able to do something. Wait here till I gather a few things."

She tried not to allow her misgivings to overwhelm her while she collected bandages and salves. Instead, she thought back to the times her father had allowed her to help him set bones and tend mangled flesh. If this was a simple fracture, she might be able to help. If it was something worse, like crushed bones, she trembled to think that more might be expected of her than she would ever be able to give.

As they set off hurrying across town, Amanda was surprised to notice an oppressive silence. Of course. The stamp mill had shut down. The unusual quiet heightened her dread of what she might find at the mill.

"The boy wasn't caught in the stamps or the crusher, was he?" she asked as they crossed Toughnut Street. When the man shook his head, Amanda breathed a sigh of relief. She did not know a lot about stamp mills; but from what she had heard, if the boy had fallen under one of those heavy machines, there would be nothing she could do to help him.

By the time they reached the mill, she was reassured to hear the machines starting up again. The boy had been brought outside and laid on a blanket on the ground. A few people anxiously clustered around him, while another man in shirt sleeves fussed about, trying to send the onlookers back inside the mill.

As Amanda hurried forward, the young man turned to meet her and she recognized Charley McDowell, one of the members of St. Anselm's.

"Thanks for coming, Miss Lassiter," he said, running his hand around the collar of his shirt. "I didn't know who could help with both docs gone, then I thought of you."

"I don't know if I can, but I'll have a look. Can we get these people back and give the boy some air?"

As Amanda knelt beside the patient, Charley began shoving the spectators away. The boy's father knelt beside his son's head and looked up at Amanda with hope and expectation written on his lined face.

"He's very young," Amanda said quietly. In fact, she was shocked that a boy who appeared to be little more than eight or nine would be working in this mill at all, much less with his father's blessing. She leaned over to smile into the child's face, as white as tallow and twisted with pain.

"You won't cut off my arm . . ." he managed to murmur.

She smiled reassuringly. "No. I can promise you that. Just try to be still while I have a look."

She saw, to her great relief, that it was a clean break. The bone protruded through the skin and would have to be set, but she had done that many times before while her father watched. Surely she could do it now without him.

"Bring me a glass of water," she said to the anxious young man hovering over her. At once Charley went hurrying off for it while Amanda laid out the items she had brought with her. "We'll need a splint. It's the one thing I don't have."

"I got something," the boy's father said and hurried off, returning a few moments later with two pieces of narrow board. "Will these do?"

"I think so." She measured out a small dose of laudanum and raised the boy's head to help him swallow it. "That will help ease the pain, Jody," she said soothingly. "Now, Jody, you just try to think about something nice and pleasant while I see if I can fix your arm."

Keeping up her quiet, calming conversation, she quickly cleaned the exposed bone and tissue, then, before he knew what was happening, worked the bone back into place. The child screamed, arching his back, then collapsed in a faint.

"He's not dead, is he?" the father cried, staring at her with wide, anxious eyes.

"No. He's just fainted. It's better that he did. If I don't set this right, his arm will never be whole again."

She worked quietly until the arm was ready for the splint. Then she bathed it in carbolic acid and bound it up rigidly to the board.

"Now you must keep him quiet, Mr. . . . I don't think I ever got your name."

"Ephraim Bennett. Jody's my only boy, though I got a passel of girls. I sure wouldn't want for him to go through life a cripple."

Amanda looked around the yard. The layers of rubble; the rhythmic, ear-splitting pounding of the stamps; the nauseous odors of the chemicals in the amalgamating pans; the oppressive, searing heat—what an atmosphere for a young child!

"Then perhaps you should put him in school instead of this mill."

"I would if'n I could. But we need the money. And it's better than down the shafts," he added, defensively.

"Well, Mr. Bennett, I've done all I can. You can thank the Good Lord that arm wasn't crushed. If you keep him quiet and let the break heal, it ought to be as good as new. I'll give you a little more laudanum to help him get through the night, but please have Dr. Goodfellow look at him as soon as he gets back to town. Just to be sure."

Amanda gathered up her implements and got to her feet. Now that it was over, she realized how tense she had been by the sudden weariness that swept over her.

"That was just fine, Miss Lassiter," Charley McDowell said quietly, stepping up to shake her hand. "I don't think Doc Goodfellow could have done no better. I sure thank you for coming."

"I'll feel better once the doctor has also seen him. Will you make sure Mr. Bennett takes the boy home? He has to stay quiet."

"I will. His ma works over at the laundry, but I'll send someone to see to him. Thanks again, Miss Lassiter."

Starting back to town, Amanda sighed with a sense of satisfaction. True, it was a simple break, but she had done a good job with it; and it pleased her to know her skills had been useful. It wasn't until she was back at the store that she realized Mr. Bennett had never thanked her.

Cole looked down at the note in his hand. The writing with its flourishes and curlicues obviously came from a woman, though not a well-schooled one, judging by the spelling and grammar. Still, since it was his first request for 'pastoral guidance,' he felt challenged as well as curious. It was true there was something about the letter that made him wonder if he shouldn't ignore it. The woman had not signed her name, so he had no idea who she was. Even her request was vague—'I feel the need of counsel from a man of God' could mean anything. He was walking on eggs here in Tombstone anyway, so why push his luck?

He laid the letter on the table and walked to the window of his room to look out over the stretch of desert beyond the town. He felt satisfied with his performance so far. His simplistic sermons had been well received; he had mastered the rituals of the service well enough to be accepted; there had been no more marriages, and he felt he had the people of his congregation eating out of his hand. He did not sense a sign of suspicion anywhere that he might not really be the Reverend Storey. His pursuit of Amanda Lassiter added spice to the masquerade, even though his nosing around to find out what Aces meant by 'rich pickings' had not yet gone very deep. At this point he felt secure enough to take on another aspect of the clergyman's life. It might even be fun to listen to a straightlaced lady confess her sins while he tried to comfort and reassure her. Why not?

Besides, Cole Carteret was never one to refuse a challenge. He put on a clean shirt, tied his string tie in a bow, ran a cloth over his boots to give them a dull shine, picked up his hat, and started off to find the address on the letter.

It turned out to be one of the new clapboard boxes

thrown up on the western edge of town. It looked simple and unpretentious, but neat and clean. Cole's boots thumped on the boards of the porch as he walked to the door and knocked. After a long pause, it was opened by a Mexican woman in a large apron; two long braids trailed over the front of her dress.

Cole gave her his name and mentioned he was expected at this hour. She disappeared for a moment, then returned to lead him into a small parlor off the tiny main hall.

As his eyes adjusted to the shadowed light, he made out a room sparse with furniture whose walls were cluttered with framed photographs and small landscapes. A woman sat in a cushioned rocker near the fireplace while two men stood on either side of the one long, narrow window. All three turned to look at him as he walked in.

Cole stopped on the threshold as he recognized Tilly Lacey smiling up at him. With a brief turn of his head, he saw that one of the men was John Behan, the town sheriff. He did not recognize the other man.

"How kind of you to come," Mrs. Lacey said, extending her hand. For a moment Cole was tempted to turn and bolt out the door. Instead, he forced himself to walk forward and take her fingers briefly in his.

"A pastor can never refuse a request for help," he murmured, trying to brave it out.

"Have you met Sheriff Behan and Marshal Williams?" Tilly asked, waving a hand toward the two men.

"I haven't yet had the honor," Cole said, forcing himself to turn toward the two men. He extended his hand and tried to smile, feeling all the while as though he had walked into a den of lions. To his relief, Behan seemed bored meeting a clergyman. He nodded stiffly at Cole then turned away. Williams shook his hand vigorously.

"Pleased to make your acquaintance, Reverend Storey. We need more respectable men like you in this town. Helps us to look better and draw a better class of people."

Cole smiled his thanks and sat stiffly down on the straight-backed chair Tilly Lacey offered him. He turned the chair so his shoulder was to the window, taking surreptitious glances at the men while Tilly talked about Tombstone needing more respectability. This was the closest he had ever been to Behan, whom he knew had bragged loudly that he would someday hang The Casket Kid from the nearest tree. He was a tall man, handsome, with bright, glittering eyes and a direct gaze. His chin had a tuft of black beard that gave him an elegance in contrast to Marshal Williams' long, full growth of whiskers.

"Mr. Williams is the Wells Fargo agent in Tombstone," Tilly added.

Cole gave him a guarded glance. "That must keep you busy."

"Indeed. The mines outside the town are bringing in millions in silver ore and all of it gets shipped to Tucson on the first leg of its journey." Williams swelled with importance. "It's a responsibility, I can tell you, Reverend Storey."

Cole briefly wondered if Williams might be involved in the murky transactions Aces had mentioned. Who better to know when silver bars were being transported than the Wells Fargo agent who was supposed to guard them? Still, there was no need to jump to conclusions.

It would be better to listen, watch, and learn all he could, then wait for Aces to put everything together.

"That stage robbery last night must have cost you dear, Mr. Williams," Tilly drawled.

"Indeed."

"Robbery?" Cole asked, sitting forward in his chair.

Tilly turned to him. "Oh, yes. They happen all the time, even though Marshal here does everything he can to protect the shipments. You can see how important it is to bring some morals to Tombstone. We seem to attract the worst men instead of the best."

Cole turned to see Behan eying him with sudden interest. He looked quickly away as Williams spoke up.

"It's a question of logistics, my dear Mrs. Lacey. These valuable shipments must cross a stretch of open desert filled with arroyos and gullies where brigands can hide to spring out on the unwary. We always provide a man to ride shotgun messenger, but these outlaws have no compunction about killing anyone who gets in their way. It is a terrible problem."

"Maybe Sheriff Behan should run these men out of town."

"Outlaws are not all from Tombstone, my dear Mrs. Lacey," Behan said shortly. "Though I will admit, these particular ones seem to always know when a valuable shipment is being made."

"Then they obviously have contacts in the town. But gentlemen, the rector has come to talk with me. You were just leaving, weren't you?"

To Cole's great relief, both men reached for their hats. Knowing he could not avoid it, he stood and looked squarely at Behan as he started for the door.

"I'd like to invite both of you men to come to church sometime," he said, deciding he would walk straight into the lion's jaws.

"I'd like that, Reverend Storey," Williams mumbled half-heartedly. Behan stopped, looking at him quizzically. Then with a shrug he mumbled, "I'm not a churchgoer," and headed out of the room.

Cole settled back into his chair as the front door closed. He was relieved that Behan had gone, yet he knew that now he must face this woman, whose sideway glances and thin smile suggested she knew more about him than she should. Yet, how could that be true? Bluster was his best approach.

"Well, Mrs. Lacey," he said, crossing his legs and leaning back in the chair. "We meet again."

"You remember me from the stage, then?"

"Of course."

Tilly fussed with a watch that hung on a long chain about her neck. "I'm relieved to hear it. You seemed so interested in that young woman, I wasn't sure you even noticed me."

"I would have remembered your name, too, had you signed your note."

"Oh, that," Tilly said with a laugh. "I was afraid you wouldn't come if you knew it was from me."

"A pastor is always ready to give moral support," Cole said, pulling out the pocket Bible he had thoughtfully brought with him. "Do you want to pray?"

"Pray! Goodness, no. It's just that, well, I have this burden that disturbs me. I suppose you could call it *guilt.*"

She said the word teasingly, turning her face to him.

She must be in her forties, Cole thought, but she was still a damned fine-looking woman. Her back was straight, and her full bosom above her tiny waist could be tantalizing if he allowed himself to dwell on it. Her face was not covered with paint as it had been in the coach that day, yet her fine eyes and thin lips showed a natural color that was becoming. If you looked closer, of course, you could see the tiny lines around her mouth that gave it a downward twist, the hard edge to her dark eyes which managed to appear seductive even when she spoke about the most mundane things. With a start, he realized he was getting the full blast of that seduction right now.

"You mentioned guilt," he murmured, looking away.

"Yes. For a life misspent. Oh, Reverend Storey, if you only knew the regret that overwhelms me . . ."

She closed her eyes and leaned her head back against the chair, thrusting her ample bosom forward. "Of course, I had little choice. What else could I do? Alone, helpless, without the protection of a strong man . . ."

Her hand went to her forehead in a dramatic gesture. Next would be tears, he thought, no doubt with the expectation that he would bound forward to comfort her. He stayed firmly in his chair.

"A misspent life?" Cole offered.

"Terribly misspent. You see, at a young age I fell the victim of . . . men. Men who used me, then threw me away. I thought it was love, but it never was." She turned to look at him through nearly closed eyes, seduction in every pore. "What is a poor girl to do, Reverend Storey? Where can I turn for . . . for solace?"

Cole sat back in his chair, his fingertips together. "Forgive me, Mrs. Lacey, but you are not a girl any longer. Surely you must have come to grips with this problem before now."

Tilly rose from her chair to stand by the window. "I thought I had. But you've no idea how guilt clutches at me, stabbing me in the vitals, right here." She balled her fists against her chest, lifting her breasts provocatively. "Right here," she repeated, turning toward Cole, invitation in her eyes. When he looked away without responding, she walked over to stand behind him, lightly resting her fingers on his shoulders.

"You must feel the burden of other people's problems keenly," she said, leaning toward his ear and speaking in a near whisper. "I could help. One of the most valuable things I learned from my misspent youth was how to help a man relax."

He could feel her warm breath on his cheek. "That's right friendly of you, Mrs. Lacey," he said, easing out of her grasp, "but I don't feel especially burdened right now. And I don't think you asked me here to confess your sins."

Tilly gave a quick start of surprise, followed by a short laugh. "You don't beat around the bush, do you Reverend Storey?"

"Not when something is so obvious. What made you think I would want to give in to your charms?"

Her eyes narrowed as she scanned him from head to foot. "I know men. First of all, you are not like most preachers I've known. I could see right off that you were a man familiar with the world. You might have given it up for the pulpit, but you've been around the barn a few times. I can tell."

Cole met her look dead on, steeling his face into a

mask that would not betray how much her words upset him.

"Looks are not always what they seem."

Tilly tipped her head to the side, her eyes appraising him. "Perhaps. But I suspect you could make a woman forget all about her past sins, once you got into the mood. Why confine yourself to a young, starry-eyed colt when you can have an experienced filly?"

Cole bristled. "And you'll be mine for the asking."

"Why not? It might be mutually beneficial."

Cole picked up his hat, turning the brim in his fingers. "Thanks for the honor, but I'm afraid I must refuse. I'm new in this town, Mrs. Lacey, and I don't think I want to be run off from St. Anselm's on a morals charge. Besides, it wouldn't be . . . right," he added lamely.

He started toward the door, but she stepped quickly in front of him. Laying her hands on his shoulders, she pulled his face to hers and planted a kiss on his lips. Cole forced himself to pull away.

"Some other time, then?" Tilly said invitingly, not in the least perturbed by his refusal.

"Perhaps."

He went quickly into the hall and opened the door without waiting for the Mexican maid. "Good day, Mrs. Lacey."

She smiled provocatively at him from the parlor doorway. "Tilly, to you, Reverend Storey."

Cole shut the front door and ran down the steps to the road, resisting the urge to wipe his sleeve across his mouth until he was far enough away for Tilly not to see, since he felt sure she was standing by the window watching him. The arrogance of the woman! The nerve! Blatantly trying to seduce a man of God!

She must have suspected he was not what he seemed as far back as the stage that brought them both to Tombstone. He would have to be very careful to avoid Tilly Lacey until Aces Malone returned. At least she had given the Reverend Cabot Storey a good excuse for staying out of her way.

"Miss Lassiter, may I have a word with you, please?"

Amanda looked up from the row of grosgrain ribbons she had been inspecting in Tippet's General Store. Though he was standing in the shadows of the doorway, she immediately recognized Dr. Goodfellow's stocky figure and her heart sank.

"Dr. Goodfellow," she said with a forced smile. "I didn't know you were back."

"Got in late last night," the physician said, walking up to reach for several small packages she had laid on the counter. "I can carry these for you if you're going back to the hotel."

"Back to the store, actually. Thank you," she said, turning to the clerk, "but I don't think I want to purchase any ribbon today."

Ignoring the storekeeper's frown, she started toward the door, followed by the doctor. It was only a short walk to the drug store, but when they had gone halfway there without the doctor's speaking, Amanda began to wonder if his anger with her would be even greater than she feared. Of course, though he had every reason to be annoyed with her, it was not her fault that she had been commandeered to set Jody Bennett's arm. She hadn't gone seeking someone to help; they had come for her. She was relieved when Goodfellow spoke casually without raising the subject.

"That was a long trip out to Horseshoe Canyon and back. And once I got there I found I had to stay longer than I'd planned. One of the cowboys got pinned under a horse and had severe internal injuries. Looks like he's going to be all right, though."

"I'm glad to hear it. I suppose you know about Jody Bennett?"

"Yes. I've just come from there, in fact. That's what I want to talk to you about."

Amanda paused before the door to her store. Pulling out her key, she opened it and motioned for the doctor to enter. He laid her packages on the counter and looked around, whistling in amazement.

"You've done a good job here, Miss. Your uncle never had the place this neat."

Amanda reached to unpin her straw bonnet. "I did it because I wanted to make a good impression on a buyer. Instead, I keep getting customers. Would you like a cup of tea, Doctor? Or coffee, perhaps?"

Goodfellow made a face. "Never touch either one, thank you. I just want to tell you, Miss, that I've never seen an arm set so cleanly and neatly as Jody Bennett's. I couldn't have done it better myself. Where'd you learn tricks like that?"

Amanda felt a great weight ease off her chest. "It was no trick, Doctor. I told you my father was a physician. He often allowed me to assist him with uncomplicated fractures. I learned a lot from watching when I couldn't help."

"Did you ever think of becoming a doctor yourself?"

Amanda laughed. "Occasionally. But there are not many women in the field, as you know, and there was never enough money to send me to a proper school. I'm relieved that you didn't think I was encroaching on your territory. When they came to me, I just did what I could to help. There wasn't any one else."

Goodfellow nodded. "I know. That's a problem here in this town. Sometimes we have three or four doctors and one of them is always around. But other times, when there are only two and we're both away for long stretches, it leaves the town without medical help for emergencies. So . . ."

He paused as though reluctant to speak. "Miss Lassiter, I don't know how to say this when I know you're anxious to sell and go back East, but I'm hoping you'll reconsider. I need to have someone like you around to help when things get busy. You could fill a real need here."

It was the last thing she'd expected to hear. She stared at him, not knowing how to respond. "But I'm not experienced enough to help you."

"You're more experienced than anyone else in Tombstone, aside from Dr. Gillingham. And I could teach you a lot. Perhaps, eventually, you might be able to strike out on your own. Meanwhile . . ."

He waved his hand around the store. "Meanwhile, you've got a good thing here. I've seen drug stores in Tucson that don't look this inviting. You could add all kinds of things, too, like tobacco and candy, soaps and perfumes. You'd have a thriving business here, and you'd be of real service to me. Won't you consider it, Miss Lassiter?''

Amanda looked away, her thoughts tumbling. Her determination to go back to St. Louis had wavered of late, but it had never completely been given up. It still seemed the most sensible, intelligent thing to do. It gave her pause to think of the risks involved in a young woman's trying to run a business in a wild, unruly town like Tombstone. She would be asking for trouble. And while she would welcome helping Dr. Goodfellow and learning from him, suppose he expected more of her than she was able to give? She would be stretching her little knowledge of medicines and their ministrations to its absolute limit.

With a clarity of sudden vision, she could see that she must make a choice between taking risks and stretching her limits or retreating back to a safe, familiar cocoon.

Was there really any question?

Thirteen

Should she buy it? Once again Amanda ran her hand down the soft fabric of the riding skirt. She had never seen one like it before—a skirt that was actually divided like trousers but full enough to appear to be a skirt. Made of buttery-soft suede with a small fringe around the hem and tiny metal beads defining the waist, it was the prettiest and yet the most practical garment she had ever seen. Added to her new riding boots and hat, the price would take the rest of her profits and part of what was left of the money she brought with her to Tombstone. How crazy of her to even think of throwing her money away like this!

And yet . . .

She would do it. After all, a girl had to indulge herself in lovely things now and then. And this would be perfect for riding out with Cabot Storey the next day.

"I'll take this, too," she said laying the skirt on the counter next to her boots and hat. Bert Tippet, the owner of Tippet's General Store, broke away from the group of men he had been talking with at the other end of the counter to fold the skirt in gray wrapping paper.

"A good choice, Miss Lassiter. It's going to look mighty pretty on you. We don't get many female garments ready-made, you know, and this one is really special. I'm glad you're taking it."

Amanda looked at the bales of cloth stacked on the counter. For a small store in a small town, Tippet's had an unusually large selection of fabrics and colors. That would be her next project, she decided. She would make herself a new dress. Two new dresses!

"You'd better be careful where you ride wearing that skirt, Miss Lassiter," one of the men at the other end of the counter drawled. Amanda looked up to see Roy Alander smiling at her, a long straw protruding out of his thin mouth. He stood next to two other men whom she recognized as idlers who often hung around the store, Jake and Lefty. If they had last names, she had never heard them.

"Why is that, Roy?" she asked, opening her purse to take out her money.

"Well, to begin with, there's them Indians."

"Them Apaches is in Mexico, Roy," Jake drawled. "Everybody knows that."

"Yeah," Lefty added. "Everybody."

"I'm not just talking about Apaches," Roy said indignantly. "There's other dangers out there, too. Outlaws like Curly Bill and The Casket Kid. They'd just love to find a pretty little thing like Missy here, riding out on the desert."

Amanda felt a sudden chill. "The Casket Kid?"

"Yeah. He's been seen around these parts—leastways some of his gang's been seen. He's as tough and mean an hombre as any you've ever come across."

"And got an eye for shootin' like nobody else," Jake chimed in. "That's why they call him The Casket Kid."

Amanda laid her coins on the counter. "Because he put so many men in their caskets?"

"That's right. It's a known fact, if you go up against The Kid, you might as well go have your pine box fitted out first."

The three men nodded at each other gravely; yet, from their smiles, Amanda had the feeling they were jesting with her. "I've heard of Curly Bill and some of the infamous gangs, but I never heard of The Casket Kid. I think you men are trying to pull a joke on me."

"No, no," they all cried at once. Roy finally shushed the others and turned to her, his lined face as serious as she had ever seen him.

"It's as true as the sunshine, Miss Lassiter. Not many people know what his real name is; but as 'The Kid,' he's struck terror into every place he's hit. He'd as soon take the gold fillings from your teeth as look at you; and if you object, he'll shoot you dead without blinkin' an eye. Just ask all the people on the stages he's robbed. He's a thief . . ."

"A murderer . . ."

"And an all-round, no-good varmint who's only fit for hangin'!"

Bert Tippet handed Amanda her package. "Now stop this, you fellows. You're goin' to make Miss Lassiter so nervous she won't go riding wearing that pretty new skirt. Besides, The Kid's no worse than any other outlaw, and he's the best shot of them all. I heard that from a man that saw him once in a shootin' contest. He won hands down."

Amanda laughed. "That's all right, Bert. I thank you, gentlemen, for your warning; but I assure you I won't be riding anywhere alone. If I go out on the desert, I'll be sure to take someone with me."

"I'd ride out with you myself, Miss," Roy said, gently. The other two men began snickering while Amanda restrained her smile. Roy Alander had spent so many years idling around stores and saloons he probably could not even sit a horse, much less ride one.

"Thank you, Roy," she said sweetly, "but I've already promised Reverend Storey I'd ride out with him."

"Oh, the preacher." The three men exchanged knowing glances. "Well, I suppose that's all right. He spoke the marriage for my boy Horace and his wife, you know, the first day he got here. He looks like he could take care of hisself, even if he is a preacher."

Lefty nodded solemnly. "And since he's a preacher, I guess you don't need to worry none about him takin' advantage."

"I don't know," Jake said. "Miss Lassiter's mighty pretty."

Embarrassed, Amanda gave a quick nod to the proprietor. "Thank you, Bert. Good day to you, gentlemen."

They nodded politely as she hurried past. "Lucky preacher," she heard one of them mutter, followed by more snickers. Amanda stepped outside into the sunshine and turned toward the hotel. The excitement she had felt earlier was tinged a little by the warnings she'd been given, yet she was determined not to let them ruin her happiness. The thought of riding out on the desert, dressed in her new clothes and accompanied by the handsome, captivating Cabot Storey, was simply too intoxicating to be overshadowed by threats from outlaws and Indians.

"Casket Kid, indeed!" she muttered as she hurried back to the hotel.

Amanda found all the expense and effort of her new riding habit worth it when she saw the admiration in Cabot's eyes as she walked down the steps of the hotel the next morning. Her skirt had required a tuck in the waist; but other than that, it fit her perfectly. She had fixed her hair in one long braid down her back tied with a gaily colored ribbon. From her smart, felt, low-brimmed hat to her shiny new boots, her ensemble looked as neat and fashionable as any riding habit back East and was far more practical.

Cole, accustomed to drab calico housedresses and sunbonnets, gave a low whistle. "You look pretty enough to charm the warts off a frog."

"I'll assume that's a compliment," Amanda said, laughing and drawing her long braid of hair over her shoulder.

He gave her his arm as they started down the street. "It is. I've rented two horses at the corral. You didn't say how experienced you were, so I got a calm animal for you."

"Good," she said with relief. "It's been awhile since I spent much time on a horse. Papa always drove a buggy on his rounds, but I rode out with him sometimes on a mare from the livery stable. After he died, I just gave up riding. It will be good to get back to it."

Cole had rented the best horse in the corral for himself, a beautiful roan with a white blaze and two white feet. When Amanda saw how skittishly the sleek animal moved around the open yard of the corral, she was even more relieved to be riding her sedate gelding. Both horses were outfitted with tooled-leather saddles, but she noticed the rector's saddlebags bulged while hers lay flat.

"Lunch," Cole explained.

They mounted and rode out of the yard and down the short length of street that led from the town to the winding, gray road stretching out across the desert toward the hills.

"Do you know where we're going?" Amanda asked, scanning the smoky blue hills in the distance.

"Yes. There are seven mines around Tombstone, but I thought we'd visit the two that are closest together, the Matchless and the original Tombstone mine."

"Seven mines?"

"Oh yes. Old Mr. Schieffelin stumbled on one of the richest silver bonanzas in the country when he found the Tombstone. One of the newer mines is right here in town, near the stamp mill. In fact they're digging tunnels for it now beneath Toughnut Street."

Amanda glanced over at Cabot Storey, admiring the easy grace with which he rode. "You amaze me, you know," she said. "You already know more about Tombstone than I do, yet we arrived here at the same time."

Cole looked away. "I'm just a naturally curious fellow."

"I suppose as the rector of a church you would have to know everything about the town you serve."

He gave a short cough. "That, too."

"Do you find these western saddles difficult to use? I've heard that people who are accustomed to English saddles dislike the western ones intensely."

"English saddles?"

"Yes. You know, those small, flat ones. Back East, everyone uses them."

"Oh, those," Cole said. "Well, not everybody likes them. The western saddle was designed for cowboys working long hours on the range. It's more practical for this rugged country. Look over there," he said, pointing to an outcrop of sandstone ledges. "I'd swear I saw a coyote disappear behind those rocks."

"A coyote? I'd love to see one. I hear them howling all the time."

With her attention focused on the non-existent coyote, Cole reminded himself to be more careful. It had been so good to get back on a spirited horse and head out into the open country that he had naturally slipped into his old ways. He'd better remember who he was supposed to be, perhaps even create a few little mishaps for himself and his mount. Just enough to convince Amanda that he was not as sure of himself as he felt.

They rode for over an hour, across dry arroyos, and up and down small gullies and draws. They skirted long vistas of cacti and thorny scrub, admired huge saguaro with their plumage of white spring flowers, rested occasionally in the shade of a cottonwood or sycamore near the thin trickle of a stream red with clay.

Once they passed a wagon team drawn by twenty mules hauling silver ore back into town and stopped long enough to verify that they were headed in the right direction. At length, the faint pounding of a pump in the distance told them they were nearing the first mine.

Amanda could hardly believe that the cluster of dilapidated buildings and dry hills they finally rode up to could yield so much wealth. A huge thirty-ton walking beam pulled water from beneath the earth with a regular, monotonous beat. She waited in the shade of a lean-to while Cabot went down inside the tunnels to watch the ore being chipped away, for she had no inclination to descend into dark, airless passages surrounded by earth. The foreman was kind enough to explain how the mine worked and that was sufficient.

The men moving in and out of the bowels of the earth were the dusty, bearded, wiry fellows she had seen coming into town by the droves every Saturday night. Their faces were lined with permanent earth stains; their hands were gnarled and encrusted, and their clothes worn and shabby. She knew they came here to these mines by the hundreds from all over the country, drawn by the lure of instant wealth; and she wondered how many of them found any riches at all, given that the owners, shareholders, managers, and foremen all took their profits first. These men had the worst job of all—wrenching the silver from the earth. From the look of them, they profited the least.

The second mine was smaller but in every other respect similar to the first. This time, Amanda ventured a little way into the dark interior, but when it came to descending down into a small shaft, she fled back outside into the bright sunshine.

When Reverend Storey at last emerged, it was already well into afternoon and Amanda was beginning to feel hungry. She was relieved when Cabot shook hands with the foreman and called for their horses. They rode away, taking the road by which they had come a short distance before Cabot pulled off and onto a path that led upward toward the hills.

"I heard about a place up here where we can eat lunch," he explained. Amanda guided her mount behind him up a hill scraggly with clumps of sagebrush. They climbed for a short time before heading over a ridge where Cabot pulled up his mount.

"What do you think of that?" he asked, resting his hand on the pommel of his saddle.

Amanda looked down on one of the prettiest little valleys she had seen since coming out West. Surrounded by blue mountains, it nestled like a small green jewel between the hills. She caught the silver glint of a pool beneath the canopy of two small cottonwoods, their white fluffy down covering the ground like a scattering of snow.

"It's lovely," Amanda said, on a sigh. "Is this where we're having lunch?"

"Yes, and I'm ready for it. Let's go."

They rode down into the valley at a canter and drew up near the pool. Cole hobbled the horses to graze while Amanda laid out the contents of his saddlebags on a large tablecloth.

"You thought of everything," she said, looking eagerly at the cold fried chicken, slabs of bread, small chunks of cheese, and tiny bite-sized pieces of fruitcake. "Everything but the wine."

Cole folded his long legs beneath him and stretched out on the ground next to the tablecloth. "I was told the water in that pool is as sweet and cool as any wine. And you can thank my landlady, Mrs. Jasper, for the food."

"Thank you, Mrs. Jasper," Amanda said, lifting a chunk of bread and cheese. "How did you know about this place, anyway?"

He hesitated. "One of my parishioners told me about it. It's a famous water hole out here, well known by travelers. If we're lucky, though, none of them will come along while we're here."

"You certainly found it easily. You must have memorized the map."

He reached for a chicken leg. "Something like that."

Once they finished the meal, Cole stretched out on the grass while Amanda knelt by the pool, drinking the sweet water from a tin cup. He watched her, studying her slim figure. Her hair, even in its long braid, reflected the light in flecks of gold among the chestnut bronze. She lifted her head to scan the open sky, revealing the graceful length of her white neck, straining the fabric of her blouse over her full breasts. As she raised a hand to shield her eyes, her sleeve fell away, baring her smooth, white arm. Her sculptured profile against the deep blue of the sky was so beautiful he had to suppress a groan.

He quickly turned over on his stomach to hide his swelling need of her, absently picking at the grass.

"You were right—it is sweet," Amanda said, moving back to sit beside him. Putting her hat on, she pulled at the strings beneath her chin. "I suppose we ought to be starting back soon."

"Oh, there's no hurry. We've plenty of daylight yet." He leaned on one elbow, drawing a straw through his lips and studying her. "Do you know you're very beautiful?" he asked impulsively.

Amanda gave a start as she felt a surge of joy warm her body. "Beautiful! I don't think so," she said, shyly looking away. "But I thank you for the compliment anyway."

"I mean it. Hasn't anyone told you that before?"

"No. Besides, it's not true. I'm lanky and thin, and I have freckles."

"All your curves are in the right places. And I don't see any freckles."

"You would, if I didn't wear a hat all the time."

Cole reached out to push her hat away, letting it fall to the back of her head. "A hat hides your lovely hair," he said, smoothing a thin strand away from her forehead and moving closer. "And with beautiful skin like yours, a few freckles don't even matter."

Amanda stirred under the warm excitement his touch evoked. His face was close to hers, his fingers lightly brushing her cheek. His lips moved closer, and for an instant she was tempted to get up and run. She resisted the urge and instead bent toward him, relishing the light coolness of his lips on hers. His arms went around her; his fingers slid across her shoulders and down her back. She felt her nipples go hard and taut against his chest, the long length of his leg pressing against her own. Giving way to the growing warmth that consumed her, she let her arms go round his neck, drawing him nearer.

Cole's lips played with her mouth, moving sensuously above and around until her lips parted with the warmth of his kiss and his tongue darted within. He sensed her resistance melting away as he tasted the depths of her sweet mouth, then drove fully within, filling her with his tongue. She fell back as he carried her over, laying

stirrup and her hand on the pommel
ircled her waist to give her a heave
of his hands on her body, she knew

ving while he waited for her to jump
ly to face him, she threw her arms
d pressed her open mouth to his. He
prise then quickly enfolded her in his
of his desire surged back to life. Her
his as together they sank to their
n embrace.
in bursts; his lips coursed her face,
lders; his hand slid upward to stroke
f her breasts. "Oh, I need you," he
you so much . . ."
ak at all. She could only revel in the
dy against hers, the warmth of his
ng, searching. She was filled with
e for him that nothing else mattered.
rs, she unbuttoned her blouse to al-
de her chemise and bare h[illegible]ast.
k as he laid h[illegible]

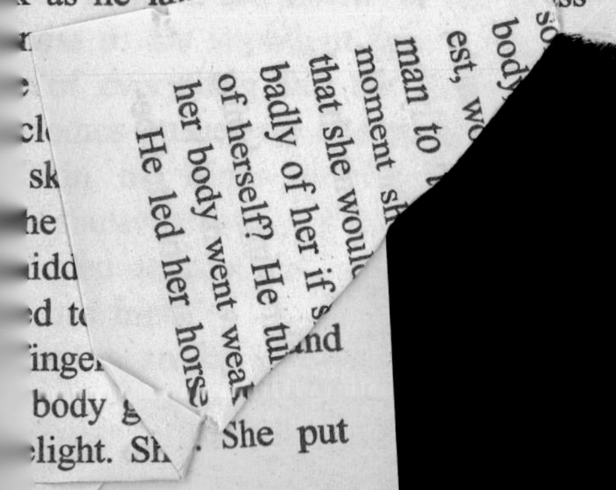

her gently on the ground, their lips still locked. Then, pulling away from her mouth, he kissed her chin, her throat, the hollow of her neck. She strained against him, lifting to his kiss. His insistent mouth covered her throat and moved downward to the opening of her blouse. She felt his fingers unloosening the buttons, the swift rush of air on her skin.

"No . . ." she murmured weakly, struggling to resist the rising tide of desire that slowly consumed her. When his hand cupped her breast, lifting it free of the confining chemise and his lips closed over it, suckling gently, the surge of wild pleasure that swept over her told her she was lost.

She forced herself to remember that they were in a solitary place, completely alone, carried on the tide of a rising passion. With a growing panic at how it would end, she turned swiftly, pulling away from him.

"Don't!" she cried. "I can't . . ."

She jerked to her knees. Instantly he was there, enfolding her with his embrace. "Don't be afraid," he murmured, lifting her hair to kiss the tender places behind her ear. "I won't hurt you."

She felt her body sinking beneath his need and her own. "I can't . . ." she cried. "I can't."

Like a cold wave washing over him, Cole realized he was going too fast. Forcing himself to pull away, he put some space between them and waited a moment until he could look back at her.

"I'm sorry. I guess I got carried away." He paused, looking deeply into her eyes. "You've never known a man, have you?" he asked gently.

Amanda looked away. "No."

She was a virgin. Yet what else had he expected? He mentally shook himself, still stirred by the reaction he had experienced when he held her in his arms. It had been a long time since any woman had affected him so strongly.

"And I suppose it's important that you save yourself for an eventual husband?" he asked, not without a note of sarcasm.

Amanda waited while the pounding of her blood eased. "Isn't that what a minister would expect?"

Cole ran his hand over his damp forehead. "I suppose most would. But. . . . Well, I'm not your usual minister."

That was certainly true, she thought. The gentle skill with which he made love was enough to prove his experience. But then, she had never known any other clergyman. Perhaps they were all this way and kept it hidden.

"It's not that I'm saving myself," she said quietly. "In truth, I don't think much about marriage. And I do want to know what's it's like to make love to . . . someone. Since the first time you kissed me, I've wanted you to be that someone."

His heart gave a leap at her honest, forthright words. Somehow he had known she would be this kind of woman and not simpering or prudish. "Then what bothers you?"

"I don't know. Fear, perhaps. And I don't know you very well."

Cole laid his hands on her shoulders and looked directly into her eyes. "Don't be afraid. I won't hurt you, I promise."

"And would you respect my wishes, if I refuse?"

neath him, but not until she cried out in desperation did she feel him enter her—hard and thrusting. For a few moments she was conscious of pain. Then the barrier was broken, and she knew the whole length of him filling her completely. She strained against him, holding him tightly to her as, pounding and driving, he joined with her in one climactic whole that was ecstasy she had never known before.

He stiffened against her, crying out as she clasped him, never wanting to let him go. Only gradually, like a wave receding, did the flame ease. He relaxed against her, drawing her lips to his in a long kiss that held both gratitude and adoration.

Exhausted, he turned on his side, still pressing her against him, his lips resting against her hair.

"I didn't hurt you too much, did I?" he whispered when he could speak again.

She laughed against his throat. "A little. At the time, it didn't seem to matter."

Her hair had come undone, spilling over her shoulders. Cole took a long strand of it and wound it around his finger. "Did you know that you are a very passionate woman?"

She smiled in embarrassment. "No. I was afraid I'd be awkward."

"You were perfect!"

"And you were very . . ." she paused, ". . . experienced."

"Experienced?"

"Yes," she said, laughing. "I thought preachers were supposed to be, well, innocent."

Cole buried his face in her shoulder. "That's a myth.

After all, I did live and work out here for several years. Cowboys are notoriously earthy. Besides, I believe if you're going to preach about heaven, you ought to first know something about the world."

Amanda lifted his head, laying her palm along his cheek and looking deeply into his eyes. "You know, you're different from anyone I've ever known."

It was Cole's turn to laugh with embarrassment. "I hope that's a compliment."

"It is," she answered, kissing him lightly. She ran her finger down his long cheek, across the firm chin, the sculptured lips. It made her tremble to think how dear this man could be, how dear he already was.

Abruptly she sat up, wrapping her arms around her knees. "Then you don't think this . . . well, sinful?"

Cole leaned on his elbow and pondered how to answer. "I don't see how anything that draws two people together in such joy can be called a sin."

Amanda laid her head on her arms, thinking quietly. She suspected that was true only if the joy also included some kind of commitment. She had no idea what this experience would mean for their future or even if, indeed, they would have any future. But for now, the world seemed infused with more beauty and contentment than she had ever experienced before. Perhaps that was enough.

Her eyes traveled over his lean body, dwelling with curiosity on the limpness of that part of him which had so recently filled her with delight. "Did you know you have a wonderful body?" Her eyes held a hint of mischievousness.

Cole laughed. "I'm not the first man you've seen in such a stage of undress, am I?"

"Oh, no. My father was a doctor, remember? But you are definitely the most . . . the most well-endowed."

"Why, thank you, ma'am." He had heard that before but never appreciated it so much. He reached for her discarded blouse and gently laid it over her shoulders.

Amanda smiled her thanks, then said abruptly, "Are you happy in your new parish?"

Caught by surprise, Cole hardly knew what to answer. He lay back, his hands behind his head. "Why, yes. They're good people. They want to get their church built more than anything else and, of course, I want to help them."

"And once you get the church built, will you be leaving Tombstone?"

"Perhaps," he said casually, thinking how he'd be gone long before then. "What about you? You'll be going back East soon, I suppose?"

He asked the question so casually Amanda couldn't tell if he were hoping she'd answer yes or no. "As a matter of fact, I've just about decided to stay. At least for a while. I think I'd like to run the drug store. There seems to be a need for it, and Dr. Goodfellow thinks I can be of help to him. He's urged me to stay."

Cole sat up quickly. "But you're not a doctor."

"I know that, and so does he. But I learned a lot from my father and there are minor things I can handle, especially when the doctor is out riding on visits."

She glanced over to see the consternation on his face. A cold pang struck her. Perhaps he wanted her to go away now that she had given herself to him. "You don't like it that I'm going to stay and run my store, do you?"

Cole ran his finger lightly down her cheek. "I don't want you to leave. But running a drug store is not a woman's place."

"And where is a woman's place? Where I was a little while ago?"

He gave her a quizzical grin. "There's nothing wrong with that. But running a business is another whole thing."

Amanda began pulling on her skirt. "Let's don't talk about this now. It's been too lovely, and it's time we got back anyway." She stood, fastening her blouse. "We don't want to get caught out on the desert by some desperado like The Casket Kid."

Cole paused in pulling on his clothes. "What do you know about The Casket Kid?" he asked, trying to sound casual.

"Only what I was told—that he's a horrible, ugly man who would as soon cut your throat as take your money. I certainly don't want to run into him."

He moved to put his arms around her, pushing aside her hair to kiss her lightly behind her ear. "Don't worry; I'll protect you. Besides, I could stay here the rest of the day and all night."

"I don't think that's a very good idea," Amanda said, feeling a thrill go up the length of her body. "I'd end up more fallen from grace than ever."

He laid his palms on her cheeks and lifted her face to his. "You're not a fallen woman, and you have more 'grace' than anyone I've ever known."

He meant it sincerely, she could tell, and her heart

overflowed. She had to fight to keep her voice from betraying all she felt.

"Thank you for those kind words, Reverend Storey."

With their arms around each other's waists, they started for the horses.

Fourteen

Amanda sat in front of the small mirror in her room and studied her reflection. She could not see that she looked any different for having lost her virginity. She'd heard that the marks of a fallen woman would tell on her face; but if they were there, she could see no trace of them. She peered closer, running her finger down her cheek and around her eyes.

Were the hazel-colored orbs that peered back at her more deeply set than before? Were the lines that defined the corners more coarse? Did the lips turn downward in sad lines suggesting depravity?

All she could see were the hated freckles more evident than ever, probably because of her long day out in the sun. Her fashionable hat had done no good at all!

No, she thought, turning away from the mirror. If there were a difference, it was within, in the bubbling turmoil of her conscience. According to everything she'd learned about society, she was wrong to give herself to Cabot Storey without a commitment of marriage or, at least, an engagement. She barely knew this man, yet she had thrown off all misgivings and eagerly, wantonly joined her body with his in a moment of passion and delight. She ought to be ashamed of herself!

On the contrary, she did not regret it at all. It had been a wonderful, delicious experience. And while it was true that she did not know Cabot very well, still her instincts told her he was a man who would not treat her shabbily. He had been tender, passionate, and loving.

He had also known exactly what he was doing. His experience had countered her inexperience. She was not sorry for that, though she still wondered at it, considering his profession.

Amanda walked back and forth across the narrow room, her arms folded against her chest. No, she would not be sorry and she would not feel guilty. She was more a woman now than ever before, more attuned to the mystery of the universe. Surely a loving God who had put men and women on this earth to enjoy each other would not condemn her for the joyous experience of love she had shared with Cabot Storey.

But was it really love? She hardly knew how to answer. The turmoil she felt, once the euphoria of that glorious afternoon wore off, had left her more confused than ever. Since last Friday she had tried to avoid seeing him again, partly out of fear that he would reject her for her wanton ways and partly because she doubted her own feelings. He professed to be a man of the spirit, but his reaction to their lovemaking had been decidedly earthy. There was something disturbing about him that she simply could not understand.

And yet she knew that when she saw him again she would want nothing more than to have him take her in his arms and carry her again to the heights they had shared on that grassy knoll. Was it love she felt or something much more base?

A brisk knock at the door of her room brought her out of her thoughts.

"Who is it?" she called.

"It's Mrs. Poole, Amanda," came the muffled voice from the other side of the door. "You asked me to let you know when the stage came in, and Jimmy just told me it's arrived."

"Oh. Thanks, Mrs. Poole. I'll go right over."

With any luck, the shipment of drugs she had ordered from Tucson would be on that stage. The small amount of laudanum she'd brought with her was nearly gone. If it wasn't replenished soon, several of her customers might suffer needlessly.

She reached for her hat, standing before the mirror to fasten her bonnet atop her hair with a six-inch stiletto of a hatpin.

"All right, Amanda, so you're not a fallen woman," she spoke firmly to her reflection. "All the same, you'd better be careful about getting carried away again. It won't do, you know. He's not interested in marrying you, and you don't need any unwanted pregnancies! So, stay away from him!"

The hazel eyes peered back at her, unconvinced.

"Well, maybe not completely away," she muttered as she picked up her parasol and headed for the door.

Cole watched the stage rattle down Allen Street as he stood in the door of the barber shop. The lathered horses thundered past in a cloud of dust with the driver shouting and flourishing his whip. In its wake, a crowd of children scurried behind, followed by the more sedate adults, all of whom were intent on seeing who and what had arrived.

"He was goin' mighty fast," the barber said, casually stepping up beside Cole and wiping his hands on a towel. "Must have had some trouble."

"Maybe he just wants to attract attention," Cole answered. He slipped on the coat he had removed to get his hair trimmed.

"He don't need to do that. Stage comin' in is the most important event of the day around Tombstone. No, when he's going like that, it usually means he got robbed outside of town. Happens all the time these days."

"Maybe I'll just wander over and see if you're right."

"Mark my words, Reverend Storey. I know."

"How much do I owe you, Sam?" Cole said, reaching into his pocket.

"Let's see, shave and trim—fifteen cents."

"Good enough. Thanks."

Sam pulled up the hem of his long apron and stuffed the coins into his pocket. "Vestry meeting tonight, Reverend Storey?"

Cole was already half out the door. "Oh, yes. That's right."

"Good. We've got to decide how to get that church built. We've been waitin' too long. We've got to find a way to make it happen."

"Yes, indeed we do."

"I've got a few ideas."

Cole glanced toward the crowd around the stage, longing to join them. With any luck, Aces Malone would be among today's passengers.

"That's good, Sam. I'll look forward to hearing them tonight," he added, moving out onto the walk. He set his hat firmly on his head and stepped off the curb to cross the street.

Building this church was fast becoming an obsession with the people of his congregation. They had some idea that he was supposed to work a miracle and make happen what they had not been able to during the last two years. He understood how important it was to them, but it was getting more and more difficult to put them off when they looked to him for answers.

Strangely, at times he found himself caught up in the problem almost as much as his parishioners. He would worry over ways to accumulate the needed funds, then realize what he was doing and chide himself for it. If only Aces would show up, he could get out from under this crazy masquerade and bring the real Reverend Storey back to solve the problem.

However, a first glance at the disembarking passengers lumbering off the stage did not look encouraging. No familiar figure stepped down from the swaying cab with a jaunty derby over shoulder-length hair, holding the long cigar that Malone was never without. On the other hand, the watching crowd appeared excited and disturbed as they grouped around the driver who was speaking in an unusually animated way. Sam was probably right—something had happened.

"Stopped us right outside of Contention," Cole heard the driver exclaim as he walked up to the edge of the crowd. "Two men, with black beards and moustaches and hats pulled down around their eyes. Made everybody get out and took everything—money, watches, a gold ring. They got the Amelia payroll. Knew right where it was. Whole thing didn't take more than five minutes."

Cole felt someone brush by him and saw Sheriff Behan pushing his way through the crowd. He couldn't hear what the law man said, but the driver's answer came ringing clearly.

"I tried, Sheriff, but they took my shotgun. One of the passengers had a pistol and shot at them as they rode away and maybe winged one. There wasn't nothin' else we could do."

A man in a black suit, whose drawn, pale face suggested he was one of the passengers, spoke up. "That's right, Sheriff. We was all feared of being killed. The driver did all he could."

"How do you suppose they knew about that payroll?" Cole heard someone near him remark. He turned to see Brody Hanlon, one of the directors of the Ameila mine, standing behind him. A second man standing beside Hanlon answered quietly.

"There's a leak somewhere. Got to be."

Cole smiled to himself. Yes, indeed, there had to be. Desperados weren't going to rob a stage in broad daylight for a few watches and a gold ring. The loss of a payroll was going to hurt; several of the men in his congregation worked at the Amelia. Brody Hanlon, on the other hand, being one of the owners, did not seem too perturbed over the loss. He chewed the end of his cigar, his fingers looped in his waistcoat pockets, and surveyed the scene with an almost bored expression on his bearded face.

Cole checked the passengers once more just to make

certain Aces Malone was not among them, then started to turn away. Another remark halted him in mid-stride.

"The Casket Kid's got a beard, don't he?"

"I heard he was in these parts. Was it him, you suppose?"

Cole forced himself to turn back. The men throwing out comments were part of the crowd and were not looking at him. All the same, he decided to wait a few moments before starting up the street.

"I couldn't tell who it was," the driver said loudly. "All that hair—could'a been anybody. But I think one of them was nicked in the leg as he rode off. I'd look for anyone around town that had a gunshot in the leg."

"In Tombstone? That could be anybody!"

The sheriff clucked his tongue in irritation. "Go on, all of you. Go back to work. Nothin's going to be solved standing around here jawin' about this." He turned to the driver. "I'll talk to you inside."

As the crowd began to thin, Cole was surprised to see Amanda standing on the walkway near the station door. Immediately Aces was forgotten in the surge of pleasure he felt seeing her there, looking so pretty in her neat, dark dress and fetching little bonnet. Forgotten, too, were the agonized moments he had spent since last Friday telling himself to stay away from her, warning himself that this decent, lovely woman was bad news for a man like him. He was playing with fire getting involved with Amanda Lassiter. She would spread her net, and he would be caught twisting and thrashing like a fish pulled from a pond. Who would have thought it? The Casket Kid risking his reputation over a soft, respectable young girl!

All the same, he had looked for her for two days,

hoping to meet her on the street. Only his sternest self-control had prevented him from going to her hotel and making a fool of himself again. And, finally, here she was, just a few feet away. Surely it couldn't hurt just to talk casually with her in public.

He hurried toward the walkway and almost stumbled over Behan who stepped out in front of him, blocking his path. Instinctively, his hand clenched into a fist, but he caught himself and put it behind him.

"Excuse me, Sheriff," he said politely, opening his hand to touch the brim of his hat. "I didn't see you."

Behan, standing close to him without moving, stared intently into his face. "That's okay, Reverend Storey. We're all a little preoccupied right now."

Cole waited for the sheriff to step out of his way and found himself growing disconcerted when the man continued to stare at him with a quizzical intensity.

"Something I can do for you?" Cole finally muttered.

Behan shook his head. "No, no. There's just something about you that's familiar. I noticed it the other day at Tilly's. Trouble is, I can't think of any place we could have met before."

"Maybe somebody else looks like me," Cole offered, knowing he didn't dare hurry on. As The Casket Kid, he had never really met John Behan, though he knew well enough that the sheriff boasted he would nail the outlaw's hide to the jailhouse door. Deliberately he pushed back his hat and looked directly into Behan's dark eyes.

"Must have been," the sheriff drawled, stepping aside. To Cole's discomfort, Behan fell in alongside him as they headed toward the walkway.

"It's going to be hard to find these robbers," Behan went on casually. "A heavy beard can hide a man's features almost as much as a mask."

"I suppose so. But then there's the gunshot wound. That ought to help, if the man comes into town, anyway."

"Perhaps. Keep an eye out, Reverend Storey. If you see anyone who looks suspicious, let me know."

Cole stepped up on the walk. "I'll do that, Sheriff."

He was relieved when Behan moved past him into the stage office. Yet by the time he turned back to the walk, he saw with alarm that Amanda had already started down the street toward town. Cole had to quicken his steps to catch up with her.

"Hello," he said as she continued to scurry down the walk.

She gave him a tentative smile but did not slow her step. "Hello," she answered nervously.

"Mind if I walk with you?"

"No. Please do."

This was not the reaction he expected after their warm experience the last time they were together, and it had the effect of immediately doing away with his sensible resolve to stay uninvolved. He skipped along beside her until she turned the corner and he stepped out in front of her, blocking her way.

"Why do I get the impression you're angry with me?" he asked, extending one arm across the walk. "I've been hoping to see you for two days, but you were never around. And you didn't come to the service yesterday."

Amanda tried to duck under his arm, but he swiveled around, still blocking her path.

"I'm sorry. I've just been terribly busy."

"Not at your store. I passed by there four or five times."

She looked away, her cheeks flaming. "I haven't felt very well, so I took some time off. I really ought to be working now, but I hoped some merchandise I ordered had come in on the stage."

Her eyes flickered in every direction except his. Cole reached out and tipped up her chin, forcing her to look into his face.

"And did it?"

"No," she answered, struggling to free her chin.

"Amanda," he said quietly. "Are you regretting what happened between us the other day? Because if you are, that would be a terrible shame."

"Regretting? Of course not. Why should I?"

"I don't believe you. You won't look me in the eye. You shrink from my touch. I thought what we shared meant something to you."

Amanda looked down at her hands. "That's just it. I don't know what it meant. I'm having difficulty looking into the mirror."

So that's it, Cole thought. Conscience and morality rear their ugly heads. Well, he shouldn't be surprised. She was a decent woman, after all. He studied her pale face and trembling lips and was strangely touched by concern for her. Reaching out, he took her arm.

"Come on, let's go round to Alahambra and I'll buy you lunch. At least we can have a friendly discussion."

"Really, that's not necessary . . ."

"I think it is." When she didn't move, he leaned closer and whispered in her ear, "Please?"

Amanda fought down a shiver at the warmth of his breath. "I ought to open the store."

"You can do that later. After all, you won't lose your customers to the competition, because there isn't any."

She hesitated, fighting, and losing, an invisible, inward battle. Then, abruptly, she smiled up at him. "Oh, all right. I suppose you're right."

"Good," he said, drawing her arm through his.

The Alahambra lunch counter was situated just behind the saloon, separated from it by a pair of swinging doors. A constant stream of traffic back and forth sent the doors flying open and allowed Amanda glimpses of the saloon interior—men grouped around tables and lined up at the mahogany bar, their boots resting on the brass rail. Through the open spaces above the swinging doors, the noise from the saloon almost drowned out the quiet chatter of the few people at the lunch counter and adjacent tables. She toyed with her food, listening to the loud buzz of conversation in the other room, punctuated by frequent laughter or some ribald remark shouted across the tables. Jangling spurs and the stomp of boots on wooden plank floors clashed with the clatter of the black-jack wheel. Amanda, who had never been inside a saloon before, found her interest piqued by the enticing glimpses of this mysterious, men's world of drinking and gambling. Once, she even saw the gaudy feathers of a woman's hat bobbing above the swinging doors and heard a girl's high pitched giggle.

"You're not, are you?" she heard Cole asking.

"What?" she said, forcing her thoughts back to the

man across the table. "I'm sorry, I was listening to the noise in there."

He smiled at her, his eyes crinkling in a way that made her heart flutter. "I asked you if you were sorry about what happened the other day?" he said, lowering his voice.

She felt her cheeks flame with color, but she forced herself to meet his gaze. "No. I'm not sorry, because it was a lovely experience. And I wanted it. That must have been obvious. It's just that I've always been told nice girls shouldn't do those things before they were married."

Cole reached out and squeezed her hand. "That's a myth, perpetrated on society by middle-aged mothers. More young women ignore it than you would ever imagine."

She reveled in the strong feel of his hand over hers. When he touched her like this, all her shame and fear seemed silly and nothing else mattered but being with him. "Perhaps they do, but I never did."

Cole studied her large, honest eyes, so beautifully fringed with thick lashes, the soft brownish color flecked with gold from the lights in the room. "I know that. And I know you are a good, virtuous young woman. I would never want to hurt you, Amanda. Remember that."

"I don't think you would, Cabot. Only . . ."

She was interrupted by a loud crash inside the saloon. People began shouting and a woman screamed. Amanda jumped to her feet as a second crash was followed by one of the saloon chairs careening through the swinging doors and across the lunchroom.

"What in the world?" Cole muttered, looking back toward the saloon.

A cowboy in chaps and a battered hat came running into the lunchroom. "Look out," he shouted. "He's got a gun!"

From behind the lunch counter, a waiter hurried out to peer over the swinging doom. "Looks like that crazy Al Dumont's at it again. Hey, Reverend Storey, you'd better go see if you can keep him from killing everybody in there."

"That's the sheriff's job," Cole replied. But he pushed back his chair and walked over to look into the saloon. People inside had scattered in all directions. Those near the front had fled to the walkway and cowered on the sidewalk, peering through the open door, while those caught at the rear of the room stood pressed flat against both walls or crouched down behind upturned tables and chairs. In the open center Cole could see two men facing off, one of them waving a long-barreled pistol.

"Someone's gone for the sheriff," the waiter muttered, "but all hell could break loose before he gets here. Go on, Reverend Storey. See what you can do."

Reluctantly, Cole pushed open the swinging door. The last thing he wanted was to call attention to himself by getting involved in a gunfight. But the waiter was right. A lot of bullets could begin to fly very quickly unless someone broke this up.

He had barely entered the room before he recognized Tilly Lacey in a green-feathered hat, cowering against a wall near the lunchroom doors. He saw her eyes light up as she recognized him, but he ignored her and walked straight up to Dumont, who was waving his pistol wildly around.

"You'd better give that to me," Cole said, in a low, level voice.

"Get away, Preacher," Dumont snarled, turning a thin face distorted with rage briefly toward him. "This is my fight. That bastard cheated me."

Cole glanced quickly over at the other man, whose striped waistcoat and fancy cravat marked him as a professional gambler. Dumont, on the other hand, he could tell in one glance, was one of the typical, shabby losers who frequented saloons all over the West trying to win a rich stake. He probably *had* been cheated, but that didn't give him the right to shoot up the place.

"You know you're not supposed to wear guns in town, Dumont," Cole said, keeping his voice calm. "Just give me the pistol, and we'll work this out peaceably."

The gambler, in an arrogant stance beside the overturned table, spoke in a voice full of contempt. "He's crazy. I didn't cheat him. He's just a sore loser."

The gambler's eyes were so black and cold that Cole knew Dumont would never have had a chance if the man had been wearing a gun. He stood with his fingers locked casually in his vest pockets, his eyes boring into Dumont, his face a mask of amused disgust.

"If you want to fight, at least go out in the street," Cole said levelly to Dumont. "Don't shoot that thing in here where you can hurt innocent people."

"I don't care about people, damn it!" Dumont shouted, his face contorted with rage. "He ain't never goin' to cheat nobody again. I'm goin' to see to it!"

Very carefully Cole reached out to lay his fingers

around Dumont's wrist. "He'll leave town on the next stage. Better that way than you should be hanged for murder. Now give me the gun, Dumont."

The sudden silence hung heavy in the room while Dumont struggled between his fury and the preacher's level reasoning. When he glanced over into Cole's eyes, Cole knew he had won. Incredibly he breathed a sigh of relief as Dumont let the pistol sink into his hand.

A murmur broke out around him, a collective ease of tension. Cole turned the pistol over to remove the bullets from the barrel while Dumont slumped beside him, his rage evaporating like air escaping from a balloon.

"Reverend Storey!" Tilly screamed. "Look out!"

A sudden burst of gunfire shattered the air. There was a high, piercing woman's scream as the men scrambled for the doors while an acrid explosion of smoke surrounded the three women standing in the middle of the room. When it cleared, the gambler was on his knees, holding his wrist in one hand; across from him, Cole stood with knees slightly bent, pointing Dumont's pistol.

All eyes traveled from the cowering Dumont, to the rector—still poised to fire, to the gambler on his knees, to the tiny derringer which had been blasted across the floor.

"My God, Reverend Storey!" someone breathed. "That was damn fine shooting!"

"And pretty fast, too."

Cole looked down at the smoking pistol. He had acted instinctively at the warning, shooting the gambler in the hand which held his concealed pistol, knocking the weapon across the room. Blood ran down the gambler's wrist and onto the white cuff of his sleeve.

"That's my dealing hand!" the man cried, wincing in pain.

Amanda burst into the room to kneel at the gambler's side and examine his wound. She looked up at the bar-keep, who threw her a napkin which she used to wrap his bleeding wrist.

"You'd better have Dr. Goodfellow see to this right away," she said quietly. "You're going to lose a lot of blood."

"Damn it!" the gambler whined, staring angrily at Cole. "You didn't have to shoot my dealin' hand!"

"You're lucky I didn't blow your head off," Cole snapped back. Throwing the pistol to the bartender, he reached down and took Amanda's arm. "Come on. Let's get out of here."

She followed him without speaking, past the woman in the feathered hat who stared shamelessly at them as they passed, through the hands that reached out with admiration to slap the rector on the shoulder, past Sheriff Behan, who came running in the door as they stepped out of it. She moved meekly along the walkway, saying nothing as they hurried away from the main road and down the side street that led to her drug store. Stopping in front, she pulled out her key, opened the door, and entered, waiting for him to follow.

Once inside, she closed the door, locked it again, snapped down the window shade, and turned with her back against the doorframe, staring angrily up at him.

"All right, Reverend Storey. I think it's time for some honest answers."

Fifteen

"I don't know what you mean."

Amanda watched Cabot amble down the aisle, pausing beside a glass case to run his finger along the handle. For a moment her certainty wavered. Was her intuition wrong? Was she making too much of all these little incidents that didn't add up?

When he did not look back at her directly, her resolve came rushing back. No, she was not wrong. A lot of things about the Reverend Cabot Storey didn't fit, and she was going to find out why.

Cole gave a short laugh. "You know your customers aren't going to take kindly to being locked out."

"They can wait until you've answered my questions. And I'd like some honest answers, please, for a change."

"Now, that's unfair. When have you ever caught me in a lie?"

Amanda stalked up to the counter and threw her reticule on it, turning back to him with her arms folded across her chest. "Perhaps you haven't lied to me directly, but there are a lot of things about you that make me wonder. I don't think you've told me the whole truth about yourself."

"I'm a simple country parson," Cole said, giving her his most engaging smile.

She countered it with a short, bitter laugh. "You're anything but simple, and I'm not so certain you're even a parson. Does a simple country parson ride a horse as if he were born in the saddle? Or walk down the street of a town like Tombstone as if he belonged in the saloon instead of the pulpit?"

Cole leaned against the opposite wall and folded his arms across his chest. "Don't I preach a good sermon? Haven't I earned the trust of my congregation? I'm even trying to help them find a way to build their new church. Why would I do that if I were an imposter?"

"I don't know about those things, but I do know that I never saw a preacher who could shoot a gun as quickly and accurately as you did back there."

He shrugged. "I was lucky, that's all. I didn't think, I just reacted."

"Your reactions include a deadly aim. You blew the pistol from that gambler's hand and left him bleeding but not dead. And all before the rest of us even knew he had a gun. That's a pretty good reaction for a clergyman."

"There's no law that says a man of the cloth can't be a good shot, is there?"

This was getting her nowhere. Amanda fought the sudden urge to walk to him, to lay her hands on his arms and look up into his face. She longed to be close to him, to touch him, to feel his arms go around her. All her instincts told her to be cautious, to force him to explain the truth about himself. Yet her heart turned over when she watched him standing there, smiling at her with that jaunty grin on his handsome face. Her body cried out for him even as her reason warned her away.

Deliberately she forced herself to face the counter, turning her back to him. "Cabot, there is something you're not telling me. I feel it without being able to put my finger on it directly. I'm asking you to trust me because . . . well, because of what we shared the other day.

"I won't pretend that I haven't felt a lot of guilt about what we did. But I tried not to let it overwhelm me because I believed in you. I believe you are a decent, good man who would not hurt me. Now, I'm wondering if perhaps I am wrong. I'm wondering if you are deliberately deceiving me about who you are and what you are doing here in Tombstone. And I'm thinking that perhaps I threw my hat over the windmill for nothing. That you were only using me for your own selfish reasons."

Walking over to her, Cole turned her shoulders toward him so he could look down into her open, lovely face. He fought against the urge to lay his palms along her cheeks and lift her soft, beautiful lips to his. He wanted to close off the questions and drive off the dismay from her eyes with his kisses, to block out her disillusion with the need for him.

But he would not do that. Amanda was not the kind of woman he could treat so lightly. Furthermore, he realized to his dismay, he truly did not wish to hurt her or use her selfishly. Somehow she had come to mean more to him than that.

He tried to smile. "All right. Perhaps I haven't been

entirely honest with you but I wasn't sure I could trust you. I wasn't sure I could trust anyone."

A great weight seemed to lift from her heart. She waited as he dropped his hands and moved away, standing with his back to her.

"I did have another reason for coming to Tombstone."

"Then you're not really a parson?"

"I didn't say that. But the truth is. . . . Well, I came here with the intention of doing more than simply building a church." He turned to face her but did not close the space between them. "You heard about the stage being robbed today. These robberies take place too often, almost always when a shipment of ore is going out or a payroll is coming in. It's obvious an informer in town is tipping off the robbers, someone possibly very high. I'm trying to find out where the leak is."

"But who wants to know? The banks? Wells Fargo?" She gave a sudden gasp. "Not . . . !"

"That's right. The United States Government."

Amanda's hands flew to her face. "You're a government agent?"

"I believe you'd call it an 'undercover' agent."

Gripping her hands, she walked back and forth, trying to adjust to this new information. "But why didn't they just send in a Pinkerton man? Isn't that the kind of thing they do?"

"I suppose because they thought a parson would be less suspicious. A *lot* less suspicious." He caught her in mid-stride and turned her around to face him, his fingers digging into her shoulders. "You realize I am trusting you with information that could get me killed, don't you?"

Amanda threw her arms around him, holding him close. "Oh, Cabot. You needn't worry. I would give up my life before I'd betray your confidence. I'm so relieved. I knew there was something about you that didn't fit, and now I understand it all. Of course they wouldn't send just any parson to Tombstone. They'd want a man who knew how to handle the people of the town as well as those in the church. You must have seemed the perfect man for the job."

Cole breathed a sigh of relief, at least for the moment. Lightly, he kissed her forehead then tucked her head against his shoulder. "I like to fancy myself the right man."

Amanda nestled against him with her arms tight around his waist. "But how did you learn to shoot and ride so well? I still don't understand."

"The truth is I've lived most of my life out here in the West, and I learned to ride and shoot at an early age. The government thought it would sound more plausible if the Reverend Storey came from somewhere else; and since the parish had written the bishop asking him to send them a pastor, it all fell into place."

"But the danger," she cried, looking up at him with alarm in her eyes. "You could be killed."

"I might, if the men in this town who are working with these robbers discover what I'm doing. I'm counting on you to help me. That little incident with the gun back there was a mistake, made before I had time to think about it. I only hope it doesn't set other people to wondering about me, as it did you."

Amanda smiled up at him. "I don't think it will. After all, I know you better than anyone else in this town."

His arms went around her and he lifted her face to his. "And I hope you'll know me even better still," he whispered, bending to touch her lips with his. She melted against him, enfolded in the deep shadows of the store, her body murmuring with the warmth of desire. It flared like a sudden flame on a candlewick, stirring to life as his hands moved across her back, then drifted down against her hips, pressing them into his own swelling hardness. His lips left off drinking from her mouth to course down her cheek to her throat. Amanda lifted her face to allow the dreamy softness of his lips to kiss the hollow of her shoulders.

"Still concerned?" he whispered as his fingers unfastened the buttons at her throat and eased the neck of her dress over one shoulder.

She arched against him. His hand slid up her waist to cup her breast, lifting it and gently stroking the taut nipple with his thumb through the fabric of her blouse. "Not at the moment," she sighed as the fire built to a slow, delicious glow within her.

A loud rapping at the door shattered the moment. "Damn!" Cole cried, lifting his head. "What a time for a customer to come calling."

Amanda jumped away, hastily buttoning her dress. "Quick, into the back room," she said, pushing Cole toward the rear of the store.

He gave her a quick kiss. "We'll continue this later," he answered before hurrying away.

She smoothed down her hair, then waited a moment for the banked fire to die down and her cheeks to regain their accustomed hue. Then she walked to the door and peeked around the shade that covered the glass.

Roy Alander! Probably wanting more of that willow decoction for his rheumatism.

Pursing her lips, she snapped up the shade and turned the key to open the door. She was supposed to be running a drug store, after all!

"I tell you, Sheriff, there's more to that parson than meets the eye."

Tilly Lacey let the curtain at her window slip from her hand. She turned to face John Behan, sitting and rocking slowly in the cushioned chair near her parlor stove. His heavy brows creased over his black eyes as he stared past her at the lace curtain lazily moving in the soft wind off the street.

"You don't believe me, do you?"

Behan crossed one booted leg over the other and rocked gently back and forth. "Oh, I do, Tilly. I've wondered about that fellow myself. He talks like a preacher and he carries a Bible, but there's something about him that's not a bit preacher-like. I just can't put my finger on what it is."

"I've never seen a cleaner shot. Or a quicker one. At the same moment I saw the pistol in that gambler's hand, he shot it across the room. Ringo himself couldn't have done it better. In fact, anyone else would have probably killed the man on the spot."

The creaking of the rocker on the plank floor was Behan's only answer. Tilly walked to the empty hearth, leaning against the mantel, her arms folded across her chest. "I always knew there was something about him, even in the stage. Something that just didn't seem right."

"Are you sure you're not just out to get even with him because he didn't respond to your 'invitation'?"

Tilly's face grew hard. "I never should have told you about that. No, I'm not, though I would dearly love to teach him a lesson. Not many men turn down Tilly Lacey."

"Oh, I can believe that. But I don't know why you were surprised. Isn't that what you'd expect from a man of God?"

"Maybe," Tilly replied archly. "Maybe not. Anyway, what are you going to do about it?"

"What do you suggest? If I arrested every man in Tombstone who was a good shot, half the town would be in jail."

"You've got to make him reveal himself. I'm sure he fired that pistol today without thinking. And afterward, he got out of there as quick as he could." She grimaced as she recalled the way he took that chit of a girl with him. "Think of some way to force him to show what he really is."

"And what is that?"

"How do I know? Maybe's he's not a preacher at all. Maybe he's an outlaw who ought to be behind bars."

"Come on now, Tilly. Your imagination is running away with you. There's no reason a preacher can't be a good shot, too."

"It's not just that," Tilly said in exasperation. "It's more. My instincts can tell, and my instincts are usually right."

"Bah!"

Behan abruptly stood up from the rocker, setting it flying back and forth. His boots creaked on the floor as he paced the room. Finally, he stopped near the window, staring out through the lace curtain at the quiet, dusty street.

"All right. I admit your intuition has been right before. I suppose it can't hurt to give it a try."

Tilly gave him a slow smile. "Good."

Behan's handsome face fell into a frown as he rubbed his chin. "Maybe we could have a little shooting contest. We haven't had one in a while, and everybody in town likes them. Anyone who handles a gun the way you say he does couldn't pass that up."

"Oh, but he could. He might even deliberately lose, just to prove that incident this afternoon was a fluke or something."

"He might. On the other hand, if there was a lot of prize money to be had by winning, maybe he would figure it was worth the risk."

"How much money?"

Behan gave her a sly smile. "A lot. Enough to tempt a man to try his best. Say, a thousand dollars?"

"A thousand dollars!" Tilly exclaimed. "Where would you get that kind of prize money?"

Behan looped his thumbs over his waistcoat pockets and chuckled softly. "I know a few men in Tombstone who would put up two hundred dollars each if they thought an imposter was snooping around town. And with a prize like that, every gunfighter and yokel in town will want to try. That should make the contest less suspicious."

Tilly's smile gave way to a sudden frown. "But suppose he doesn't want a lot of money."

"Come now, Lacey, every man wants a lot of money. That's why people come to Tombstone. Besides, isn't that church of his trying to raise money to put up a building?"

Tilly's frown slowly evolved into a satisfied grin. "So they are, Sheriff. So they are."

By the end of the week, the prize money had increased to fifteen hundred dollars and word of the contest had swept through the town. It was the subject on everyone's lips, the first thought in everyone's mind. There had not been this much excitement over anything since the discovery of the latest mine.

The members of St. Anselm's vestry could talk of little else at their next meeting.

"One thousand, five hundred dollars! *Fifteen hundred!*" Leander Walton breathed, lightly pounding the table with his fist. "With fifteen hundred dollars, we could put up the best little church in the Arizona Territory."

"It's the answer to a prayer." Charlie McDowell added. "We would never be able to get that much money anywhere else."

"It would take years to save it."

"And hundreds of potlucks and auctions."

"Even then, we'd probably never accumulate that much."

Cole looked with growing dismay at the faces of the men around the table. "Wait a minute now," he cautioned. "Remember, every gunslinger in the territory will be after that prize. It's not likely any of us could win."

Leander leaned toward him. "No, Reverend Storey. You're wrong. Sheriff Behan told me hisself that they planned it for Saturday just so the word wouldn't spread to other towns and bring in more competition. It's only for those of us who are already here. And we all know who is the best of that lot," he added, smiling broadly at Cole.

"That's right," Lucas Stone spoke up. "Ain't nobody going to shoot any better than you did when you winged that card shark at the Alahambra."

"Now, that was just a lucky fluke," Cole countered. "The truth is, I don't shoot nearly that good as a rule."

"Some fluke!"

"I never seen a cleaner shot."

"It was an accident, I tell you."

Walton waved a hand to shush the others. "Wait just a minute, boys. Let the rector speak. After all, maybe he thinks a man of God like hisself ought not to be so good with a gun. Is that what it is, Reverend Storey?"

Cole shrugged, looking away. "Well . . ."

"Don't let that bother you," McDowell said. "Out here a man has to be able to shoot or he runs the risk of being shot. We don't hold it against you that you're better than most with a pistol."

Horace Alander added, "In fact, we respect you more for it. That's the God's truth."

"Thank you, Horace," Cole mumbled, "but I don't think God is impressed by guns. They hurt a lot of people, you know."

"Not this time." Walton shouted down the others.

"This contest just involves shooting a few targets and tin cans. Nobody will be hurt."

Cole felt his authority slipping away. "Isn't there anyone else in the congregation who can win this money for us? Surely one of you must be good with a shotgun."

Lucas shrugged. "Leander here is a pretty good shot. So's Charlie, and Grady Corum. But none is as good as you, judging from the other day."

"And none could stand up to Wyatt Earp or Johnny Ringo or even Buckskin Frank Leslie. Those guys make their livin' with guns."

"And they're already lickin' their lips over that fifteen hundred dollars."

"Not Johnny Ringo. He's left town."

"Well, there's still Luke Short and the Clantons."

Leander leaned across the table toward Cole, earnestness on his face. "Don't you want to win that money for our church, Reverend Storey? It's for a good cause. The Good Lord wouldn't hold it against you that you used a gun to get it."

Cole felt every eye studying him. He shifted in his chair, uncomfortable under the scrutiny of these innocents who were so impressed by the way he used a gun they could think of nothing else.

"I don't know. It just doesn't seem right," he muttered. But he knew he was going to lose this one. He suspected even a silly man like the real Cabot Storey would jump at the chance to try to win that money for St. Anselm's. For him to do anything less was going to make the entire congregation as suspicious of him as Amanda had been. And the last thing he needed right now was more people asking questions. Damn! If only Aces would get here.

"Oh, all right," he mumbled, ignoring the cheer that went up around the table.

As Saturday approached, Cole suffered second thoughts. One moment the idea of winning so much money with his talent for shooting a gun seemed natural and enticing. That moment was usually followed by the unsettling thought that by doing so he might raise even more questions about his identity.

To his surprise, he found himself really wanting to win that fifteen hundred dollars—not for himself, but for St. Anselm's Church. It seemed preposterous that he could care that this church ever got built, and yet somehow he did. Without realizing it, he had gotten caught up in the burning enthusiasm of the people of St. Anselm's. He wondered how such a thing had happened. The humor of it, as well as the unusual situation of wanting something constructive for a change, continued to amaze him. The result was that by the time Saturday morning rolled around, he had decided he would risk winning this contest. After all, as he said to Amanda, where was it written that a clergyman could not also be good with a shotgun?

Dressed in his cleanly brushed long frock coat, freshly washed white shirt, and well-polished boots, he ambled over to the courthouse, where the contest was to take place. He had spent most of the day before practicing with his pistols, then cleaning them to a polished perfection. In addition, he had borrowed a Winchester .44 rifle from Lucas Stone and brushed up on his skills. He had one of his own he'd used for years but, of course, there was no way to retrieve it from the camp. He felt relaxed and ready, even excited about competing in a shooting contest once again. It should be a good morning.

A large crowd was already gathered behind the courthouse. The group from St. Anselm's surrounded him at once, offering encouraging remarks that suggested their church was as good as half-built already.

"Don't be too certain," Cole tried to caution them. "Look at Earp, and those other gunslingers. I never had to stand up to competition like that before."

His caution sounded overly-modest even to himself. Wyatt Earp and the others might be good with a gun, but Cole knew from experience he had a better eye than anyone here. It might be a different story, of course, had word of the contest spread to other parts of the territory and brought in a few notable gunfighters from Kansas or Colorado. Without them, he was confident he'd win the day.

"We're countin' on you, Reverend Storey," Leander Walton said, pounding him on the back. He leaned closer and whispered, "Some of us even made a few bets on the side. Don't let us down, now."

"Gambling, Leander? Don't know as how I can approve of that," Cole answered, winking at the man. "But I'll do my best."

"That's all we ask."

Through a break in the crowd, Cole spotted Amanda walking toward the spectators. He was about to push through the group to join her when he saw Tilly Lacey walking beside her, the two of them chatting and laughing together. Holding back, he waited until Tilly had walked away, then ambled over to Amanda's side.

"Come to watch the fireworks?" he asked, smiling down into her upturned face.

"Of course. According to my customers, this is the most exciting event in town since that touring company brought *The Pirates of Penzance* to the Bird Cage Theater. I wouldn't miss it for anything."

"I didn't know you were so friendly with Mrs. Lacey," Cole commented absently as they started back toward the shooting area.

"I'm not. But we did arrive on the same stage, remember. And she's been in the shop one or two times."

"I'd be careful of her if I were you. I've learned she has a shady past, and it might not do your reputation any good to be too friendly with her."

Amanda laughed. "Why, Reverend Storey, you're getting positively stuffy. Shady women from the Tenderloin District often frequent my store, and I'm quite accustomed now to associating with them. Besides," she whispered, leaning close and giving him a wicked wink, "there's only one person in this town who is in a position to endanger my reputation."

"All right," he said with a grin. "Forget I mentioned it."

Amanda slipped her hand through his arm. "Do you think you're going to win today?"

"I've got a good chance. If you'll stand over where I can see you and keep smiling encouragement at me, I ought to walk away with all that money."

"For the church?"

He looked down at her in surprise. "Of course. That's

why I'm here, isn't it? I didn't want to compete, even when they offered to pay the ten dollar entry fee. They insisted."

"I know," she said, looking away. "And I hope you win the prize for them." How could she tell him she never knew when he was simply a pastor and when he was something more? His plausible explanation of being sent to Tombstone by the government should have put all her qualms to rest. She wanted to trust him completely; she *would* trust him completely. It was just that, now and then, she could still not make him fit into any kind of correct image. She still wondered . . .

Cole squeezed her hand on his arm, completely unaware of her thoughts. "This is probably the best chance St. Anselm's will ever have of getting the money to build a church, and I intend to win it for them."

Their eyes held for a moment. Looking up into his strong, handsome face, Amanda felt the familiar stir of desire he awoke in her so easily, that delicious desire that washed away all her misgivings. She moved as close to him as she dared in this public spot, her body thrilling to the feel of his long thigh against her skirt. He leaned toward her, and for an instant she thought—she hoped—he might bend and kiss her lips. But, of course, that would be foolish here in front of the whole town. She was not surprised when he abruptly moved back.

She squeezed his hand before he pulled it away. "Good luck."

By this time the crowd was dispersed along a fence and into a semicircle surrounding a cleared area where the contestants were to stand and face three targets set up far down the narrow roadway. Cole stood to the side while Sheriff Behan stepped forward and announced that there would be six sets of target shooting, eliminating all but the best until a final contest decided the winner. Each set would progress in difficulty. The winner of this fantastic prize would have to prove his mettle or the prize would go to no one.

The crowd cheered as the first line of contestants took their places. There were thirty contestants, three at a time shooting at the target placed fifty yards away. Cole was among the last group of three, so he had plenty of leisure to judge the competition and study the faces of those he considered the best. Wyatt Earp leaned against the fence near him, chewing on a straw, his cold black eyes focused on the target. His brothers—Virgil, Morgan, and Jim—straddled the fence to one side of him, making loud comments on the ineptitude of many of the marksmen. On the other side, convulsed by a fit of coughing, the invalid Doc Holliday watched quietly, awaiting his turn. Both Wyatt and Holliday were the men to beat, Cole figured, though there might be a surprise or two among those he didn't know.

The easy target of fifty yards successfully eliminated half the field, mostly the poor shots in town who felt the prize was worth taking a chance that they might get lucky. Once they were gone, the targets got more difficult and the shooting more serious.

Cole had no problem moving on through the next three sets. He was pleased to find that his eye had not lost any of its accuracy through recent disuse. He easily won the first two sets and allowed himself to come second and third in the next two. By the time the fifth set was reached, the field had narrowed to Cole, Earp, Holliday, Frank Leslie, John Folger—one of the cowboys of the Clanton ranch—and a surprise entry—Ethan Simms, a foreman at the Amelia mine whom no one had suspected of having such skill with a gun.

The fifth set required some setting up, so the contestants took a break. Cole found himself surrounded by the people of his congregation, happily encouraging him and delighted that he was among the finalists. He took the glass of lemonade that was handed him and worked his way through the crowd to where Amanda sat perched on the fence under a sycamore tree that shaded them from the worst of the sun.

"You've done well," she said, squeezing his hand beneath the folds of her skirt. "I think you're as good as any of the men who reached the finals."

Hidden by her skirt, Cole rubbed his hand along her thigh. When a telltale blush reddened her cheeks, he pulled it away and leaned his arms on the fence, smiling up at her. He was satisfied that the money was as good as won, though he wouldn't say so for fear of jinxing his luck.

Amanda looked out over the crowd to regain her composure. "I wonder if Sheriff Behan has gotten what he wanted out of this," she said absently.

He was instantly alert. "What do you mean? I thought this was just an ordinary shotgun contest."

"It is, but it's also something more. At least, that's the impression I got talking to Tilly Lacey earlier. When I commented that Sheriff Behan hadn't entered, she said something about his getting a lot more than money from this contest. And look at him. He's positively smug."

Cole glanced over at the sheriff, laughing as he pounded Ethan Simms on the back. He did look smug—and unusually animated for a taciturn man. The hairs on the back of Cole's neck came to life.

Suddenly Amanda gave a gasp. "You don't think he's looking for a government . . ."

Her hand flew to her mouth. Cole turned to face the fence, his back to the crowd. "Careful, Amanda," he said softly. "I'm sure they don't suspect me; and even if they did, winning a contest like this isn't going to prove anything."

Amanda gave a sigh of relief. "That's true. I guess I got carried away for a moment. I'm sorry."

"You didn't say anything to Mrs. Lacey about me, did you?"

"Of course not. Your secret is safe with me, Cabot. I promise you that."

"Good girl."

He left her and ambled back to the contestants' area, thinking hard. John Behan had pushed to the front of the crowd and was eyeing him curiously. Over Behan's shoulder, the gay feathers on Tilly Lacey's hat bobbed lightly in the wind. Beneath them, her eyes fastened on his face.

Cole felt a coldness creep down his spine, a sure sign that something was wrong and he was in danger. It was possible, of course, that he might be making too much of Tilly's remark to Amanda; but somehow he knew he wasn't. With that fifteen hundred dollars almost in his grasp, he now faced the question of throwing the contest. Angrily he toed his boot in the dirt. Damnation! What a lousy turn of affairs.

The fifth contest involved shooting over his shoulder, using a mirror. Most of the gunslingers—who were accustomed to shooting a target walking toward them—were eliminated, leaving Cole and Ethan Simms in the final trial. Cole, who had practiced this kind of trick many times in his youth, tried half-heartedly to miss but still hit the target, a fact that told him how much he really wanted to win. He looked around at the radiant, joyous faces of his congregation and something in him died a slow death. The competition, the use of his skills, the thought of winning this money to build a church, all had brought him to wanting this prize more than anything in recent memory. Yet, one glance at John Behan's excited, triumphant face, and he knew he would be risking more by winning than it might be worth.

The final test would be made on horseback, riding at full speed, shooting at two pigeons released from a wire cage. As Cole mounted up, he still had not made up his mind. He sat in the saddle and watched as Ethan Simms roared down the road, blasting at the target. One bird fell to earth, the other soared away.

Lucas Stone, smiling broadly, threw him the Winchester. "All right, Reverend Storey. It's yours for the taking."

Cole caught the rifle and lifted it to sight down the barrel, not bothering to reply. Then he heard another voice at his knee.

"Go ahead, Preacher. It's your turn."

Cole looked down at Sheriff Behan who had his hand lightly on the bridle. Though the sheriff's dark face was as blank as a mask, he could not keep the satisfied triumph from his eyes. He stepped back and gave the cry; and Cole, his rifle cradled in his arm, spurred his horse forward. As the birds soared up into the sky, he closed his eyes and blasted into the air.

Pulling on the reins, he brought his horse to a stop and opened his eyes to see both pigeons soaring up toward the clouds. Disappointment was dust in his mouth as he turned his mount and cantered back down the track to the stunned crowd.

It gave him a pang to see the surprised disappointment on the faces of his congregation. "I'm sorry, Leander," he said as he swung down from the saddle. He refused to add that he had done his best, since he knew he hadn't.

"That's all right, Reverend Storey," Walton said in a half-hearted, choked voice. "We'll get the money somehow. It'll just take us a little longer, that's all."

Lucas and McDowell could barely look him in the eye. They stood, stone-faced, staring at Ethan Simms as he was hoisted to the shoulders of a group of miners.

"It's one thing to stand still and shoot at a target," Cole added lamely, "and quite another when you're on the back of a running horse."

"We understand, Reverend Storey. Don't worry about it."

Sheriff Behan stepped up to shout to the crowd that all guns were to be either turned in to him or carried away at once. Before Cole knew what was happening, the sheriff grabbed his shotgun from his hand and turned it over, examining it closely.

"Pretty nice rifle you got there, Reverend Storey," he said, snapping it open. "Especially for a preacher."

"It belongs to one of my parishioners," Cole snapped, grabbing it back. "If there's a problem with it, see him."

As Ethan was carried off to spend a good part of his winnings in the saloon, Cole spotted Amanda coming toward him. Her eyes, too, were full of disappointment, but she smiled bravely. "Well, you came in second anyway."

"Yeah. I guess that's something."

"Would you like to have supper later?"

"Thanks, but not tonight. Tomorrow, maybe. I'll stop by the hotel."

She could see how hard it was for him to handle his disappointment, so she simply touched his arm and moved on. Cole turned his horse over to the livery stable owner and started back to town. He passed Behan and Tilly, still watching him with quizzical expressions on their faces. He wondered if he had really put their questions to rest by throwing the contest or if he had given away fifteen hundred dollars for nothing.

As he approached Allen Street, he saw that most of the pedestrians were noisily celebrating inside the saloons, leaving the street deserted except for a group of cowboys riding in from one end and a lone rider from the other. The cowboys whooped and hollered as they churned up the dust before the Oriental Saloon, where they slid from their horses. The solitary man, his hat pulled down around his eyes, slumped in the saddle as though he had been traveling for a long time. As Cole stepped off the curb, the horseman ambled over in front of him to hitch his horse before the Cosmopolitan Hotel. Cole absently glanced up at him, then stopped dead in the street as he found himself staring up into the startled, dust-covered face of Aces Malone.

Sixteen

"I swear to God, I didn't recognize you."

Aces Malone leaned over the table, his face close to Cole's, his voice barely above a whisper. "I nearly went right by you. It was the eyes that done it. They always do."

Cole glanced around the lunchroom. Only three other tables were occupied—two men at one, a man and a woman at another, and a single man reading a copy of the *Nugget* in the corner. Two men sat at the counter talking to the waiter behind it. All these people seemed intent on their meals or their conversations, and none even glanced in his direction. If they did, Cole hoped they would assume nothing more than the good preacher was giving a drifter a square meal.

"I don't like this," he muttered to Aces. "The sooner I get out of here, the better. We ought not to be seen together."

"Don't worry about it. I never seen none of these people in the saloons when I was here a'fore. Once I get back in my card-shark clothes, I won't never see 'em a'gin. But how the hell did you manage to pull this off? Convincin' people you're a preacher! I'd of never believed it."

"I'll explain later. But we better not get together again in town. Sheriff Behan already looks at me as if he can see right through me."

"Oh, Behan. He suspicions everybody." Aces leaned close to his plate and shoveled in the food like a starving man. "Have you figured out what my letter meant yet?" he whispered.

"Not without you. I have a few ideas though. There are a few too many knowledgeable thefts to put down to plain old luck."

"The Earp gang?"

"My guess is they're part of it. I think it goes deeper, though. Probably a leak at the Wells Fargo office. Maybe some higher-ups at the mines."

"You're on the right track. Keep goin'."

The man in the corner folded his newspaper and rose to his feet to leave. Cole recognized him as one of the customers he often saw in the barber shop. At the same moment, the man recognized Cole. He doffed his hat as he passed Cole's table.

"Afternoon, Reverend Storey. That was pretty fine shootin' today. Sorry you didn't win the big prize."

Cole leaned casually back in his chair. "Thanks. It was a fair contest and I lost. What I regret the most is not winning the money to build our church."

"I know. It's too bad, especially since right now that prize money is being swilled down the gullets of a lot of worthless bums in the Oriental Saloon. Better it should have gone to your congregation."

Cole shrugged. "That's true."

"Well, better luck next time. These contests are always croppin' up." Doffing his hat, the man moved out through the door, leaving Cole to glance everywhere around the room but at Aces.

"Build a church!" Aces mumbled. "Good God a'mighty, what's the matter with you. You gone crazy or somethin'?"

"I have to let people think that's what I want," Cole muttered.

"Maybe, but it's some kind of joke, I'll give you that."

"Look," Cole said, abruptly sitting forward in his chair. "I've got to get away from here. But first I want you to tell me exactly what you meant by 'rich pickin's.' "

"I could have got you in on some of those robberies, that's all. When you know for sure a payroll box is on a stage, there ain't much risk in stoppin' it. I figured that would be right up your alley."

Cole eyed his friend with suspicion. Aces's long, thin face had always reminded him of a sly ferret. The narrow eyes that had seen too much of the seedy side of life never lost their hard edge. Right now, his cheeks were covered with a blondish stubble of beard and his face still bore the yellow streaks of dirt from the road. But once he shaved and dressed in his cravat and striped vest, Cole knew he would look like the quintessential gambler he was. His skill was manifested in the easy grace of his figure, in the eyes that darted appraisingly around a saloon, and, most of all, in the elegant, almost ladylike, slender hands that could shuffle a deck of cards to his specifications before you knew what was happening.

"I don't believe that was all you meant," Cole said, meeting Aces's gaze directly.

Aces glanced away. "Well, maybe not. But I can't talk about that here."

Cole reached for his hat. "I agree. We'll have to meet privately the next time. Let's say, at night, behind Boot Hill. That's far enough outside of town to be alone."

"That spooky place? I don't know . . ."

"You're not afraid of ghosts, are you?" Cole said, giving him a thin smile.

"I don't like 'em. You know that."

"I'd forgotten how superstitious you gamblers are. All the same, it's the safest place."

He watched Aces's head bob a 'yes,' then neatly fingered the crease in his black hat before setting it on his head. "We can't make it tonight, though. It's Saturday, and I have a sermon to write."

He was on his feet and looking down into Aces's gaping mouth before the man could speak. Throwing a coin on the table, he said loudly enough for the rest of the patrons to hear, "There, my good man. Maybe a bath and some clean clothes will help you change your wicked ways. Good day, and God bless you."

He walked out feeling Aces's astonished gaze on his back and trying to suppress the satisfied smile that played about his lips.

The following Saturday, Amanda once again rode with Cole into the desert. She told herself she was only going for a leisurely ride and a picnic, but her heart knew better. The barest touch of his hand on her arm, the brief brush of his thigh against hers as their horses came alongside, was enough to set her blood singing.

Every nerve in her body felt alive and responsive to the slightest stimulus. A cursory sideways glance at his profile beneath the broad brim of his hat, the strain of his wide shoulders against the checkered fabric of his shirt, the taut stretch of muscled thigh above his high boots—sent a stirring through her that no amount of reasoned denial could contain.

She knew she wanted him again. She wanted his arms around her, his long body against hers. She wanted him completely.

She kept her face turned from him, sure that her obvious embarrassment gave away every thought in her head. Yet he seemed unaware of it, chattering idly as they rode, pointing out an abandoned Apache wickiup, a bone-dry draw that a sudden spring rain could turn to a raging stream in a few minutes time, a stunted cactus that looked like a dead shrub but could supply an Indian with enough food and water for a day's journey. As they climbed again up into the blue hills, she became certain he felt none of the wild desire for her that burned in her for him.

She was wrong. Cole forced himself to talk about stupid, foolish things only because he thought Amanda still meant to pull away from him. Ten times he longed to stop and draw her from her horse and into his arms, but he knew he could not. She must come of her own free will. Anything less would turn her away from him forever.

Once again he silently cursed himself for ever getting involved with a decent woman.

Finally they reached the place he planned to stop, a grassy bank below a cluster of cottonwoods that grew next to a thin stream of reddish-brown water. He slid out of the saddle and moved to lift her from her horse. As he looked up at her, their eyes locked. The air between them came alive with a force like electricity, binding them together. His hands on her waist were hot, burning into her skin like brands. She slid down against him, melting her body into his, acutely conscious of the molds and swells of his lean, hard body against her own.

Amanda gave a short gasp that he cut off with his mouth. His kiss cried out with the need for her and she responded by opening her lips to him. He drove his tongue deep within her, searching out the hidden depths; and, like a flower blooming, her lips widened.

Then he felt her body trembling in his embrace and forced himself to calm the raging need within. Withdrawing, he reached up to clasp her chin in his fingers, deliberately closing her mouth and kissing her lightly on her soft lips.

"Amanda . . ."

"No," she whispered. "Don't say anything." She buried her head in the hollow of his shoulder. "Talk is useless."

Cole laid his hands on her shoulders, forcing her to look directly at him. "You know I want you. But I won't, unless you agree. We can still mount up and ride ba—"

She stopped his mouth with her own, kissing him fiercely and hard. His arms tightened around her, his hands slipped down to press her hips into his.

"Does that answer your question," Amanda gasped when she could tear her lips away.

"Wait here," he whispered. He tethered the horses

while Amanda knelt beside the stream, dabbing her hot face with the warm, brackish water. Deliberately, she forced away all the arguments she had honed for a week, all the reasons she should not get involved with this man. Nothing mattered but wanting him. Reason was useless against the delight, the wonder, the joy of being part of him.

She turned back to the bank to see that Cole had spread the saddle blanket on the grass and was sitting on it, watching her. She went to kneel beside him, and he turned to face her, gently unbuttoning her loose blouse, starting with surprise when he realized she wore only a thin chemise beneath it. His hand slid deep inside to cup her breast and Amanda moved against him, gasping with delight at the stab of pleasure that went through her.

"You are so beautiful," he whispered, before bending to lift her breast free for his lips. Deftly, his tongue circled and darted, teasing her as her pleasure mounted. Her little moans of delight encouraged him, and he licked at her taut nipple until she thought she could bear no more. Only then did his lips close over it, and he suckled greedily while Amanda gasped with mounting ecstasy.

She sought him, rubbing her hands along the huge mound of the swelling manhood that pressed against his trousers. He loosened his clothing, and it was free to fill her hand. Hardly knowing what she was doing, she stroked its firmness, sensing that he, in his rising passion, had become filled with the flame that consumed her.

He laid her back on the blanket, pulling away her

gown. Still suckling her breast, he guided his hand between her white thighs to cup her, his fingers thrusting into her, working her to a fury of exquisite longing until she cried out with desire.

"Not so soon," he gasped against her throat. Turning, he rolled over to pull her atop him, his arms clasped around her. Her unbound hair fell like a cloud around his face. With her lips she teased his mouth, now *her* tongue driving into his mysterious depths. Spreading her legs on either side of him, she carefully let her hips descend to enclose the thrusting prong that promised so much delight. He entered her, while she rocked gently back and forth, driving him to a despair with need for her.

"Not so soon," she whispered, chuckling, delighted with the knowledge that she could tease him as he had her.

"Oh, yes . . . now . . ." he said, swiftly pulling out and turning her on her back. Gentleness was forgotten as he plunged into her depths, thrusting deeply. She felt his hard body driving into her, rubbing against her, driving her to a wild longing where she could only cry out for fulfillment. It seemed to build forever, the pounding in her body and her brain, the swirling void of stars that circled and grew, exploding into a torrent of vivid colors that filled the universe. She felt him stiffen, heard him cry out, and she clasped him to her, their bodies melded into one.

The quiet after the storm descended. The delicious completion after the frantic journey engulfed them. They lay, clasped together, their breaths coming in short gasps. She felt the pounding of his heart against her chest, saw the jagged pulse in his throat. Nestling against him, she waited for her own body to ease, filled with a joyous calm.

Only gradually did the joy subside and reality come sluggishly back, reminding her that nothing had changed. She pushed it from her mind and rested against him, giving herself up to a half-dozing daze of satisfaction that was only broken half-an-hour later when they roused themselves to open the picnic basket and nibble at the lunch Mrs. Jasper had prepared for them.

Once that was finished, they packed up the remains, then lay together on the blanket once again.

Lacing his fingers in the long strands of Amanda's hair, Cole smoothed the tendrils across his face. "Your hair always smells so clean," he breathed. "And there's always a faint tinge of flowers on your skin."

"Heliotrope," she sighed, leaning against him and rubbing her cheek along his arm. "It's a cologne water I use."

"I'm used to women smelling of lye, when they smell of soap at all."

"What kind of women do you know, Preacher?" she asked, laughing.

"Oh, housewives, shopkeepers—you know the type." His lips ranged across her cheek and down her neck. He felt her tremble beneath the waves of delight that coursed through her body. His hand drifted across her back, sliding beneath her arm to cup her breast.

No need to tell her that these last few years the only women he had been this close to never smelled of soap at all. Underneath the oppressively heavy odors of French perfume, there had always been an unpleasant staleness he never wished to identify. Layers of cosmetics were the least objectional ingredient.

Yet, with Amanda, there was something familiar, from long ago. An almost forgotten fragrance he associated with his mother.

The afternoon was waning, giving a softer glow to the quiet glade. The sense of isolation, of being alone in the world, engulfed them both, but Cole, particularly, welcomed it. Here there were no pressing worries, no other people to guard against, no troubled past. There were only the quiet sounds of the mountains, a flock of mourning doves flapping their wings in the tree as they settled on a limb, the scuttering of a lizard in the bush near the stream, the whinny of his horse as it shook out its mane, the buzzing of a bluebottle fly.

And the lovely woman stretched at his side, her beautiful brownish-gold hair spilling over his arm and half-hiding the milky whiteness of her breast.

His wandering thoughts came roaring back as she moved beneath his hand, reaching up to draw his lips to hers. He sighed, shifting his weight to cover her body with his, his knee pushing her legs apart. With a gentleness, as surprising as it was unusual, he entered her, claiming her as part of himself. She raised her hips, and he felt her legs lock over his back. His need for her rose on swelling waves of consuming passion, carrying him along, driving him further and further toward a climax that consumed them both in its ecstasy. He heard her groan; their cries mingled in staccato bursts of sound. He stiffened as he emptied himself into her, giving her all that was of his essence. Beneath the roar of his own pounding blood he heard her shrill cry, and he clasped her closer, as though to forge her with him into one whole being.

Then there was only their labored breathing as passion ebbed.

Cole rolled over on his side, pulling her against him, tucking her head beneath his chin. For a long time neither of them spoke. Instead they lay, reveling in the feel of their mingled bodies and the sense of wholeness they enjoyed.

A few feet away, one of the grazing horses lifted its head and whinnied.

"We ought to be getting back," Cole whispered, smoothing her hair from her forehead and kissing the spot.

"I don't want to leave."

"Nor do I. But though we've had this spot to ourselves all afternoon, you never know when someone might come along. I'd better just check on what's bothering my horse. Be back in a minute."

He pulled up his clothes and rose from the blanket, ambling off toward the grazing horses. Amanda watched him leave, then sat up and began dressing. Though it seemed they were out on the edge of the world, Cabot was right. A rider could come along at any moment. Even a secluded glen was no guarantee of solitude.

He swung back beside her. "Must have been some small creature. We have to be starting back soon anyway."

She pulled her hair back to fasten it at the nape of her neck. Cole pulled her face to his, kissing her deeply and long.

"You are so beautiful," he breathed.

Amanda laid her palm along his cheek, her heart

near to bursting with happiness. "You make me feel beautiful."

Wanting to make the moment last a little longer, Cole pulled her into the circle of his arms. "No regrets?"

"Only one. Though it's terribly romantic to make love out here under the open sky, I long to be with you in a proper bed. Do you think we might risk my room at the hotel sometime?"

"No. People always know, and I wouldn't want to harm your reputation. For the same reason I won't bring you to my room when Mrs. Jasper is away."

"That might harm *your* reputation."

"Exactly."

Or the reputation of the real Reverend Cabot Storey. It amazed him that he should care, but he did. He supposed there was something about Amanda's direct, trusting honesty that affected his usually cynical nature.

Unaware of his thoughts, Amanda snuggled against him, musing on her own situation. "I am a grown woman, you know. I have no relatives watching over me and no one to care about my reputation except myself. Why shouldn't I be free to 'step out' if I want to."

He laughed. "That's not the way you were talking a few days ago. As I remember it, you didn't want me near you."

"I know," she sighed. "And even now, I go back and forth between dreadful shame one minute and defiance the next. Sometimes I don't know what I really feel, except that when I'm with you, all the arguments don't seem to matter."

Cole turned her to face him. "Stepping out is one thing, Amanda, but losing the respect of decent people is quite another. Do you want to have the town putting you in the same category as those ladies of the line? That's what would happen if you brought a man to your hotel room. At the very least, it would be bad for your business. And it would give people the wrong idea about you. You're a fine, decent girl."

"But why does a woman have to be either straight-laced or loose? Why can't a decent woman have an affair?"

Cole gave an exasperated sigh. "Because the Bible has a lot of 'thou shalt not's.' That's just the way it is. And I won't have you being hurt by what's been between us."

Amanda caught her underlip in her teeth. She knew the other, unspoken reason—because the woman was the one who bore the telltale baby if a relationship ended in pregnancy. Well, she was a doctor's daughter. She knew a few tricks to help her avoid that peril.

"Oh, all right," she sighed. "So we'll continue to ride into the desert, I suppose."

Abruptly, Cole rose to his feet and led the horses to the stream for a drink. "We can't even do that too often or people will begin to talk." He took a deep breath. "I guess it's just as well that I'll probably be going away soon."

"What?"

He had spoken it, against his better judgment, throwing caution to the winds. Still, it was said now and might as well be faced.

"You're going away?" Amanda repeated, getting to her feet. "You're leaving?"

"Not immediately—just eventually."

"But why? Where?"

"Well, it's this business of trying to get the church built. I may go looking for sources for the money, that's all."

"Oh. Then you'll be coming back?"

He stared down at his horse's arched neck, unable to look at her, knowing he ought to say frankly that he might not return. The words hovered on the edge of his tongue, but he couldn't bring himself to speak them. Turning, he saw her watching him with relief and affection in her eyes. She was beautiful and decent, and she trusted him. For the first time in years, he felt a pang of remorse that he would cause hurt to another person.

But not yet. "I'll know more about it in a few days. We can talk about it then."

Smiling, Amanda picked up her hat and pulled the strings taut under her chin. When he led the horses over and reached down to help her mount, she allowed her fingers to linger on his hair before swinging up into the saddle. Once she was seated, his arms went around her hips and she leaned down as he raised his face for her kiss.

"If we keep this up, we'll never make it back to town," she said, laughing.

"If we keep this up, I may cease to care about both our reputations."

There was no moon. Stepping into the night was like walking into a closet and closing the door behind you, Cole thought. The day had been hot, but now the cold night air seeped beneath his jacket and laid cold fingers along the back of his neck. He scratched at the thick, false beard he had fastened to the lower part of his face, remembering how irritating whiskers could be. Standing in the black shadows of the lean-to behind Mrs. Jasper's house, he let his eyes become accustomed to the darkness and listened for any sound. When he was sure there was no one around, he slipped down the street.

Though the evening was still early, this end of town was pretty much deserted. Decent folk had retired to their parlors and kitchens, readying their families for bed. There were lights and noises in the saloons, but they were so far away he could only hear tiny echoes of a tinkling piano. His boots on the graveled road resounded louder.

Earlier that day he had stabled his rented horse in the McDowell barn on the edge of the desert, telling them he would need to take it out at sunrise the next day. The McDowell house was already quiet, making it easier for him to saddle the animal and lead him out. Once he was clear of the houses, he mounted up and quietly rode out toward the hills, keeping in the shadows as much as possible.

He had scouted out the area the day before and so knew exactly where to go. He'd received his actual instructions at his meeting with Aces behind Boot Hill three days ago. If Aces had his facts right, he should be there well ahead of time, allowing him ample opportunity to seclude himself before the others arrived.

If Aces had his facts right.

Once in the desert, Cole let his horse set the pace, unwilling to gallop across the uneven terrain in such darkness. The slow canter allowed him time to reflect once more on whether or not Aces could be trusted. When it came right down to it, how well did he really know the man, even though they had been friendly for years? This little enterprise might at least have the advantage of showing him if Aces knew what he was talking about. If it turned out to be a mistake, he ought to be able to get out of it without anyone knowing.

With all his caution, he arrived at the bluff he had selected later than he had planned. He hadn't been there ten minutes when the whinny of a horse below alerted Cole to a group of riders who were just cantering up. He dismounted and fastened the reins, then crouched along, low to the ground, to the edge of the bluff where he could see below. A dim, silver thread weaving across the desert marked the Bisbee road. Directly below, a series of rough sandstone outcroppings made a perfect hiding place for four men who were dismounting, talking to each other in low tones. Cole couldn't make out the words, but when the cloud cover parted to reveal a late rising moon, he glimpsed their bearded faces. One of them wore a long coat and carried a rifle. The other three cocked their pistols and pulled their hats down over their eyes, waiting.

They did not have to wait long. Cole heard the rattle of the approaching stage before they did. He watched as they mounted and pulled handkerchiefs up around their faces. Cole smiled with satisfaction. He had picked this spot as the best place for an ambush and obviously the outlaws agreed. As the stage came roaring around a bend in the road, the gang spurred forward, crossing its path and shouting to bring it to a halt.

He heard one of the men yell for the money box to be thrown down. He saw the guard sitting next to the driver reach for his rifle. A shot screamed through the night and the guard doubled over, crying out in pain.

"Dang it! Why'd you do that?" he heard one of the gang exclaim. "You killed him."

"No time for that now," another answered. "Get the box."

The man in the long coat swerved his horse around in a circle while one of the others leaned down and scooped up the box. Cole waited for them to order the passengers out, but they were in too much of a hurry to bother. He scrambled over to his horse and edged up close enough to watch as the four men galloped away. Keeping his eyes on the one with the box, he took off after them.

As he expected, they rode together only a short distance before pulling up near a dry arroyo that formed a dark depression in the desert. Crouching, they broke open the box and quickly divided the bags. They didn't linger there either. In a matter of minutes, they were back in the saddle and riding off in separate directions.

Cole followed the one nearest his hiding place. The man was traveling at such a gallop that he was unaware he was being pursued. Stalking him, Cole waited until he was sure his quarry was headed for the darkened, adobe town of Bisbee, then circled around to cut him off before the man cantered on to the main street.

The thief was more relaxed now, riding slower and probably looking forward to spending some of his loot in the cantina at Bisbee. The moon was high, and even with the clouds, Cole could make out the figure of the man on his horse, ambling now toward the first of the low buildings. As the rider approached, Cole pulled his kerchief up over the lower half of his face and stepped out into the road, leveling his pistol at the man.

"Git off'n that horse," he snarled in his best western slang. "Put your hands over your head and throw down your gun."

The thief stared at him in shocked surprise. "Who the hell . . ."

Cole leaned forward and jerked the man off his horse and into the dirt. Jabbing the end of his pistol in the man's chest, he waited until the outlaw threw down his pistol. Kicking it ten feet away into the brush, Cole snarled, "Now gimme them bags you took off'n the stage. Now!"

He knew he mustn't say too much or his voice would be recognized. He could see the thief's eyes above his fake moustache darting desperately around, but there was no one in sight to look to for help.

"You got one more second," Cole muttered through gritted teeth. Though he would rather not shoot this worthless creature, it clearly showed in his eyes that he was ready to do so if necessary. Reluctantly, the man nodded toward his pockets.

Reaching in, Cole grabbed out two heavy, corded bags and thrust them into the pocket of his jacket. Then he yanked the outlaw to his feet and shoved him toward the town. "Now, start walkin'."

"You can't . . ."

The cold end of the pistol dug into the man's back. Muttering curses, he began shuffling dismally toward the town while Cole grabbed up the reins of the second

horse. Jumping up on his own mount and pulling the outlaw's horse with him, Cole thundered off in the opposite direction, back into the darkness of the desert, ignoring the outlaw's shouted curses behind him.

Leander Walton fastened both hands behind his back and bounced lightly on the balls of his feet. He looked out over the hotel dining room with satisfaction. His starched collar pinched his neck, and his Sunday suit, fashioned of some devil's concoction of blended wool, set his skin to itching. His weekly annoyance at the way his wife always made him late arriving was beginning to fade under the general good will that always came with going to church. It was Libby's way, after all, and she'd probably never change. If only she'd let their dinner wait until she got home, they wouldn't have this problem. Somehow she'd gotten the notion in her head that a good wife had to put Sunday dinner on the table the moment she walked back in the door, and nothing he said could change her mind.

The room filled quickly, much to Leander's satisfaction. He tried not to register his surprise at seeing that ne'er-do-well Roy Alander follow his son and daughter-in-law down the aisle to one of the front rows. Old Roy might even be converted one of these days, if he came often enough.

"Good morning, Mr. Walton," said a pleasant voice behind him. Leander looked around to see pretty Amanda Lassiter entering the room, looking as fresh as a bowl of peaches in her lacy pink frock and bonnet.

He smiled and gave her his hand. "Nice to see you, Miss Lassiter. Pretty day for a church service, ain't it?"

"That it is."

Walton admired Amanda as she walked on, thinking how nice it was that she was getting so regular in attendance at worship. They really ought to start working on her to get confirmed next time the bishop came round.

He frowned as he spied Reverend Storey arranging things on the altar at the other end of the room. The rector looked tired after his trip out of town. Never did say where he'd been; but then, like doctors, preachers often had to take long trips of a private nature. Still, you'd think he'd confide in his senior warden, if nobody else.

Down in the front row, Horace Alander shifted restlessly in his seat, not daring to look around at the shocked surprise on the faces of the congregation. Everybody in town knew what Pa was. The old man thought he could fool people by coming to church and sitting between his respectable son and his wife as if some of their hard-earned reputation would rub off on him. He probably only wanted to borrow money, anyway.

He recoiled as Roy leaned closer and said in a loud whisper, "I hope there's singing. I like a good rousin' hymn now and then."

The old man's alcoholic breath left him gasping. For a moment Horace toyed with the thought of getting up and leaving. Then Clara peeked around his pa to give him one of her dimpled smiles, and he thought better of it.

Idly he wondered what kind of sermon they'd get today. Something to change Pa, with any luck. Reverend Storey's sermons weren't anything to write home about; but then, the pastor had married him to his dear Clara, so he couldn't be too hard on him. Clara was the best and dearest thing that had ever happened to him. He settled back on the hard chair and tried to ignore Mrs. Jasper's loud whispering two rows behind.

Mrs. Jasper pretended she didn't see Horace's irritated glare and leaned closer to Mrs. Ellis's ear.

"Didn't think I'd make it today. The colic, you know. It bothers me something dreadful."

"You need a good dose of peppermint tea. Works every-time."

"I tried it. Don't do a thing for me. No, nothin' ever helps but Glauber's salts. It sits heavy, but it does the trick every time."

"I know. I suffer terrible with the gas. I just know it's aggravated by worryin' about my Lucy. She's enough to give a mother gray hairs. Sometimes I don't think I'll ever find a respectable husband for her."

"Oh, you don't need to worry about Lucy," Mrs. Jasper said, patting her friend's hand in a motherly way. "She's a girl can take care of herself. What about the rector? Is there any chance there? He's a good quiet boarder and I'd hate to lose him, but a man needs a wife."

"He just don't show her much interest. Only girl he looks at is that eastern lady who runs the drug store. Though why any man would be interested in a woman what runs a business is more than I'll ever understand."

Mrs. Jasper nodded solemnly. "That's true. That's true."

Their whispers carried to Amanda, sitting three rows away. She smiled to herself, unconcerned about the implied criticism. For the most part, she always received a warm welcome when she worshiped with the people at St. Anselm's. Even though their service took place in a refurbished dining room, there was still an aura of reverence about it.

Still, she hadn't come among them today simply to pay her respects to the Lord. She wanted to see Cabot, to be where she could smile at him and have him smile back at her. She knew he had been out of town and felt a little miffed that he hadn't told her where he was going. It was his business, of course, or so she tried to tell herself. Even so . . .

When the service ended, she took her time moving to the back of the room where Cabot stood, greeting people as they left. By the time she reached him, most of the congregation had moved on and did not see the warmth in his eyes as he reached for both her hands.

"You look fresh as the morning dew," he said, smiling down at her.

"Thank you, sir," she replied archly. "It must be those rides in the open air."

"Don't go away. Maybe we can walk over to the Alahambra and have breakfast."

Amanda was about to reply with an enthusiastic 'yes,' when she was interrupted by Leander, running in from the alcove off the dining room.

"Reverend Storey! Come quick. We need to show you something."

"Of course," Cole said. He squeezed her hands, then

followed Leander into the alcove. Amanda waited by the curtained doorway.

The men were grouped around a table, staring at its surface in astonishment. Amanda's eye was caught by the glint of a pile of gold coins, and she moved closer.

"Good heavens, what's this?" Cole asked, pushing away the empty basket in which the offering had been collected.

"It's a miracle; that's what it is," Leander cried, reaching for the coins and allowing them to run like golden rain through his fingers. "Great jumpin' Jehoshaphat, it's a miracle!"

"But I don't understand."

"It was all in the offering," Charlie McDowell said, his eyes as round as saucers. "Twelve hundred dollars! I never seen this much money at one time in my whole life!"

Cole looked up at them blankly. "But where did it come from? Isn't there any note with it to explain?"

Horace Alander spoke up. "Nothin' at all. It's an an-non-ie-mous donation. And it's just what we need to get our church built."

Leander picked up a greenish-colored cloth sack with faint white letters on it. "It was in this bag. I dumped it out and nearly fainted flat on the floor. We got us a miracle."

"It would seem so," Cole said, gingerly touching the coins. "Someone must have wanted to help us out."

"I bet it was one of them bankers or mine directors. Though it does seem they'd want credit for it."

Leander began to pile up the coins in neat stacks.

"Who cares? What matters is we got the money now to build our church. And we're goin' to do it."

"May I see that bag?" Amanda asked. As she turned it over in her hand, the hairs on the back of her neck seemed to come alive. Of course she recognized it. It had once contained several packages of scented soaps she'd brought with her from St. Louis. She recalled wanting to keep it because it was made of good strong worsted. And she was certain she had put it away with several others in the back room behind her store.

"Have you seen that before?" Cole asked, watching her intently.

"As a matter of fact, yes. It held some special brands of soaps."

"You must have thrown it out and someone picked it up from the trash and used it to keep his donation a secret."

Amanda hesitated a moment. "Yes, I suppose that's exactly what happened."

"Leander's right," Cole said, turning back to his delighted parishioners. "Someone wanted to help us out, someone who has a lot of money. Who knows, maybe that person wanted to make up for some secret sin that's caused him a lot of guilt. We'll probably never know. What matters is, all this money is here; it was in the plate, and it's ours."

Leander smiled broadly. "That's right, Reverend Storey. And we're goin' to use it. After saving and working for so long, now we can finally build our church."

"But where can we keep it until tomorrow when the bank opens?" Horace asked, thinking he'd better not let his pa know about this.

"I can speak to Mrs. Poole," Amanda answered. "I believe she has a safe here in the hotel."

Cole nodded. "Good idea. Leander, you and the other vestry members start making up a list of all the supplies we're going to need. I think tomorrow we'll take a little trip into Tucson."

Seventeen

Amanda heard the pounding of hammers two blocks away. Once again she felt a pang that her responsibilities at the store kept her from joining the men and women of St. Anselm's who were putting up their church. Since today was Saturday, however, she had worn her oldest frock, closed the store at noon, picked up a basket of food Martha Poole had prepared for her, and was now on her way to spend the afternoon assisting in any way that would be helpful.

It was amazing how quickly the building was going up, especially since the work was being done almost entirely by volunteers from the congregation. As she rounded the corner of Third and Fremont, she could see they were working on the roof, the unfinished bell tower rising raggedly above it. With half its roof in place, the building had begun to really look like a church. As she drew nearer, she spied Cabot Storey crawling along the roof timbers, hammering shingles in place. He waved at her with his hammer.

"I brought lunch," Amanda called to him. "Whenever you're ready."

"As soon as we finish this section."

A table had been set up near the sycamore tree to

hold the baskets of food brought for the workers. Several women stood around the table waiting to serve lunch, while a few of the more adventurous were helping to paint the exterior walls. Amanda made up her mind that she would join the adventurous group once lunch was over.

Seeing Libby Walton nearby, she was about to join her when she heard her name and turned back to the street. She recognized Nora at once, standing in a faded calico dress with a thick woolen shawl around her shoulders in spite of the heat. Nora waved listlessly at her.

Amanda could almost feel the disapproving looks of the church women on her back as she moved to join Nora. They were quickly forgotten, however, when she saw how ill the woman looked. The first time Nora came into her store, she knew the girl was dying of consumption. During the weeks she had been in Tombstone, Nora's illness had ravaged her severely. Her thin frame was skeletal in its gauntness. Pale, parchment skin stretched over the bones of her face. In the shrunken face, her huge eyes bulged unnaturally and were dark with despair. Amanda's heart went out to her.

Nora opened her mouth to speak but was convulsed in a spasm of coughing instead. Blotches of red blood dotted the handkerchief she held to her lips.

"You're very ill, Nora," Amanda said, laying her arm around the girl's emaciated shoulders.

"I suppose I am, Miss. It's never been as bad as this a'fore. I was hopin' you could give me somethin'."

Amanda shook her head, knowing what Nora needed was quite beyond her powers to give.

"Your store was closed," Nora went on, "but one of the men on the walk said he'd seen you coming this way."

"I'm glad you found me. Possibly I can give you something to ease the coughing, but you really need to see a doctor."

"No. Don't want no doctors."

"But Nora, Dr. Goodfellow can help you more than I. And he doesn't care about your . . . profession. He won't hold that against you."

Nora shook her head vehemently. "No. Don't need no doctor. It's just the cold nights that's made me sick, that's all."

"The cold nights?" Amanda frowned with a sudden suspicion. "Aren't you still living in the cribs?"

Nora looked quickly away. "No. I could still work long as I could get a drink when I needed. But when even that didn't help no more, Big Gert threw me out."

"So where have you been sleeping?"

Nora shrugged. "Under porches. In sheds when I could find one that wasn't locked. Anywhere out of the night cold."

"Merciful heaven!" Amanda muttered. "This is an outrage. When was the last time you had a real meal?"

"I don't know. Couple of days, I guess."

Amanda gripped the girl's arm. "Come with me. I have a basket of food over here, and you're going to eat some of it right now."

Nora summoned up all the strength she still possessed to hold her ground. "I can't go over there, Miss. It wouldn't be right. Please don't make me."

Amanda glanced around to see every female eye focused on her in shocked disbelief. For a moment she almost gave in to her desire to affront them all by bringing Nora to the table. But when she looked back to see thin tears beginning to trickle down Nora's white face, she relented.

"Very well. Wait here. I'll bring you some food, then we'll walk around to the hotel. You can stay in my room."

"Oh, Miss, I couldn't do that!" Nora cried, her eyes widening. "I'd only be gettin' you in trouble."

Amanda frowned. It was true that Martha Poole would be scandalized if she found out a diseased whore was staying in her hotel. And Martha had been very good to her.

"All right. I have a room at the back of my store with a cot. You can stay there until we find you something better. At least you'll be out of the cold."

Nora pulled her heavy shawl closer around her shoulders and smiled weakly at Amanda. "Thank you, Miss. I'd be grateful to lie down on a bed, that's the Lord's truth."

As Amanda moved back toward the table, the formidable Mrs. Stone stepped up to bar her way. "You're not bringing that fallen woman among decent people, I trust," Mrs. Stone muttered in shocked tones.

Libby Walton stepped up beside Amanda. "Now, Georgina, get off your high horse. I'm sure Miss Lassiter doesn't want to do anything that would discredit her or the rest of us."

Amanda reached for her basket as several of the other women clustered around her. "Nora may be a 'soiled dove,' but she is very, very ill. She's been sleeping in the open and has had almost nothing to eat for two days. Where is your sense of Christian charity?"

"The just desserts of a sinful life," one of the women in the back snapped.

"She's in need," Amanda snapped back. "Isn't that what matters?"

Libby laid a hand on her arm. "Amanda, we're all good Christian women and I'm sure we want to help anyone in need. I'm willing to give you some food from my own basket for her, and I'm sure the rest of us are, too."

"But you won't allow her to sit here at the table with you and eat it."

Libby's plump face creased with concern. "It's just not done, my dear. It wouldn't be right."

"Why is she sleeping in the open?" Mrs. Jasper asked, leaning around Georgina Stone.

"She was thrown out of the cribs because she can no longer work. She can't be more than twenty-two or three, and she's dying of consumption. Frankly, I see good decent people of this town treating their horses and dogs with more compassion."

The women exchanged agonized glances. "Maybe she could sit over there," one of them said quietly.

"I'll make her some hot coffee."

Mrs. Jasper nodded. "And I'll allow there must be someplace we can find for her to stay, at least for a while. Someplace out of the cold, anyways."

Amanda looked around at their faces. They were good people and they did care. No doubt they would find a place for Nora to stay and would make sure that she had something to eat. But not at their tables or in their homes. She shook her head at the strangeness of it.

"Well, you needn't worry about it right now," she said with resignation. "Nora doesn't feel she belongs here anymore than you want her. Besides, she needs to lie down and rest. I'm going to let her stay in the back room of my store tonight. If you really mean what you say, maybe you can come up with some other plan for her after that."

Draping the basket over her arm, she went back to the street where the girl waited. "Come along, Nora," she said, laying her arm around the girl's shoulder. "Let's get you to bed."

Cole watched as Amanda walked down the street, accompanied by one of the whores from the cribs. That girl! Would she never learn that she should not associate with some people? He knew she was being kind, but she really ought to be more concerned about her reputation.

My God, he was beginning to get as priggish as the real Reverend Storey! He smiled to himself as he went on hammering the roof shingles in place. It didn't take much reflection for him to realize the real reason he was annoyed with Amanda was because she'd left, not because of the company she'd left with. When he'd seen her walking toward the church, the sun shining on her hair and her legs coltish beneath her skirt, he had felt warm inside just thinking of being near her. Of course, he had to be careful around his congregation. He might burn to take her into his arms, to let his fingers drift over her back and cup her breast in his hand; but, naturally, he could do nothing of the kind. It was all lingering glances, playful smiles, and warm, dancing eyes when other people were around. The brush of her hand on his arm, the casual smoothing away of a spot on her collar, the occasional press of their shoulders as they sat together—these were the only tantalizing bits that were allowed to them in public.

Yet somehow these bits made it all the sweeter on those infrequent occasions when they were alone and free to give way to the hot need they felt for each other. Yes, he had been looking forward just to being near her.

Then she walked away with a whore!

Suppressing his annoyance, he finished hammering his share of shingles, then crawled down the ladder and walked over to the table.

"I guess you won't get any lunch, Reverend Storey," Mrs. Stone said, stepping up to him almost before he arrived. "Miss Lassiter went off with the basket she said was meant for you. Now, you're welcome to some of mine that my Alice put together this morning."

"The pastor can share my lunch," Mrs. McDowell broke in. "I brought plenty just in case some of the men didn't have any."

Libby Walton shoved a plate toward Cole. "Reverend Storey don't need to worry about eating. We've got enough food for the whole town if they wanted it."

Mrs. Stone glowered at Libby. "Well, he ought to worry about that young woman. It ain't fittin' for her to be seen in broad daylight with one of those sportin' women."

"That's right," echoed Mrs. Ellis. "You ought to have

a word with Miss Lassiter, Reverend Storey. She seems like a nice enough girl, but she doesn't have any sense of what's proper."

"Now, just ease off," Libby broke in. "The woman was sick and she needed some medicine. Give Miss Lassiter credit for wanting to help. Remember Mary Magdalene in the Bible was a fallen woman, too."

Cole backed away as the women crowded around him, trying to draw him into their argument. "Is that true, Libby? Amanda just went to get some medicine?"

"I heard her offer that woman a place to sleep in the back of her store," Mrs. Stone interjected. "Just imagine if she tries to set up her . . . business there. It would be an outrage."

"Oh, for heaven's sake, Georgina," Libby snapped. "The poor girl is three-fourths dead already. If we had a hospital in this town, that's where she ought to be. Amanda was only trying to get her off the streets."

"Is that true, Libby?" Cole asked again.

"Of course it is. Anyone could see it."

"In that case," Cole said, reaching for his coat and slipping it over his arm, "perhaps I'd better go along and speak to both of them."

"And while you're doing it, give Miss Lassiter some advice on how decent people behave."

"Now, the preacher ain't goin' to deliver no sermons. That poor sick girl is about to face her Maker and mayhap she needs some advice."

"Mayhap she needs to repent!"

"Ladies," Cole said, raising his hands. "I'll handle it my way, if you please. Libby, tell Leander to see about finishing up that roof. I'll be back to help later."

He took off down the street, leaving them still arguing about the propriety of Amanda's efforts to help Nora. For it was Nora, he was certain. Once, at Amanda's urging, he had gone round to visit the girl in the miserable hovel that served as her home and place of business. It turned out to be a disastrous effort. He was extremely uncomfortable in the close, squalid little cabin. He could think of nothing to say, for any words of comfort coming from him for someone so ill sounded too false to utter. He had sat there, trying not to touch any surface and struggling to lean away from her constant coughing, wanting only to get away as quickly as possible. It had probably been the least successful of all his attempts at playing the Reverend Cabot Storey.

He admired Amanda for trying to help a woman like Nora, but the other ladies were right. He had a duty to tell her to be more careful about the proprieties. After all, she would have to go on living in Tombstone after he was gone.

After he was gone . . .

"Good day, Reverend Storey."

Cole was jolted out of his thoughts when a dark-green piano-box buggy pulled up alongside in the road and Tilly Lacey, with the reins in her hands, peered around the curtain at him. He looked back to see that while he had been so deep in his thoughts, he had turned the corner away from the church. There was no one on the walkway and only a lone horseman in the opposite direction on the street.

"Mrs. Lacey," he said, his voice full of reluctance. If only he had been paying attention, he might have avoided her before she'd caught him like this.

"Out for a walk, I see," Tilly said, smiling brightly. "Or perhaps on a call?"

"Yes, that's it. I'm just on my way to see . . . a parishioner."

"Oh, please, then allow me to give you a lift. Since we're both heading in the same direction." She squirmed over on the seat.

"Thank you, but I'd rather walk. It's not far."

"Now, Reverend Storey, I insist. After all, we don't get too many opportunities to chat, do we now?"

"No, really . . ."

"Now, you just come right on up here and allow me the chance to do my good deed for the day."

Cole looked longingly down the street. Short of taking off at a run, he could see no way out of refusing her request, and to do that might add to her suspicion. Reluctantly, he climbed up beside Tilly sitting as far away from her as possible on the seat.

At a snap of the reins, the buggy rolled off while Tilly managed to ease her body over until her thigh lay flat against his leg. "Were you headed for Allen Street?" she said cheerily.

"Yes. That's right. Allen and Fifth."

"No trouble at all. Lovely day, ain't it?"

Cole squirmed around on the seat as the buggy rolled merrily past Fifth Street. "I think you missed the turn."

"Oh, I know. I just thought we'd take the long way round. After all, like I said, we don't get too much chance to chat, you and me, and there's things I feel I ought to talk to a preacher about. That's your business, ain't it? Listen'n to people's troubles."

"Well, yes, but . . ."

Tilly caught both reins in one hand, leaving the other free to reach out and fold over Cole's, which lay on his leg. "I declare, it is a comfort to talk to a man of the cloth. I haven't done much of that in my lifetime."

"I'll bet you haven't," Cole muttered.

"What's that?"

"Nothing. I understand. But really, Mrs. Lacey, I need to . . ."

"Oh, I know you got people to see and things to do. But you won't begrudge me a few moments of your time, now, will you? A kind-hearted parson like yourself."

Gritting his teeth, Cole looked straight ahead without replying. Other than leaping out of a moving vehicle, he had no choice but to remain trapped in the buggy until she decided to release him; and that did not look promising. She turned down the last side street and emerged onto the main road that led out into desert."

"I don't remember saying that my appointment was in Bisbee," he commented dryly.

Tilly giggled. "My, Reverend, you are a card, ain't you? I don't intend to drive all the way to Bisbee. I just wanted a nice quiet place where we could talk private-like."

She squirmed closer to him on the seat, forcing him to grab one of the slats of the top-bows to keep from falling off. It was useless to comment, however, so he pursed his lips and waited for her to find the right place to stop. Whatever Tilly Lacey wanted with him, he was certain it was not to unburden herself of some fancied problem. He was even more certain when she finally pulled up beside a low chaparral shadowed by a towering saguaro cactus nearly fifteen feet tall. There had been a rare early-summer rain a few days before and as a result, all around them, the desert bloomed with Mexican poppies and purple owl's clover, spreading a mantle of color over the harsh, brown earth. His thoughts briefly went back to the joyous times he had shared with Amanda out in the wild, but he was quickly brought back to reality by his companion.

Tilly fastened the reins and looked at him coyly. "Help me down, please, Reverend Storey."

Half-amused at the woman's brazenness, Cole climbed out of the buggy and reached up to give her a hand. Lifting her skirt, she managed to bare half her leg encased in a black sheer stocking and a high-buttoned boot before laying her hand in his. He tried to step back as she lowered herself but wasn't quick enough. Before he knew what had happened, she was up against him, her arms around his neck.

"Oh, Mr. Storey, you really are a finely built man." Tilly breathed into his face. Her lips sought his, but he lifted his head, leaving her free to kiss his neck. "I love a finely built man," she muttered, trying to kiss his cheek and searching for his lips.

Cole stumbled backward and forced her hands away from around his neck. "Mrs. Lacey, please . . ."

"Tilly."

"Your horse is about to run away."

"Oh!" That got her attention. Leaving him for a moment, she caught up the reins and handed them to Cole. "Why don't you just fasten them to that big saguaro?"

He moved toward the cactus, as much to get away from her as to hold the horses. Before they were half-tied, she had come up behind him and slipped her arms around his waist, plastering herself against his back.

"Mrs. Lacey!" Cole snapped. "I don't think you drove out here to discuss your problems." He pulled himself out of her grasp and turned to face her.

"Oh, a girl can have all kinds of problems," Tilly crooned, moving closer against him. Growing more exasperated by the moment, Cole backed away, stumbled and fell to the ground. She was on him before he could regain his footing, shoving him on his back. He could feel the rounded force of her ample breasts against his chest, the quick thrust of her tongue between his lips, the grinding of her hips against his body. In an instant his mild amusement and bored exasperation flamed into full-fledged disgust.

"No! I don't want any part of this," he cried, shoving her to one side. Quickly he sprang to his feet and began slapping the dust from his trouser legs. It helped to disperse some of his anger, even if it did little to make him cleaner.

Tilly sat on the ground staring up at him, a cold fury congealing in her chest. Her painted lips formed a grim, red slash in her powdered face.

"I'm not good enough for you, I suppose."

"It's nothing like that. It's just not . . . right."

He reached down to give her a hand, but she ignored him and struggled up by herself.

"Now I suppose you're going to try to give me some kind of pious sermon about what's moral and what's not. Well, it won't work, Reverend Storey. Not with me. I been around men since I was twelve, and it don't take so many years as that to know that you ain't no preacher."

Cole caught his breath. "What do you mean?" he asked coolly.

"You might fool all those dumb yokels back there in town, but you don't fool Tilly Lacey. I been out here in the West too long to fall for a snake game like that."

He could feel a muscle in his cheek jumping. He moved away to lean against the horse's rump, watching her with what he hoped was composure. "Just what is it you're trying to say?"

Tilly flipped her skirts into place and straightened her straw hat. The anger on her face revealed her age. "I don't know what your game is, but it's going to be up soon. I'm not the only one who knows you ain't what you pretend to be."

"This is ridiculous."

"I don't know who you really are, but I got my suspicions. There's a few men I heard about but never met, and you could fit the ways they was described to me. They was all good with a gun, too. Some was law men, and some was nothin' but rope-bait. Jack Rivington, Cole Carteret, Moses Rivera . . ." She cocked her head, staring at him through half-closed eyes. "You could be any of them."

Cole felt something go cold in his chest. He forced his face to remain mask-like and casually reached over to pick up the reins. If he didn't get into that buggy first, it would be just like Tilly Lacey to leave him here to walk back into town.

"Your imagination is carrying you away, Mrs. Lacey," he said with exquisite politeness. "And my patience is wearing thin. I didn't ask to come out here, and I really do need to get back."

When she realized what he intended, Tilly grabbed for the reins, but he evaded her and jumped up on the driver's seat.

"Coming?" he asked, tipping his hat.

"Damn you!" she muttered under her breath. Then, gaining control, she gave him a false smile and climbed up beside him, leaving a wide space between them on the seat.

"Of course, *Reverend*."

"I should have left long ago."

"You're right about that." Aces Malone dug the heel of his boot into the graveled soil, creating a shallow trench that reflected the moonlight in a silver pool. "I never could see why you did this in the first place—pretendin' to be a preacher! It's the most cocky-brainy idea you ever come up with."

"I never expected it to last this long. I only intended to come here and see you, then go right back. If you had been where you were supposed to be . . ."

"How did I know you was goin' to do anythin' so crazy? Besides, I had to go to Tucson to check on them deeds. It was the only way I could make sure that what I suspicioned was true."

An eerie howl shattered the night. Aces jumped and cast furtive glances around the desert. "Geezes, Cole, I tole' you I hate this place in the dark of nighttime. Why can't we meet somewheres else?"

Cole chuckled. "You're even more superstitious than I remember. It's a sight, comin' from someone who's so sure of himself at a gaming table."

"That's different. You know I don't like the out-of-doors, and especially not no graveyard!"

Cole looked around at the ghostly light that fell on the short crosses of the Boot Hill Cemetery. He thought it looked rather striking with its shadowy, low mounds, haphazard crosses, and moonlight reflecting off thousands of tiny agate stones scattered like diamonds across its surface. It must be the idea of so many bodies beneath the ground—and not many of them respectable folk, either—that made Aces nervous. As though one of them might rise up in a spiral of ectoplasm, pointing a long, ghostly finger to remind both mortals of their sins.

"This is the one place I know where we're safe from nosey people," Cole said in a matter-of-fact voice to counteract Ace's jumpy nerves. "And I can't risk being seen with you at this point. There is too much suspicion already."

"Then you ought to leave Tombstone, and soon. Otherwise you're goin' to get me in as much trouble as you already are in."

"I plan to. But first I want to know what you've found out."

Aces's tiny eyes narrowed in the bronzed light. "I don't think I want to tell you. I thought to cut you in on some rich pickings, and what do you do? Go and give away everthin' you take! Dumbest, craziest thing I ever heard of!"

"That's no business of yours. Besides, it was a one-time thing and not likely to be repeated."

"Yeah, but don't you see what you done? There ain't no way you can muscle in on those gangs now. They'd never accept you. I was hopin' to get a cut of whatever you took, but that ain't goin' to happen now."

Cole leaned closer to Aces's face, lowering his voice. "Maybe I'm not interested in penny-ante change. I want something bigger. Just what did you learn in Tucson?"

Even in the dim light he could see Aces's face fall into the mask he used when playing high-stakes card games.

"Give me another few days," the gambler muttered. "By then I'll know everything for sure."

"I may not have another few days."

"Well, that's a risk you'll have to take." Aces started as something darted through a mesquite bush near his foot. "Damn! I told you I don't like it out here."

"Oh, it's just a scorpion, or maybe a rattlesnake," Cole said, taking satisfaction from the way the whites of Aces's eyes gleamed in the moonlight.

"God a'mighty! Let's get out of here."

Cole reached out and gripped the man's arm. "All right, but I want that information before I leave. Understood? You brought me into this, now you help me to get out with profit enough to make it worth my while."

Aces shook off his hand. "I intend to. Long as I get my share of it. Also understood?"

Cole studied the man's frightened face before answering. "Right."

He chuckled to himself as he watched the nervous gambler bolt off into the shadows almost before the word escaped his lips. He was still chuckling when he heard the clatter of Aces's horse heading back to the town.

* * *

A knock on Amanda's door brought her head up from the ledger book in which she was writing. At first she did not recognize the tall man standing in the doorway, but then as he walked forward, he pulled off his black plainsman hat and she saw it was Sheriff John Behan.

"Good morning, Sheriff," she said politely, trying to mask the frown that sprang spontaneously to her brow. Though she had met Behan several times, he had never given her more than a few perfunctory words and had certainly never set foot inside her drug store before. She was both surprised and alarmed to see him now. Closing the book, she stepped back from the counter as Behan leaned against it.

He gave a cool, appraising glance around. "You've really made this into a nice place," he said, smiling at her. "I was only in here a few times when old George . . . when your uncle owned it, and it was so cramped and disorderly, I never knew how he could find anything." He ran his hand along the curved glass surface of the counter, admiring the rows of ribbons and buttons beneath. Beside it stood a large glass jar holding peppermint stick candy. Casually he lifted the lid and removed one stick.

"Seems you're selling more than just medicines here. How much for this?"

"A penny," Amanda said. "But you can have it with my compliments since this is your first visit." Carefully she took the candy from his hand and closed it inside a paper bag. "I intend to expand even more. You see, I remember the drug stores in St. Louis. The most successful ones sold many other items along with medicines. I think there is a place for that here in Tombstone."

"Bert Tippet might not be too happy about that, since it creates some smart competition for him."

"Oh, I'll only sell the small things he's not likely to carry. I've already spoken to him about it. What can I do for you today, Sheriff? Did you need some medicine?"

John Behan laid his hat on the counter and smiled at her. In spite of herself, Amanda was caught in the pleasantness of that smile. The sheriff was a comely man with long dark hair, a square face and black, mischievous eyes. He had a tall, wiry body that suggested a taut alertness underneath. He was not as muscular as Cabot Storey, nor did he have the engaging grin and twinkling, intelligent eyes the rector possessed, but he was a handsome man who had probably made many conquests among the ladies of the town.

"Actually, I came to talk to you, not to buy anything. Have you got a free moment or two?"

Amanda found herself smoothing back her hair. "Why, yes. We can sit at the back of the store if you like."

"That would be nice."

Closing the ledger, she led the way to the two slatted Windsor chairs flanking the potbellied stove at the rear of the room. Taking one, she smoothed her skirts and waited while the sheriff sat down, crossing his legs and laying his hat on the stove's cold surface.

There was a long moment of silence while Amanda ran through her mind all the possible reasons for this visit and Behan stared at the floor, wondering how to begin. At length he cleared his throat and plunged in.

"I know what you've done for Nora down in the cribs. That was kind of you, Miss Lassiter."

Amanda looked quickly away. "She's very ill."

"All the same, some folks might see it as a just punishment for a misspent life. It speaks well for you that you didn't."

"Is that why you came here today, Sheriff?"

"No. I just thought I'd mention it, now that I'm here." He shifted uncomfortably in his chair. "No, I want to ask you about Reverend Storey. You seem to know him pretty well, about as well as anyone in this town. I'd like your impression of him."

"Why, Sheriff," Amanda spluttered, her cheeks flaming, "I'm sure there are others you might ask. People in his congregation . . ."

He looked at her through narrowed eyes. "I think I'd trust your judgment more, simply because you're not one of the flock, so to speak. Tell me," he said, suddenly leaning forward, "what kind of man do you think he is? Has he told you anything about his background? He doesn't seem quite the typical preacher to me. Does he to you?"

Amanda caught her underlip with her teeth. Typical? How could she tell when she'd never known another clergyman? Certainly he was nothing like she imagined the clergy to be, but that could be her mistaken image. She resolutely pushed down the uneasiness he had at times aroused in her mind. No need to go into that with the sheriff.

"He's a good man. His background is varied, so much so that at times he surprises me with all he knows. But I trust him completely. Why do you ask?"

Behan shrugged. "Just curious. How much do you know about the West, Miss Lassiter? Have you ever heard of Johnny Ringo? The Casket Kid? Moses Rivera?"

"I heard some of the men at the store talking about The Kid. And Johnny Ringo has a wide reputation. I've never heard of the other one."

"Ringo is a man you don't want to meet. He's in and out of Tombstone because he's a friend of Wyatt Earp's—another man you'd do well to stay away from."

"I've never even met him, or any of his family," Amanda said. But she had heard gossip that Earp had taken away a girl the sheriff was courting and the competition had led to a bitter enmity between them. This was not something she wanted to get involved in.

Behan settled back in his chair. "Let me tell you about The Casket Kid. His real name is Carteret—Cole Carteret. He came from a good family but threw it all over to become a gunfighter and an outlaw. He's the best with a gun anyone ever saw, I'll grant him that. But he's left a trail of robbery and murder as thick as your arm."

"Why would a man from a good family want to follow such a path, Sheriff? I don't understand it."

"Pride, and a bad character. He was so good he thought he could get away with anything. He's been caught a few times but never held long, except once when he spent nearly two years in the prison at Yuma. A year ago, he and his gang hit a stage I was on bound for Cortez. They took a cash box and every bit of money and jewelry the passengers had with them. Some shots were fired as they took off, and one of the passengers was killed. I swore then I'd put him behind bars someday, and I will."

"Why are you telling me all this?" Amanda asked, trying not to let her growing uncertainty show. All this had nothing to do with her, yet the peculiar sinking feeling in her stomach would not go away.

"Because . . ." He hesitated. "Because I want you to know that people out here are not always what they pretend to be. You're a fine-looking woman, Miss Lassiter, and you got a good heart. You ought to be on your guard all the time. I'll be frank with you. I don't trust that preacher. Now I never got a good look at The Kid. He had a handkerchief over his face, and he wears a full set of whiskers. But where my intuition tells me something's not right, I believe in taking a good look around."

"Are you trying to tell me that Reverend Storey is this . . . Carteret person?"

"I won't go that far. But if there's anything suspicious about the preacher that you've wondered about, I'd be obliged if you'd tell me."

Amanda got to her feet. "Really, Sheriff. That is a preposterous idea. Cabot Storey is a good, fine man, and I don't think I want to hear any more of this kind of talk."

Behan stood and reached for his hat. "All right. If you say so, I'll believe you. I'm sorry if I offended you, Miss Lassiter."

"Not me, but Reverend Storey."

He shook his head. "I've got to take a good look at everything. It's my job."

"I understand."

He started toward the door but stopped halfway across the store to turn back to her. "By the way, Miss Lassiter. There's something else I've been wondering. How would you feel about stepping out with me some evening? Maybe we could visit the play that's coming to the opera house or have supper or . . . something."

Amanda stared at him, too surprised to answer. "I . . . I don't think so right now, Sheriff. Perhaps when we know each other better."

He smiled. "Sure. That's something we'll have to work on, isn't it? Well, good day, Miss Lassiter."

"Good day, Sheriff."

She closed the door behind him and leaned against it. Handsome as he was, she had no interest in stepping out with John Behan. *Especially* not John Behan, whose foolish talk about outlaws had stirred up uncomfortable suspicions. It was nonsense, of course, and yet . . .

"It's not possible," she said out loud, thrusting her chin in the air. "I refuse to even think about it."

Yet she wished she could feel as certain deep down inside as she sounded. She wished her words could make this nervous pressure in her chest go away.

While Amanda chatted with the sheriff, Cole stood in the middle of Third Street looking up at the newly framed bell tower of St. Anselm's. The tower added the finishing touch to the small building and gave the final definition of a church to the structure. Though a lot of work still remained to be done, particularly inside, just having the frame up gave him a splendid feeling of satisfaction. It had been years since he had worked at anything that required so much physical labor, and to see it this near completion was a special kind of pleasure.

"Coming to supper, Reverend Storey?" he heard Leander Walton ask. Walton was just rolling down his sleeves after the work on the tower. He carried his coat over his arm, and his hat was shoved back on his head.

"I'll be along shortly," Cole said. "I want to have a last look around first."

"Don't be too long. Libby's made one of her apple pies."

"Save me a piece."

As Cole watched Leander stride off down the street, a quiet settled over the raw, new building. With his hands on his waist, his feet spread apart, he looked up at the square tower silhouetted against the deep blue sky. Yes, it was a good feeling.

The slow clopping of a horse on the road behind him brought him back to reality. He reached down for his coat and swung away from the building, beginning to roll down one sleeve. The horse stopped; its rider, slumping forward with both hands resting on the pommel, looked down at Cole.

"Well. So you ain't dead or in jail after all."

Cole stood rooted to the ground, his hand frozen over his arm as he stared up into the man's thin, lizard-like face and cold, steely eyes.

"My God," he breathed. "Jim Reily!"

Churning his jaw, the rider turned his head to spit a stream of tobacco juice into the dirt. "Leastways you ain't forgot my name!"

Eighteen

Reverend Storey had disappeared.

Word spread throughout the town, first among the members of his flock, then outward to the clerks in the stores, the office workers at the mine, the men who lounged around the stables and cracker barrels, the doctors, judges and lawyers, and, lastly, the long, lean hombres idling around the saloons, their hard eyes showing a glint of surprise.

Tilly Lacey pursed her lips with bitterness and nodded knowingly at Sheriff Behan, whose handsome face betrayed not a glimmer of emotion. Big Gert shook her head sadly, sorry she'd never gotten to know the rector better. "But then, he never seemed like your typical man of the cloth," she commented to Eugenie and Roxy. Leander Walton and Charlie McDowell ran to check the church money box, feeling guilty even as they did it. But they were realists, after all, and one couldn't be too careful. Much to their relief, they found everything intact.

Amanda first realized her suspicions might be confirmed when Libby Walton came hurrying round to her drug store, her face somber and drawn.

"He's not coming back," Libby intoned. "The vestry is sure of it. He's never been gone this long before."

Unable to meet Libby's eyes, Amanda ground a pestle against the powders in her mortar, forcing herself not to let her face reveal the turmoil she felt inside.

"They're wrong. He went on a trip. He often goes into Tucson on business."

Libby's little straw hat bobbed as she shook her head. "No, not this time. He's been gone too long. We'd made arrangements for Netty's son to be baptized last week and I thought sure he'd be back for that, but he wasn't. The last we saw of him was the Friday after that day at the church when you met . . . you know, that girl."

"You mean Nora," Amanda said listlessly.

"That's right. When Leander left him that afternoon, he said he would see us in a little while for supper. But he never came. When he didn't show up for Sunday service, Leander went round to Mrs. Jasper's to see if anything were wrong. She hadn't seen hide nor hair of him, but when she checked his room, everything was lyin' there, just like he had stepped out for a walk. Clothes in the drawers, an open Bible on the desk."

Libby folded her arms and leaned back, pursing her lips. "Nothin' was gone but his hat and his spurs. Now, surely if he were goin' on a trip, he'd of told somebody and he'd of taken his clothes with him."

"There must be some explanation," Amanda said lamely. "You don't suppose he's hurt or . . ."

"If he were hurt or dead, where's the body? The vestry went all over town looking for him. They even rode out across the desert as far as Contention. I tell you, he's gone without a trace. Of course they checked the money box right away, because, naturally, that's what you think of first."

"Cabot . . . Reverend Storey wouldn't steal money from the church." Amanda hoped her voice sounded more convincing than she actually felt. Though she wouldn't admit it to Libby, this conversation confirmed her worst fears. She hadn't seen Cabot Storey since he'd waved to her from the church roof nearly three weeks before. How many times had she told herself he must have been suddenly called away? How often had she pushed down her growing sense of desolation and anger with reasoned excuses for his absence? Surely he wouldn't go off without speaking to her first? Not if he were who he said he was . . .

"Oh, the money was all there. That last Sunday's offering and everything left from the gift to build the church. No one can accuse him of stealing."

Amanda turned away to reach for the pill-mold, recalling the green bag that gift had been wrapped in. She was almost certain that money had come from Cabot Storey, though where he got it was still a mystery. Naturally, he wouldn't run off with money he had given the church in the first place. But why would he run off at all? Her chest constricted, making it difficult to breathe. Hadn't he mentioned having to go out of town? But to leave without a word, an explanation, a kiss goodbye . . .

"I'm sure there's a simple explanation. Perhaps he was called away to see someone, like Doc Goodfellow often is." Though she couldn't tell Libby, she remembered that, after all, Cabot was a government agent and this disappearance could easily be related to his job. Then, too, there was that mysterious confrontation with the Apache weeks ago. Perhaps the Indians had called him away. She tried to smile with assurance. "He'll probably come riding in sometime today or tomorrow, and we'll all feel foolish for worrying."

Libby leaned close to Amanda's face, speaking in low tones. "Why just walk away without tellin' nobody? A preacher wouldn't do that if he was just riding out on a call. No, I'd bet my life he's gone for good. There was always somethin' a little different about him, you know. He just wasn't like no minister I've ever seen."

Amanda felt a stab of pain. How often had she said those words to herself?

"I don't remember your saying anything about it while he was here. In fact, everyone at the church seemed to think he was pretty wonderful."

Libby brushed at a speck of dust on her sleeve. "Well, things look different from hindsight, you know."

"I think it's all nonsense," Amanda exclaimed, pushing the powder gell into the pill-mold with such force that part of it spilled onto the counter. "Not all preachers are the same. There are bound to be a few like Reverend Storey—men who are familiar with the ways of the world but who long to bring a spiritual dimension to it. When you think about it, what other kind of man would choose to come to a place like Tombstone?"

"Well, you can defend him, my dear," Libby said, disappointed she had not gotten more of a reaction from Amanda, "but it's mighty strange and that's a fact." She slipped her purse strings over her arm. "Of course, he did a good job while he was here and he got our church built for us. I suppose we owe him the benefit of the doubt until we know for sure."

"Know what for sure?"

"Why, where he is. *Who* he is."

For all her brave words, Amanda suffered a traumatic few moments once Libby left her store. She was grateful there were no customers since it allowed her the opportunity to flee to the back room, sit on the edge of her cot, and wring her hands in solitude.

It couldn't be true. Cabot wouldn't just up and leave Tombstone without taking his clothes. He must be coming back if he left all his things. Surely he would never go away without saying goodbye to her. After all they had shared, all they had meant to each other . . .

Her body flamed with the memory of the times they had made love, clinging to each other on the blanket, lost in wild abandon. She saw his long, hard body, the familiar sweep of his shoulders, the feel of her hands on the swell of his hips, the soft tufts of dark hair that broadened on his chest then narrowed to a thin line leading below to his . . .

Abruptly she jumped up, striding back and forth across the narrow room. The tears hovering at the edge of her eyes had to be forced back. No one could knew the turmoil she felt, and she couldn't give way to her urge to weep and wail. After all, it might not be true. Everything she had said to Libby was still possible.

And yet, that thought was not enough to stem her swelling grief. She caught her arms across her waist and pushed against her body to hold back the fear threatening to explode inside her. A fear which had been there for a long time and which she had tried in so many ways to expiate. The fear this man to whom she had given so much was not what he claimed to be; the horrible realization that she had no inkling who he really was.

She was saved by a slow, seeping anger that swelled into a rush of pure fury. She turned to the wall, banging it lightly with her fist. How dare he do this to her! How dare he use her, take her love, then disappear without a word.

As she slammed her fist against the wall a second time, she heard the bell on the front door jingle. Forcing herself back to a measure of composure, she smoothed her skirt and brushed back her hair, then returned to the front of the store with a grim smile on her lips to meet her next customer. Beneath the frozen smile she made a silent vow. If Cabot Storey truly had run away, she would make him pay for it if it were the last thing she ever did.

Roy Alander's hangover was worse than usual. His head felt three times the size of his body and was filled with tiny creatures pounding away like workers in a mine. His mouth couldn't taste any worse if it were filled with desert gravel. It had to be that lousy whisky Jonas Dole had foisted off on him last night at the Bird Cage. Just because he hadn't got the money for the good stuff, Jonas fed him rotgut culled from the bottom of the barrel.

Pulling himself together, Roy crawled gingerly out of the big, empty keg in which he'd slept off the worst of last night's excesses. He squinted against the gray light just dawning over the desert and shivered with the cold. Dragging himself to his feet, he took two steps before giving it up as hopeless and sinking back against the raw wood of the keg. Behind him a rooster in the yard of the Mexican's house on the edge of town crowed the arrival of dawn, and he knew that soon now the housewife, Marietta, would be stirring. If she found him there, she'd chase him off with her broom again. He ought to be moving, but not yet . . .

He ran a callused hand across the gray stubble covering the lower half of his face. If only he could have a drink of good Cyrus Noble whisky. He rolled his tongue across his dry lips just thinking about its smooth, mellow taste. That was all it would take to get him going again, a shot of Cyrus Noble.

At first he didn't notice the shadow falling across his hunkered form. Dimly through the fog in his brain, he became aware of a horse clopping along the road beside the house, its hooves keeping rhythm with the pounding of the miners' little hammers in his brain. He raised his head, slowly, against the increased drumming within, and stared upward.

The man who looked down at him was sitting on a horse that seemed twice as huge as it ought to be. The man had his back to the light so his face was indistinct, yet Roy could swear he was smiling. Shielding his eyes with his hand, Roy squinted up at him, straining to make out the face beneath the hat.

"Good morning, my good man," said a cheery voice.

Roy groaned at the echoing reverberations of the man's voice in the clear, dry air.

"God damn it, not so loud!" he muttered, covering his ears with his hands.

"Oh. Sorry," the man said, lowering his voice. "I didn't realize you were suffering. Is this better?"

Roy gingerly rolled his head to enable his eyes to look upward without setting off the miners inside again. "What do you want?" he mumbled ungraciously. "Go away."

"I assure you I will be on my way as quickly as I can. I simply want your assistance. Is this, by chance, the metropolis of Tombstone?"

"Met—what? Yeah, it's Tombstone. What else would it be, stuck out here by itself in the desert?"

"I thought as much. Thank you, my good fellow."

"I'm not your good fellow," Roy snarled, gathering strength even as he made the effort to respond. "Now, git, before Marietta hears you and comes roarin' out here with her broom."

Much to his consternation, the rider did not gallop away but, instead, climbed down from his horse. Roy shied from the man in horror as he bent over him.

"My dear fellow, you look terribly ill. Is there anything I can do for you?" The man reached out and laid his hand on Roy's shivering arm. "And you're cold. Here, take my coat. I don't need it. I rarely ever suffer from the cold."

Roy watched in amazement as the man pulled off a jacket lined with sheepskin and laid it across his shoulders. The warmth of it brought immediate comfort to his thin body. He grabbed the edges and yanked it closer around him, expecting this crazy man to take it back any second.

"Who are you? Some kind of angel or something?"

The man gave a good-natured laugh. "No, I'm certainly no angel."

Roy saw the angel turn his face away as he caught a whiff of what must be his stale, alcoholic breath. "I can see now why you are suffering. It must have been some party last night."

"No party," Roy grumbled, gripping the warm jacket tenaciously.

The man stood with his hands on his hips looking down at him. "No, I suspect it's a nightly routine, not a celebration. Look here, my man, if I gave you the blunt for it, would you buy yourself some breakfast and a strong cup of coffee?"

"Blunt?"

"Brass. Money."

A sudden thrill shot through Roy's wasted body. "Coffee? Sure. Why, that would be real nice."

The man laughed, shaking his head. "Somehow, I don't think it's coffee you'd buy. But I bet you would like a drink."

Roy's tongue automatically went journeying around his dry lips. "I sure would, mister. And that's the God's truth."

"I'm sure it is. Very well. Take this and get yourself a drink. At least it will get you going, and away from the formidable Marietta and her broom."

Roy stared only a moment at the dollar bill the man thrust toward him before grabbing it out of his hand. "What's the catch?" he asked, squinting up at him with sudden suspicion.

"Well, as a matter of fact, there is one. I'd like to see you in church very soon. St. Anselm's, to be exact.

I'll be in town a long time, so I'm sure we'll see each other again. You can return the jacket to me later."

The angel—for by now, Roy was convinced he was hallucinating and seeing beings that did not really exist—bounded energetically back into the saddle, and politely doffed his hat.

"Good day to you my man."

Tugging on the reins, the rider turned his horse and cantered down the street toward town. Roy peered around the barrel, staring after, half-expecting to see him disappear in a cloud of smoke.

"I'm not your man," he muttered, settling back against the keg. He pulled on the tabs of the warm jacket. It was real! He looked down at the paper bill in his hand. And it was real, too. An Eastern bank's legal tender, not one of those fly-by-night Western issues. Enough for a few drinks of good Cyrus Noble.

Staggering to his feet, he took off at a stumbling lope down the street for the nearest saloon.

"We're the laughingstocks of the town."

Leander Walton leaned his elbows on the table and dropped his head into his hands. Opposite him, Charlie McDowell drummed his fingers on the surface in a rhythmic drumbeat of frustration.

"It wasn't our fault. Everybody was fooled. We weren't the only ones."

Leander raised his head and looked around the table at the rest of St. Anselm's vestrymen. Their expressions mirrored his own. And they radiated in waves from one to the other, alternating disbelief, shock, anger, embarrassment.

"Charlie's right," muttered Lucas Stone. "Everybody in town was flummoxed by this impostor."

Joseph Donnely wagged his finger in Lucas's face. "I never thought he was what he pretended to be. There was just something about him, right from the first. He wasn't like no preacher I ever known."

"I'm hearin' that a lot now," Leander grumbled. "But I don't recall hearin' it when he was here buildin' our church."

"He gave awful good sermons," Charlie offered tentatively.

Donnely snorted. "Anybody can give a good sermon. It don't take no preacher to speak from the heart."

Leander shook his head. "That's just it. Was he speaking from his heart? He must have been lying the whole time, and we never saw it."

"Well, it was a mighty good act, you got to admit," Lucas retorted. "He ought to be on the stage of the Schieffelin Opera House."

Horace Alander leaned forward, his elbows on the table. "So what are we goin' to do about this new one? In a few minutes we got to go out there in the church and introduce him like we was behind him one hundred percent. Suppose he's an impostor, too?"

"I don't think so," Leander answered. "Everything about this one rings true."

"Yeah, but to just walk in out of the night, off the desert, calling himself Cabot Storey. We got took by that once, you know."

"That's true. But I'd swear this one is genuine. He talks big, like back East. And he knows the services and the Prayer Book like the back of his hand."

"He knew right where his diplomy was in that trunk, too. The impostor never did produce it when we asked."

"The impostor had the bishop's letter."

"He could have taken it off the real rector. He was pretty slick when you think of it."

Charlie McDowell ran a hand over his forehead where the hair was beginning to thin. "All I know is I been livin' in sin these past weeks. I trusted that preacher to marry Jane and me. All the time we thought we was wed and we wasn't!"

"You had every right to think you was wed," Lucas said. "It wasn't your fault you wasn't. And this new pastor is goin' to make it legal first thing."

A warm flush crept up Charlie's cheeks. "All the same, it'll never be forgot. I'll be teased about it the rest of my life. And poor Jane, she's fit to die from shame."

"You ain't alone," Horace said quietly. "Me and Clara and the Taylors got the same problem."

"We got bigger problems than your marriages," Leander said sadly. "At least the impostor didn't run off with the money box."

"I wonder why he didn't? I wouldn't have put it past him."

Leander's lips pursed into a tight line. "I just got this to say. I'm not going to rest easy till I know who he really was. But the meantime, we've got to do something to give St. Anselm's back its good name and learn this town to respect all of us on this vestry. Right now we look like the biggest durn fools God ever made!"

* * *

It had only taken a few hours for the news to spread all over town that another man calling himself Reverend Storey had ridden into Tombstone. The principal bearer of this astounding information was Roy Alander, basking in the fame of having been the first to see the new preacher. But who, then, had the first Reverend Storey been? That was the question on everyone's lips. Speculation spread like fire on a dry prairie. While there were all kinds of suggestions, no one had any way of knowing for sure.

Once again Libby Walton hurried over to Amanda's store, hoping to be the first to break the news. She found Amanda waxing her counter top and knew the instant the girl looked up with a "now what?" expression on her lovely face that she would be difficult to convince.

Libby hurried forward, fairly bursting with excitement. "You're not going to believe this, Amanda."

Amanda paused her brisk polishing as a leap of expectation flamed in her eyes. "Has he come back? He's returned, hasn't he? I told you he would."

"No, no. It's not that at all," Libby said, ignoring the disappointment on Amanda's face. "Reverend Storey has returned, all right; but he's not the one we knew."

"What are you talking about?"

"I mean a young man rode in a little while ago, calling himself the Reverend Cabot Storey. He says he's the real one. The one we had wasn't real at all."

Amanda stared, her eyes widening. "That can't be true."

"I tell you it is." She grabbed Amanda's arm. "Come with me. I want you to meet him. He's over at the church. Everyone's going there to look him over and . . . compare."

Though Amanda started to pull away, it only took a moment's reflection to change her mind. "I'll get my hat."

Amanda walked beside Libby the few blocks to the church with a smothering constriction in her chest. The news did not surprise her, and yet, it was dismaying and disturbing all the same. At the new building, people clustered around the steps. A larger crowd gathered inside, spilling down the center aisle and grouped where the altar would go. The throng parted as Amanda and Libby approached, allowing the women a view of a young man standing at its center. He was tall with a long thin, esthetic face and blue, twinkling eyes—the very picture of what Amanda had imagined a preacher should look like.

The smile he gave them reflected a genuine pleasure. "I've yet to meet these ladies," he said, stepping forward. "Are they members of the congregation?"

"This is my wife, Libby," Leander said quickly, laying his arm around his wife's shoulder. "And this is Miss Amanda Lassiter. She runs the drug store here in town."

"I'm so pleased to meet you both," Cabot Storey replied, taking first Libby's hand and then Amanda's in his long fingers. He lingered a moment, staring down at Amanda. "I didn't expect to find such loveliness out here in the desert."

Amanda colored as she realized he meant the compliment sincerely. "You're very kind," she murmured. "And you talk like an Easterner."

He laughed. "What else should I talk like?" Noticing her embarrassment, he coughed politely. "I'm sorry. I keep forgetting someone else has been here before me. I keep thinking this is my first day in my new parish." He smiled down at Amanda. "I hope the comparison between us doesn't put me in too bad a light."

Amanda hardly knew how to respond, but she was spared from having to by Leander's saying, "You haven't told us yet who that impostor really was, Reverend Storey."

Cabot laughed. "I don't know any more than you. I was on my way here when I was stopped on the road by a gang of very rough men. I knew they intended to rob me, and I only hoped they wouldn't do something worse. But when their leader found out who I was and where I was going, he took off, leaving me a prisoner with the rest of the gang."

"You mean you was there with them all this time?"

"No. I spent part of the time with Heronimo at his Apache camp down near Sonora."

"You were with the Indians?" Amanda gasped.

"Yes. And it was a most revealing experience, too. I enjoyed seeing what an Indian camp was like and even had hopes of converting, a few of them. But a day or so ago, one of the gang's members came for me and brought me back to their hideout. They gave me a horse and sent me on my way."

"Outlaws and Indians! You were lucky you didn't get murdered by one or the other," one of the men muttered.

"Yes, that possibility crossed my mind several times," the minister said lightly.

Leander shook his head. "I declare, Reverend Storey, it doesn't make any sense at all. I don't understand it."

"I don't understand it either. But, by the grace of God, I am safely here now. Whoever this fellow was, he did me a service by building so much of our church. Now we can finish it and have a proper place of worship."

Amanda looked at the satisfied, smiling faces of the people of St. Anselm's, happy that now they finally had their proper shepherd. She eased away from them, sick at heart, more confused than ever. Slipping out of the church, she determined to return to her store and not dwell on the fact that the man she knew as Cabot Storey was gone and she might never see him again and to try to ignore the pain that thought caused her.

She was nearly there when someone fell in beside her on the walkway. She looked up into the black, unsmiling eyes of John Behan.

"Mornin,' ma'am," he said, politely touching the brim of his hat. "May I escort you back to your place of business?"

He was the last person she wanted to see, but she was too polite to say so. "Good morning, Sheriff. Of course."

"I guess you've heard the news," he said, helping her down the low walk and across the street.

"Yes. In fact, I was just over at St. Anselm's to meet . . ." She couldn't say his name. "To meet him."

"What did you think of the 'new' pastor?"

"From what he says, I think he's lucky to be here."

Sheriff Behan nodded grimly. "I talked to him this morning, the moment I heard he'd arrived in town. Considering the cutthroats who took him captive, he was fortunate indeed."

"Cutthroats?"

He gave her a sideways look. "Yes. From the descriptions he gave, we're pretty sure he was taken by the Carteret gang."

Her voice was a whisper. "Carteret gang?"

"The man I was telling you about the other day. Cole Carteret, The Casket Kid."

She could not breathe. "Does that mean . . ."

"It does indeed. I can tell you, Miss Lassiter, the people of that church are embarrassed at having had a bloodthirsty outlaw pretending to be their pastor. But their chagrin is nothing compared to mine. To think I had that criminal walking around town, right under my nose, and I never knew it!"

"I suppose we were all fooled," Amanda mumbled, feeling more sick to her stomach by the moment.

"Of course, in his wanted-pictures he has a full set of whiskers, which tends to hide the features. And when he robbed the Cortez stage, there was that handkerchief over his face the whole time. Still, I should have recognized the eyes."

The eyes. Amanda could see them, looking down at her with such tenderness it gave a wrench to her heart.

"Those cold, calculating, greedy eyes," Sheriff Behan went on.

"But he didn't seem like an outlaw. Or talk like one."

"Oh, he was convincing, all right. Remember, I told you he comes from a good family. Probably had a good education. He sure pulled the wool over everybody's eyes, though I have to say, I did have my suspicions."

The door to her shop loomed ahead like a beacon.

Once it was reached, she turned to the sheriff and thanked him.

"May I come inside? I'd like to ask you more about this impostor."

"Could we talk some other time? I'm not feeling very well."

The sheriff studied her for a moment, then smiled. "Of course."

She hurried inside, closed the door, locked it, and leaned against it, fighting back hot tears.

Cole. His real name was Cole. Not Cabot, not Reverend Storey, but Cole Carteret, the man they called The Casket Kid. He wasn't a government agent, and he certainly wasn't a preacher! He was an outlaw, a thief, a murderer.

Cold, calculating, greedy eyes, the sheriff had described them. Yet they had never seemed so to her. She remembered them as pale as the desert, filled with love and longing, with hunger for her, and later, with laughing mischief. And all the time he had been telling her lies . . . lies . . . lies . . .

Once again she was strengthened by the slow fury that began to burn in her heart. The swine! she thought, yanking out her long hatpin and jerking her hat from her head. With a swing of her arm she sent it flying down the length of the shop.

The unconscionable, lying, treacherous rat! To pretend that he loved her, to use her, to take her precious virginity, her respectability, then walk away without a word! To make her fall in love with him and then . . .

She didn't love Cabot, or Cole, or whoever he was.

She hated him! And someday she'd show him just how much.

Stalking to the end of the room, she grabbed up her crumpled hat. "Casket Kid, indeed!" she exclaimed, then threw the hat down and crushed it under her foot.

Nineteen

"You *what?*"

Cole's head shot forward, his mouth gaping. Across from him, Floyd Barrow stared down at his feet, digging the heel of his boot into the graveled earth.

"Well, you was gone so long. We never thought you'd be gone so long."

Cole turned his head away so Floyd could not see the twitching at the corners of his lips. He struggled to make his voice stern. "By God, I leave you alone with a prisoner a few weeks and he just about takes my place. What were you thinking of?"

"We never planned it. You don't know this fellow. He had the smoothest tongue you ever heard. He could talk the warts off a frog. We all figured he was just a big sissy; but it turns out he could outshoot Scorpion, outride me, and like to beat Grady to a pulp when we matched them up in a fight."

"You let him have a gun?" Cole asked in a steely voice.

"It was a shootin' contest. A slick Easterner like that, we thought he couldn't hit the side of a barn from twenty yards. Besides, he gave us his word he wouldn't turn it on us and, by that time, we knew we could trust him."

With an exclamation of genuine disgust, Cole pulled off his hat and threw it on the ground beside his saddle. "All right, so this paragon could out-cowboy all three of you. I accept that. But *Bible* study!"

A slow flush darkened Floyd's ruddy cheeks. "That was another thing we never meant to do. It just kind of happened. Grady's grandma raised him, and she was a real Bible thumper. So once, when this preacher was spoutin' off about the Good Book, Grady thought to catch him. He asked him, if Adam and Eve were the only two people on earth, where did their sons get their wives? It didn't even make him pause for breath. He started in so slick-like, talking all about these old people and such, and the next thing you know, we was arguing near about every night. It got kind of interestin'. Funny, too. I tell you, he had the smoothest tongue I ever heard."

Cole, beginning to tire of hearing about the Reverend Cabot Storey's many accomplishments, walked over to the camp fire and crouched beside it to pour a cup of coffee from the porcelain pot bubbling on a rack. "It's a wonder he didn't take all three of you down to the San Pedro for a baptism," he said, his voice dripping sarcasm.

"I tell you, Cole, I was kind of relieved when he went off with them Apaches. They came through here looking for you; and once he knew there was an Indian camp to visit, nothing would do but he had to go."

"He probably planned to convert them, too. I'm surprised Heronimo didn't flay him alive."

"We wasn't converted," Floyd protested. "In fact, once he was gone, we went out and robbed the Bisbee stage just to prove we was still what we'd always been.

And Heronimo didn't kill him because we told him what you said—that he wasn't to be hurt."

"That may have been a mistake," Cole mumbled. Yet he knew it hadn't been. He had never yet killed a man out of pique and he wasn't about to start now.

Floyd noted with relief that Cole's barely disguised hilarity at the way the minister had taken over the camp was settling into calm resignation. He pulled a dirty deck of cards from his vest pocket and sat on the other side of the camp fire, listlessly dealing the cards in a row in front of him. He still didn't understand quite how that eastern greenhorn had worked his way into their gang. Like Grady and Scorpion, he considered himself a hard man who thought nothing of taking advantage of people to rob them—even, when it was necessary, to kill them. Somehow this tinhorn preacher had upset everything about himself that he had always taken for granted. He was profoundly glad the man was gone.

Opposite him Cole drew up his knees and rested his elbows on them, his cup dangling in his fingers. His thoughts went back to the town he had left so abruptly, without a backward look when Reily showed up to tell him he had been gone too long and if he did not get back, there would be no gang to return to. Somehow he could not get Tombstone out of his mind. He had expected to shrug it off as easily as he might a soiled shirt once he returned to the life of an outlaw. But he was finding it increasingly difficult to do so. He thought about the Reverend Cabot Storey and wondered how he was managing to pick up the pieces of the ministry Cole had left him.

As he stared at the tiny tongues of fire leaping in a

golden frenzy about the pile of mesquite, he realized with a sudden jolt why he missed the town so much. The truth was he had enjoyed the respect he had received there. He enjoyed people smiling at him when they passed him on the walkways of Allen Street, the honor they gave him simply because he represented the church, the friendly way they greeted him.

Mornin,' Reverend Storey, bankers and mine owners and store clerks would say, lifting their hats to him.

Beautiful day, ain't it, Reverend Storey.

Pastor Storey, me and Hannah would like you to come for supper some night. We never went to church much, but we got a little one now and thought we ought to start thinking about it.

Reverend Storey, my sister back in Philadelphia, sent me some of her homemade crabapple preserves. I'd be proud if you'd take some for your own use.

He liked the feeling of warmth these people had created for him with their kindness. He liked the feel of the Prayer Book in his hand as he spoke the words uniting people in marriage or a congregation in communion, even once for a burial. Even more, he liked not having to look over his shoulder every minute for some smart-ass kid trying to make his reputation as a gunfighter by out-drawing The Casket Kid. Or some sheriff trying to better his career by dragging Cole Carteret to the gibbet.

He missed all that.

Most of all, he missed Amanda.

He had a sudden vision of her lovely heart-shaped face, her glistening eyes looking at him with tenderness, with hunger, with longing. He ached to run his hands over her lithe form; to lay his palms on her cheeks and draw her lips, soft as down, to his own; to slide his hands up her waist and cup her full, rounded breasts. A rush of desire filled his body and he turned to throw himself lengthwise on his stomach. He ached for her with a strength that astounded him. How had she become so dear to him? She was just another woman, after all.

Yet he knew that wasn't true. There had never before been any woman he couldn't walk away from. The thought of never seeing Amanda again, of never holding her in his arms, of never again seeing her laugh up at him, or never pressing the length of her soft body against his—the thought was intolerable!

He had to find a way to speak to her once more, to explain to her why he was forced to leave so suddenly. Of course, it was possible she might be so angry with him and so hurt by his sudden departure, she might not want to see him. But he felt sure he could overcome that once he had her back in his arms. The real question was how?

Sally.

Cousin Sally and the Bar M.

He rolled over on his back, resting his head on the curve of his saddle and staring up at the stars that crusted the black night like glistening sands on a shore. It might work. It had to work.

He would ride over there tomorrow.

Cole picked his way through the Dragoon Mountains, then swung west across the San Pedro River, avoiding the main stage routes and the Southern Pacific railroad lines into Tucson. Because he thought it best to approach the Bar M Ranch from the west, he had a lot of range land to cross and he did not want to be seen by the ranchhands and cowboys. As he had planned, he arrived near dusk. He secreted himself in the deep shadows at the back of the barn, and waited for Sally to ride in.

He hadn't seen Sally or her father Hiram for over a year; and, in truth, he hadn't thought much about them during that time. But now they were probably his best means for accomplishing his goal—if he could talk them into it.

He didn't have long to wait before Sally rode in. She swung off her lathered mount and began doing her own tack work, as he knew she would. He watched her from the shadows, his eyes playing over her slim, taut body as she pulled off the saddle and blanket and began to brush down her horse. As always, she was dressed in men's clothes—he couldn't remember the last time he had seen her in a dress. The only child of Hiram Mahone, she had taken it upon herself at an early age to be more of a son to him than a daughter. By now, with Hiram growing old, Cole supposed the running of this large ranch with its three thousand head of cattle fell mostly on her slim shoulders.

In spite of her tanned skin, she had a woman's body with a woman's curves—tight, rounded buttocks, long coltish legs, and full breasts that filled out her checkered shirt to perfection. She had braided her hair in one long rope that swayed gently as she worked over her mount, humming to herself. Cole made certain she wasn't wearing a gun before he stepped from the shadows.

She swerved, her hand automatically going to her hip.

"Don't shoot. It's just me, your Cousin Cole," he commented dryly, smiling at her.

"Cole Carteret! You mangy bastard! What do you mean sneaking up on me like that?" Her shoulders slumped with relief as she angrily threw her brush hard against his chest. He laughed as he bent to pick it up and casually lobbed it back to her.

"I wanted to see you private-like, and I knew if I went to the house that would never happen."

"You might at least have warned me. If I'd been wearing a gun . . ."

"I made sure you weren't."

Sally pulled her mount into the stall and piled the manger full of hay. After giving the horse an affectionate slap on the rump, she closed the stall door and turned back to Cole. Leaning one hip on an upturned barrel, she folded her arms across her chest and looked at her cousin with an expression both quizzical and pleased.

"Well, Cousin, once I'm over the shock, I have to say you look pretty good."

"Well, you don't. You look more like an old weather-beaten ranchhand than ever. Do you even own a dress, Sally?"

"Pshaw. I can see me running this ranch in a dress. Those hard-nosed cowhands wouldn't pay a bit of attention to a thing I said."

"Maybe so. But you're never going to get married

looking like that." Cole pulled a straw from the pile and chewed on one end.

"That's all you know. If you came around here more often, you'd know I got me a beau. Andrew Leslie. He's got a big ranch down near Contention."

"Humph. One of those Leslies. I'd watch out for him. That's bad blood." He moved closer and lowered his voice. "Listen, I better say what I came for and get going before the rest of the hands come in."

Sally glanced toward the empty yard beyond the open barn doors. "I guess you'd better. How've you been? I been hearing bad things about you."

"Sally, you ought to know by now a man's reputation and the truth are two totally different things. Besides, I had nothing to do with killing that passenger on the Cortez stage. I fired into the air. It was Scorpion who fired at the stage."

"That hasn't stopped them from putting your picture on the wanted posters. Why don't you explain the truth to the law?"

"Because once they had me, I doubt they'd wait long enough to listen. But I didn't come here to talk about my past. I want you to do something for me, Sally. Something important."

Sally frowned at him. "I should have known. We never see you until you want something from us."

"But this really is important."

"It always is. Just because your pa and my ma were related don't mean I have to come running every time you crook your finger. Seems to me you gave up all claim to kinship long ago."

"Now, Sally, don't read me a sermon. I came here in good faith."

They both knew she didn't mean a word of her protests. She smiled up at him, her face becoming soft and feminine as it relaxed. "Oh, all right. I was always a sucker for those sandy eyes and all that charm."

"Do you know a girl in Tombstone named Amanda Lassiter?"

"I've met her once or twice. She's trying to keep that drug store going that her uncle opened."

"That's right. I want you to invite her here for a vacation like. Get her out of town. Give her a change of scenery."

"But, Cole, I don't know if she'd come. I hardly know her."

"Then get to know her better. You'll like her. She's a lot like you—honest, direct, straightforward. And she's never seen a real ranch before. Make an effort, for me."

Sally's eyes narrowed. "And what's behind this sudden invitation? You planning to rob her blind?"

"No, no. Nothing like that."

Suddenly her eyes widened and she stared at him open-mouthed. "Why, Cole Carteret, don't tell me you went and lost your heart to her." Her delighted giggling quickly gave way to full-fledged laughter.

Cole glared at her. "Never mind my reasons. Just do it."

"I never thought I'd see it—and a respectable woman, too. Why, I figured if you ever got married, it would be because one of those dance hall girls trapped you into it."

"Who's talking about marriage? Now stop laughing and be serious. How long do you think it would take?"

"I don't know. About a month?"

"That's too long. Two weeks."

"But, Cole, I've got to get to know her."

"All right. Three weeks, then. I'm counting on you, Sally. It'll be worth your time. Amanda would be a good friend to you."

Muffled sounds of horses riding into the yard drew their eyes to the open doors. Sally quickly grabbed Cole's arm and pushed him toward the back of the barn where a single small door led onto a corral. They hurried across it and into the shadows of a small shed leaning against the fence.

"I don't know why I should do this, but all right. I guess you don't ask much of us."

Cole settled his hat on his head, creasing the brim with his long fingers. "Give my regards to Hiram. I'll see you in three weeks." Bending down, he kissed her on the lips. "You and your pa are my only kin, Sally. For a cousin, you're a good sport."

Sally gave an embarrassed laugh. "Take care of yourself."

She was still smiling as she watched him easily clear the fence and head for a cluster of sycamores on the other side of the house.

After leaving the San Pedro, Cole leisurely worked his way southward toward Mexico and the Sierra Madre mountain hideout sheltering Heronimo and his band. Though he had no idea exactly where the Apaches were holed up, he was not worried. They would find him long before he found them.

Once across the border, he could almost feel their eyes watching as he picked his way along the barren flats toward higher ground. He met few Mexicans. The farming was so poor that few peasants bothered to try. As for the Mexican Army, they had encountered Heronimo's hatred too many times in the past to venture into these mountains with anything less than an overwhelming force.

Once he entered the mountains, the desolate desert gave way to such incomparable beauty that more than once Cole halted his horse to admire it. Gamma grass, swaying gently in the soft breeze, covered the low hills. As he climbed higher, scattered oaks and junipers melted into forests of ponderosa pines. Cottonwoods lined the blue thread of the Bavispe River, flanked by canyons and labyrinths of hidden cliffs, gleaming ruddy in the sun.

Admiring the scenery, however, was only one reason he frequently paused. The other was to allow those hidden eyes to assess who he was and that he came peacefully. He was relieved when finally his path was blocked by two ragged Apaches cradling rifles in their arms and watching him with black, impassive eyes.

Cole recognized Little Vitorio at once. He made the requisite hails, then allowed them to take the reins of his horse and lead him the rest of the way into Heronimo's camp. They climbed higher in such a convoluted series of trails, he knew he would never have found it on his own.

Heronimo's band was larger than he'd expected, considering the way they had been hounded by the United States Army these last two years; and the collection of brush wickiups that made up their camp appeared more permanent. The old war chief greeted him warmly, though only Cole could tell that the slight softening of the Indian's sharp features meant that. After a lifetime of treachery and tragedy in dealing with Mexicans and Americans, Heronimo trusted few white eyes. Cole felt honored to be one of them. He sat cross-legged on the ground with the famous fighter across from him. Beside Heronimo sat the Chiricahua chief, Naiche; and next to Naiche sat the brilliant Apache military strategist, Jhu. To Heronimo's right sat the young warrior, Little Vitorio, who was always the one sent to contact Cole. Cole politely drank the strong beer, *tiswin,* which the Apaches brewed and loved, and waited patiently for Heronimo to reveal why he had called him all this way.

"May Goyahkla live long," he said, addressing Heronimo by his Apache name. The down-turned slash forming the Indian's grim mouth lifted slightly at the edges.

"Not if General Crook has his way," he replied in his native tongue. Cole knew enough Apache to get the gist, if not the nuances.

Cole sipped at the strong beer and looked around at the well-secluded camp. "The spirits of the mountains have been kind to Goyahkla."

The old Chiricahua nodded solemnly. "The spirits protect us from our enemies. But *Ussen* has spoken in a vision to Jhu. In this vision, a thin cloud of blue smoke became a long line of General Crook's soldiers. He will drive us out eventually."

Though Cole wished he could deny the truth of Jhu's

vision, he knew he could not. General Crook was a wise and practical man with unlimited resources of men and arms. One day he would get enough of this ragged band of fugitives and would round them up and bring them back to the San Carlos Reservation. Heronimo had to be over fifty—an ancient age for an Indian. He couldn't hold out in these mountains forever.

Cole glanced over to see Naiche glaring at him, his prominent cheekbones glistening in the fading light. Though Naiche was the son of the famous Cochise, his reputation was insignificant compared to that of his heroic war chief, Heronimo. Clearly Naiche wasn't happy that Goyahkla had brought this white eyes into their secret camp.

"We have been friends for a long time," Cole said to Heronimo to remind the rest of them that he was under the medicine man's protection. "If there is anything I can do for you, you have only to ask."

"I did not call you here for me," Goyahkla muttered, "but for my people. There are men raiding into Mexico, stealing horses and cattle. They take them back and sell them to the army for big prices. Often we are blamed."

Cole nodded. "I know of this."

"These men make great trouble for the Chiricahua. Trouble we do not need. We want to be left in peace."

Cole kept silent, waiting for the details.

"There is a large ranch, two days ride into the dawn from Fort Huachuca."

"That would be the Clantons."

"And another, one day to the north and west."

"Frank Leslie's place."

"And one north from there by one day's ride."

For a moment Cole wondered if Heronimo was referring to the Bar M. But that was unlikely. He probably meant Asa Bradley's Setting Sun Ranch. Asa was thick with the Clantons. Put the whole bunch together and they would be worth about one bullet.

"What do you want me to do?"

"Speak to General Crook. Tell him the Chiricahuas do not steal these horses and cattle."

Cole almost laughed, but he caught himself in time. "Surely Goyahkla knows if I tried to see General Crook, I would be arrested and jailed, possibly even hanged. I could not be of any help to you that way."

Out of the corner of his eye he saw Naiche and Jhu lean their heads together, nodding gravely. His answer was about what they had expected.

Heronimo's sharp features became a frozen mask. He rattled off a long string of Apache, of which Cole only understood enough to realize that his answer had been most upsetting. He waited until the old warrior finished, then sat forward, speaking earnestly.

"For long years I have been honored to call Goyahkla my friend," he said, choosing his words carefully, "as my father did before me. While I cannot speak to General Crook, I can promise you I will do all I can to show these men for the mean-spirited thieves they are."

"What other way is there, save by General Crook?"

"Oh, there are other ways. General Crook is not the only white eyes with power to stop this kind of thievery."

Heronimo glanced at Naiche and Jhu. "Perhaps not. But he is the one that matters."

Cole was relieved when the old Indian reached out to hand him more of the *tiswin,* indicating that the

Apache's irritation was forgotten, at least for the moment. He drank deeply of the appalling brew so beloved by the Apaches and wondered how soon he could get away. Of course he would have to spend the night, but that didn't bother him. Heronimo and his band would never betray the hospitality they had offered in bringing him here. However, what the old warrior really wanted was for Cole to get General Crook off their backs, and that was something completely beyond his power to accomplish. He wished he could be honest enough to say so.

Heronimo spoke gruffly. "My friend Cole took his time coming to see Goyahkla."

So the irritation was not completely gone. "When Little Vitorio came to summon me to you, I was busy with other matters. Once they were completed, I journeyed at once to the mountains."

Immediately the four Indians exchanged amused glances. He felt as though they could see right through him, yet surely they could not know about that crazy masquerade he took on when he went to Tombstone.

"Oh, yes," Heronimo said with a low, raspy chuckle. "The white eyes, Cabot."

Naiche's shoulders began silently heaving. *"Loco, loco,"* he muttered, pumping Jhu's arm. Cole watched in amazement as Naiche, Jhu, and Little Vitorio broke into spasms of quiet laughter.

"You found Cabot amusing?"

Heronimo actually smiled. "Yes. Most amusing. I never saw a man so eager to know so much."

"But *loco?* You thought him crazy?"

"Goyahkla did not," Little Vitorio answered, holding

a hand in front of his mouth to hide his smile. "All the rest."

Cole turned to Heronimo. "And what did you call him?"

The old medicine man's obsidian eyes, hard as ebony, took on an almost dreamy aspect. "I call him *Mangos Wassun*. He Whom the Spirits Touch."

Cole wondered at this and would have wondered more except his mind was beginning to be affected by the strong beer. They were all staggering drunk by the time they broke up. Cole managed to keep his head only because he had pretended to drink more than he actually had. He politely declined the use of one of the women to warm his bed and climbed into the warm skins, eager for dawn. In spite of his rational belief that the Indians would not go against the laws of hospitality, he still ended up waking at every little creak outside the brush hut. Not that he didn't trust Heronimo, but all the stories he had ever heard of finely skilled Apache torture crowded his memory. Near dawn, he finally fell into an exhausted sleep and had to be shaken awake by Little Vitorio only a short time later.

They left the camp without seeing Heronimo or Naiche, Little Vitorio leading him back along the convoluted path out of the mountains until they reached a place where he could ride on alone. He left word with the Indian to renew his promise made to Heronimo the night before.

It was a long trek back, and he had plenty of time to think about all the great Apache had told him. This scheme of stealing cattle, then selling it to the army was just one part of the whole rotten mess emanating out of Tombstone. Robber gangs, stock frauds, thefts of silver and payroll that found their way back into the pockets of bankers and managers—it was all part of a puzzle in which the pieces were beginning to fall into place. Soon now he would put a crimp in the whole operation.

But not yet.

He thought of Amanda. There was something more important he had to do first.

Twenty

Amanda was kneeling on the floor behind the counter sorting through a box of patent medicines when she heard the jangling of the bell at the front of her shop. Gripping the counter, she raised up enough to recognize the woman coming through the door, her feathered hat bobbing as she turned to close it. Since it had been a slow morning, Amanda was glad to see a customer. She rose to her feet and smoothed down her hair, smiling at Tilly Lacey.

One look at Tilly's tight, hard face and Amanda sensed she was not a customer.

"Miss Lassiter."

"Mrs. Lacey. What can I help you with today?"

Tilly closed her hands together at her waist and stared at Amanda through half-closed eyes, as if appraising her for the first time. "I don't want anything, thank you. I just came to bring you a bit of news."

Amanda wondered at the hostility in her tone and manner but, searching her memory, could think of no reason for it. Though she seldom spoke to Mrs. Lacey, they had been polite enough to each other since arriving in Tombstone on the same stage. On the day of the shooting contest, she had been positively friendly.

"Oh. Well, would you like to sit a moment?" she asked, indicating the chairs at the rear of the store.

"No, thank you. I won't keep you from your work. I wanted to tell you about Nora."

"I heard that you had taken her to Tucson to the hospital there. That was kind of you, Mrs. Lacey. Not many people wanted to help her."

"I know. That wretched Gert at the Bird Cage threw her out on the street—lock, stock, and barrel. It is to your credit you allowed her to stay here."

Amanda looked down in embarrassment. "It was only for a day or two until Mrs. Lockwood at St. Anselm's allowed her the use of a back room. I assumed she was still there until they told me you took her into Tucson."

"Yes. Well, I have known quite a few 'Noras' in my life. Her condition was not entirely her fault. She was very ill and belonged under a doctor's care."

"I hope she is doing better at the hospital."

Tilly's lips pursed in a tight line. "She did recover a bit once she began getting proper care. But a week ago she began to lose ground, and last Friday, she died. That's what I came to tell you."

Amanda caught her breath. "Oh, dear, I'm so sorry." She turned away, staring at the front of the shop but seeing Nora's gaunt, pale face and huge, empty eyes. What a waste! The poor creature. It crossed her mind that perhaps the poor girl was better off, but she refused to make such a simpering statement to Tilly Lacey, who, out of all the women in Tombstone, had done the most to help her. When she turned back, it was to see Tilly studying her intently.

"Thank you for telling me," she said, wondering why

Tilly didn't leave. "And thank you for helping her. She didn't have many friends."

"She was a whore. She was used up by men and by greedy women, then discarded like yesterday's trash. They never saw the young, sick girl she really was. I think maybe you did."

"And you, also."

For the first time, Tilly looked away. "Yeah. Well, maybe we have that much in common." She turned angrily back to Amanda. "There's something else we have in common. We were both taken in by that lying preacher."

Amanda felt a flush creep up her neck. "I'd rather not be reminded of that," she said in a tight voice. "I'm not very proud of it."

"You were close to that devil in a frock coat," Tilly said, ignoring Amanda's embarrassment. "Surely he must have confessed who he really was to you, if to nobody else."

"No, he did not."

"You mean to say you never asked him? You never wondered why he was so different from what a preacher ought to be?"

"That's right," Amanda answered, biting her lip. Of course she had, but that was none of Mrs. Lacey's business and she'd be damned if she'd say so. "I never knew any preachers to compare him with."

"And he doesn't try to see you now?"

"He'd better not!"

Tilly studied her a moment, then shrugged and started for the door.

"Mrs. Lacey," Amanda called as Tilly laid her hand on the knob. "Do you have any idea of his true identity?"

Tilly gave her a thin smile. "Why, Miss Lassiter, if you don't know, how in tarnation would you expect *me* to?"

The door barely closed behind Tilly before Amanda turned and slammed her hand down on the counter. She wished the woman had never come in. It was bad enough hearing Nora had died, without all the anger, shame, embarrassment, and bitterness mixed up with Cabot Storey surfacing again. The false Cabot Storey, that is. She still had to call him that, for she refused to believe Sheriff Behan's absurd statement that Cabot Storey was actually the outlaw Cole Carteret.

"Stop thinking about it!" she said emphatically to herself. It was a command that had worked so far, every time her emotions threatened to get the better of her, and it worked now. She forced down all her fury and regrets and went back to sorting through female remedies, stomach bitters, and childhood balms, letting her mind focus on more pleasant things.

Like the trip she was going to take tomorrow.

She was still amazed at how quickly it had come about. Amazing how Sally Mahone, a girl she had only met once or twice, should appear in her shop one day and strike up a conversation that grew so beguiling they continued it over lunch together at the Maison Dorée Café. Amanda had not realized how much she had missed the company of a congenial young woman friend. She and Sally found they had much in common. They had both lost their mothers early in life and had both grown up close to strong, dominating fathers. They both wanted more from life than to be just a housewife, and both now had some experience with a career. And the more they talked, the more they found they both were drawn to the same kind of men—strong, dangerous, anything but average.

Sally's invitation to visit the Bar M Ranch had grown easily out of their budding friendship, and Amanda had jumped at it, always supposing she could find someone to run the store for her. She had never seen a real working ranch and she was as curious about it as she was eager to get away from Tombstone, where everything reminded her of Cabot and the humiliation he had caused. When Doc Goodfellow ordered her to take a few days vacation and promised her he would see the store was kept running, she gladly agreed to go.

Now her portmanteau was packed, and tomorrow Sally would ride in to town to take her back in the Mahone buggy. She could hardly wait.

Soon she was humming to herself as she worked, all thoughts of Cabot Storey pushed resolutely from her mind.

Amanda was ready and waiting an hour before Sally arrived at the hotel to pick her up. Though it was still early morning, the day promised to be hot, and she was glad they would be riding in a buggy rather than astride a horse.

Sally Mahone greeted her warmly, then motioned for one of her ranchhands to throw Amanda's small bag in the back of the carriage. Behind the covered chaise in which the women would ride, Amanda saw a second weathered cowhand fussing with the harness on a bay horse standing quietly between the slats of a buckboard wagon.

"Zeke and Ed are riding shotgun for us," Sally commented dryly as she climbed up on to the buggy seat. Zeke moved quickly to help Amanda climb up beside her.

"I'm relieved to hear it," Amanda said, settling back. When she saw Sally was attired in men's working clothes she was glad she wore her riding skirt instead of the calico dress she had originally planned. That was now packed inside her bag alongside two others, one of them fancy enough for more formal occasions at the ranch, in case the need arose.

Sally picked up the reins and slapped them across the back of the roan horse. "I told Papa I can take care of myself, but nothing would do but they had to come. However, since they've still got to collect some bags of feed from the lot, we'll be riding on ahead of them."

Amanda wondered if that were wise, but since Sally obviously felt strongly about taking care of herself, she made no comment. Once they passed Boot Hill and began to leave the town behind, she forgot all other concerns except sheer relief to be getting out of Tombstone. For the first time in weeks, she looked forward to seeing new places and meeting new people. Regrets, recriminations, and her sore heart were forgotten as the road lengthened behind her. This trip marked the beginning of a new time in her life, the turning over of an old page to a fresh one. She was determined to enjoy it.

Her lightened mood was enhanced by the beauty of the world around her. A clear, azure sky beamed over a desert still scattered with the remains of a few colorful wildflowers. The summer heat that would frazzle the landscape later in the afternoon had not yet wilted the fresh newness of the morning. As they rode north toward the San Pedro River, they began to see more trees and the lush, green growth water encouraged. Dry arroyos gave way to rolling hills covered with grass. She had almost forgotten this kind of scenery, so accustomed had she become to the dull desert landscapes.

Their ride was punctuated with spells of chatter followed by long comfortable silences. Sally assured her she would enjoy getting to know Hiram Mahone, who was one of the earliest pioneers in the area and could spin tales of the territory when it was the province of Indians and wildlife. She described the Bar M in great detail—how the open range was giving way to the newfangled, barbed-wire fences separating neighbor from neighbor, how the threat of cattle rustling and horse thievery cut into the profits of a working ranch, of the need for a strong law enforcement that would curtail the harm outlaws and thugs caused to hard-working honest men.

"I don't think I've ever met anyone quite like you, Sally," Amanda finally commented. "You talk more like a rancher than a young girl; and you know as much about men's work, I would guess, as anyone on the Bar M. You even dress in men's clothes. I've never known a woman who could get away with all that."

Sally seemed pleased by her comment. "It's this country, I suppose. It's not an easy place to live in, and it forces people to grow and change in order to tame it. Also, I've got an indulgent papa who allows me to go my own way, bless him. I'm his only child, and he wants to be sure when he goes that the ranch will carry on. So do I, if it comes to that."

Amanda thought of her own long-ago wish to be a doctor like her father. It was an ambition Robert Lassiter could never quite countenance, even though he trained her to be proficient in many of the required abilities. Ultimately, he wanted her to be a wife and mother, as her own mother had been. How different her life might have been if only Robert Lassiter had been more like Hiram Mahone!

When Sally pulled the buggy up beneath a cluster of cottonwoods to allow the horse a brief rest, Amanda got out to stretch her legs.

"I still don't see the men with the wagon," she said, peering down the empty road.

"Oh, they're back there all right. If we wait long enough, they'll catch up with us, but I'd rather push on. I'd like to get home in time to ride out and check on some new calves that were dropped last spring." Sally looked up at Amanda from the edge of the creek where she was splashing her arms with the cool water. "You're not worried, are you?"

Amanda laughed. "If you're not afraid, Sally, then I'm certainly not."

"Good. We don't often have any trouble on this road."

Amanda lifted her face to the sun, closing her eyes and enjoying the feeling of serenity and ease washing over her. How good it was to be out of Tombstone with all its terrible memories! How nice to be going to visit a new place in the company of a congenial friend. Even if she did have to return to the same old problems in a few days, this welcome respite surely must help her to forget the past and concentrate on rebuilding her future.

A few moments later, they were back in the buggy and heading northwest, away from the river and toward the hills. For several miles they rode in companionable silence while Amanda watched the rising ground and rocky outcroppings they passed. She was so deep in her thoughts it startled her when Sally spoke.

"Over that ridge is Canisteo," Sally said, pointing. "Once past there, it's only about half-an-hour till we reach the first limits of the Bar M."

The words were barely out of her mouth when her horse shied, half-rearing in its traces as a rider spurred out from between two large boulders to block their path.

"What the devil . . ." Sally cried, yanking on the reins, trying to hold her horse. As the buggy swayed wildly, Amanda grabbed hold of the seat to keep from being thrown forward.

The buggy grew still as both women stared at the rider who turned his horse in a small circle in their path. Their dismay gave way to fear as they realized he wore a kerchief over the bottom half of his face. His black hat was pulled down over his forehead, allowing only a glimpse of dark eyes. The bright sun glinted silver on the long barrel of a pistol he pointed straight at them.

"I'm not carrying any money," Sally started to say, but he cut her short.

"Get down."

Sally's hand edged down to the seat where, behind it, Amanda remembered seeing a rifle.

"No," Amanda whispered. "Don't fight him. Do what

he says and maybe he'll just take the buggy and let us go."

Sally's tight lips pursed in frustration, but she removed her hand. Both women started to climb down out of the buggy.

"Just the driver," the man snapped in a low, growling voice.

Amanda felt the blood leave her face. "But . . ."

"Now!"

Sally climbed down to the ground where the man motioned her over to one side. Waiting for an explanation, she watched in amazement as he jumped down from his horse and fastened it to the back of the rig, all the while keeping his pistol pointed squarely at her chest. Then, in a smooth, fluid motion, he jumped up to take her place on the seat and grabbed up the reins.

"You can't leave her here alone!" Amanda cried. She still could make no sense of this. Everything was happening so fast.

"Someone will be along. Yehaw . . ." he called, slapping the reins on the roan's back. The horse tried to rear, then took off at a run. Amanda grabbed wildly for a handhold.

"What are you . . . Sally! Help!"

But there was nothing Sally could do. As she watched the buggy wildly gyrating down the road, she saw a dark object come flying from it to land just a few feet away. Recognizing her rifle, she ran and grabbed it up, cocked it quickly, and fired at the disappearing rig. Since it had already dodged behind the scattered boulders, her shots did no good whatsoever. Still, she continued firing until she realized she had better save a few bullets in case she ran into any more trouble while waiting for the buckboard to pick her up.

"Of all the crazy, nitwitted, gol-blasted stunts to pull, this takes the cake!" she muttered furiously as she sat down in the shade of a huge boulder to wait for her men.

Amanda was so busy trying to keep her balance on the bouncing seat, she didn't think at all. The buggy continued its jarring journey until the horse grew winded. When the driver finally pulled up, allowing the horse to stop, its lathered sides heaving, her fear finally soared to the surface. The driver jumped down to see to his tethered horse behind and Amanda looked wildly around, wondering if she could get away. All she could see were rolling hills and bare ground. There were no trees, no large boulders, no places to hide. If she tried to run, he could come after her on his horse. She had no weapon, no idea where she was, and no way to escape.

"Sorry you had such a rough trip," Cole said from the rear of the buggy. "I couldn't think of any other way to get you here."

She recognized his voice at once. He stepped up to her, pulling the kerchief away and smiling while she stared open-mouthed.

"You? It was you?"

"Of course. Who would want to rob two women in a buggy who obviously weren't carrying anything of value? I thought you might recognize me right off. I'm sure Sally did."

Amanda struggled to get her breath as her choking fear gave way to a hot mix of fury, shame, and embarrassment.

"You know Sally?" she said through clenched teeth.

Cole hopped up on the seat. "She's my cousin."

"You mean, the two of you . . . you planned . . . you got me out here on purpose?"

"Well, not exactly," Cole said, picking up the reins. "Sally didn't know I was going to carry you off."

In a sudden motion, Amanda grabbed the side of the buggy and propelled herself off the seat. She half-stumbled to the ground, her skirt catching on the side until she yanked it free. Then she set off at a run, not knowing or caring in which direction.

It all happened so quickly, Cole was caught off guard. He jumped down and started after her with long strides that caught up with her after only a few yards. Grabbing her around the waist, he tried to pull her back but was so pummeled by her fists that he nearly lost his grip. Amanda fought with all her strength against him, nearly breaking free before they both went tumbling to the ground.

"You . . . you bastard!" she cried, half-choking with the dust and struggling against his tight grip.

Cole pulled her arms around and pinned her against him. "For God's sake, calm down. I'm not going to hurt you."

"No, you're not," Amanda exclaimed hotly, "because I'm going to kill you first!"

Lifting her off the ground, Cole half-carried, half-dragged her back to the buggy and threw her up on the seat. She tried to climb off the other side, but he caught her wrist in a viselike grip, then climbed over her to grab the reins.

"I certainly didn't expect you to act like this," he

muttered as he lifted the reins. The buggy swayed and bounced while the roan horse, unable to understand any familiar signals, danced in its traces. "You might as well calm down because we've got a long way to go."

"Never!" Amanda cried, pounding his arm with her fists.

He gripped both her wrists. "Behave yourself, Amanda. Look around you. There's no place you can run to and no one to help. You have to come with me."

"Never!" she cried, trying to climb out of the buggy as the confused horse started forward. His arm went around her waist and he yanked her back.

"Godammit! Either you sit still or I'll tie you to the seat!"

"Then that's what you'll have to do." Bending swiftly she sank her teeth into his arm. With a yowl of pain, he relaxed his grip and she threw herself forward, half-out of the buggy.

"You're going to kill yourself, you crazy woman," Cole cried, pulling her back. Yanking on the reins he brought the horse under control. Then, in a swift motion he unfastened his leather belt and tugged it free. Forcing her backward on the seat, he fastened her hands together.

Though she struggled against him, he was too strong for her. "How appropriate for an outlaw!" she gasped, her chest heaving with her exertions. "Tying up a helpless woman."

"You don't give me any choice," Cole mumbled. "Now sit quietly until we get where we're going."

"And where is that? Some hideout in the mountains, I suppose. Or maybe a church!"

He glared at her without answering and slapped the reins on the horse's rump. They rolled off at a sedate pace while Amanda leaned her head against the side bow of the buggy, struggling to get her breath and resigning herself to the situation. There was nothing she could do now; but surely, when they stopped, she would find a way out. And, if this lying, deceiving, wretch to whom she had given her love and her body, who had casually thrown them away and then callously abducted her, were thoughtless enough to allow her near a gun, she promised herself she would use it on him first.

They rode most of the afternoon, stopping only for brief rests at springs filled with a trickle of rusty-colored water. By the time the day had droned on toward evening, she had grown too tired to fight him or even to care where they were going. Cole had loosened her bonds once he saw her spirits flagging, but he hadn't trusted her enough to remove them and her wrists were chafed by the leather belt. Her bottom ached from the hard seat, and every muscle in her body protested the long confinement. The thought of making camp on the hard, cold, rocky ground only added to her misery.

"Well, there it is at last," Cole said, pulling up.

Amanda peered through the gathering darkness across an expanse of bare plain to a low hill in the distance. Along the ridge lay the dark, rambling shape of a Spanish-style house amid a cluster of outbuildings and a few scattered trees.

He turned to her, unsmiling. "You'll feel better once you've had a night's rest."

She glared at him, pursing her lips and refusing to answer. In truth she felt relieved to know they would not be camping outside, but she wasn't about to let him know it.

Twenty-one

The house surprised her. By the time they rode into the yard, there was just enough light for Amanda to make out its spacious design. It was larger than it looked at first glance, with a two-story section in the center flanked by single-story wings on each side. The center portion had a long balcony running the length of the upper floor, with doors opening onto it. Lamplight from one of the upper rooms spilled out onto the balcony.

Amanda scorned Cole's helping hand and climbed out of the buggy by herself—no easy task since her hands were still fastened with his hated belt. She glanced around wondering if she might try to run, but the yard was too open and she was too weary to even contemplate it. As she turned back to the house, she saw a woman emerge from the front door carrying a lighted lamp. The woman was plump, with the dark skin and Indian features of a Mexican peasant. Her black hair hung down her back in two long braids.

"*Buenos días,* Señor Cole, she said in a thick Spanish accent.

"*Buenas noches,* Conchita," Cole answered. "This is our guest, Miss Lassiter. Is the room ready?"

"Like you say, Señor. It has been a long time . . ."

Amanda looked up in surprise when Cole answered the woman with a long string of Spanish, none of which meant anything to her. Conchita gave him a few curt phrases back, also in Spanish. Then Cole turned to Amanda and took her arm firmly in his grasp.

"Come on. I'll see you inside."

Amanda yanked her arm away. "So I'm a guest, am I? Dragged here with my hands bound. You have a strange sense of hospitality."

"Now, Amanda, if I hadn't done all that, would you have come with me? I'm sorry it had to be this way, but you're here now. Why not relax and enjoy it?"

He reached to untie the belt, freeing her wrists. Then, taking her elbow, he propelled her onto the veranda and through the open door. Once inside, Amanda rubbed at her chafed wrists, trying to mask her surprise at the loveliness of the room. It was a hall opening along one side onto an atrium filled with plants surrounding a small fountain. The walls were lined with colorful tiles arranged in geometric patterns. Lamps in brass fixtures along the wall made it bright and inviting, while the growing moonlight spilling through the open ceiling of the atrium bronzed the water flowing from the fountain into the center of a pool.

She was impressed, but she only allowed herself a moment of admiration before recalling how affronted and furious she was with the man standing behind her.

"Shall I take the señorita to her room?" Conchita asked.

Cole kept his iron grip on her elbow. "I'll show her

where it is. Why don't you lay out supper? I'm famished, and I'm sure the señorita is also."

"I don't want anything to eat," Amanda snapped. "And I have no intention of sitting at the same table with you."

"Come now," he answered genially, pushing her toward a stairway. "You must be hungry. Conchita is a good cook, and the house has some fine wines in stock."

She was famished, but she wasn't about to admit it. Shrinking as far from him as possible, she made her way up the stairs. "They're probably poisoned, and I'm not hungry."

Cole chuckled. "Now why would I bring you all this way just to poison you? Come on, Amanda, let's call a truce. I told you I was sorry."

Amanda caught herself grinding her teeth in frustration as he pushed her toward an upstairs door. Opening it, he stood aside while she walked stiffly by him to find herself in the brightly lit room she had noticed outside. It wasn't large, but it was neat and comfortable. The bed was covered with a colorful quilt in an Indian pattern. Opposite it, two French doors stood open, revealing the balcony beyond.

"See," Cole said, motioning toward the open doors. "Hardly a prison. And all the comforts of home. It's a pleasant house. Why not enjoy it? Freshen up, then come down and we'll have a good dinner."

She stalked across the room before turning back to him. "Followed by what?"

He had the grace to look uncomfortable. "Why don't we just see? I have never forced myself on you."

"What other reason did you have for kidnapping me and dragging me here? Why not rape? It would fit the rest of the pattern beautifully."

Cole felt a hot flush on his cheeks. "Now that's not fair."

But Amanda was just warming up. "Oh, isn't it? This house. . . . Where did you get it? Steal it, by any chance? Win it cheating at the faro table? Or perhaps you just murdered the owner."

"He's in a dungeon beneath the atrium," Cole said sarcastically.

"It wouldn't surprise me. It's just the kind of thing an outlaw would do. Or maybe a lying preacher, or even a government agent!"

"You might at least let me explain."

"Explain what? How you took advantage of me, lied over and over, pretended to be someone you never were?" She could hear her voice becoming shrill, but she couldn't stop. All her bitter fury poured out.

"Now, Amanda." He moved across the room trying to get near her, certain if he could just take her in his arms all would be made right. She darted the other way, keeping the distance of the room between them.

"Don't you come near me!" she exclaimed. "Don't you ever touch me again! Stay away from me."

"You're being ridiculous, Amanda. I can explain everything if you'd just stop screaming long enough to let me get a word in edgewise."

"I haven't even started screaming yet!" she yelled even louder.

"For God's sake, you'll have Conchita running in here thinking I'm murdering you."

"Let her come," Amanda screamed. "Ow . . . w . . . w!" She gave a banshee wail. "If I thought there was anyone outside, I'd scream from the balcony. Ow . . . w . . . w . . ."

"Godamnit! STOP THAT!"

Running across the room, Cole tried to grab her, but she was too quick for him. She darted away, still screaming at the top of her voice. Looking wildly around, she grabbed a large pottery pitcher from the washstand and threw it across the room, straight at him. He ducked, and it shattered against the wall, scattering fragments.

"Damn it, Amanda . . ." he yelled, running and ducking as a bowl came soaring across the room followed by a brush and a bottle of toilet water."What's the matter with you . . . ? NOT THE CHAIR!" he cried as she raised one of two latticed chairs flanking a dresser.

He made a wild dash for the hall door and yanked it open, turning back to her with his hand on the knob. His face was twisted with anger and his eyes blazed.

"Go ahead and act like a crazy woman if you want, but it won't do you any good. You're here now and you'll do just what I say."

"Get out!" Amanda yelled, lifting the chair in her two hands.

"Godammit, you'll straighten yourself up and come down to supper if I have to drag you every step of the way!"

"GET OUT!"

Cole just managed to pull the door closed before the chair crashed against the other side. He stood in the hall a moment, shaking his fist at the door before stalking off to one of the other rooms.

Amanda heard his retreating footsteps. She stood, her chest heaving, listening until all was silent, then made her way over to the bed and sank onto it, spreading her arms out and waiting for her pounding heart to ease. She felt as weary as ever in her life, but strangely exhilarated as well.

It was good to get all that anger off her chest, to let the venom she felt toward Cole-Cabot-preacher-government agent-Storey-Carteret come pouring out. She only wished she had managed to hit him with the pottery. It was no more than he deserved.

A common outlaw! He had tricked her with smooth words and gestures of love, and all the time he had been nothing but a robber and a thief. Her cheeks flamed with the shame of it. She would never forgive herself for believing him, for swallowing his lies. Trying to convince the world he was decent, when all the time . . .

Amanda rolled over on her side, fighting back the hot tears which the catharsis of her outburst threatened to unleash. She would not cry, and she would not give in. The idea of his dragging her here against her will, forcing her to stay, to endure his company . . .

She hadn't realized how weary she was. The next thing she knew, Conchita was digging her fat fingers into her shoulder, shaking her awake, and hollering in her ear.

"Señorita! Wake up, wake up. Supper is laid, and Señor Cole is waiting!"

Amanda stirred groggily. "Let him wait. I don't want any supper."

Conchita shook her again. "Señorita, you have to go to supper. If you don't come down, Señor Cole says he will beat me."

Forcing her eyes open, Amanda stared at the woman's round face. "He wouldn't dare . . ."

"Oh, but Señorita, he would. Believe me, I know . . ."

"That would be just like the miserable cur," Amanda groaned, dragging herself up. "Very well, I'll go down, but only so you don't get a beating."

"I have hung up your gowns. Which one will you wear?"

"None. I'm not changing."

"I bring you a pitcher of warm water for washing, too, but the bowl, *madre de Díos,* it is lying all over the room!"

"Yes, well, it fell. Anyway, I'm not going to wash. He'll just have to look at me as I am." She threw her legs over the side of the bed. "However, I would like to brush my hair—not for him, you understand, but for me."

"I find the brush on the floor here, Señorita. Please, allow me . . ."

Amanda gave in and sat before the dresser so that Conchita could pull the brush through her tangled hair. Some of her weariness fell away with the strokes of the brush, and she would have stayed longer except that Cole's voice, yelling for Conchita, came soaring up from below.

The Mexican woman tied Amanda's hair at the nape of her neck with a ribbon, letting the long strands cascade down her back. "There. The señorita looks very pretty."

"The señorita doesn't want to look pretty. She wants to look like an old hag. Go on and tell him I'll be down in a moment."

Conchita paused beside the door, frowning. "You really will come?"

"Yes, yes. I'll be there."

She kept him waiting just as long as she felt she could without earning poor Conchita a beating, then slowly made her way down the stairs. He waited at the bottom, scowling as he noticed she still wore her dusty riding clothes and boots.

"Supper is getting cold."

"I told you I don't want any supper."

"Very well. Then you'll sit at the table and watch me eat," he snapped, taking her elbow and propelling her down the hall and into the dining room.

The dining room was even more lovely than the entrance hall. One whole side opened onto the atrium, allowing an airy view of plants with huge, spilling leaves glimmering in the moonlight. The opposite wall was hung with Indian blankets in colorful patterns. In the center of the room, a mahogany table was laid with silver candlesticks and expensive china. Cole plopped her down in a chair at one end of the table, then took the chair opposite. They sat stiffly eying each other as Conchita hurried in, bearing fragrant, steaming dishes.

Amanda forced down the urge to grab her fork and, instead, stared at the Indian blankets on the wall while Cole dug in. Surreptitious glances revealed a plate of some dumpling delicacies covered with a sauce floating with pieces of green and red peppers. When Conchita returned bearing a basket of hot, yeasty rolls, she almost relented. But she wouldn't give in. She ignored Cole while he ate heartily, even refusing to touch the wine which he poured into the glass beside her plate.

"You're going to have to eat sometime," he said between mouthfuls. "You can't refuse food the whole time you're here."

"And how long will that be?"

"Oh, I don't know. A week maybe."

"May I remind you I have a business to get back to in Tombstone. I told Dr. Goodfellow I would only be gone three days."

Cole waved his fork. "Don't worry about that. I sent him word you would be delayed."

"You thought of everything, didn't you?"

"Everything but the possibility that you might die of starvation while you're here. Go on, taste it. Conchita makes mostly Mexican dishes. They're a little spicy but delicious."

"I don't want any of Conchita's Mexican dishes." She looked around the room. "This is rather grand for an outlaw, isn't it? I suppose you're going to tell me it belongs to you."

"That's right."

"Another lie, of course. Who does it belong to? Where is the owner?"

Cole leaned toward her across the table. "I told you, he's locked in a dungeon below. In fact, underneath this very room."

"It wouldn't surprise me. Nothing about you will ever surprise me again."

Annoyed, he glared at her; but before he could answer, Conchita appeared at his side, whispering that her husband Pedro wanted to see him. With a reminder he would be right back, Cole rose and left the room.

He had hardly disappeared through the door before Amanda grabbed her fork and began wolfing down the dumplings. Breaking a roll, she stuffed half of it into her mouth, then washed it down with huge gulps of the wine. By the time she heard Cole's boots on the hall tiles, she was sitting disdainfully before a half-empty plate, ignoring it as before.

Cole did not fail to notice that part of the food and wine was gone and that only half of a roll was still in the basket. He smiled to himself as he took his place again and picked up his fork.

"I can't manage to leave you during every meal," he said casually. "Of course, I could send them up to you."

"I would prefer that."

"But I don't think I will since it would deprive me of the pleasure of seeing you across the table."

Amanda glared at him. "It would offer me the pleasure of never having to look at your face while I'm here."

Cole threw down his fork. "Now see here, Amanda. You're stuck here with me for a week, so you might as well make the best of it."

"I didn't ask to come! The truth is, I never wanted to see you again."

"That is just the reason I brought you. I want to clear the air, to explain. You might at least listen and try to understand."

"What is there to understand? You're a lying, deceiving, wretched . . . bounder!"

Cole chuckled. "I've been called many things before, but 'bounder' is surely the least of them."

"That's because I'm a lady and can't say what I really want to."

"Well, you're not acting like a lady. Anyone with breeding would behave in a civilized way. She would try to enjoy herself, make the best of the situation, and listen with an open mind."

"You dare to talk to me of breeding!" Amanda gripped the edge of the table, leaning toward him. "You of all people . . ."

Cole's voice dropped to a cold intensity. "Amanda, don't you even think of throwing these dishes. They are Haviland china, and they belonged to . . . to the owner's mother."

"So why should you care?" She slumped back in her chair. "I'm too tired to throw anything. All I want is to be allowed to return to my room and go to bed."

Cole sat back, noticing for the first time the lines of fatigue on her face and the black smudges beneath her eyes.

"All right. I can see you are worn out. Very well, go to bed. I'll have Conchita bring up a tray so you don't go hungry."

Amanda looked away, refusing to even say 'thank you.' After all, it was no more than her due.

"Get some rest, because tomorrow I want to show you around the place."

"I believe I'll just stay in my room tomorrow."

He started to reply, then thought better of it. Perhaps

a day or so of confinement in one room would wear down her resistance. "Have it your way. We've plenty of time."

She swept from the room and up the stairs. Once inside her bedroom, she closed the door and locked it. Then she hurried over to the veranda doors and fastened them as well. It made the room close and warm, but it gave her—for the first time—a feeling of security. That was worth some discomfort, she thought, as she pulled off her clothes and climbed into bed.

The following afternoon, she began to have second thoughts. She had slept deeply and long, only waking the next morning when Conchita banged on her door to bring her a breakfast tray. Amanda was astonished to realize it was nearly nine-thirty in the morning, but she was grateful that part of the day was already gone. Since the night had been cool, she hadn't really noticed how close the room had grown. However, by three in the afternoon, the room was stifling and she was bored nearly to death. Although Conchita brought up one or two books from the shelves below, it wasn't enough to keep her occupied. It was simply too hot to read. Finally, in exasperation, she threw open the double doors to the veranda and stood basking in the breeze.

"I wondered how long it would take for this desert air to get you to open up."

With a start, Amanda turned to see Cole leaning against the railing in front of the doors next to her room. His arms were crossed over his chest and his hat was pushed back on his head, allowing a shock of sandy hair to fall in a wave over his forehead.

"I hope you haven't been standing there all day waiting," she snapped.

"Hardly. I was up at six and finished riding over the place by ten. This is siesta time, so I decided to see if the heat had driven you out yet."

"Well, it hasn't," Amanda said and turned to pull the doors closed behind her again. He got to her before she could secure them and drew her onto the veranda.

"You don't have to let yourself be broiled alive in there. I promise I won't bother you."

His fingers on her flesh were like hot brands. Angrily, Amanda snatched her arm away and rubbed it. "I know what your promises are worth."

He glowered and leaned against the railing again, folding his arms over his chest. "There. We have ten feet between us. Is that enough?"

"Not nearly enough," she snapped, walking away from him to stand farther down the veranda. The breeze had the desert heat in it, yet it felt cool after her steamy room. She lifted her face and wiped at her damp neck with a handkerchief. She was acutely conscious of Cole's tall body not far away. It set her skin tingling with a warmth of its own, a response which she furiously fought down. She wished he would go away and leave her to nurse her anger in peace.

Cole watched her with half-lidded eyes, admiring the way she tilted her head back, the expanse of white neck which he longed to kiss, the arch of her back that lifted her breasts and molded the fabric of her blouse tightly to them. His fingers itched to lace themselves in the long cascade of hair down her back. His body ached with the need to take her into his arms, to lift and carry her to the bed . . .

He must be crazy to allow her these limits. There was no one to stop him from throwing her down and making wild, delicious love to her. No one but himself. For he knew that if he did so, with the anger she was feeling toward him now, it would be the end of any future they might have together. It would prove to her he was the scoundrel she believed him to be. There had to be a better way.

He shook off his growing desire for her and started toward his room, resigned to leaving her alone.

"I hate to admit it, but I'm bored," Amanda muttered in a voice full of reluctance.

Cole stopped and turned back to her.

There was anger still in her eyes, and suspicion as well. But she faced him squarely for the first time. "If you really mean what you say—that you'll keep your distance—then I would like to see what this place is like."

"You mean, you could stand my company?"

"You don't have to be so sarcastic. I left Tombstone hoping to see a ranch. If I can't see Sally's, I might as well see this one. I presume it is a ranch?"

"It was once. There's little left of that now, but the country is still very beautiful."

Amanda shrugged. "If you'd rather not . . ."

"No, no," he said quickly. "I'd be delighted to show you around. You don't even have to talk to me if you don't want to. Just promise not to throw anything."

She ignored his grin and went to don her riding skirt

once again. Conchita had brushed it, but it still looked the worse for wear. However, that was the least of Amanda's concerns. She hoped she wasn't making a mistake by giving in to him this much, but the thought of sitting in her stifling room for a whole week was more than she could bear. Better to have a cold truce and at least be able to move around. Just let him try something, and he'd find out soon enough that she had not relinquished one bit of the furious anger she felt toward him.

Downstairs, Amanda found Cole waiting with a brown-and-white pinto mare for her to ride. There were three or four other horses in a corral beside the barn, but surely this was the best-looking of the lot. The animal turned out to be gentle and good-natured as well, and Amanda had not ridden more than half a mile before she was enthusiastically enjoying the freedom and exercise. She cantered ahead of Cole for a while until the road disappeared in an expanse of sagebrush that fanned out into a wide plain. At its far edge, the blue haze of a range of mountains lifted their jagged heads against the sky.

He rode up alongside her. "The path is overgrown, so follow me. There's a pass through these mountains. I thought we'd go along it a little way."

Amanda dropped back without answering to follow him at a sedate pace. Once they left the grassy plain, the path began to slope upward, carrying them on a gentle climb into the mountains. They traveled for nearly an hour before Cole pulled up on the brow of a hill. Though the soil was rocky, there was enough clumpy undergrowth to let his horse graze while he sat overlooking the plain below.

After giving it some thought, Amanda dismounted and walked over to look out at the valley, standing a safe distance from him.

"I expected to see cattle," she said finally.

"There used to be a lot of them. Nearly five thousand head. But they've been gone a long time now. The owner made a mess of running this place and had to give it up."

"I suppose that's the man who's chained in the dungeon of the house?"

He grinned, though she looked as stern and serious as ever. "Now you know I wasn't serious about that." He debated whether she would believe anything he said. "Actually, the owner moved on long ago."

Amanda sat down, tucking her legs beneath her. "So this is not really a working ranch?"

"No."

"Well, the view is very pretty anyway."

They sat in silence for what seemed a long time. Then, abruptly, Cole rested his arms on his drawn-up knees and began to speak.

"I know you don't want to hear this, Amanda, but I went to great lengths to get you here so I could talk to you and I'm determined to do it. When I went to Tombstone as Cabot Storey—Reverend Storey—I had no intention of creating a complicated disguise. I expected to go in, speak to a man I was looking for, and get out right away without anyone even knowing I was there. I figured a poor clergyman in a town like Tombstone—

who would even care? It was, well, a kind of joke. A lark. I thought it would be one day's amusement.

"Then I met you in the coach. Right from the first, I knew you were different. I felt there was going to be something special between us. Yet I still would have gone in and left right away, except things happened so fast. All those church folks were there waiting—three couples to be married, for God's sake! They kind of swooped me up and carried me off in their arms, so to speak. And then I learned Aces Malone wasn't in town and wouldn't be back for two weeks. It was really important that I talk to Aces, so I figured, why not give it a little time, just until he got back."

Amanda stared out at the dun-colored plain below dotted with the gray-green of barrel and cholla cactus, yucca, and mesquite. Her tight face betrayed nothing of what she was thinking. She refused to reveal anything of the confusion his words evoked and concentrated on her stubborn will to stay angry, her determination not to allow more lies to affect what she thought of him.

"Things sort of built from there," Cole went on. "I found I kind of liked being Reverend Storey. Most of all, I liked being with you. In the end, what we had together meant more to me than anything."

Amanda jumped to her feet. "If this is supposed to be an apology, you can save your breath."

Cole gradually unbent his long legs and stood up, his hands on his hips. "It's not an apology. I just want you to understand I didn't set out to deceive you. It just happened."

"And I supposed it just 'happened' that you were a

government agent? And The Casket Kid was only a lark, simply—what did you call it?—part of a day's amusement."

Cole looked away from her blazing eyes. Obviously, her opinion of him wasn't going to be affected by anything he could say.

She stalked over to lift the reins of her grazing pinto. "I'm ready to ride back now."

He made an exasperated clucking noise with his tongue. "All right, stay mad if that's what you want. I've said my piece. But we still have the rest of the week to get through."

Amanda climbed back in the saddle. "I'm aware of that." She turned the mare around toward the path they had come up.

Cole put a boot in the stirrup and heaved himself onto his horse, muttering.

"Women!"

Twenty-two

They rode back without speaking. Amanda went straight to her room, still nursing her anger and refusing to accept Cole's explanation as anything other than more lies. Summoning Conchita, she asked for a bath to be drawn, then spent nearly an hour luxuriating in its warm, cozy depths. With her hair newly washed and her body still tingling, she decided to put on one of her dresses—one of her most drab and ordinary dresses—and go down to supper.

She sat without speaking unless it was to answer a question Cole asked of her, but she no longer bothered to pretend she wasn't hungry. The ride and the bath, in addition to her stringent dieting of the day before, had left her ravenous, and she plowed into Conchita's excellent dinner with an enthusiasm that had Cole chuckling.

Once the meal was finished, he suggested they take coffee beside the fountain in the atrium. Amanda admitted—to herself—that it was a pleasant place indeed. The small, tiled fountain made a gentle pattering noise while above them the black sky sparkled with a million diamond lights. A cool breeze rustled among the potted trees and heavily fringed plants, making her grateful she had thought to bring along her shawl.

In fact, she soon found herself so pleasantly occupied that she quickly drank her coffee and went back to her room. It was obvious he was trying to wear down her defenses with all these pleasantries, and she was determined it wouldn't work. Not for all the comfort in the world was she going to forget how he had deceived and betrayed her, then dragged her here against her will!

She woke late the following morning, rested and ready for another ride. Yet when she went downstairs to the dining room where her place was laid at the table, she found the house quiet and Cole nowhere to be seen.

She had barely sat down before Conchita appeared carrying a plate of potatoes and eggs and a basket of fresh bread.

"You sleep late today," the Mexican woman lamented dryly as she set Amanda's plate before her. "Food probably not good anymore."

"It looks all right to me," Amanda replied brightly. If her lateness had inconvenienced the servant, so be it. "I suppose everyone else has already eaten."

"Señor Cole, he rode out early. He say to give you your breakfast and, if you want, show you the house. But you not to ride until he return."

Amanda bristled at this presumptuous order. "I suppose that means Pedro wouldn't saddle the pinto for me if I asked?"

"No, Señorita. Pedro and me, we do as Señor Cole says."

It briefly crossed her mind that she could saddle the horse herself until Conchita went on.

"It is not safe for a woman alone to ride these lands. Too many *bandoleros* and bad men all around."

"I didn't see any yesterday. In fact, I didn't see anyone else at all."

"That is because Señor Cole was with you. Does the señorita wish some chocolate?"

Amanda nodded, mulling over the servant's words. She had no wish to run into any *bandoleros* herself. Perhaps it might be better to spend the day exploring this fascinating house. She made arrangements to meet Conchita later, then spent part of the morning reading and fussing around her room. When she went back downstairs, she found the servant in the kitchen peeling potatoes.

"Un momento, Señorita. When I finish these, I give you the 'tour.' "

Amanda pulled up a stool, admiring the open, airy kitchen made mostly of tile and stucco and spotlessly clean.

"Whoever built this house put a lot of care into it," she commented absently. "I never saw so many beautiful tiles."

"They are hand-painted from Mexico. The old señor, he wanted the best. And his wife, she loved beauty."

"I suppose you mean the owners. Who were they, Conchita? Where are they now?"

Conchita looked up, her black eyes widening in surprise. "Why, Señor Cole is the owner."

Amanda looked quickly away. "Señor Cole owns this house?"

"Sí, Señorita. His father, the old señor, build it. When he died, it went to Señor Cole. He is not much here, though, so it is not now nearly the grand *ranchero* it was when the old señor was alive. Ah, it was something to see then. I was only a girl when I first come here

with my mother to work in the kitchen. Now I have been here so long, I feel it is my home, too."

Amanda brushed an invisible speck from her skirt. "So this is Señor Cole's home?"

"*Sí,* except that he does not live here much. He comes back now and then, bringing a few horses with him like those in the corral. Pedro and I, we keep the place ready for him always." The paring knife in her hand stilled and she looked out into space, remembering. "Such a place this was before. So many horses and *vaqueros.* And cattle, big, big herds of cattle. Always there was noise and people coming and going. And music and dancing. The old señora, she loved dancing. It is too bad you could not see it as it was then."

Amanda smiled, "Yes, it's too bad." So much for the owner incarcerated in the dungeon! Of course, she had known all along the house belonged to Cole. She just didn't want to believe it. "Tell me, Conchita, why doesn't Señor Cole live here? Why didn't he continue to run the ranch his father had made so successful?"

Conchita dumped the potato into a bowl of water and gathered up the peelings in a towel. "Ah, that was before all the trouble. He was wild, Señor Cole. He never appreciate all his father made for him. When he went away, it broke his mother's heart. When she die, the old señor was not long in following."

"Why did he go away? What happened?"

Conchita pursed her lips, set aside the bowl of potatoes and dropped the peelings in a basket at her feet. "I think the señor will have to tell you about that, Señorita Amanda. But if you like to see the rest of the house, I can show it to you now."

Amanda could sense the invisible door that had closed between the Mexican woman and herself. "I'd like that very much," she said, getting to her feet.

That evening she put on one of her prettiest dresses, brushed her hair until it shone, then tied it at the nape of her neck with a ribbon that matched the color of her dress. After all her fussing, she was disappointed when she went downstairs and found Cole was still not back. She took her place at the table, telling herself it didn't matter and that she would enjoy the solitude more. Yet when she heard the jingle of his spurs as he walked down the tiled hall, there was a stir of excitement in her breast that annoyed her no end.

He came striding into the room wearing riding clothes still covered with desert dust. Though Amanda meant to ignore him, her eyes were drawn like a magnet to his broad shoulders beneath the fringed leather jacket, the wide silver buckle at his waist, the tight-fitting denim pants.

"Sorry I'm late," he said, pulling off his hat and sending it sailing over to the sideboard. "You can take me as I am or I can go clean up first."

Amanda shrugged. "Suit yourself. I've already started."

"In that case, I'll start too. I'm too hungry to wait."

She had hoped to ask him some of the questions Conchita refused to answer; but, for once, he seemed more interested in eating than starting a conversation. And Amanda was determined not to start one herself. The only time he spoke was to explain he had been called away to see someone and it had taken longer than he had expected.

"I trust you weren't too bored," he added.

"Not at all. I would have preferred to ride; but since Pedro refused to saddle the pinto, I spent the time with Conchita instead. She showed me around the house."

"Good," Cole answered, turning his attention back to his plate. This could have been her opening, she thought, but she could not bring herself to break the silence he seemed to want. Once he finished his meal, he excused himself to go clean up, telling her she could take her coffee alone in the atrium if she wished.

"Perhaps I will."

She watched him leave, her eyes again drawn to his tall figure. She had never noticed before how smoothly he moved. Perhaps it was the riding clothes, dusty as they were, that showed his lithesome, athletic grace to perfection, that accentuated his masculine self-assurance. For a moment she allowed herself to recall that long back beneath her fingers, the narrow hips, the muscular thighs, the astounding maleness.

Shaking herself, Amanda grabbed her coffee cup and stalked out among the plants. The air was cooler here and she lifted her face and throat to it, hoping it would breeze through her mind as well. Nothing about Cole Carteret—the name still seemed strange to her—had changed. He was still the man who had deceived and betrayed her, walked out on her with no word of explanation or goodbye, then dragged her to this isolated spot without so much as a by-your-leave. She must never forget that!

It was frustrating there had been no opportunity to

ask her questions, yet she still had four days left. She'd ask them sometime before he returned her to Tombstone. He owed her the answers.

She stayed in the atrium enjoying the cool evening for nearly an hour. Cole never came back down so she assumed he had gone to bed, tired after his long ride. The house was quiet when she finally walked up the stairs to her room, planning to read awhile before going to bed.

Through the open doors to the balcony she could see the brilliant night sky, with stars glimmering like jewels against black velvet. A rising moon bathed the world below with golden bronze. She walked out onto the balcony to stand by the railing, overwhelmed by the cool radiance around her. The air was so crisp and clear she felt as though she could reach out and pluck a handful of diamonds from the sky or run her fingers along the curve of the bright moon. She lifted her arm, half-convinced she could touch its luminous magic.

"It's beautiful, isn't it?"

Amanda gave a quick gasp and turned to see Cole standing a few feet away. He was smoking a cigarillo which burned a tiny red glow against the darkness. He moved closer and she could see he had thrown off the riding clothes for a white shirt, open at the throat, dark pants, and slippers. His hair lay in damp curls against his forehead, and there was a faint odor of citrine water about his skin.

"You gave me a start," she said, her hand going to her throat.

"I'm sorry. I should have spoken sooner, but while you were admiring the sky, I was admiring—something else. It's glorious, isn't it?" he said, gesturing toward the heavens. "I don't think I've ever seen prettier night skies anywhere than here at Paso Diablo."

"Paso Diablo? Devil's Pass? That's a strange name for such a lovely place."

"I always thought so, too."

"Was it your idea?"

He laughed. "No, as a matter of fact, it wasn't."

"Your father's then? Or your mother's?"

There was an ominous silence. "Conchita has been talking."

"Yes," Amanda said, turning to lean against the balcony and folding her arms across her chest. "She told me you inherited this lovely place from your parents and that it was once a lively, successful, working ranch. She refused to tell me what happened to make it the empty, fallow place it is now."

Cole drew deeply on his cigarillo. "And you would like to hear that from me, I suppose. Well, that's only fair." He was silent a moment longer, as though unsure of his decision. Throwing down the cigarillo, he stepped on it to put it out, then rested both hands on the railing, staring out into the night.

"My parents were good people, hard working and successful. My father was a wealthy man once. Unfortunately, they only had one child and they spoiled that one terribly. I grew up thinking I could have anything, do anything I wanted. In addition to a swollen opinion of myself, I also had some special talents. Between the two, by the time I was fifteen, I figured the world was mine to do with as I pleased.

"Of course I got into trouble. At seventeen, I killed

a young punk who pushed me into a shoot-out. He wasn't blameless either, but with a little more self-control, I could have prevented all that followed. Instead of facing the music, I ran off, trying to see how much more I could get away with. By the time I was caught, I had a list of crimes as long as your arm and had dispatched several more young punks to their eternal reward. My father spent everything he had trying to keep me out of jail, but it was useless. I was finally sent to Yuma, and he and my mother died soon after, leaving only this house and the land around it."

Amanda listened to his quiet voice without speaking. When he grew silent, she was afraid he wouldn't finish. Then he began again.

"At Yuma I had a lot of time to think. I also met a man I wish I had met ten years earlier. He helped me straighten out my head, and he arranged to have my sentence reduced if I would do a little work for him on the side."

"The government agent?" Amanda asked.

"Something like that. I could have come back here to Paso Diablo and tried to rebuild the ranch, but the thought of all the hurt I had caused my parents made that unappealing. Instead, I got a gang together, engineered a few robberies, and started building a reputation which I could use to get the kind of information my friend needed. He was the man I went to see today."

"You do love to play a part, don't you?" There was an edge to her voice which Cole didn't miss.

"Aces Malone wrote me there was something going on in Tombstone. I had already been asked to look into it. Pretending I was Reverend Storey was just a way to get into the town, see Aces, and get out again. Unfortunately, it didn't work out quite that easily."

"What about Tilly? She came to see me after you left, asking about you."

"Tilly Lacey used to run a whorehouse back in Newton, Kansas. I recognized her in the stage out of Tucson. She'd never met me, so I thought I was safe. However, she had heard of me and she suspected right from the first I wasn't the man I pretended to be. She was also very thick with Sheriff Behan, something I hadn't planned on."

"Sheriff Behan? Is he in on this, too?"

"One of those smart-alec punks I killed was Behan's cousin. He's been trying to get me back in jail ever since I was released early from Yuma."

Amanda gave an exasperated sigh. "You men! He asked me to walk out with him, you know. I suppose that was just so he could get at you."

"You underestimate yourself, Amanda. No man needs any such reason to try to get near you."

She hadn't realized how close he was. Suddenly he was there, beside her. She could feel the light hairs on his arm next to hers, smell the citron scent on his skin mingling with the faint pungent odor of tobacco. The air between them came alive; she could sense the throbbing warmth of her body calling to his.

This would never do! "Good night. I'm going to bed," she snapped and started toward the door to her room.

Cole watched her for a moment while his blood surged with irritation, fueled by his desire for her. She was so beautiful—and so arrogant, so haughty. How dare she treat him with such contempt?

He darted after her, catching her next to the door, where he spun her around until her back was against the wall, pinning her arm above her head.

"No, not tonight," he said huskily.

"Let me go!" Amanda cried, squirming against him. His body pressed her into the wall. She was acutely conscious of his chest pressing into her breasts, his hips flush with hers, the swell of him against her thighs. "Let me go . . ."

"Not yet. Not when I've poured out everything to you, revealed everything about myself. Then you walk away as though none of it mattered."

"You said you wouldn't force me—" Amanda writhed against him, twisting her head away from his hot breath.

"Then tell me you don't want me here. Tell me not to touch you, not to kiss you, not to hold you in my arms ever again. Tell me I'm nothing to you, and then I'll walk away."

She opened her mouth, but the words would not come out. Slumping against him, she looked up into his dark, burning eyes, wanting to tell him and wanting not to, but most of all, wanting him with a longing that cried for him to fill all the empty places, to do away with all the hurt.

"Tell me, Amanda," Cole said, leaning into her, his lips brushing her skin like brands of fire.

She clenched the fist caught fast in his grasp, digging the nails into her flesh. Her free arm went around his neck and wildly, wantonly, her mouth opened to his.

Instantly he recognized her surrender. He opened to her, his tongue seeking deeply within her depths to probe and search. Pressing her against the wall, he released her arm to slide his hand down her body, avidly feeling the length of her, reveling in the touch of her side, her waist, her hip. Urgently his hand moved across her thigh to clasp the skirt between her legs, forcing it upward, probing with his fingers through the barrier of her skirt.

Amanda lost all sense of feeling for anything except the wonder of having him in her arms again, his hard body pressed against hers, his hands and lips searching out every inch of her skin. With a desperation of long need, she arched her back, lifting her throat to his wild kisses.

He murmured against her neck, "Oh, if you only knew how I've wanted you . . . longed for you . . ."

"Take me, then," she cried, nearly half out of her senses with desire for him.

Swiftly, he lifted her in his arms and carried her to the bed. He threw himself on top of her, his weight pressing her down into the deep feather mattress. Gripping her hands, he yanked them over her head and pinned them there while his tongue drove deep inside her mouth.

Amanda felt herself giving way beneath his conquest. Twisting her head, she writhed beneath him.

"Say you want me," Cole demanded, his voice husky with desire. With his free hand he bunched up her skirt and thrust under it, plunging his fingers into the damp, mysterious depths of her body.

"Say it," he demanded, his tongue darting into the crevices of her ear, licking and probing until her senses reeled. "Say you love me," he muttered huskily.

All her reluctance went up with the soaring flames of her body's hot need. "I love you. I love you . . ."

Her wild, impassioned response was more than he could take. Entangling his fingers in her tousled hair, he pushed her down and thrust deep within her. She cried out in delight, and he heard his own cries mingling with hers as he drove to master the ecstatic sweetness of her body.

He felt her clasp him to her with the strength of her arms. Driving into her, he lost all sense of anything but the delights of his body, parched for the moist wetness of hers until, with a cry, he planted his seed deep within.

Clasped together, their bodies poised for a moment in bright eternity before falling back through the quiet spaces of satisfied longing. Cole rolled over in exhaustion, cradling her in his arms. She could hear the pounding of his heart, feel the damp perspiration on his skin. As her own breathing eased, she snuggled against him, content and utterly spent.

When Cole could speak again, he smoothed the long strands of her hair from her forehead and tucked her head beneath his chin.

Gingerly, she touched the thin, red scratches on his shoulders. "I think I hurt you."

"Isn't that what you wanted?"

True as it was, she hated to admit it. Lightly, she ran her lips over the long welts.

Cole enjoyed the softness of her lips for a few moments, then he pulled away, looking into her flushed face. "Still mad at me?"

Her arms went about his neck. "Yes." She moved her hand to lay her palm against his cheek. "No."

He smoothed away her hair and kissed her brow. "I never thought I would hear the word 'love' from your lips again."

"It was in the heat of the moment."

He gave a deep, husky chuckle. "I don't believe that."

She smiled up at him. "Well, you know, there was a point there when I would have said anything."

She snuggled against him, so happy and content that all the troubles of the past no longer seemed to matter. She knew they would come back, but for now, she would not allow them to intrude on the joyful delight of being in his arms again, out here in this solitary place with no one to know or care. She felt as though they were suspended in some magical world of their own, away from all everyday concerns, from all the questioning reasoning of reality. And she decided she would enjoy it while it lasted.

For a long time all she heard was his quiet breathing and she assumed he had fallen asleep. She almost drifted off herself until the slow, languid wandering of his hands on her body brought her senses fully alert. They both still wore their clothes, tousled and rumpled as they were. Now Cole began to slowly, methodically remove them.

She lay back, enjoying the easy movements of his hands as he pulled off her blouse and unlaced her chemise. Pulling it away, he bared one breast, kissing the swelling softness of it, teasing her by allowing his lips to roam everywhere except the hot tip. Only when she groaned and moved to raise it to him, did he enclose the pouting nipple in his lips, suckling greedily.

She lay in his arms, enjoying the slow arousal he

evoked until once again the need for him began to build. Then she moved over him to divest him of his shirt. Throwing her legs on either side of his body, she worked her way down the length of him, easing away the clothes he still wore. With her lips she teased him, watching him grow long and firm beneath her fingers and her mouth. She heard him groan with pleasure, but not until he cried out for her did she ease herself over him, taking his hard shaft within her. He reached for her, clasping her in his arms, rolling her over to drive deep within. Then slowly, languidly, he rode her, building with delicious slowness to the moment when she could bear it no longer.

"Take me," she heard herself cry and no longer cared about her pride.

"Yes, yes," he murmured, prolonging the ecstasy of his gift as long as possible. Their hips moved together in the timeless dance of love until their bodies climaxed into one perfect meld. Holding each other as though nothing on earth could ever part them, they fought to keep the delight of the moment.

Too swiftly it was gone and there was only the lingering sadness of separation, the joyful contentment of having for a few moments been complete.

Utterly exhausted, she nestled against him, prepared now to say anything he wanted, to declare how much she loved him in spite of everything. Then she heard his heavy breathing and knew he had fallen deeply asleep. And no wonder, when she thought about it. He had been tired before they ever reached the bed, and their exertions there had not been light!

Amanda ran her fingers lightly down his cheek and

smoothed away his hair. Then snuggling down against him, she, too, fell into a satisfied sleep.

She woke once to glimpse the first rays of dawn and to feel the slow drift of Cole's hands over her body. She stirred warmly beneath them until they became insistent and demanding for her love once again. She woke next to light flooding the room. Sensing how late in the morning it was, Amanda jumped up, threw her legs over the side of the bed, and stretched her arms high over her head.

"Wake up," she said, shaking Cole's inert body buried under the covers. "It's late. Past time for breakfast. What will Conchita think?"

He murmured and turned over. "Who cares? She knows to keep her observations to herself."

Amanda threw back the quilts and reached for a robe, belting it around her waist while Cole watched in approval.

"Come back to bed," he said. "Who needs breakfast?"

"I do. I'm starving. I feel as though I've been riding all night."

"You have." He yawned in contentment, spreading out his arms. "I'd like to stay here all day. Come and join me."

"I'd never survive," Amanda said, laughing. She reached in the press for a casual blouse and skirt. "Get up, lazy bones. I want to ride a horse today. I couldn't yesterday, remember. There is so much I want to see of the countryside around this ranch. Come on. We've got four more nights to spend in that bed."

She had the blouse and skirt over her head and fastened when she saw he still lay there, spread out in the recess of the feather mattress, his eyes closed. Quietly she picks up the pitcher from the washstand, tiptoed to the bed, and poured a thin stream on to his face.

He came up with a roar. "What are you doing, woman! That's cold."

Amanda laughed and threw him a towel. "I'm going down to breakfast. You can stay here and sleep all day if you want."

Cole dabbed at his wet face and grinned at her. "Oh, all right, I'll get up. But I warn you, tonight I'll take my revenge for that dousing!"

The five days passed all too quickly. For Amanda they were like living a dream—riding and exploring by day and wrapped in a deliciously ecstatic bliss by night. They laughed together, enjoyed playful little jokes on one another, talked endlessly of the way the ranch used to be. But they were both careful to avoid speaking of the future or even the events that had brought them together here. When, once or twice, the future was mentioned, they came so quickly to an impasse that they both felt it was better dropped. This precious time together should not be tainted by any thought beyond the present.

Then the idyllic days were over and it was time to go back. While Cole waited for her downstairs, Amanda stood in the doorway of her room, staring for the last time at the high feather bed, an aching void in her heart. He rode with her as near to Tombstone as he dared.

Once they reached the road leading into town, he pulled up beside the buggy.

"Get out and walk with me before you go on."

Without answering, Amanda climbed down, fastened the reins, and, her arm around his waist, walked with him over to a small bluff where she could look out on the valley. The winding road below was a pale, thin thread across the flat desert plain. Far in the distance, she could see the low roofs of the town and, behind them, the tall frame bulk of the stamp mill. The air was so clear and pristine she almost caught the faint echoing drum of the heavy metal stamps wafting across the desert.

Cole turned her in his arms and looked down at her lovely face. "Am I forgiven?" he asked, grinning.

Her arms went about his neck. "Well, for some things, I suppose." She lifted her face to his and kissed him. "These last few days have been so beautiful, so happy. I wish they could go on forever, but I know they can't."

Cole ran his finger down her cheek. "You could stay at Paso Diablo, you know."

"And wait with Conchita for you to show up when you felt like it? Wondering, when you didn't, if you were dead in a ravine somewhere or sitting in a jail waiting to be hanged? That's not the kind of life I want."

He pulled her close and hugged her fiercely. "It's not the kind of life I want either. Oh, Amanda, if only I could go back and change these last ten years!"

"We've said all this before," she said, pulling away. "It's the way things are, Cole, and nothing we can do will change it. You can't come into Tombstone, and I won't live like an outlaw, waiting for the axe to fall. It's better we try to forget."

Placing his palms on either side of her face, he looked deeply into her eyes, the color of the desert after a rain. "I will never forget you. I love you, Amanda. You are the only woman I've ever said that to, the only woman I've ever loved. How can I let you just walk away forever? Especially after what we've had together."

"You did it once before," she said, not without bitterness.

"No. I knew I would see you again somehow."

"But you didn't bother to tell me. Oh, Cole, don't you see? It's better this way. Let me get on with my life."

"Running a drug store? What kind of life is that?"

"What kind of life is the one you've chosen?"

He gave an exasperated sigh. "Very well, if that's what you want."

"It's for the best," she said softly, knowing it was not what she wanted at all.

He bent to kiss her, clasping her to him, melding her body to his, his lips draining every iota of sweetness and remembrance from hers. She clung to him, dreading to let him go, knowing this memory must be burned into her mind to last through the long, empty time ahead. When at last he released her, she slumped weak and miserable against him. With their arms around each other, they walked back to the buggy, where he helped her up.

"Goodbye, Cole," she murmured, turning her face away so he could not see the tears that blinded her.

"If you ever need me, send word."

She nodded and slapped the reins against the mare's back, sending the buggy rolling down the road toward the town. Though she felt certain he still stood on the bluff watching, Amanda refused to turn around and look. She could not have seen him anyway through the tears streaming down her cheeks.

Twenty-three

Amanda had barely driven the buggy through the wooden fence of the OK Corral before she spied Libby Walton hurrying out of the back door of Artimus Fly's photographic studio, which opened onto the yard. Libby came bustling over to wait for her as Amanda climbed down and handed the reins to one of the ostlers.

"I'm so glad you're back," she cried, lifting her round, homely face to Amanda. "I've been needing my special tonic something fierce these last two days, and there's just no other place to get it."

Amanda fell in step beside her. "Wouldn't Doc Goodfellow make some up for you?"

"Oh, you don't know, do you? Doc was called out to Bisbee last Friday and hasn't come back yet. Mrs. Dawley's laying-in, I expect. Anyway, the drug store's been closed since he left and there's been nobody to open it."

"Merciful heavens! And I thought things would be running smoothly while I was gone. Well, come on. I'll get you the tonic before I go round the hotel."

"Oh, thank you, Amanda. I'm obliged to you. And you can tell me all about Sally and her pa while we're walking over there. How's she doing?"

Amanda evaded Libby's question long enough to give the ostler word to send her bag round to the hotel, then made some vague answer while the two of them started for the drug store. It wasn't difficult to turn the conversation away from Sally since Libby was full of other news which Amanda had missed while she was away.

"You remember that awful fracas over Bud Philpot gettin' shot during that stagecoach robbery last March, and how the word was all over town that it was Holliday who done it because his horse was spotted runnin' away."

"But Holliday and the Earps formed the posse to look for the robbers."

"Humph, that don't mean nothin'. That was just a blind. Everybody knows they was involved. Even last Tuesday, when some prime horse flesh was stole from Dabney's ranch, at first everybody blamed the Earps and Doc Holliday again. But it turned out this time it wasn't them. It was some sportin' gambler here in town who was behind it all."

Amanda's steps slowed. "What gambler?"

"Somebody called Aces Malone. They haven't caught him yet, but they will. The Earps got together another posse and are out looking for him now. It's just another blind, if you ask me."

Amanda fussed in her reticule, searching for her key. "Are you certain his name is Aces Malone?"

"It was printed in the *Epitaph*. I declare, you can't know how relieved I am to get this tonic. I been suffering with the female problems something terrible." Libby pulled a handkerchief from her pocket and dabbed at her damp brow with it. Her usually bright eyes were dull, Amanda noticed, and her complexion more florid. It was time this store got running again.

Inside it was dark and dusty, as though the building had been closed far longer than four days. Amanda hurried behind the counter to look for the tonic, then remembered it was in the back room. Excusing herself, she walked to the rear of the store and opened the door to her small storeroom, moving to the shelf where she kept refills. Her hand was on the bottle when she had the eerie feeling something was different. She glanced around, noticing that the cot was rumpled as though someone had been lying on it. Of course, it might have been Doc. Perhaps he took a nap or just lay down for a rest while he was watching the store. Still, it was strange.

She completed Libby's purchase, assured her she would see her in church on Sunday, then locked up the shop and went round to the hotel to freshen up. Staring at her reflection in the mirror over the washstand, she noted the puffiness of her face and the circles under her eyes. She knew they were the lingering residue of her sadness at perhaps leaving Cole forever. Too many tears, she thought, splashing water on her face. Well, there was work to do now and no time for thinking about lost loves. The lovely glow from the happy days she had spent with him would simply have to overcome the ache in her heart when she thought of the future without him.

She had barely reopened the store before a steady stream of customers appeared. For two hours she never stopped working. It was a kind of relief, for it kept her from thinking about Cole, and more than ever convinced her that the town really needed her services.

When the door finally closed on the last customer, she decided to begin making an inventory of what was left, for the sudden demand had made her realize she was low on many of her more popular medicines. She went carefully over the shelves in the front, then, with paper and pencil in hand, moved to the storeroom to list what was left there.

Pulling up a small stepladder, Amanda had just reached to sort through the packages and jars stored on the top shelf when a sudden noise arrested her hand in mid-air. She turned quickly, looking around the room.

It was empty and silent, except for her shallow breathing. She turned back, but once again heard the same shuffling noise. She gripped the edge of the shelf in a sudden panic and nearly lost her footing on the spindly ladder.

"Who's there?" she called, grabbing at the shelf to right herself.

No answer and no sound.

"I know someone's here. Come out, right now."

For a moment she thought perhaps she was imagining things. When a hand appeared from under the cot. Amanda gave a gasp, threw down her pad of paper, stumbled off the ladder, and darted for the door. A man's voice called out, stopping her.

"Don't run! I won't hurt you."

She stood in the doorway ready to take off again in an instant and watched fearfully as a figure rolled from under the cot. A man emerged, dressed in checkered pants, spats, a biscuit-colored coat, and a striped cravat.

As he unbent and got to his feet, she saw that his shoulder-length hair was tangled and in need of combing, his thin cheeks dark with several days' stubble of beard. The clothes, which once must have been quite natty, now looked as rumpled and forlorn as his face.

"Who are you? What do you want?" she cried, with terrible visions of robbery and rape running through her mind.

He lifted a hand toward her. "I won't hurt you. Please don't make a commotion. I been hiding here waiting for you for days. My name's Malone."

Amanda felt an easing of her fear. "Aces Malone?"

"That's what they call me. I'm a friend of Cole Carteret's."

She hesitated, thinking he looked too pitiful to be violent. "Yes. He told me about you."

Relief flooded the ravaged face. "I'm glad he mentioned me. I'm in trouble, lass. They say I stole them horses, but I didn't. They just want to get rid of me 'cause I'm on to them."

"They? Who?"

"That don't matter. It's no business you ought to know about, anyway. I'm fixin' to head out of here, but I thought maybe, if you saw Cole . . ."

Amanda looked away. "I probably won't see Cole Carteret again, certainly not anytime soon."

He gazed at her in surprise. "No? But I thought . . ."

"I'm afraid you thought wrong, Mr. Malone. And I'd prefer not to have someone a posse is searching for hiding in my store. You put me in a dangerous position."

"I don't mean you no harm, Miss. Since there weren't

nobody here, it looked like the best place to hole up. Now you're back, I'll be on my way."

"Good. Please go."

Aces gave her a long look, then turned and pulled a battered saddlebag out from under the bed. Reaching inside, he removed a green whisky bottle with a cork stopper in the top.

"If you see Cole, tell him he might like to finish this for me," he said, throwing it on the cot.

"I told you, I won't see Mr. Carteret."

"I know." He shrugged, making a soft clucking noise. "The best laid plans. . . . Well, I'll be on my way then."

He moved to the rear door that opened on to the back yard. His hand was on the knob when Amanda called to him.

"Wait. Is there anything you need? Food? Medicine?"

"I helped myself to what you had here, Miss, but I left you some extra money to pay for it. No, I'm all right. It'll be dark soon, and I can get out of town then." He paused, studying her face for a moment. "You sure ain't like most of the girls Cole went for. You're . . . different. But you're OK. Most of Cole's women wouldn't have bothered to ask."

Amanda wanted to ask him more about the kind of girls Cole liked, but he was out and gone before she had the chance. She opened the door a crack and peered out into the yard but could see no sign of Aces Malone. Closing the door, she walked over and picked up the bottle, a grungy thing, half-filled with a dark brown sludge that looked as though it would poison anyone who had the nerve to drink it. She placed it on the shelf among the other assorted bottles, then went back inside the store, too upset by Malone's comments about Cole's *other* women to finish taking inventory.

Amanda had never had occasion to enter Banker McKeithan's hallowed inner office, but she'd heard from others of its forbidding elegance. When the note arrived asking her to stop in at two o'clock that afternoon, it gave her a sudden twinge of anxiety, even though there was no reason for it. After all, she hadn't applied for a loan or sought protection against creditors or any of the other bits of business a store owner might pursue with a bank.

Still, McKeithan had a reputation for power in the town and—who knew?—the day might come when she would need to see him about those concerns. On an impulse she decided to return to the hotel and don her nicest dress and her newest straw hat. It couldn't hurt to make a good impression.

Her first glimpse of McKeithan's private office confirmed her worst fears. In a town where the mahogany and brass decor of the Oriental Saloon was the last word in elegance, Louis McKeithan's inner sanctum offered the understated but expensive comfort of an illustrated salon in Godey's *Ladies Book.* Amanda sank into one of the overstuffed chairs that flanked a highly polished cherry-wood table. In the center sat a silver tray with a crystal decanter and two small glasses. Amanda made an effort to appear at ease while McKeithan offered to pour her a little Madeira.

"No thank you. I have to get back to the shop."

"Oh, of course. It was good of you to stop by, Miss

Lassiter, the banker said, settling in the opposite chair. "I could have come to you, but I've always found the comforts of my little room here make the carrying out of business so much more pleasant."

Amanda smiled, thinking, *yes, and so much more intimidating!* McKeithan looked as expensively turned-out as his surroundings. A short, homely man with a balding head and a thick, gray moustache, he made up for his lack of comeliness by dressing in a smartly tailored suit and gray spats, a diamond stickpin and a heavy gold watch chain across his striped silk vest. He might have been one of the high-stake gamblers at the Alahambra, Amanda thought. Probably there wasn't all that much difference between the two.

"The truth is," he went on, oblivious to her scrutiny, "I have a business proposition to put to you. One which I feel sure you will find to your liking."

She looked at him in surprise. Until this moment she had been more than certain it was Cole the banker wanted to discuss. It had never crossed her mind her store might be involved.

"I have a . . . a friend . . . who has asked me to convey to you that he would like to purchase your drug store—and at a very nice price. Far higher than the going rate would suggest."

"Purchase my store? But I haven't offered it for sale."

"I'm . . . we're aware of that. My buyer feels a drug store will have a strong future as Tombstone grows and wants to invest in that future. So much so, he is willing to make you an offer you won't want to refuse."

Amanda glared at the dapper little man in the chair opposite. "Why then didn't he come to me? Why not offer me a partnership? What ever gave him the idea I would want to be bought out?"

Keithan placed the tips of his fingers together and smiled thinly at her over them. "He felt it would be more professional to have me present his offer. He is not at all interested in a partnership. He would like to take your little store and expand it considerably beyond drugs and medicines. It would offer him the kind of challenge he especially relishes."

"Well, Mr. McKeithan, you can tell your buyer I'm not interested, whatever his price. My uncle left this store to my father and through him, to me. I have found it a challenge which has given me much satisfaction. As for expanding, that is something I hope to do myself someday."

McKeithan's smile faded. "Come now, Miss Lassiter. We all know the problems a women faces competing in a man's world. You have enjoyed a modest success since coming to Tombstone, but how long do you think you can hold out if a competitor opens up another drug store, one larger and grander than yours? As for expanding, you will need bank loans for that. A bank might not be interested in backing two such stores."

"Are you threatening me?"

"Of course not. I never threaten."

"What else would you call it? Either I sell or I'm run out of business."

"Really, Miss Lassiter. You cut me to the quick."

Amanda caught back the derisive laugh she wanted to make. McKeithan, for all his gracious ways, was as hard as flint underneath. She could see it in his eyes, in the satisfied smile around his narrow lips, in every nuance of his assured body. She draped the strings of her purse over her arm and made ready to rise.

"I think there is nothing more to be said, Mr. McKeithan. Please tell your buyer I am not interested in selling my store under any conditions or for any price." Standing beside the chair she lingered for a moment, looking down at him. "It is true I may someday need to appeal to another bank for a loan and you could, with the power you have in this town, keep me from getting it. But, in the meantime, I will continue to work to build the store my uncle started and hope, in time, your sense of fairness will overcome any need for revenge. Good day, Mr. McKeithan."

Amanda moved to the door where she waited for him to get out of his chair and open it for her. When it became obvious he wasn't going to move, she turned the knob herself.

"Good day, Miss Lassiter," she heard him mutter as she swept out. The jovial smile she had received when she entered had completely disappeared.

She paused for a moment, collecting herself before crossing the bank to the street door. She could feel the eyes of the clerks on her as she walked, and she saw one of them, a parishioner from St. Anselm's, give her a brief nod. She was almost to the door when a small, plump, well-dressed gentleman came striding briskly into the bank, nearly bumping into her.

"Miss Lassiter, is it?" he asked, removing his bowler hat.

"Yes."

"Brody Hanlon, Miss Lassiter. I don't think we've

ever met. I always meant to thank you for helping that Bennett boy the day he was injured at the stamp mill."

Amanda remembered then. Brody Hanlon was the owner of the Amelia mine and had an interest in several others in Tombstone. "It was nothing," she murmured. "I did what I could while Goodfellow wasn't available."

"All the same, I feel sure you saved his leg."

"It was his arm."

"Oh, yes, of course. He's back at work, good as new."

"That's too bad since he ought to be in school. Good day, Mr. Hanlon."

She took some satisfaction in the way Hanlon's smile turned to a sudden frown as he stepped aside to let her pass. She ignored the sharp little bow he gave her, as well as the feel of his eyes on her back as she went out into the street. Brody Hanlon and Louis McKeithan. Two of the town's richest, most powerful men, and two of a kind, if she were any judge. She walked on, squinting against the bright sun and wondering idly if Hanlon was McKeithan's mysterious buyer.

She wondered that same question often in the days that followed. When a month went by, and then two months, without the competing drug store opening in the town, she began to think Louis McKeithan's threat had been an idle one. Surely if there were a serious entrepreneur hoping to drive her out of business with a grander store, there would have been some sign of it by now.

In the meantime, she was too occupied with her own business to give the problem much thought. What with frequent gunshot wounds, a brief epidemic of whooping cough, and the extent to which the townspeople had come to rely on her for medicines and advice, she barely had time during the busy days to think at all. Twice, she made quick trips to Tucson to purchase more supplies; and even then, she could not keep enough of the popular physics in stock—Hostetter's Stomach Bitters, mandrake root nostrums, and Dr. Kilmer's Female Remedy were gone almost as quickly as she put them on the shelf. Her brisk business had the added advantage of keeping her too busy to think about Cole.

When she did think about him, the pain seemed almost too much to bear. She would wake in the night aching to feel his arms around her, longing to have the long length of his body against her own. Tears constantly welled behind her eyes, threatening to spill over at the most awkward times. Sudden memories would twist her chest with a pain so terrible she could barely breathe.

For two long, empty months she fought these awful spasms by forcing Cole Carteret from her thoughts. She stopped attending services at St. Anselm's because the sight of Cabot Storey in his clerical robes awoke too many painful memories. When Libby Walton or John Behan or any other acquaintance brought up his name, she refused to talk about him. Forcing herself to concentrate on her work, she let her social life die on the vine, refusing to step out with Sheriff Behan or Reverend Storey, who both made tentative offers to share her company. She knew it wasn't healthy or wise, but it was the best she could do to protect herself from thinking about a future that looked increasingly bleak.

The busy events of the town helped keep her thoughts at bay. Everyone was talking about the escalating feud between the Earps and the Clantons that went back to the shooting of Bud Philpot last spring. Every week rumors flew through town that one or another of the silver mines had played out and would fold. When that proved false, word would spread that a rich new vein of silver ore had been discovered. Gunfights erupted in the saloons and knifings in the brothels. Stagecoach robberies continued unabated, and thefts of cattle and horses in Mexico occurred weekly.

Meanwhile, amid all the violence and disruption, the stamp mills continued their relentless pounding, the mines yielded up their riches, men went on making money, and the town continued to grow. Much of that growth was in respectable areas—a new courthouse, the first school, two more churches. Amanda observed it all as she kept aloof from the violence, concentrated on making her little store a success, and watched every day for some sign that Louis McKeithan's threat of opening a competing drugstore was about to come true.

And then Aces Malone was captured and brought back to town in irons.

Twenty-four

Amanda was walking along Fremont Street on her way to Papagao's Cash Store when Sheriff Behan passed her, tugging at the reins of a second horse. She recognized Aces Malone at once, slumped in the saddle, his hands tied behind his back. She had thought the man had looked pitiful the last time she saw him, yet he appeared even more bedraggled now. His beard was long and scraggly, his eyes sunken, his cheeks pallid, almost yellow; and his clothes looked as though he had slept in them during the time he had been away. She paused, looking up to meet the captive's eyes, and read in them a silent plea for help. He mouthed a word to her as he passed by, but it was only as she watched the two men disappear down the street on their way to the jail that she realized Aces had said, 'Cole.'

Amanda went on her way, feeling even more depressed. How could she contact Cole? She had no idea where he was or how to begin trying to get in touch with him. She did not even know the way to Paso Diablo, had she wanted to go there. She tried to tell herself it was none of her affair, that a gambler like Aces would have been brought to justice sometime, even if he weren't responsible for stealing those horses. She could do nothing to help him.

Yet she remained unconvinced by her own argument. Feeling against the horse thief ran high in the saloons and brothels, possibly fueled by the card shark's dishonest dealings in the past at the faro and keno tables. There was even talk of a lynching. Why wait for a trial and the possibility of an acquittal? A vigilante hanging was a terrible possibility, for if there was one never-changing factor in Tombstone, it was the mercurial temper of its more violent citizens. In such a place, anything could happen.

Amanda decided the only help she could offer Aces was to go round and see him. Yet once she set out to do so, she found Sheriff Behan vehemently against the idea. In the end, he only agreed to it if he could accompany her and Amanda was forced to agree though she knew Aces would not say much in front of the sheriff. Only when Behan was called back into the office for a moment did Malone's face take on any semblance of life. Gripping the bars of his cell with both hands he poked his bony nose against them and whispered: "Get Cole. I'm in trouble here. He'll know what to do."

Amanda glanced through the open door to the jail office where Behan talked to one of the deputies.

"I can't get him. I don't know where he is."

"You got to, missus. They're after me cause of what I know. They'll get me, too, lessen Cole saves me."

"You'll have a trial . . ."

"Hell, lady, there won't be no trial. And even if'n there is, it's gonna be fixed. I tell you . . ."

Amanda heard Behan bark a command to the deputy and start back toward the cells. "But how?"

"There's an Indian comes into town. Little Vitorio."

She nodded as Behan approached.

"Send him," Aces whispered quietly, then backed off to stand against the wall, folding his arms over his chest, his long face once more an unreadable mask.

"Well, Mr. Malone," Amanda spoke loudly, "if you're sure there's nothing you need in the way of medicines, I'll be going along then."

"Thanks anyway, Miss, but the only tonic I need is a good slug of whisky."

"I'm afraid that's one thing I can't get for you."

"I told you this was a waste of time," Behan said, taking her elbow to guide her back to the office. "You can't reach hardened men like Malone. They're so used to taking what they want, they don't have any softness left in them to respond to decent people."

Amanda paused in the doorway, looking back at the forlorn row of cells. "He says he's innocent."

"They all say that."

"But if he is, he ought to have a chance to prove it."

Behan's face grew guarded. "What makes you think he won't?"

"I don't know. I hear wild talk in the town about mobs and lynchings."

"Look, Miss Lassiter. As long as I'm the sheriff here, no mob is going to hang one of my prisoners. But you got to realize, Malone stole five of Mr. Dabney's prime horses and tried to sell them to the army. Nobody gets away with that."

Amanda tied the strings of her bonnet under her chin,

preparing to go back out in the sun. "But if he didn't do it?"

"Then we'll find that out, won't we?"

She walked out into the bright light of the afternoon feeling a strange heaviness. Why should she care about what happened to Malone, innocent or guilty? It could only be because he was Cole's friend and his dangerous situation gave her a reason to reach out to Cole again. Her common sense told her this was the last thing she should do, but her common sense was overruled before she walked half a block. She didn't realize it though, until she found herself searching the streets for a glimpse of Little Vitorio.

She found him the following afternoon, hurrying away from the rear door of the Oriental Saloon with a small bottle under his arm. Amanda had never talked to an Apache before and she hardly knew how to manage. Still, she went running after him, thankful they were on the back alleys and not in full view of the town. Once he heard her, he stopped and waited, gripping the bottle against his chest as though he thought she was going to try to take it away from him.

"I'm . . . Amanda," she said, trying to catch her breath and hoping he could understand English. The Indian stood staring at her, his face a blank. "You . . . Vitorio?" she went on. "I want to find Cole. Cole Carteret."

She thought she saw a flicker of recognition in the dark eyes. "Where? Where Cole? Find him."

I sound like an idiot, she thought to herself, but that mattered little now. "You," she said, poking her finger toward Vitorio's chest, "find Cole. I," pointing at her chest, "give two," holding up two fingers, "of those," and she pointed at the bottle. Her heart sank when she received no response. Thinking this was hopeless she was about to turn away when the Indian muttered, "Three."

Amanda smiled and held up three fingers, nodding vigorously. "Yes. Three. But now, find Cole. Find fast."

"He has a camp in Apache Pass," Vitorio said quite clearly.

Amanda caught back her exasperation. "Where is that?"

"One day's ride."

"Then go today. It's important. Tell him Amanda Lassiter needs to see him right away."

Vitorio's eyes narrowed as he stared at her. "Three whiskies. Now."

"Oh, no! When you get back. I promise."

The Indian thought a moment, then shoved the bottle toward her hands. "Keep this. When I bring Cole, I want four!"

"Yes, yes," she nodded. "But hurry. It's really very important."

She never saw a horse, but she supposed he must have one. As he went loping out of sight, she placed the bottle beneath her jacket and held it in place with her arm. No need to have the townsfolks thinking she was taking up drinking in the middle of the day.

Late the next morning, Vitorio appeared at the back of her store and knocked lightly on the door. When she opened it, he slipped into the back room as silently and easily as a whiff of smoke.

"Whisky," he said, handing her a folded piece of paper.

"It's in there," she said, nodding toward the shop. Stepping away from the Apache, she opened the paper and saw that it was a note from Cole telling her to have Vitorio bring her to meet him at the spring. She gave the Indian a guarded look, wondering if he could be trusted. He spoke English far better than she had expected, yet she felt certain he could not have written a note like this. She would have to risk it.

"I'll meet you at the corral in half-an-hour," she said crisply. "Once we meet Cole, you'll have all the whisky."

For a moment she thought he would protest, then his face reassumed its impassive mask and he slipped out as quietly as he had entered. Though it meant lost business, Amanda closed the shop, hurried to her hotel to don her riding skirt and hat, then walked across the street to the corral. Vitorio waited beside a sable-and-white pony while she hired a horse and placed the carefully wrapped bottles inside the saddlebags. As they went cantering down the street out of town, yellow dust swirling around their horses' hooves, she received several strange looks from people along the walkways. One of the Mexican women, who was hanging out wash, paused to stare at them, then took off running back toward town. Amanda thought it strange, but was too intent on seeing Cole again to linger over it.

She recognized the route they took as the one she and Cole had taken the day they rode out to visit the mines. Though she could never have found the spring by herself, Vitorio seemed to know exactly where he was going. He rode hurriedly ahead of her, often stopping to wait for her to catch up on her slower horse.

The churning in her chest grew stronger with every mile. Now that she expected to see Cole again, she was beset with a hundred doubts. Was this whole thing just a wild-goose chase? Had she dragged him from his camp into dangerous proximity of Tombstone for nothing? After all, Sheriff Behan had assured her Aces would get a trial. What was the big hurry, anyway? The sense of urgency Malone felt was probably all in his mind.

And what of Cole? Would he be as eager to see her again as she was to see him? Or would he resent her dragging him here or be annoyed, even angry, for trying once again to rekindle their relationship after she had broken it off? With every mile, Amanda's reluctance grew until she was almost ready to declare this whole thing a mistake and turn back.

Then, as they climbed up into the low gravel paths of the Dragoon Mountains, she saw him standing far off on a bluff, waving his hat at her. Her blood raced and her heart leaped with anticipation and relief. She spurred her horse upward along the path, outdistancing Vitorio, until she came round a sharp bend of rocks and saw the green valley below with the blue thread of the stream winding through it. Cole stood beside his grazing horse, smiling at her as she cantered forward.

She slipped out of the saddle and into his arms before her feet touched the ground. He wrapped her tightly to him, knocking her hat backward and catching her hair in his hands as he pressed his lips into hers, drinking from them as a man with a long thirst.

Amanda's arms went around his neck and she hugged

him fiercely to her. All the longing and need she had forced from her came surging back as she felt his hardness against the length of her body. Her hands slid round to cup his face and she broke away, just to look at him, to know he really was here in her arms again.

Cole wanted to do more than look. He kissed her face, brushing his lips along her cheeks, her eyes, her mouth, and down along her throat. "You feel so wonderful," he murmured, gasping for breath. "I've missed you something terrible."

Amanda laughed with delight as he picked her up in his arms and swung her around. "Something terrible," he echoed as her arms went around his neck and she clung to him. Even as he set her down, his lips sought hers once more, his tongue gently probing into the sweet recesses of her mouth, flicking against her teeth.

"Mmmm . . ." Amanda murmured, pointing at Vitorio, who sat on his pinto staring at them.

"What? Oh, don't worry about him," Cole said, his fingers slipping to the buttons on her blouse.

Amanda pulled away, catching his fingers in her hands. "Cole, I'm as glad to see you as you obviously are to see me, but I won't make love in front of anybody. Especially an Indian. Besides, we have something important to talk about."

Reluctantly, Cole looked around, smiling at the Apache. "Oh, all right." He spoke a stream of Indian words Amanda did not understand, which were followed by a sentence or two from Vitorio. She caught one of those words—'whisky.'

"I think I know what he wants," she said, walking to

her saddlebags and pulling out the four bottles. “Here. You’ve earned it.”

“Amanda!” Cole exclaimed in mock indignation. “Don’t you know it’s against the law to give whisky to an Indian?”

“It’s against the law to sell it. But Vitorio and I made a bargain and he kept it. Take it, and have a good time,” she added.

For the first time she saw the ghost of a smile on the Apache’s face. He took the wrapped bottles and cradled them under his arm. “Cole want me to stay and see the Missy back?”

“You wouldn’t even if I asked,” Cole said, smiling at him. “Go on. I’ll see she gets safely back.”

Without a word, Vitorio turned his pony and rode back down the path. They watched him only a moment before moving toward the stream and settling down on the grass. Amanda fought the urge to slip into Cole’s embrace again and, instead, sat opposite him, looking intently into his eyes.

“Your friend Aces Malone asked me to contact you,” she said.

“And I thought you needed me to make love to you again.”

“Be serious, Cole,” she said, trying to ignore his dancing glances. “Aces is in big trouble, or at least he thinks he is. He was arrested for stealing some horses from Dabney’s ranch and trying to sell them to the army. Once they brought him back to Tombstone, talk started linking him to Bud Philpot’s shooting last spring. He thinks they mean to hang him.”

“Aces never robbed a stage. There’s no way in the

world they can link him to Philpot's murder. Besides, everybody knows it was Doc Holliday who murdered Bud Philpot."

"But Holliday was acquitted, remember? Evidently Aces believes the murder is just an excuse to get him out of the way."

"Why would anyone trouble themselves about a second-rate cardshark? He's no threat to anyone."

"He thinks he is. He begged me to find you and get you to help him."

Cole inched nearer her on the grass, his fingers sliding along her arm. "He's just scared. Stealing horses is a serious charge out here in the West. But I know Malone. He might cheat you out of the gold in your teeth at the faro table, but he doesn't rob stages and he doesn't steal horses. I think he's making too much of all this."

"Cole, I've talked to him. I tell you he is really frightened."

Cole dropped his hand, pursing his lips. "Then there must be something more involved. Of course, framing Aces for Philpot's murder would be the perfect way to clear Holliday. But why should Behan want to do that? He has no use for any of that Earp gang." Absently, his fingers began their light drift over her arm once again.

The feathery touch on her skin sent warm shivers coursing through her body. "Then you think there might be a plot against him?" she murmured, trying to ignore the awakening waves of desire that caught at her throat.

He slipped his arm around her shoulder and pulled her against him. "No, I don't," he murmured, lifting her hair to lightly kiss the back of her neck. "But just in case there is, I think I'll try to find out who really stole those horses."

Amanda felt the short, hot jabs of his tongue against her skin and shivered from head to toe. "But, suppose you're wrong?"

Gently, Cole pushed her down to lie stretched out on the soft, spongy grass. His hand slipped up her side to cup her breast, and he bent to taste the nipple through the fabric of her blouse, teasing it into hot, firm life and sending wave after wave of delicious ecstasy through Amanda's body. She arched against him, lifting her breast to him. with his lips, he pushed away the fabric to bare it to his longing lips.

"I'm never wrong," she heard him murmur before she lost all sense of anything except the joy of his cool lips on her tender skin and the hot desire of his hands against her flesh.

They stayed there until late in the day, when Cole thought it safe to ride with Amanda back to Tombstone. He left her on the outskirts of town, with a message for Aces to keep up his spirits.

"But suppose you aren't able to find out who really stole those horses?" Amanda asked, reluctant to loosen her grip on his hand. Being with him again had awakened all her love for him and washed away all her efforts to put him out of her mind. She knew now she could never forget, never turn away. And yet their future together was just as bleak as it had been when she left Paso Diablo.

"Don't worry, I'll find them. I know whom to ask."

"You'll have to have proof or it won't do any good."

He leaned toward her from his horse to kiss her lightly

on the lips. "I know that. You just tell Aces I'm out to prove him innocent. That ought to make him feel better."

"I'll tell him in the morning," she said quietly, laying her palm against his cheek. "Will I see you again?"

He cuffed her lightly under her chin. "You can count on it." Then, slapping her mount's rump, he sent her cantering toward the town.

Amanda didn't look back, though she could feel his eyes on her until she was swallowed by the darkness.

She went straight to the jail first thing the next morning to give Cole's message to Aces. It seemed to buoy his spirits a little, though it was difficult to detect any change in Malone's guarded eyes or in his face, covered as it was by an increasingly heavy growth of beard.

"I hope he hurries," Aces muttered as she turned to leave. Amanda thought him overly pessimistic. She felt certain once Cole put his mind to finding the real horse thieves, they were as good as caught. And since she had no other reason to continue to visit the jail, she went on about the business of her life without trying to see the prisoner again. Even as the days went by with no word from Cole, she didn't worry. After all, trials and sentencings took time and the court never seemed to be in any hurry.

She was shocked, therefore, to pick up the *Nugget* one morning and read that Malone's trial was scheduled for 9:00 that day. Amanda threw down the paper, ran upstairs for her hat, and hurried from the hotel to the courthouse with an increasing sense of urgency. Why hadn't Cole returned before now? Was he waiting for the last moment to appear with the evidence to save Aces? Surely he wouldn't come into town himself. She had expected him to bring whatever evidence was needed to her, yet she had heard nothing from him since the night he left her outside Tombstone.

The courthouse was already filled, mostly with the idlers of the saloons who were interested in seeing a known gambler and cardshark get his just desserts. Amanda squeezed into the crowd and worked her way toward the front of the gallery where she was able to glimpse the heads of the lawyers and the prisoner. The rowdy court grew comparatively silent once Judge Spicer entered and started the proceedings. During the presentations, murmurs of approval or disagreement swept through the throng; and twice, when evidence was given of which they approved, the crowd erupted into applause and bravos to the accompaniment of the judge's gavel.

From the beginning, it looked bad for Aces. The men who testified against him claimed to have seen him hanging around Dabney's ranch the day before the theft. An army officer testified Aces had approached him, offering to sell the animals. When John Slaughter took the stand and, under relentless questioning, admitted he couldn't be certain it was Doc Holliday and not Aces Malone he had seen the night Bud Philpot was killed, it was the last nail in Malone's coffin.

The jury only deliberated for half-an-hour before returning a verdict of *guilty as charged.* Judge Spicer pronounced sentence of hanging right away and Aces was led from the courtroom amid a loud clamor. Amanda caught his eye only briefly as he passed. He did not try to say anything; he just looked at her with a blank stare that suggested he had accepted his fate long before now.

As the courtroom emptied and the crowd swept out to the gallows in the rear, Amanda sank into one of the chairs, twisting her hands in her lap. She felt as though something had broken inside. Not that she had any real feeling for the gambler—she barely knew him. Yet somehow she felt a terrible injustice was being done. Why hadn't Cole come back before now to help his friend? Was it deliberate or had something interfered to keep him away?

"Not going to watch the fun?" asked a voice behind her. She turned to see Sheriff Behan studying her from the doorway.

"I don't consider watching a man die a form of entertainment."

"Then you're different from the rest of the people in this town. Or throughout the West, for that matter."

Amanda stood to face him. "I don't believe that man was guilty," she said, lifting her chin.

"A jury convicted him."

"Do you believe he was a horse thief?"

Behan shrugged. "It doesn't matter what I believe. I know this. When a man is desperate, he can be driven to do all kinds of things he would never consider under more ordinary circumstances."

Amanda walked to the door as if to pass him. Then she paused. "Suppose the jury was wrong? What if he's proven innocent in the end?"

Behan tried to smile. "Then we'll write on his tombstone that he was hanged by mistake."

His callous remark left her furious. She gripped her

hand to keep from slapping his smug cheek. "That will be cold comfort to Malone," she muttered, stalking out the door.

When she had told Sheriff Behan she intended to leave, she had really meant to do so. Yet, as she started across the yard, three men appeared from the side door of the jail, hauling Aces Malone toward the gibbet in the courtyard at the rear of the building. As they crossed Amanda's path, she stopped and caught her breath, hoping Aces would not see her.

He spotted her right away, leaning toward her as he passed and forcing the deputies to slow for a moment. There was a thin, ironic smile on his narrow lips; and his eyes, as Amanda looked into them, were dark as still black pits of stagnant water.

"I'm so sorry," she muttered. "He's still out there, trying."

"Tell him this was the first time I wasn't able to draw against a spade flush," Aces said, giving her a macabre grin. "And be sure to tell him to have a drink on me."

Amanda nodded, her hand at her throat, as the deputies dragged Malone across the yard. She wanted to call out some words of comfort but was unable to think of anything helpful to say. Sick at heart, she turned away before the crowd closed in around the condemned man and hurried back to her store. The noise of the execution followed her down the street, like a spectre of gloom dogging her footsteps.

By the time she put her key in the lock, a distant roar from the courthouse told her it was all over.

Twenty-five

It had been a busy week. Aces's body was barely cold before a spectacular shoot-out on the street in front of the livery stable drove the memory of his hanging from the town's collective mind. Amanda found herself faced with a steady string of customers seeking solace from all the excitement in nerve tonics and stomach pills. At least all the activity had the added effect of keeping her too busy to dwell on Malone's death and her disappointment that she had not been able to prevent it.

She'd heard nothing from Cole and could only imagine that he either had given up after finding no proof Aces was innocent or that other concerns had lured him away from even trying. Either way, as the days went by, the euphoria she had felt at seeing him again was overshadowed by an ever increasing anger at his silence.

Amanda was trying to help three customers at the counter when the bell over her front door told her another one had entered. She looked up to see a man's slight figure standing near the window casually observing a row of labels on the shelf. When the man reached up to remove his gray peaked cowboy hat, allowing a long braid to fall down his back, Amanda gave a start of surprise. It wasn't a man at all but a women dressed in the serviceable clothes of a ranchhand.

Sally Mahone! What on earth had brought her back to Tombstone?

Amanda threw Sally a tentative smile and served her customers quickly, praying no more would appear before she had a chance to talk privately with her friend. The three chatty women she was helping were matrons of the town who wanted to talk about the gunfight that had occurred the week before and what Amanda thought of it. Only by forcefully putting them off was Amanda able to ease them out of the store and turn her attention to Sally who, by that time, had worked her way to the middle of the counter.

Sally appeared embarrassed and uncomfortable. As Amanda turned to face her, she found herself feeling the same way.

"Let's go sit at the back," she suggested. "At least, until someone else comes in."

"I guess you're surprised to see me," Sally said, laying her hat on the cold stove and settling into one of the chairs. "I haven't been able to get back into town since, well, the last time I saw you. But when I heard about all the excitement, I thought I'd ride in. I was curious, too, about . . . well . . ."

"About how my abduction worked out?"

"Well, yes. You see, I've known Cole for a long time and he's done some pretty strange things before, but I never thought . . ."

"Then you didn't know he was going to carry me off?"

"Not at all. He asked me to invite you for a visit

and, once I got to know you, I gladly obliged him. I really thought we might get to be friends, and I hoped we would. I could have strangled him with my bare hands when he showed up like that."

Amanda smiled. "So could I! In fact, it took some time before I forgave him. Eventually, though, well, I guess it was the place, and the fact that we were alone . . ."

Sally gave her a knowing smile. "He can be persuasive when he wants to be. I suppose he took you to Paso Diablo."

"Yes. And I fell in love with it." She sighed. "And with him, all over again. Though what good it will do me, I can't see."

Sally studied her face. "I can only tell you that I've never seen Cole go to such lengths for a woman before. He must care for you very strongly. I hope that's some kind of consolation."

"Not much. He went off days ago to find evidence that might have saved a friend from being hanged, and I haven't had a word from him. It's too late for the friend, of course, and now even I am beginning to wonder if that week at Paso Diablo was just a fantasy."

Reaching out, Sally squeezed her hand. "The way my cousin's life has gone these last few years, I can't offer you much encouragement. But I believe at heart he is a man worth waiting and fighting for. If any woman can change him, I think you can. I hope you will find it in your heart to try."

Amanda looked down at her hands. She was moved by Sally's words and felt a tremendous relief just to be talking with someone who knew Cole and could understand the conflicting emotions she felt for him. She jumped when she heard the bell at her front door jingle as two more customers entered.

"Thank you, Sally. Will you wait while I take care of these people?"

"I can't," Sally said, rising. "But I'll stop back by after I finish my errands. I want to hear what all the excitement is about."

Amanda shrugged. "Oh, that was nothing but a bunch of gunfighters feuding among themselves. Some are calling it cold-blooded murder because one of the men killed—Tom McLowery—wasn't armed. The talk is the Earp gang wanted the Clantons and McLowerys dead because they could implicate them in all these robberies."

"So that's it. Well, as the saying goes, 'Live by the gun, die by the gun.' " Sally picked up her hat and set it on her sandy-colored hair. "I'll see you later, then."

"Thanks for stopping by," Amanda said, giving her a grateful smile. She walked toward the two matrons who waited patiently by the counter with Sally's words echoing in her mind. *'Live by the gun, die by the gun.'* Would that be true for Cole? Would he someday lie sprawled in a dirt street, shattered and bleeding?

Mentally she gave herself a shake and forced a smile for the ladies waiting at the counter. Her attention had to be given now to preparing salves and powders; but, once she was alone, she knew she would be grateful to Sally for coming to see her. As for Cole, she refused to think about him.

* * *

Two weeks later, the town of Tombstone buzzed with excitement over the indictment of the Earp brothers and Doc Holliday for the murders of Billy Clanton and Frank and Tom McLowery. The indictment dominated every conversation, while the long, conflicting stories run by both newspapers added fuel to the fire. Most of the decent people of the town looked on with amusement as the *Epitaph* lined up supporters for the Earps and the *Nugget* tried to be impartial. The *Nugget* attempted to print only the facts, but the truth was so damaging that the paper appeared to be decidedly against the Earps. Readers followed the lead of both papers by lining up on either side.

Amanda only half-listened to the impassioned arguments of the customers who came into her drug store. She wished she could get excited about a passel of worthless gunslingers because that might take her mind off wondering where Cole had gone. He was so much in her thoughts she could not even share in the town's indignation when Justice Wells Spicer dismissed the indictment against Holliday and the Earps in spite of the overwhelming evidence against them.

Sally's visit helped her to regain some of the trust she had lost in Cole. But so many days went by with still no word from him that she found that trust once again eroding. She began to think it might be better for her to leave Tombstone for a larger city like Tucson. Perhaps she should even reconsider the offer of Louis McKeithan's mysterious buyer.

With December, nights began arriving earlier, and soon Amanda found herself trudging back to her hotel in the dark. This didn't worry her too much since Fremont Street was not nearly as tumultuous as Allen, which held most of the saloons. Besides, she had been in town long enough now to recognize most of the people she passed.

This night seemed darker than most when she snapped down the shade on the window and stepped outside to lock the door. Pulling her shawl around her shoulders against the cold night air, she hurried toward Fremont and home. The sounds of revelry grew dimmer as she walked farther from Allen Street, but she could still catch the distant jangle of a piano, the hoops and hollers of men on the street, and even the occasional blast of a gun. She was so accustomed to it all by now that she didn't even flinch when the guns went off. Most of the time it was just some hotshot cowboy showing off.

As she turned the corner onto Fremont, she noticed that the street was unusually deserted. Then she remembered there was a performance of a traveling play at the Opera House that evening and most of the people who would normally be on the streets were probably inside watching it, as much to keep warm as to enjoy the entertainment. Her heels clattered on the wooden walkway as she hurried on, eager to get to the hotel before the last supper call.

"Amanda."

She stopped, her breath catching in her throat. The whisper came from the dark recesses between two buildings and though Amanda strained to make out who was there, she could see nothing. But she recognized the voice. She stepped back from the shadows, her hand going to her throat.

"Who's there?"

"It's me. Cole."

He stepped out of the narrow blackness far enough to let her make out his figure. The dim glow of the street lantern cast gaunt shadows on the long planes of his face. She leaned closer, not recognizing him at first. He had grown a fairly full moustache since she had last seen him, and it made his face more mysterious than ever.

"It can't be. I don't believe it."

"For God's sake," he whispered. "Do I have to step out here in front of God and everybody? Who else would it be?"

Amanda struggled between relief and fury. "Cole . . . Oh, Cole," she cried, moving toward him. His arms went around her and he pulled her back into the darkness of the alley. Still, she struggled against his embrace, unwilling to give up her righteous anger so easily.

"You came too late. Aces is dead."

Sensing her reluctance, Cole eased his grip on her waist. "I know that. I wanted to see you."

Her senses reeled with the nearness of him, the scent of leather and musk, the dark outline of his lips and chin, the hardness of his body against hers, the feel of his hands drifting across her back. She fought the urge to throw her arms around his neck and press her lips to his.

"Where have you been? Why didn't you come back in time to help Aces?"

For a long minute he was silent. "If we can go someplace safer than out here on the street, I'll try to explain." He dropped his hands and stepped back. "Are you headed for your hotel?"

"Yes, but you would not be safe there. The back room of the store is better. Can you manage to get there without being seen?"

"Of course."

"All right. I'll meet you there in fifteen minutes."

He gave her shoulder a squeeze before being swallowed up by the darkness. Amanda stepped back on the walkway, made certain no one was watching, then retraced her steps. She did not light a lamp until she was safely in the storeroom with the door to the inside of the shop tightly closed. She sat on the cot to wait for him, hoping she would not be disappointed once again. Her heart turned over at the realization he had come back to her in spite of the danger, knowing it was too late to help his friend. Perhaps it was time to give him the benefit of the doubt and let the residue of her anger drift away.

She jumped at the short, soft knock on the back door. Quickly she opened it just wide enough for Cole to slip through. Relocking it, she turned to lean against the wood, studying him.

She could see he had been traveling hard. His clothes were covered with the yellow dust of the desert. Even his eyelashes looked sandy pale, and his face appeared jaundiced. His lips were cracked with the sun and his hard hands callused. His shoulders, normally so straight and tall, were bowed with fatigue. Amanda regretted her curt comment back in the alley when she realized what a toll it had taken on him just to get here.

Cole looked longingly at the cot as though he wanted nothing more than to throw himself along its length.

Instead he turned to face her, looking deeply into her eyes, his own dark with longing.

"I hoped I could save him," he muttered.

Amanda flew across the narrow room and into his arms. "Oh, Cole. I hoped so, too. So much."

It was all he needed. He caught her up and swung her around before drawing her face to his and kissing her lips. She clung to him, molded against him, pressing her body against him, reveling in the feel of his mouth on hers. Warmth flowed between them, heightening to a rich desire. Cole tightened his arms around her, lifting her off her feet. He buried his lips in the hollow of her neck while she made soft cries of longing and pleasure. Lifting her in his arms, he carried her to the cot and laid her on it, kneeling beside it. Deftly he worked at the buttons of her dress, teasing her with his fingers and his lips as he worked away her confining clothes. Pulling the laces of her bodice free, he warmed her skin with his tongue, tasting every sweet inch, until she writhed beneath him. Lifting her breasts free, he pressed them together and caressed them with his mouth.

Amanda's body floated on waves of delight, twisting with the need for him that grew with every kiss. She moaned softly as he slid his hand beneath her clothes and down the length of her to cup between her legs. Gently he stroked the fire there, flaring it into wild life. She was moist, ready for him, desperate for him, yet still he teased and tormented her. Not until she thought she could bear no more did he stretch quickly along the length of her body, thrusting his rock-hard, elongated shaft deeply into the damp, willing recess of her body.

She clasped her arms around him, holding him tightly

as with lunge after lunge he drove into her. Dimly she heard his cries as his need built. He filled her with his manhood, joined with her as one creature that sought completion in the wild, ecstatic joy of raging desire. He was not gentle now. There was a desperation in his drive to possess her. She was as wild as he in her wanting. He cried out in the emptying of himself and she clasped her legs around him, melding her body with his in the joyful completion of their joining.

Like waves pounding on a shore, her senses reeled. Then came the slow subsiding, the draining, the quiet. There were tears on her cheeks. He brushed them away with his fingers, kissing the damp spots.

"I didn't hurt you, did I?"

"No. Did I hurt you?"

He laughed. "My back is so burned from the sun that your nails didn't help. It hurts now, but I don't recall noticing it a few moments ago."

She snuggled against him on the cot. "The town band could have marched through here a few minutes ago and I wouldn't have noticed!"

"I'm glad they didn't. As I remember, you don't perform in public." His arms tightened around her as he lay breathing the scent of her hair. "You smell so fresh and good. God, it's been a long time. I didn't realize how much I missed you until I had you in my arms again."

Amanda nestled her head in the hollow of his neck. "I had almost given up waiting for you. If Sally hadn't encouraged me . . ."

"Sally? She was here?"

"Yes. She came into town after the big shoot-out at

the corral. She told me not to stop trusting you, that you would come back when you could."

Cole gave a soft chuckle. "My cousin Sally. Well, she's right. I tried my damnedest to get back sooner, but it took longer to find the evidence I needed than I thought. When I did find it, it was so feeble it might not have saved Aces anyway."

Amanda raised up on one elbow, looking down into his thin face. "Aces told me nothing would do any good, that they wanted to get him out of the way because of what he knew. What did he mean, Cole?"

"I'm not sure, but I think I have an idea. And he was probably right." Cole shifted to sit up, turning to put his feet on the floor and rest his elbows on his knees. "What I don't understand is how Aces could have died without leaving something behind to show what he knew. It wasn't like him not to make the people who wanted him dead pay for it. He didn't say anything to you, did he?"

"No, nothing. But then, we never had much of a chance to be alone. Except once . . ." She jumped up. "He did leave something. A bottle of whisky which he told me give to you to 'have a drink on me.' Where did I put that?" she said, rummaging among the bottles stacked on a top shelf. "I don't know how it could mean anything, though. It was so grimy and awful-looking. Here it is."

She pulled the green bottle from behind a row of tonics and handed it to Cole. He turned it over, inspecting it. The brownish-gray liquid inside appeared thicker and even more unappealing than when Aces had given it to her.

"You're not going to drink that?" she asked hesitantly.

Cole pulled out the stopper and held the bottle to his nose. "I don't think so. It smells as if it would kill anyone who did. You're sure this is all he left?"

"It's all he gave to me. He might have left something more with another person."

Cole shook his head. "I don't think so since he knew you were the only person in town I would be talking to." He replaced the stopper and shook the bottle furiously, setting up a brown froth on the surface. "I think there is something besides old whisky inside. Where can I pour it out?"

Amanda felt a twinge of excitement as she handed Cole a wooden bowl and watched him pour the liquid into it. Only half streamed forth before the neck was plugged by a dark object.

"There is something," she said excitedly. Cole worked at the neck of the bottle with his finger, gradually drawing the object outward until he grasped it. Peering over his shoulder, Amanda saw that it was a small piece of leather, tightly wound and tied with a thin thong. She took the bowl and set it aside while Cole cut the wet binding with his knife and unwound the leather strip.

"Clever Aces," he murmured. "He used treated leather that's waterproof. And here is the reason."

Carefully, he spread out a small strip of paper with crabbed writing on its surface, hardly large enough to read.

"What does it say?" Amanda asked, straining to make out the words.

Cole held it to the light. "It's too small to be very important. Yet he wouldn't have gone to all this trouble for nothing." He peered closer to the writing. "Boot Hill, Gold Dollar."

"That's all?"

"That's all I can make out. I know what Boot Hill means, but 'Gold Dollar'? Does that make any sense to you?"

"I've never been to Boot Hill; it's such a creepy place."

A faint memory stirred in the back of Cole's mind. He turned to Amanda, frowning. "Isn't there a whore at the Bird Cage called Gold Dollar?"

"There used to be. She killed another woman in an argument over her boyfriend, and I heard she left town soon after."

"That must have been after I left. Do you suppose her name would be on one of those markers on Boot Hill? Who was the girl she killed?"

"I think her name was Marguerite. She was a Mexican girl and hadn't been in Tombstone very long."

Cole gathered up Amanda's clothes and handed them to her, then began pulling on his own which had been so hastily discarded a short time before. "Come on, my love," he said. "We're going to make a trip to Boot Hill."

Amanda shrank back. "Now? In the dark? Oh, no. Not me."

"I can't very well go poking about out there in the daylight now, can I? I have to go at night. Bring that lantern, and your cloak to mask it. And a shovel, just in case. I have a hunch Aces buried the evidence he collected out there, and if we can find anything with Gold Dollar's name on it, that will be the place to look."

Reluctantly, Amanda pulled her dress over her shoulders. "But Cole . . ."

He yanked at his belt, buckling it, then reached for his jacket. "Come on, Amanda. I promise not to let the ghosts get you."

Cole's light-hearted assurances did not help Amanda nearly as much as the tight grip she kept on his arm as they moved silently around the dark cemetery. Sporadic moonlight cast long shadows on the graveled earth and the short crosses marking each grave. Amanda averted her eyes from the freshly piled earth she knew had been turned for Billy Clanton and the McLowery brothers and tried to concentrate on reading the names as Cole's lantern fell on them. It took only a few minutes to find what they were looking for—crude lettering marking the grave of 'Marguerite, stabbed by Gold Dollar.'

"This has to be it," Cole said, setting down the lantern and reaching for the shovel. "But where?" He fell to his knees and felt the earth around the cross.

"Why would Aces come out here alone at night to bury evidence when he could have left it in a dozen places in town? He could have even given it to me. It doesn't make any sense."

"It does to me," Cole said, patting the earth. "He wouldn't want to put you in any danger, and he knew I wouldn't mind coming here. I used to meet him in this place, in fact. He didn't like it, but he came. Look at this . . . the ground's softer here, as if it might have been recently turned. This is the place to start digging."

Amanda glanced around the deserted cemetery. Out

in the desert the sudden mournful howl of a coyote sent shivers up her spine. She dropped to her knees beside Cole. "I don't like this at all. Can't we leave?"

But leaving was the last thing on Cole's mind. He dug the shovel into the ground, pushing and lifting until he had a hole a foot deep. Only then did he hit something hard.

"A royal flush!" he cried, digging at the earth with his hands. When he touched a circular shape, he worked at it until he could grasp the ring in his fingers. He yanked up a small iron chest from the hole, brushed off the dirt, and set it down near the lantern.

"It's got a padlock," Amanda whispered. "And it's awfully small."

"Big enough," Cole said, picking up a good sized rock to break the padlock. The metal gave way, and he opened the lid to find the box stuffed with papers. He took one off the top and held it to the light, his lips pressed tightly together as he read.

Amanda leaned close to him. "What is it? Is it important?"

"A bill of sale. Something quite a few people in Tombstone would be interested in seeing. Come on," he said, stuffing the paper back in the box and closing the lid. "Let's get this hole filled in again and get out of here."

"It can't be too soon to suit me," Amanda whispered.

Once back in the storeroom of Amanda's shop, Cole took out the papers from the metal box and spread them, one by one, on the plank table. Amanda peered over his shoulder trying to make sense of them, but could only tell that they appeared to be copies of legal documents and lists. After a long silence, she turned to Cole.

"Will these help you?"

"They aren't of much use to me, but they will certainly be of interest to my friend." He looked up at her, noticing how the lamplight emphasized the deep planes of her cheeks and set dancing glimmers in her honied eyes. "They do one thing more. They show in no uncertain terms why some people in this town wanted Aces dead. He knew too much."

Amanda sank down in the chair opposite him. "He said that to me, in just those words. I didn't believe him."

"It's true. According to these papers, the Earps own lots all over this town. They own mining properties as well, most of which they have transferred to other grantees. These are pretty rare financial doings for a saloon keeper, a faro dealer, and an assistant marshal. How did they have the means to accumulate such large holdings in the town and in these rich mines?"

"You aren't suggesting . . ."

"I certainly am. Some influential people are behind them. Look at the names here. Mayor Clum transferred property."

"He's also the owner of the *Epitaph,* a paper that consistently defends the Earps."

"Justice Spicer served as a mining broker."

"He's the one who threw out the indictment against Doc Holliday for killing Bud Philpot and dismissed the charges against Holliday and the Earps for that shooting at the OK Corral."

"You get the idea. How did these men raise the bail they needed for all these indictments? Somebody had to pay it."

Amanda stood up abruptly and walked back and forth a few paces. "You don't understand, Cole. In this town there is the lawless element—the Earps, Curley Bill, the Clantons—and there are the respectable people, the lawyers, judges, bankers, mine owners, shopkeepers. One group has little to do with the other, except when a crime is committed. At least, that's how it appears to me."

He gave her an indulgent smile. "My dear, I guessed more than that when I was pretending to be Reverend Storey. It was clear to me then that some big money was behind these outlaws. Otherwise, they could never have gotten away with it for so long. These men never robbed stages unless there was a strongbox aboard. How did they know? Someone, probably Williams at Wells Fargo, tipped them off. It wouldn't surprise me if those boxes never had any money in them at all. The payroll probably stayed right here in town and was pocketed by the men behind the robbers. Where else did the money go? Did the Earps spend it on high living?"

Amanda laughed. "Hardly. They live in squalid little boxes on the east end of town, their wives always look shabby when they're allowed out at all, and—as far as I know—they never throw money around."

"Exactly. They get their share, but you can bet the bulk of it goes right back to the big fellows at the top."

Amanda gave a short gasp. "McKeithan. He tried to buy my store for an anonymous buyer. He wouldn't say who it was, but I suspected Brody Hanlon. He owns a lot of the town already."

"I remember them both. Hanlon has McKeithan and Justice Spicer in his pocket. I can't see why he would want this place, though, unless he thought you were too close to me and might pose a danger. These men are very good at covering their tracks."

"You mean they were trying to get me to leave town?"

"Probably." Cole stuffed the papers back into the box and closed the lid. "And I wager the Earps will never be convicted for that murder at the corral, either. They'll get off, just as they have in the past."

She watched him as he reached for his hat. "What will you do?" she asked, her heart sinking at the realization that he would be off once more.

"I'm going to take these papers to my friend and hope they do some good. Come on. I'll walk you back to your hotel."

"Is that wise?"

"No, but I don't intend to leave you here alone. It's late enough that there won't be many people about."

That was true. Amanda draped her cloak about her shoulders and bent to turn out the lamp. Cole waited by the door until she brushed against him. Closing her in his arms, he kissed her deeply and long, his hands entwined in her hair.

"I'll come back. I promise."

She didn't answer. She did not believe him. Yet she was too tired to worry about it, too tired even to give in to the rushing surge of desire his lips awoke in her body. Instead, she wrapped her arms around him and clung to him, resting against his hard body, savoring its firmness and comfort.

Cole gripped both sides of her cloak and pulled it tightly around her. "Come on, my girl. It's time you were asleep."

They walked down the empty, darkened street, their footsteps echoing softly on the wooden walkway. Amanda pulled the hood of her cloak over her hair while Cole yanked his hat close down around his eyes. With any luck, they would appear to be just another loving couple ambling home in the early hours of the morning. The streets were so deserted, however, their precautions did not appear to be necessary. They only passed one lone cowboy before they reached the hotel, and he was so staggering drunk he paid them no mind.

Cole stopped in the shadows before the hotel doors, taking Amanda in his arms once again and kissing the tip of her nose. "You'll be all right?"

She tried to smile. "Of course. I just need a little sleep. What about you?"

"I'll slip out of town quietly until I'm far enough away to ride hard. The sooner I can get this box to my friend, the better."

She ran her finger lightly down his moustache. "I think I prefer you clean-shaven."

"So do I," Cole said, chuckling. "But I haven't had time to grow a beard and it didn't seem wise to come back here without some kind of camouflage."

Amanda knew she had to let him go. She threw her arms around his neck and hugged him tightly, the pains she felt over his leaving her again numbed by the need for sleep and rest for which her body clamored.

But she wasn't to have that rest yet. As she looked over Cole's shoulder, her eye was caught by a yellow glow wavering over the rooftops of the houses across the street. She gave a short gasp and dug her fingers into his back.

"What's the matter?"

Perhaps it was the dawn, yet surely that was still hours away. Then the light flared suddenly upward, jetting into the sky.

"Oh my God!" Amanda exclaimed, breaking away and gripping his arm. "It's a fire!"

Twenty-six

Fire—the most dreaded word in Tombstone. Amanda knew the collection of ramshackle, wooden buildings that made up the town had already been purged and rebuilt after several destructive fires. Everyone in Tombstone lived with the constant fear of its happening again.

Cole turned swiftly to stare at the yellow glow, his fingers tightening on her arms. "Where?"

"I think it's coming from the houses near the church."

That was all he needed to hear. Thrusting the metal box into her hands, he took off, calling back over his shoulder: "Hide that for me."

"But . . ." Amanda stared after him, wanting to rush off as well. Yet she knew these papers were too important to treat carelessly. Dashing through the hotel doors, she ran up two flights of stairs to her room, fumbled for her key, and rushed in to throw the box under the bed. She paused beside her window long enough to see a wall of flames in the distance reaching into the black sky. Against them she could make out the dark silhouette of St. Anselm's square bell tower. Even as she paused, the tower bell began to toll wildly, accompanied by the sharper clang of the fire alarms in town. By the time she reached the street again, people were streaming along the walkways, dark figures of men in shirt sleeves and women clasping big shawls over their night-robes. Amanda joined them, urged by the need to see what danger the fire caused, as well as a nagging fear for Cole's safety.

As she darted down Third Street, she could see that the church was still intact though the house next to it was totally consumed by flames. Two others across the street were beginning to catch fire from sparks whipped and carried on the strong winds. She peered through the light seeking Cole and finally spotted him in a line of men ferrying buckets of water to wet down the sides of the church. Up on the roof, two other men perched precariously, slapping the drifting sparks with wet burlap sacks before they could take hold on the shingles.

As she ran toward Cole, she spotted Reverend Cabot Storey hurrying up the street from the opposite direction, stuffing his shirt into hastily donned pants.

"Is the church all right?" he called to her.

"They're wetting it down." She pointed to the line of men and looked back to see Cabot staring at Cole, shocked disbelief on his face.

"Is that . . ."

"Just go help," Amanda cried, shoving him toward the line. He took off at once, leaving her to run to the well, where several of the women had formed a line to receive the empty buckets and refill them. Libby Walton, shrouded in a printed flannel robe, made a place for her.

"I can't believe it," she said between gasps as she passed the empty buckets along to Amanda, who quickly sent them on. "That he'd come here!"

Amanda did not answer. Obviously the word had spread that Cole was helping to fight the fire, though everyone was too busy to try to do anything more about it than express surprise. Yet, for his own good, she hoped he would leave quickly. She glanced across the street to see that the fire had moved along toward the town, veering toward the Schieffelin Opera House and her hotel just across the street!

Her arms ached and she had a mental picture of losing all her belongings, yet she couldn't rest from the constant passing of the life-saving buckets. Thank goodness Aces had had the foresight to put his papers in a metal box. Perhaps at least *they* would be safe.

Bells could be heard all over the town now, clanging a warning as much as an alarm. They sang an accompaniment to the sobs of the women whose homes were going up in flames and to the shouts of the men as they moved off to fight the newest conflagration. Amanda kept her eyes on Cole, who seemed to be concentrating on the church alone. She lost track of how long she was there, her arms aching from the constant lifting. The house next door burned completely to the ground while the one on the other side of the church caught fire but was extinguished before it could do much damage. Gradually the flames moved with the wind toward the center of the town, and the men trying to save the church turned their attention to new blazes.

When she felt she could leave the line, Amanda hurried over to Cole. His eyes stared out from a face blackened with soot. He had thrown off his jacket, and his shirt was so wet with perspiration it molded his muscular shoulders. He wiped at his brow with his arm and tried to smile at her.

"I think we saved the church anyway."

Amanda resisted the urge to throw her arms around his waist. "You crazy fool. Do you know the risk you're taking?"

Cole looked up at the damp bell tower. "Maybe. But I wasn't about to watch something I built and paid for be burned to a cinder."

Amanda looked around, muttering through her teeth, "All right, you've saved St. Anselm's. Now, please, get out of town."

"You have a nerve comin' here," said a voice behind her. She turned to see Leander Walton step up to Cole. Leander looked almost as tired and dirty as Cole himself. "I couldn't believe it was you at first. Can't say I'm glad to see you, but it was good you were here." He turned to Amanda. "For all his sinnin' ways, he took charge when the rest of us was standin' around wondering what to do. I guess you could say he saved our building for us."

Her anxiety rose a few notches as she saw that several of the other people of the congregation had recognized Cole and were gathering around them. "Please . . ." she murmured, pushing him backward toward the shadows. But the parishioners were not about to allow him to escape so easily now that they could turn their attention away from the danger to their church.

"That was some trick you pulled, 'Reverend Storey.' "

"It was a joke on us, all right."

"Say, are you really The Casket Kid? I just never believed it."

One of them turned to call to Cabot Storey. "Hey, Preacher, you ought to come over here and meet your twin."

Laughter broke out among the small crowd grouped around Cole. He looked at Amanda, uncomfortable and embarrassed.

"Now, folks, we saved the church," he said lamely. "Don't you think you ought to go help some of those other people whose homes are burning? I've really got to be off."

"Not so fast, Carteret!"

Amanda caught her breath as she recognized John Behan's voice. Someone must have gone for him, for she was certain he hadn't been among the crowd before now. He pushed through the group to face Cole, a triumphant, satisfied smile on his thin lips.

"Cole Carteret, you're under arrest for the robbery of the Cortez stage and the murders of passenger O.T. Gibson and Jamie Behan."

Cole looked wildly around, judging his chances of making a run for it. The crowd rimmed him in, and he had laid aside his gun belt to fight the fire. There didn't seem much chance there.

Amanda threw herself in front of him, facing the sheriff. "You can't arrest this man. He stayed to help save the church. You've no right!"

Sheriff Behan's eyes narrowed as he looked down at her. "I have every right, Miss Lassiter. Now get out of the way."

She felt Cole's hands on her shoulders as he set her aside. "Don't threaten the lady, Behan. I'll go quietly.

But I remind you I served my time for Jamie's murder and you've got no proof I robbed that stage."

Behan roughly grabbed Cole's hands and clapped them in a heavy set of iron cuffs. "I got all the proof I need, Carteret. And just because you got some weak-kneed judge to let you off once, don't mean it can happen again. Get going."

Cole turned just long enough to throw Amanda a wink before being pushed again toward the courthouse jail. "Take care," he said softly, and she knew he was referring to the iron box. She stood among startled parishioners watching Cole being taken away, her heart failing within her.

The fool, for coming here to save a building! The crazy fool!

Amanda felt her knees wobble and she reached out to grab something, anything, to steady her. Libby Walton, who had been standing beside her, laid an arm around her shoulder.

"Now don't you worry, Amanda. The Reverend might have flummoxed a lot of people in this church, but, after they got over being mad, they realized they really liked him. They aren't going to let anything bad happen to him. We'll solve all this somehow."

Amanda did not share half of Libby's confidence. With surprise, she realized it was almost daylight. While they had been fighting the fire, the day had dawned and was now rapidly moving toward full light. Its harshness fell on the charred ruins of the house beside the church, revealing the stark, sooty stubble of what just hours ago had been a pleasant home. The air reeked of smoke and tar. Scalding whisps of eerie plumes of smoke rose from the embers.

"They think it was a heater that done it," Libby said absently. "These cold nights and kerosene heaters in clapboard houses—it's a wonder we don't have more fires than we do."

Amanda looked around at the rest of the street. The little church showed damp streaks where it had been watered down. Across the road, half the roof was gone from another house while the one next to it showed the scorched remains of a porch standing against a house which was mostly intact. She could see the way the fire had marched along the road toward town by the damage to the row of homes it had touched. If the wind had been from the opposite direction, St. Anselm's would be a charred ruin as well. Now, thanks to Cole . . .

Tears stung behind her eyes as much, she knew, from weariness and lack of sleep as from the agony she felt at watching Cole being taken away.

"I must go after him," she muttered, trying to pull away from Libby's grasp.

Her friend's round face was full of concern. "Now, girl, anyone can see you are about to drop from fatigue. You need to rest. Get some sleep, and then we'll all put our heads together and see what can be done. It isn't going to help him for you to fall in your tracks."

There was some truth in Libby's observation, Amanda realized. She had been up the entire night and had endured such emotional ups and downs since Cole first stopped her on her way home that her body felt drained of all strength. A little sleep might help, though she doubted if the agitation that consumed her was going to allow it.

"Where's Miss Lassiter?"

Recognizing Doc Goodfellow's voice, Amanda looked up to see the doctor pushing his big form through the crowd. He spotted her at the same time and headed toward her. Libby, still holding tightly to Amanda's arm, blocked his way.

"Oh, Doc, I'm so glad to see you here. Can you give poor Amanda something to help her rest? She's about dead on her feet, and if she doesn't get some sleep . . ."

"Get out of my way, woman," the doctor said, brushing Libby aside. With his long practice of dealing with fussing women, he made short shrift of Libby Walton's concerns and got straight to the point.

"You'd better come with me, Amanda."

She looked at him blankly, wondering if someone had been injured and he needed her help. "I don't think I'd be much good as a nurse right now, Doc," she began.

"I don't need a nurse. It isn't that. It's the fire."

Amanda's hand went to her throat. The hotel! All her clothes, her few treasured possessions, the metal box . . .

"It's the hotel, isn't it?" she whispered.

"I wish it were. No, it's your drug store. The fire whipped up Fifth Street completely out of control. We tried as hard as we could, but it was too much for us. It's a damn shame. All those saloons on Allen Street are spared while a useful drug store goes up in flames.

"Up in flames?" Her voice sounded as though it were coming from a long way off.

"Entirely consumed. I'm so sorry, Amanda, but I'm

afraid there isn't much left of your uncle's . . . oh, my God!"

He caught her as she slumped forward in a dead faint.

She slept all day and most of the following night, thanks to a heavy dose of laudanum Doc Goodfellow administered as soon as she was conscious enough to swallow.

"She might as well rest," he reasoned. "She can't do anything about the store now, and what's left of it will wait for her."

Once or twice she woke briefly, trying to remember why she had this awful pressure in her chest before the drug carried her off again into merciful sleep. When she did finally come to full consciousness, her head felt as though it were full of cotton wool while her sluggish limbs almost refused to move at all. Her body ached all over; and every time she thought of Cole in jail and her store in ruins, her heart stabbed with pain.

By the time it was light enough to see, she was dressed and ready to go downstairs. Without even bothering to take breakfast, she made her way along the chilly streets to stare at what was left of her drug store.

It was worse than she had imagined. All that was left standing was part of the back room. The body of the store was a blackened rubble, with the twisted forms of the stove and the metal register poking haphazardly up from its embers. A few of the shelves in the storeroom still looked as though the tin containers and some glass bottles had survived, but the rubble was still too hot for her to go back and see. The long twisted shape of the little cot on which she and Cole had made love just two nights ago tore at her heart. She turned away, fighting tears.

"Here. Have some of this."

She looked up to see Doc Goodfellow holding out a glass. "It's whisky," he added. "I thought you might come around here as soon as the laudanum wore off, and I was sure you'd need something."

Amanda took the glass and sipped at the searing liquid. With a little encouragement she would have downed the whole thing, but a nagging voice at the back of her mind told her that would not be wise. She must keep her wits clear—to help Cole, if nothing else.

"Thank you. It's worse than I thought."

A tentative smile creased his broad face. "Take heart, dear lady. After all, it's nothing every other store owner in Tombstone hasn't faced. It can be rebuilt. Why, Elton's Barber Shop has been rebuilt three times already."

Amanda turned her huge eyes on him. "Do you really think so?"

"I'm certain of it. This town has to have a drug store."

But she would need a loan in order to rebuild. What banker would give her one when she had so little to offer as collateral? Certainly not McKeithan. She wished she had accepted his offer to buy her out. It would have served the new owner right!

"Come on," the doctor said, taking her arm. "It does you no good to stand here staring at this rubble. Let me buy you breakfast. I'll wager you haven't eaten in two days."

"Nearly that." Food did not sound appealing right

now, yet she allowed him to lead her down the street and around the corner to the Alhambra lunch counter. She needed to ask him an important question if she could find the strength to do it. They were inside the small restaurant before she got up enough courage.

"Doc, there hasn't been anyone hanged in town while I was sleeping off that laudanum, has there?"

He pulled out a chair and helped her sit at the little table in the corner of the shop. "You mean that phony minister they arrested the morning after the fire?"

Amanda could barely breathe. She gripped the edge of the table, struggling to mask the dread she knew was written all over her face.

"Yes."

"No, no hanging yet," the Doc said, flipping open a large white napkin. "No thanks to John Behan for it. He wanted to string him up right away, but the vestry of St. Anselm's insisted on a fair trial. I don't know why. That man made suckers out of all of them."

Amanda stared down at the white cloth on the table. "I believe he helped them get their church built," she said in a soft voice.

Doc picked up the paper on the plate in front of him with the menu written on it. "Well, they're more forgiving than I would be. I'd say good riddance."

Amanda tried to focus on the printed menu and get her breathing back to an even keel. Her worst fear had been that John Behan might have hanged Cole straight out, he hated him so much. At least, with a trial, there was time to try to figure out how to save him. *If* he could be saved.

"I'm really not hungry," she began.

"Nonsense." The doctor's voice boomed in the small room. "You've got to keep up your strength. I'll order for both of us."

Breakfast helped to revive her, even though she had to force most of it down. She left Doc Goodfellow and walked straight to the jail, feeling more ready to face Cole behind bars than at any time since his arrest.

Yet, as she neared the grim building, she felt her strength giving way to fear. There was something so helpless about being a prisoner. Ever since she had first met Cole, he had seemed so strong, so "in charge" of every situation. When she had thought he was a clergyman, that trait had added to his attraction. As an outlaw, it at least gave him a sense of directing his own destiny. Now, as a prisoner in a cell, she felt his impotence, his loss over the direction of his life. The truth was that his life now lay in the hands of a vindictive sheriff and a crooked judge. If this were difficult for Amanda to accept, it must be ten times harder for Cole himself.

A block from the jail, she ran straight into John Behan. He tipped his hat to her politely, but his dark eyes glared at her with undisguised malevolence.

"Going to console the prisoner, are we?" he asked, without the slightest hint of humor.

Amanda lifted her chin. "Is that against the law?"

"You'll have to get in line. There's been a steady stream of Job's comforters since yesterday. Half of St. Anselm's has stopped by leaving books, food, and God knows what else."

"Maybe they're grateful to him. After all, he helped them build their church and he helped save it from being burned. That ought to count for something."

Behan frowned and pulled on the lapels of his black coat. "Not in my book. It's minor when you put it up against robbery and murder."

"You'd better have proof of those charges, John."

He smiled thinly. "Oh, I will. I've waited a long time to see Carteret get his just dues." He stared at her, his dark eyes riveting. "What I don't understand is how a respectable, lovely young woman like you can be so concerned about a good-for-nothing outlaw like The Kid. How has he blinded you? Can't you see what he is?"

She tried to go around him, but he stepped in front of her. Looking up into his face, Amanda said firmly, "Am I blind? Then so is half of the congregation of St. Anselm's. They have reason enough to hate him, but they don't. Perhaps that's because we all know the real Cole Carteret better than you."

"Horse feathers! A bunch of sentimental fools!"

"Please allow me to proceed."

"All I can say is you'd better bring your Bible to the hanging. He's going to need real consolation there."

Grudgingly he stepped aside, allowing her to walk on. Amanda kept her head high and tried to ignore the chilling fear his words had sent through her body. Her courage carried her up to the door of the jail, where she paused, taking a deep breath before going inside. Behan's deputy, Bobby Lunger, was sitting with his boots propped up on the desk. He swung them down when he saw her and gave her a broad smile.

" 'Mornin', Miss Lassiter."

Amanda knew Lunger well since he suffered from attacks of asthma and often visited her shop looking for any remedy that might help ease the symptoms. A few that she had suggested had actually helped, winning her his lasting gratitude.

"I was sorry to hear about your drug store," he went on. "Don't know what I'm going to do till you get it built back up."

"We'll think of something, Bobby. Perhaps Doc has a few of the same remedies on hand. Can I see the prisoner, please?"

Lunger pulled up his lanky body from behind the desk and reached for a set of keys on a ring six inches in diameter.

"Don't see why you can't. Just about everybody else in town has. This way, Miss."

A metal door formed completely of bars led into the row of cells. Lunger unlocked it and allowed her to pass by him. "The second one on the right," he said, locking the door after her. "I'll be right here when you're ready to leave."

There were four cells grouped together with an open aisle around them. Amanda was grateful that Lunger had left her alone and even more glad to see that the first two cells were empty. She made her way to the end of the row where she could make out Cole's body stretched on a cot with his back to her. She breathed a sigh of relief to see that the fourth cell was empty as well. At least they would have some privacy.

He stirred and turned over. Seeing her face outside the bars, he jumped up, moving toward her. Amanda grasped the bars, leaning toward him, and he wrapped his big hands around hers, gripping them like a lifeline.

"I wondered when you'd come," he murmured, bending to kiss her knuckles.

She reached through the bars to lay her palm along his cheek, rough with the stubble of a two-days' beard. "It was the laudanum Doc gave me. I slept all through yesterday."

"I'm sorry about your store." He reached through the bars as far as he could, pulling her against him.

With their faces pressed to the metal bars, Amanda kissed his lips. "Oh, Cole, that doesn't matter now. We have to get you out of here. Sheriff Behan is determined to see you hanged."

Cole abruptly pulled away. "I know. But I don't figure he has any real proof."

They kept their voices at a whisper. "Will that matter if he owns the judge as you said he did?"

Cole shrugged. "It's worse than that. The real people who run the court are the ones mentioned in those papers I gave you. If they learn about that box, I might as well start saying my prayers now. Is it still safe?"

Amanda glanced at the doorway to make sure no one was there. "As safe as I can make it. Cole, everything hangs on this trial. You need a lawyer."

"And who is going to defend me in this town? I've been amazed that the people at St. Anselm's have been so forgiving, but I don't think their compassion will reach to robbery and murder."

"Surely there's someone among them who can help."

He shook his head. "No, I thought I'd handle my own

defense. No one knows better than I what really happened when that Cortez stage was robbed."

"If anyone will believe you!" She felt tears stinging behind her eyes. "Oh, Cole. I don't want to lose you again."

He pulled her to him. "Don't start hanging crepe yet, Amanda. I'm not going to let Behan get the best of me without a good fight."

She laid her head against his chest, against the cold steel that kept them apart. If only she could be as confident . . .

Twenty-seven

Amanda left the jail and went straight to Warren Peters' office. Had she been less agitated, she might have reflected on how much she had changed since the first day she sat in this same chair looking at the lawyer across his desk. The defiant set of her chin, the straight-back angle of her shoulders, the challenge that darkened her hazel eyes were a stark contrast to the retiring, wary Amanda who had first entered here months before.

Peters noticed the change right away. The timid, frightened young thing who had been so shocked to hear her uncle was dead had given way to a mature, self-assured young woman who, before this awful fire, had made a modest success of running a drug store. Although he had not had occasion to visit her store, he had an ear to the ground in Tombstone and he knew Amanda was well thought of among the people of the town. She knew her remedies, and her skill in helping out the doctors had won her much good will. Her new confidence showed in her face, adding a deeper wisdom to the innocent loveliness that had been there before.

"I kind of figured you'd be in to see me," he said, settling back in his chair.

Amanda looked up in surprise. "You did?"

"Yes. You'll need some legal guidance in going about getting a loan to rebuild your store. These bankers will fleece you alive unless you have someone with you they respect. I know all their tricks, and they know it." He leaned forward, resting his arms on the desk. "I've been thinking about it, and I'd recommend . . ."

"Mr. Peters, you don't understand. I'm not here about my store. Right now, I don't want to think about that at all."

He paused, one eyebrow lifting in surprise. "But . . ."

"No. It's something quite different. I want to hire you to represent . . . a friend of mine at his trial. He thinks he can be his own lawyer, but I'm afraid that will only lead to his conviction. He needs someone who knows the law to help him."

Giving a sigh, Peters sat back in his chair and folded his hands across his paunch. "Let me guess. Cole Carteret."

Amanda felt her cheeks warming. She lifted her chin, ignoring her discomfort over her obvious involvement with Cole. "That's right," she murmured.

"My dear lady, he's nothing but an outlaw. A stage robber and—if the sheriff is right—a cold-blooded murderer. Why in the world . . ."

"Never mind the reasons," Amanda said forcefully, her embarrassment fading. "He needs a good defense, and I'm asking you to take it on. I'll pay you . . . that is, when I can. Right now . . ."

She stopped as she saw Peters chuckling quietly. "It's not funny, Mr. Peters. Cole's life is at stake."

"Forgive me, Miss Lassiter. If I'm amused, it is not because of Carteret's predicament. It's because the good folks of St. Anselm's have already offered to pay me to represent him."

She stared in amazement. "They have?"

"Yes. And I declined the offer."

"Oh, but you can't!" Amanda cried, leaning toward him. "Please, Mr. Peters. It must be obvious to you that if so many people care about Cole, he can't be as awful as the sheriff says. John Behan hates Cole. He'd do anything and say anything to get him hanged. You don't want to be a party to an injustice, do you?"

"It wouldn't be the first time that has happened in Tombstone. Nor the last."

"Then all the more reason it can't happen now. He didn't murder that boy. He was called out, challenged. He was defending himself."

"Then let him explain that to a jury."

"Would they believe him? They'd think he just said it to save his own skin."

Peters gave her a long look. "Perhaps he is. Why do you believe him?"

She sat back in her chair, looking the lawyer straight in the eye. "Because I know him, Mr. Peters. He wouldn't kill in cold blood."

The lawyer sat quietly observing her for a whole minute, his mind working. "But you don't understand, Amanda. Sheriff Behan may want to extract revenge on Carteret for killing his young kinsman, but that is not the reason Cole is on trial. He's accused of robbing the Cortez stage and killing one of the passengers. What kind of defense can there be for that? Are there any witnesses to prove he wasn't there?"

"I don't know; but if there are, we'll find them. I'll help, if I can."

"There isn't much time to go searching." Peters shook his head. "I don't know, Amanda. I hate to lose a case."

She leaned forward, earnestly pleading with every nerve of her body. "Please, Mr. Peters. You're our only hope."

Peters frowned. The pleas of a pretty woman could always get to him, feeble man that he was. He threw up his hands. "Oh, all right. Though I don't know what good it will do without witnesses to corroborate his story."

Amanda felt her body relax. "You'll find some way to save him. I know you will."

"I hope so; but without a strong alibi, it's going to be difficult. Behan will bring every witness he has to prove Cole guilty, and we'll have to try to find out who they are." He pulled off his round glasses. "When is the trial scheduled?"

"In two weeks, right after New Year's. Behan wanted it sooner, but the Christmas holidays got in the way."

"That doesn't give us much time." He dangled the wire stems of his glasses in his hand. "I have a feeling I'm going to regret this."

Impulsively, Amanda planted a kiss on Peters's round cheek. "You can save him; I know you can. Thank you, Mr. Peters."

Peters's already florid complexion deepened. "Now, now," he said, waving her off. "Enough of that. Let's get to work. I want you to tell me anything you can about The Kid that might be in his favor.

* * *

For Amanda, Christmas brought no joy. In fact, she would have been happier if Cole's trial had taken place right away, without having to first endure festivities which, for her, had no meaning this year. She vaguely remembered how difficult it had been the year before with her father's death so recent. This year was even worse. The foreboding and dread overwhelming her every time she thought of Cole's trial were made even more depressing by the uncertainty of the outcome. Yet there was nothing to do but grit her teeth and try to make it through the two long weeks, consoling herself that, at least she could visit him in jail.

Libby begged her to spend Christmas Day with the Waltons; but Amanda had no heart for being around a family or, indeed, any people at all. Until she had an unexpected visitor.

She was sitting in her room trying to force herself to concentrate on a novel when Martha Poole knocked on her door.

"You've a visitor downstairs, Amanda," Martha said through the door. "Better come on down."

Grateful for any diversion, Amanda laid aside her book and hurried down the stairs, more than half-convinced she would find Libby trying to cheer her up again. Halfway down, she saw the trim figure of a young woman rise from one of the burgundy-velvet settees against the lobby wall. She wore a dress of cheerful yellow calico and had a pert straw hat decorated with artificial daisies and blue ribbons perched on her blond hair. It was so different from her usual ranchhand costume that at first Amanda did not recognize her.

"Sally!" she cried, stopping in surprise. "Sally Mahone. I had no idea you were coming back to Tombstone."

Running down the stairs, she grabbed Sally's hands and squeezed them with delight. Seeing Sally gave her both pleasure and relief, though she could not explain why. Perhaps it was because she had known Cole so well and so long. If anyone could share Amanda's concern and fear over this awful trial, it would be this lovely, golden haired girl who smiled back at her.

"I came on an impulse," Sally said as the two of them sat on the settee. "I couldn't just sit out there at the ranch wondering what was happening to my cousin. My pa offered to do without me for a week or two, so I just up and decided to ride in." She looked around the pleasant lobby. "Do you think Mrs. Poole could find a room for me?"

"I'm certain," Amanda said, reluctant to let go of Sally's hands. "And if she can't, you can share mine. Oh, Sally, it's so good to see you." She glanced around the nearly empty lobby, then drew Sally off to a bay window where two chairs offered a greater privacy.

"I've been so worried," Amanda said quietly. "Cole is in serious trouble."

"I know. That's why I had to come. Cole and I, we've always been friends as well as cousins. Though he drives me crazy sometimes, I love him all the same. How is he?"

Amanda shrugged. "You know Cole. He pretends he doesn't care how this turns out, but I can tell he's concerned. He doesn't expect the trial to be fair."

"He's probably right. But I have some influence with

a few people in this town. I just may go round and pay a few calls once I'm settled in."

Amanda could feel the weight lifting from her shoulders. "That would be wonderful. Let's go find Martha and ask about a room for you."

Having Sally around made all the difference for Amanda. Finally, she had someone to whom she could freely admit her feelings, her love and her fears for Cole. She soon found that Sally shared many of those same feelings, even to being angry with him for not doing more with his life. In addition, Sally had known Cole since they were both children and could talk for hours about what he was like then and how those years must have affected the man he was now. To Amanda, such conversations were balm to her soul. Gradually, she found herself able to find time for some of the pressing matters that she had forced from her mind before Sally arrived, such as what to do about her store. Her renewed confidence washed away some of her reluctance to observe the holidays; and when Libby Walton asked again about Christmas dinner, extending the invitation to include Sally, Amanda quickly accepted.

When that day arrived, both women dressed in their Sunday finest and, after their daily visit to the jail, walked round to the Walton house carrying a box of peppermint taffy and a jar of orange marmalade that Amanda's old friend, Mrs. Abernathy, had sent her from St. Louis. The little house, decorated with artificial garlands brought from back East, smelled wonderfully of roasted meats and home-baked bread. Both Leander and Libby gave them a warm welcome, while their children dove into the candy with enthusiasm.

As they walked into the parlor, Amanda looked up in surprise when Cabot Storey rose to welcome them. The lean young clergyman wore the black frock coat and string tie she was accustomed to seeing on Cole, and for a moment it brought a sharp pang to her heart. But Cabot's friendly smile and cheerful manner quickly dispersed her pain. When she thought about it, it made perfect sense that the bachelor clergyman would be invited to the home of his senior warden for Christmas dinner. Cabot shook her hand with his usual exuberance, then turned to Sally. Noticing the admiration in his eyes, Amanda took a closer look at her friend. She had been so accustomed to seeing Sally in her workday ranching clothes that she hadn't noticed how pretty she looked when she dressed up. Her blue, sprigged-muslin dress modestly accentuated her handsome figure. She had arranged her golden hair in a full chignon, leaving two soft ringlets on either side that flattered the delicacy of her face. Small dangling pearl earrings added a feminine elegance. Her warm glow of good health and her open, honest smile accentuated her attractiveness and reminded Amanda poignantly of Cole. Sally and Cole shared the same blood. How ironic their fates could be so different.

"I've heard of the Bar M," she heard Cabot saying as he shook Sally's hand. "It has the reputation of being one of the best-run outfits around here."

Sally actually blushed. "Yes, it is, thanks to my father. He's put his life into it, and he's refused to ever be intimidated into doing anything that might not be absolutely honest."

Leander directed the women to a couch against the

wall. "That's to his credit. You can't say as much for most of the ranchers around Tombstone."

Cabot took a chair opposite them, leaning forward with his arms on his knees, his gaze trained on Sally. "What brings you to town at this time of year, Miss Mahone? Is your father with you?"

Sally glanced at Amanda. "No, he stayed on the ranch. I'm here to give moral support to my cousin, Cole Carteret."

There was a collective gasp around the little room when Cole's name was mentioned in front of Cabot Storey, but Sally ignored it. "I know he's an outlaw, but he's my family and I care deeply for him. In spite of everything he's done, I know him to be a good man at heart."

"I think you are right," Cabot said quickly. "Personally, I'm grateful to him for getting our church built. I even believe God may have been using him for some purpose. I was treated well, both by the men at his camp and by the Apaches, only because of Cole. What other way would I have ever had to reach men like those?"

"You are very forgiving, Reverend Storey," Sally said, looking at him in wide-eyed surprise.

"Isn't that what we are called to be?"

"Well," Leander drawled, "I don't condone that trick he pulled on us; but when all's said and done, he did some good things while he was here. The church don't hold it against him that he played them for a bunch of fools. As the rector says, the Good Lord preached forgiveness and charity."

Amanda, remembering Warren Peters's words, knew the truth of that. Then Libby appeared to call them to dinner and Cole's name was dropped in the ensuing enjoyment of a festive holiday meal.

They sat around the table for nearly two hours enjoying the long, leisurely meal and the pleasant conversation. They talked about the church, the fire, Amanda's store, the growth of the parish, the recent events among the lawless elements in town—almost everything but Cole, though she felt sure he was at the back of everyone's mind, like an unseen presence. It was the Reverend Storey who finally mentioned him once again.

"What do you think of your cousin's chances?" he asked Sally, leaning across the table to fasten his gaze on her.

"I think Amanda could speak to that better than I."

All eyes turned to Amanda. "I don't think his chances are very good," she said, absently running a fingernail down the white linen tablecloth. "Mr. Peters doesn't think so either."

Libby Walton spoke up. "Well, I'm just relieved Peters decided to defend him. He refused at first, you know. I don't know what changed his mind, but I do know a man who defends himself has a fool for a client. If the reverend—that is, Mr. Carteret—is going to have any chance at all, he's got to have a good lawyer."

"He was good at pretending to be a clergyman," Leander said dryly. "He'd probably be good at pretending to be a lawyer, too."

Cabot laughed. "I think it was a wonderful, harmless joke. Even those three weddings weren't too far off the mark. After all, in any wedding it's not the clergyman who marries people, but the two people themselves who make vows to each other in the sight of God." He turned toward Sally's admiring glance. "If your cousin hadn't done what he did, I might never have had the experience of visiting a real outlaw's den, much less an Apache camp. I enjoyed both immensely. It's easy to preach to good, decent people like the congregation of St. Anselm's. It's another matter altogether when you face criminals and heathen."

Amanda listened while Cabot Storey related stories of his time with Cole's gang and Heronimo's camp. As she mused on her lover's situation, she came to a tough decision. Once she and Sally got back to the hotel, she would take out the metal box and go over those incriminating papers. Cole might not approve, but it would be a relief for her just to share them with someone. And she was more sure every day Sally could be trusted to be discreet.

Yet, later, in her bedroom, when she opened the box, Sally took only a cursory glance and shoved them back inside.

"I don't want to know about these," she said, closing the lid, "and I don't think you do either. Isn't there someplace safer you could stow them than under your bed?"

"I thought perhaps Martha Poole's safe. She sometimes keeps valuables there for her guests."

"Good. First thing tomorrow morning, in they go."

"But Cole feels they are important."

Sally turned her direct gaze on Amanda. "My cousin is involved in many things which I wouldn't touch with a ten-foot pole. This is one of them. There are men in this town who would go to great lengths to prevent these papers from falling into the wrong hands. The less we know about them, the better."

"I suppose you're right. Cole even said as much."

"Exactly. I think he only wants you to keep them in a safe place until he can handle them himself. Now," she said, shoving the metal box under the bed and flouncing back down on the quilt, "tell me about the Reverend Cabot Storey."

Three nights later, Amanda was in her hotel room, ready for bed but with her coal oil lamp still burning, when she received a sudden summons from Doc Goodfellow to rush to the Cosmopolitan Hotel. A few moments before, Virgil Earp had left the Oriental Saloon and stepped into the street, where he had been cut down by a fusillade of bullets and buckshot erupting from the roof of a nearby building.

Badly wounded, he had been carried to the nearest hotel room, where Doc Goodfellow was struggling to save his life. Amanda threw on her clothes and hurried to Allen Street to do what she could to help. By the time she got there, Virgil's wife, Allie, was hovering near the bed, her little body tight with anxiety but her eyes dry in her stoic face. Her husband was bleeding badly, with slugs and buckshot all through his left side and one arm nearly destroyed. Remembering how Allie had been shunned by the 'good people' of the town, Amanda could only admire her spunk and her obvious love for her husband as she moved quietly around the bed, doing what she could to help and comfort him.

As Amanda knelt beside the doctor, she heard the

wounded man whisper weakly to his wife, "Never mind. I still got one arm left to hug you with."

When Doc Goodfellow turned Virgil over, the assistant marshal was bleeding so badly he fainted. At that moment, a tall man with steely eyes and a heavy moustache came barreling into the room. Amanda recognized Wyatt Earp right off, though this was the closest she had ever been to him.

Virgil came back to consciousness and saw his brother standing behind Doc Goodfellow. "Wyatt, when they get me under, don't let them take my arm off. I want to be buried with both arms."

Amanda felt sure the arm would go, and probably the patient with it. But she was wrong. Nobody knew how to treat bullet wounds better than Doc Goodfellow; and when Virgil Earp did not die by the next morning, or the two days after, it began to look as though he might make it.

The talk around town was that the Clantons and McLowerys had been behind the shooting, out to get the revenge for the death of their kinfolk which the courts had denied them. By then, however, Amanda had ceased to care about the Earps and their problems. The day of Cole's trial had arrived, and there was no room in her mind or her heart for anyone else.

The crowded courtroom had already grown oppressively hot by the time Amanda pushed her way through. About half the group was made up of the people from St. Anselm's, while the other half appeared to be the idlers who usually hung around the saloons or the stores out looking for a little excitement. Amanda ignored the pungent odors that emanated from them along with their jeering comments about looking forward to a hanging. Her eyes searched the front of the room for a glimpse of Cole.

He sat at one of two tables facing the judge's bench, talking with Warren Peters. He was wearing the same riding clothes he had been arrested in, but they looked freshly washed and ironed. His face was scrubbed and his hair neat, and he looked so ruggedly handsome that Amanda's heart turned over with sudden longing. When he looked up to meet her eyes, he smiled and tried to rise before Peters laid a hand on his arm and pulled him back to his chair.

Amanda forced her way close to the front of the room, up against the wall. While she did not relish the idea of standing through the trial, it seemed important to be as near Cole as possible, no matter how uncomfortable. Then she heard Libby Walton calling across the room.

Libby was sitting on the first row of benches, where she squirmed to make room for Amanda. By the time Amanda had worked her way over there, Judge Spicer had entered and was banging his gavel on the bench for order. Amanda squeezed in beside Libby as the room hushed for the trial to begin.

"I thought you weren't coming," Libby whispered. "Where's your friend?"

"Sally's out making a few last-minute appeals, but she'll be here soon. Do you think we can make room for her, too?"

"Sure. It'll be close, but we'll manage."

That was not a bad description of the trial itself, Amanda mused absently. If only it would turn out that well!

Her hopes diminished with the waning morning. The six people sworn in as a jury were not especially encouraging. Judge Spicer quickly ruled out any of St. Anselm's parishioners, saying they might be prejudiced toward the prisoner, or even possibly against the prisoner. Either way, they would not be allowed to serve. That meant that the people who could serve, although they might be close friends and associates of Sheriff Behan, had no reason to be dismissed. Though Peters did his best, the jury ended up comprised of six men who, in Amanda's eyes, could easily be under Behan's influence. Two worked in the mine offices, one clerked in a store, one in a bank, and the last two had temporary jobs at the livery stables in town. It was not a jury to raise her hopes. Even less encouraging was the speed with which the judge approved them. With every passing minute, Amanda began to feel that the outcome of this trial had already been decided.

By the time Sally squirmed in beside her on the bench, her worst fears were beginning to be realized.

She took one look at Sally's grim face, and her hopes fell even further.

"No luck?" she whispered.

"No. Even people who have always claimed to be my father's friends refused to get involved. They've already written Cole off as a gunslinger and a stage robber."

"So were the Earps," Amanda whispered, "and they got off."

"They had people behind them who couldn't afford

to let them be tried. Unfortunately, Cole doesn't. They also had a sympathetic judge. The feeling now is that Spicer owes Behan one after allowing the Earps to go free."

As a chorus of shushing sounds came from the people around them, the women turned their attention back to the front of the room where Warren Peters was trying to tear down the testimony of a witness who claimed he had been on the Cortez stage which Cole and his gang had robbed the year before.

The lawyer's voice boomed. "You say the robbers all wore masks?"

"Yes."

"And their hair was close around their faces, that is, between their hats and their masks?"

"That is correct."

"It was also nighttime, wasn't it? Was there a full moon which allowed you such a clear view?"

"It was pretty cloudy as I recollect."

"Then will you please tell me how you are able to definitely assert that the prisoner here was a member of that gang? Look at him. His hair is not close to his face and he wears only a neat moustache. How can you be so positive that this was one of the men who robbed that stage?"

The witness glanced quickly at Cole. "It was the eyes. I'll never forget them eyes. Besides . . ."

"Besides what?"

"When they rode off, at least two of the other people in the stage said they was The Casket Kid's gang. They knew what they was talkin' about."

"Then why aren't they here?"

"Don't ask me. Maybe they ain't around Tombstone anymore. All I know is what I saw; and, as sure as the Lord made green apples, it was that man sittin' right there who robbed me that night."

To Amanda's surprise, the next witness was Leander Walton. The town prosecutor, and the judge as well, pressed him hard on where the money that had suddenly been given to finish the church had come from, trying to link it to Cole and one of the string of robberies in the area. Leander held his ground; but every time he tried to speak of the good Cole had done, he was cut off. Only when Peters questioned him, was he allowed to speak in favor of Cole's character.

That testimony in Cole's favor was quickly cut down by the prosecution's redirect.

"Mr. Walton," the lawyer asked with the arrogant slowness of a man who is sure of where he stands. "No matter how much you claim the defendant helped St. Anselm's, isn't it true that he lied about his real identity, tricked the congregation and the good people of this town, and even presided over services which he had no legal right to do? That's the truth, isn't it?"

"Yes, but . . ."

"No more questions."

When Judge Spicer finally called a midday break, Amanda hurried over to where Cole sat. Ducking into Peters's chair, she squeezed his hand and tried to smile. "It isn't going too well, is it?" she said, knowing it was useless to try to give false encouragement.

"It's going about how I expected. Are you all right?"

His face looked leaner than usual, haggard. Amanda realized the toll this was taking on him, even though he professed to have expected everything that had happened. "I'm fine. It's you I'm worried about."

"They have no real proof. I'm banking on that." He leaned over and quickly laid his cheek against hers, lacing his hands in her hair. "I'm glad you're here," he whispered in her ear.

"Cole, please let me use the letters. If these people knew you had . . ."

"No. We've been all over that. I want them to go to the one man who can use them best."

"But if they hang you . . ."

"Then it will be up to you to get them to him. I'll give you his name before they string me up." He gripped her shoulders, looking deeply into her eyes, his own dark with concern. "This is important to me, Amanda. Promise me you'll do as I ask."

She hugged him tightly, whispering against his cheek. "You know I will. Only, how can I go on if . . . if . . ."

"Don't think about that now," he said, trying to smile with the old jauntiness. Then, spying Sally standing just behind her, he rose to embrace his cousin.

"Got to go, Cole," Peters said, taking his arm to pull him away.

Both women watched as Cole was led out back to the jail. Though the break had been planned for lunch, Amanda and Sally both felt they couldn't force down a bite. Instead, they waited outside, walking fitfully and talking over the events of the morning until everyone began to gather for the rest of the trial.

To Amanda's surprise, the first witness was Tilly Lacey. She glared at Cole with venom in her eyes as she testified she recognized him the first time she saw him on the stage into Tombstone.

"That's not true," Amanda whispered to Sally. "I was on that stage, too, and I would swear she didn't know who he was."

When asked why she hadn't said something about Cole's identity during all the weeks he had stayed in town, Tilly claimed she hadn't been absolutely sure. Yet she had been certain enough to say something about it to Sheriff Behan, and the sheriff would surely back her up in that.

"I'll bet he would," Amanda whispered between clenched teeth.

Though Peters tried his best to paint Tilly's testimony as the grousings of a spurned woman, and a woman whose reputation was none too good at that, he could not budge her from her stubborn avowal that she had known Cole's true identity. Amanda felt her heart sink even further as Tilly left the stand, her eyes glaring triumphantly under her feathered hat.

And then the third and last witness appeared.

Amanda knew he was bad news when she saw the shock on Cole's face. She had never seen the man before, but his cold eyes and hard, leathery face made her uneasy even before he opened his mouth. His name was Jim Reily, but he was commonly called "Scorpion." And his testimony had the desert scorpion's poisonous sting. He sat in the chair, pointed to Cole, and proceeded to catalogue two years' worth of robberies and gunfights which he had witnessed as a member of The Kid's gang.

Peters did his best to tear down Reily's statements. Reily had participated in the Cortez robbery, after all.

He had not stood around as an uninterested observer. And the only possible reason he could freely sit there and recount all these events had to be because he had been promised immunity. His character was, at the least, unreliable; and his motives were suspicious. When Reily tried to recount what he remembered about the fight with Jamie Behan, Peters quickly stopped him. That trial had been concluded long ago, and the defendant had already paid the price of his conviction.

After only three witnesses, the lawyers made their summations. Then Judge Spicer spoke to the jury before sending them off to deliberate. He told them that even though this trial was not about the murder of Jamie Behan but the robbery of a stage and the cold-blooded killing of an innocent passenger, still they might consider Jamie's killing since it touched on the defendant's character. That comment seemed to Amanda to put the last nail in Cole's coffin. When the jury returned after only half-an-hour's deliberation, she was not even surprised that they returned a verdict of guilty on all counts.

She sat in a daze, hearing the judge intone that Cole should be hanged by the neck until dead and good riddance to the world. Because it was so late in the day, the sentence would be carried out at dawn the next morning. She stood like a marble statue, watching as Cole threw her a thin, crooked smile while they led him away. When she felt Sally take her hand and pull her toward the door, she followed numbly through the crowd.

"Let's get out of here," Sally cried in a choked voice, pushing through the press of people. "I need some fresh air. And so do you."

By the time they got outside, Amanda's rage over this miscarriage of justice began to revive her strength. Standing on the steps of the courthouse, she looked at her friend who had translucent tears standing in her huge blue eyes.

"Oh, Amanda," Sally murmured. "My poor cousin. What can we do? There must be some way to save him!"

This time it was Amanda who grabbed Sally's arm and pulled her down the street. "Come on, Sally. We've got until dawn. We'll think of something."

Twenty-eight

Amanda and Sally went straight back to the hotel, where they forced themselves to eat a little supper, though food was the last thing on their minds. Afterward, they sat on one of the tufted velveteen sofas in the lobby, desperately trying to think of some way to comfort Cole when they saw him later in the evening.

They had only been there a few minutes when Amanda looked up to see Cabot Storey coming through the door from the street. His lean face was pink from the cold, and he unbuttoned his long black coat as he walked toward them. Pulling up a chair, he leaned forward with his elbows resting on his knees.

"I tried to catch you before you left the courthouse, but you were too quick for me. After that, I had to make a call on a sick parishioner, but once it was over, I came immediately. I thought perhaps you might need to talk to someone."

"That was kind you, Reverend Storey," Amanda said, fighting back the tears stinging her eyes, but it's not comfort we need. It's some way to get Cole out of this horrible predicament. We have to do something, but I can't think what."

Sally wiped at her eyes with a crushed handkerchief. "I suppose the jail is too strong to break him out of?"

"Yes," Amanda answered. "And that wouldn't work even if it weren't. Cole has some friends in this town, but I don't think they'd go to those lengths to save him. And certainly his outlaw friends won't either, if that scorpion is any example of them."

Cabot smiled thinly. "I remember meeting Jim Reily when I was in the camp. It didn't surprise me a bit that he'd try to save his own skin at Cole's expense."

Sally leaned toward the clergyman. "My cousin is not a bad man, Reverend Storey. He may have done a lot of wrong things, but he has a good heart. I know he does."

Cabot reached out to squeeze her hand. "I surmised a few things about your cousin when I was with his gang. Though he did rob many people, he never intentionally harmed anyone. And the other men in the camp told me he was constantly being challenged by young hotheads who wanted to build their own reputation by outshooting him. That's something all gunslingers have to deal with."

"Unfortunately," Amanda said, "one of those youths was related to Sheriff Behan. This whole thing is nothing but John's attempt to extract revenge for that boy's death. The passenger who was shot on the Cortez stage is just Behan's excuse. Cole swears he didn't fire at anybody that night, and I believe him."

Cabot reluctantly released Sally's hand and turned to Amanda. "Perhaps so, but I can't see any legal way to save Cole from this hanging."

"Legal!" Amanda cried. "Who cares if it's legal? Any way will do if it works."

Cabot studied her distraught face for a moment. "Do you mean that?"

"Of course I mean it!"

"In that case, I have an idea . . ."

It was late in the evening when Amanda and Sally appeared at the jail accompanied by Reverend Storey in his best clerical frock coat with his Bible under his arm. Cole had been stalking the narrow cell for an hour, wondering when Amanda was going to show up; and he was not pleased at first to see Sally, much less the preacher. He wanted to speak to Amanda privately, to settle the unfinished business of those papers in the metal box. But the moment he heard her voice in the anteroom, speaking to Deputy Lunger, he knew then what he really wanted was to hold her in his arms, to kiss her soft, sweet lips, to run his fingers through the thick warmth of her shining hair. He wished they could have a private moment to make love together, to experience one last time that supreme joy of melding his body with hers. It would be his way of affirming life once more before it was taken away from him, of shaking his fist at fate.

The last thing he wanted was some damned preacher intoning prayers over him!

To his surprise Deputy Lunger took out a ring of jangling keys and opened the cell door, allowing the three visitors to join him inside. Cole reached for Amanda and enclosed her in his arms. She clung to him, pressing her body against his, holding him as though she could never let him go.

"I was desperate to see you," he murmured against her hair. "Can't we have a few moments alone?"

"Here's your cousin Sally," Amanda replied, loudly enough for the deputy to hear. "And Reverend Storey thought you might want to talk to a man of God."

Cole opened his mouth to object but closed it when he saw Amanda put her finger to her lips. Instead he turned to his cousin. "I'm sorry you have to be a witness to all this, Sally. You should have stayed at the ranch."

Sally threw her arms around him. "Haven't we always helped each other when trouble came?"

That wasn't strictly true, Cole thought, but he let it pass. Extending his hand to Cabot, he said, "The only praying I've done lately, Reverend Storey, was when I took your place in the church. It seems a little hypocritical to start doing it on my own behalf now."

Cabot paid him no mind. Setting Sally's large bag-purse on the cot, he gently pushed Cole down next to it, while Amanda and Sally gathered in front, shielding the two men from view. Cole gaped in surprise as Sally opened the bag and pulled out a razor and a small bowl wrapped in a face towel. While Cabot Storey began loudly intoning a long, impassioned prayer, Amanda poured some water from a small jar into the bowl and thrust the razor into Cole's hand.

"Quickly. Get rid of that moustache," she whispered.

"But . . ."

"Don't ask questions. Just do it!"

The water was cold and there was little soap. Cole

flinched as he scraped away his facial decorations; and Amanda gathered up the results in the towel which she stuffed along with the bowl inside the bag-purse. Cabot went on working himself up into a fervent tirade of prayer while Amanda and Sally quickly threw everything else back in the bag and closed it. Then, without a break in his voice, Cabot shrugged off his black coat.

Cole was beginning to get the idea. Once again he started to protest, but Amanda cut him off.

"I can't let you do this . . ." he whispered.

She hastily began unbuttoning his checkered shirt. "You can't stop us. It was the rector's idea. Don't argue!"

Sally suddenly began making loud crying noises. "Oh, Cole!" she sobbed. "I can't bear it."

"Say something!" Amanda whispered, jabbing Cole in the chest.

"There, there, Sally," Cole said loudly. "Don't cry. We all have to die sometime."

Sally gave another loud burst of sobs while Cabot and Cole exchanged shirts. "I've just about run out of prayers," the pastor said, his voice muffled as he pulled his shirt over his head. Amanda grabbed the Bible, opened it, and read loudly in a steady voice.

Though the entire transformation only took a few moments, it seemed much longer. Cole watched in amazement as, for the final touch, Cabot Storey plastered a fake moustache to his upper lip. Though the clergyman was several pounds leaner than Cole, the two were close enough in size that once they exchanged clothes they could pass for the other. When Cole pulled the minister's black hat down over his face, Amanda thought even she would have trouble telling them apart from a distance.

While Sally's loud crying grew in intensity, Cole pulled Cabot Storey down on the cot to whisper, "This is crazy. I can't let you take such a chance. What will happen to you when they find out?"

Cabot smiled. His pale blue eyes were dancing with delight, and Cole realized he was enjoying this. "Oh, I don't think they'll do more than give me a large fine. Lord knows, they won't hang a man of God. Besides, you took my place once and you gave me the challenge of preaching to the lost and the heathen. I'm only returning the favor."

"I can't bear it!" Sally wailed loudly. "I can't stay here any longer! Let me out!"

Amanda stepped to the bars and called out. "Deputy Lunger. Please, let us go. Miss Mahone is too upset to stay."

She thrust the Bible into Cole's hands, hearing the rattle of the deputy's keys as he unlocked the door to the anteroom. By the time he reached the cell door, Amanda was cradling Sally in her arms and Cabot was ensconced on the cot in his shirt sleeves, his legs drawn up and his face in the shadows. Cole pulled Cabot's hat close around his face and fell in step behind the two women.

"I'll come back early in the morning," Amanda said, talking nonstop to the deputy. "Mr. Carteret doesn't want to see the rector or his cousin. In fact, he doesn't want to do anything but sleep. I declare, I can't understand it. You try to console a man when he's about to meet his Maker, and he doesn't want your comfort!"

"That's the way a lot of outlaws feel, Miss Lassiter. It's hard for decent folks to understand."

Amanda could hear the deputy throwing his keys into a desk drawer and sliding it shut as she and Sally made their slow way toward the outside door. Cole walked solemnly behind them, shaking his head and staring at his boots. Still talking, Amanda laid her hand on the knob. Outside she could see the darting dance movements of night insects in the dim glow of the lamplight near the street. Almost there . . .

"Oh, Reverend Storey . . ." Lunger called.

All three froze in place. Amanda turned to see Bobby Lunger approaching them from around the desk. Cole turned his head slightly, trying to keep away from the light.

"I was thinking maybe I'd have my kid baptized . . ." Bobby began. He was interrupted by Sally, who gave a sudden loud wail, flaying her hands wildly.

"My poor cousin . . . I can't stand it!" She threw herself at Lunger, gripping his shirt. "You can't do this! You can't hang him!"

Lunger backed swiftly away, clawing at Sally's grasp. "Now, Miss. . . . It's not my fault."

Amanda grabbed at Sally's arm just as the outside door was pulled open and a man appeared on the threshold. "Don't mind her, Bobby," Amanda cried, tearing Sally's hands away and pulling her into her arms. "She's distraught."

She glanced nervously around to see a short, portly gentleman in a natty checkered coat and a Vandyke beard staring at Cole. Thrusting herself in front of Cole, she turned him away and at the same time pulled Sally toward the door. The portly man was forced to step to the side, still watching them intently.

"Excuse me," Amanda muttered. "We're in rather a hurry."

"Oh, Mr. Slaughter," she heard Lunger say in a friendly way. "You're back in town. Good to see you again."

The man in the checkered coat pulled off a high-peaked Stetson hat and nodded to Lunger. "Deputy."

"Come along, Reverend Storey," Amanda cried, pushing past the new arrival. "I'm sure Miss Mahone could use your help, even if the prisoner didn't want it." She held her breath, waiting for the expected cry of recognition at any moment.

Cole quickly took his place on Sally's other side, laying his arm around her shoulder. With Amanda pushing them, they ducked quickly through the door and out onto the street. Sally kept up her wailing all the way down the block to the first darkened alley, where they ducked inside.

"My God! I've never put on an act like that in my life," Sally cried, leaning back against the wall of the livery stable.

"You were wonderful," Amanda said. "But I thought we were lost when that other man came in. The way he kept watching us!" Ignoring Cole's stare, she began pulling off her dress, revealing riding clothes underneath. "At least we've made it this far. We never could have without you and Cabot, Sally."

"Would someone like to tell me what is going on?" Cole exclaimed as Amanda's transformation became complete.

"There's no time now," Amanda said. "Come on.

We've got some hard riding to do." She turned to Sally. "Will you be all right?"

"Of course. I'll go back to the hotel and wait for the fireworks. What about the two of you?"

"We'll be fine." Amanda paused, then threw her arms around Sally's neck and hugged her. "Thank you. Thank you for everything."

"Thank you," Sally said, smiling into Amanda's glittering eyes.

"What for?"

"For introducing me to Reverend Storey. I don't intend to let him get away. Ever."

She turned to Cole and gave him a quick hug. "Take care, Cousin. And behave yourself."

"I don't think Amanda will allow me to do anything else."

Cole quickly kissed his cousin's cheek. He still had a lot of questions, but they could wait. What mattered now was to get away from Tombstone, fast.

He didn't object when Amanda grabbed his arm and pulled him toward the livery stable. "Come on, Love. The horses are saddled and waiting."

They rode most of the night, heading north until they could pick up the old stage route westward. Because Cole knew it very well, they were able to continue well along it until fatigue forced them to rest. With the horses hobbled near by, they wrapped themselves in the warm saddle blankets and clung close together, dozing fitfully.

Amanda had finally dropped off into a deep sleep when Cole shook her awake. The first rays of dawn were beginning to tinge the far horizon with an opaque rose. The deepest cold of the night chilled her body, yet she knew it would soon give way to the desert heat. She dragged herself to a sitting position and pulled the blanket around her while Cole thrust a tin cup of steaming coffee into her hands.

"You've been busy," she said, sipping the comforting liquid.

"I couldn't sleep. I'm anxious to put as many miles as possible between us and Tombstone. Are you rested enough to ride?"

"I think so. But first we have to decide where we're going. Last night I only wanted to get away as quickly as possible. I thought we might head for Paso Diablo, but I wasn't sure of the direction."

Cole sat down beside her, drawing up his knees and resting his arms on them. He stared at the brightening line of blue-gray hills. "I don't think that's wise. Too many people know it was my home. No, I think we should head westward. At least in the beginning. You did bring the papers with you, didn't you?"

"They're in the saddlebag. I had to throw things together quickly once Cabot Storey got our plan together, but I certainly wasn't going to forget that box. I knew it meant too much."

Cole laid his arm around her shoulder and pulled her head against his. "I didn't think I would see this day dawning, much less be here with you. I owe Cabot Storey one."

"We both do. He's given us back our lives."

Abruptly, Cole rose to his feet and walked over to the edge of a bluff, staring at the desert plain below.

Amanda watched him for a moment in confusion, then stood beside him, pulling the blanket around her.

"I think we have company," Cole said suddenly. Amanda looked closer and gave a small gasp as she saw the dark shape of a rider making his way up the hill. She looked frantically around for the expected posse to take shape behind him, but he appeared to be alone.

"Cole, we've got to get out of here," she cried, throwing aside the blanket to rush back to the fire. He caught her arm, and she saw he was laughing.

"It's all right. I know who it is."

Without any further explanation, he walked past her to the edge of a sandstone outcropping to wait for the man and his horse. When the rider emerged on the path around the rock, Amanda shrank back toward her horse, ready to take off at any moment. The short, straight-backed man slipped out of the saddle and extended his hand to Cole, who shook it gravely, then turned to Amanda.

"Meet John Slaughter, Amanda. A special friend of mine."

Amanda recognized the gentleman who had entered the jail the night before. Hesitantly, she moved forward. "Mr. Slaughter. I think we sort of met last night."

The portly man gave a deep laugh. "Indeed. I knew something was up, but I couldn't tell exactly what until I came face to face with Reverend Storey in Cole's jail cell."

"And you didn't give us away?"

"Of course not. I have as much interest in seeing Cole get out of this as you do."

"Amanda," Cole said, "you can get that metal box

now. This is the man who will know what to do with it."

She looked from one to the other. "This is the man who hired you to work for the government?"

Slaughter gave another deep chuckle. "Is that what he told you? Well, it's not exactly the government; it's Wells Fargo. Either way, I say, those papers are going to help me clear up a very nasty situation. Well done, Cole."

While Amanda moved to the saddlebags to retrieve the metal box, Cole poured a cup of strong coffee and held it out to Slaughter. "You can thank Aces Malone," he said. "Though he didn't intend to use them in quite the same way. What will you do with them, John?"

Slaughter took a sip of the hot coffee. "I've been thinking about that. First I'm going to change the ways of a few greedy bankers and politicians. Next, I'm going to clear your name. After that, I believe I'll run against Behan for sheriff in the next election. And I'll win, too. It's time Tombstone got over its wild ways and began to settle down."

Amanda had only heard one part of his reply. "Can you really clear Cole's name?" she asked, stepping up beside him.

Slaughter nodded. "They don't have a shred, I say, a shred of proof that you robbed that stage or shot that passenger. Once I've proved Jim Reily was bribed, I think the charges against you can be dropped. John Behan was a little too anxious for revenge to be very careful. If those papers contain even half of what you described in your letter, Cole, I don't think you'll have to worry about being hounded in the future."

He threw down the contents of the cup and wiped at his mouth with his hand. "But you still can't make a decent cup of coffee! Thank heaven you're going to have a wife who can do it for you."

Once more Cole reached for Slaughter's hand. "Long ago you turned my life around. Now, here you are doing it again. How can I thank you, John?"

"Just don't let anybody talk you into doing any more undercover work. And marry this pretty little gal."

Cole laid his arm around Amanda's shoulders and pulled her to him. "I won't have any trouble following that advice."

With the box under his arm, Slaughter climbed back on his horse and gave them a wave. "Come back and say hello someday," he called and disappeared around the blue rock.

Cole squeezed Amanda's shoulder. "I imagine there will be some big changes in Tombstone in the near future."

She kissed him lightly on the lips. "I'm glad we won't be there to see them."

She was startled when he abruptly turned away and walked back to the edge of the bluff to look out over the valley, watching Slaughter's retreating form. After studying him for a moment in confusion, she went to stand beside him, pulling the blanket around her.

"What's wrong?"

He looked down into her upturned face, its lovely lines so dear to him, her eyes reflecting the glowing dawn. "Have you thought about this, Amanda? I mean, it has all happened so quickly. Do you really want to tie yourself to a man like me? It's not too late for you to go back, you know? The town wouldn't hold it against you. You have a business there, friends, respectability. You'll have none of those things with me."

Amanda slipped her arms around his waist, allowing the blanket to fall around her feet. "I'll have you. That's more important to me than anything in the world."

He bent to kiss her lips. "Are you sure? I don't want to ruin your life like I've ruined mine. I have nothing now. No money, no means of making a living. I couldn't bear to have you suffer because of me."

To his surprise, he saw she was laughing. "This isn't funny," he exclaimed. "I'm really concerned."

"I know," Amanda said, nestling her head against his shoulder. "But, my dear, I was very busy yesterday, once Cabot figured out his plan. I don't have a store anymore. I sold it. What was left of it."

"You what?"

"To Louis McKeithan. Of course, he wouldn't give me anything like what he offered before the fire. But he was willing to pay a little cash for the land and the rubble. It's all right there in the saddlebags."

"Amanda, you're amazing!"

"So you see, we're not destitute. And if John Slaughter is right, you won't be a wanted man any longer. We're going somewhere far away, where we can buy another drug store for me to run—California or Oregon or Montana. After all, I still have all that knowledge in my head. McKeithan couldn't buy that. Maybe we'll make enough money from the drug store so you can buy a ranch and build another Paso Diablo. And who knows? I might even do some studying and become a real doctor. There are all kinds of possibilities. Except one . . ."

"And what is that?"

"No more stage robberies!"

He closed his arms around her, pressing her against him. "My God, not only will I be respectable, I'll be a store clerk! That it should come to this!"

Amanda looked up at him, laughing. "Saved by the love of a good woman."

He bent to kiss her, laying his palms against her cheeks and lifting her lips to his. "Did I mention that I love you?"

"Not that I recall. Did I mention that I love you, too? More than anyone in the world."

Her lovely face was bathed with the soft shell-pink light of the growing dawn. He kissed her again, then, giving her a light slap on the rump, turned her around and pushed her toward the grazing horses.

"Come on, woman. The day is almost here, and it's a long way to California."

From the Author

Was Wyatt Earp noble lawman or outlaw opportunist? Of the two schools of thought, I choose the second. I freely admit this choice was strongly influenced by the reminiscences of Virgil Earp's wife, Allie, as told in Frank Waters' wonderful, *The Earp Brothers of Tombstone* (U. of Neb. Press). This delightful book is as entertaining as a Hollywood movie, and much more factual.

No disrespect is intended toward Tombstone's St. Paul's Church and its historic first rector, The Reverend Endicott Peabody, in using them as models for St. Anselm's Parish and the Reverend Cabot Storey in *Outlaw's Embrace.* Although I had a little fun with both, it was done out of a deep affection for the Episcopal Church, my long-time home, and for my favorite clergyman, my husband, Bill, to whom this book is dedicated.

I welcome reactions from my readers. Please write Ashley Snow, P.O. Box 8694, Tampa, Florida 33674-8694.